Child of the Sword

Book 1 of *The Gods Within*

*When gods and wizards go to war . . . it's best to just find a
good shadow and hide.*

by

J. L. Doty

TELEMACHUS PRESS

This book or eBook is a work of fiction. Names, characters, places and incidents are either the product of the author's imagination or are used fictitiously. Any resemblance to actual persons, living or dead, or to actual events or locales is entirely coincidental.

Child of the Sword, Book 1 of *The Gods Within*
This book or eBook is licensed for your personal enjoyment only. This book or eBook may not be re-sold or given away to other people. If you're reading this book or eBook and did not purchase it, or it was not purchased for your use only, then you should return it and purchase your own copy. Thank you for respecting the hard work of the author.

The publisher does not have any control over and does not assume any responsibility for author or third-party websites or their content.

Cover designed by Telemachus Press, LLC

Cover art:
Copyright © ThinkstockPhoto/96635409/iStockPhoto
Copyright © ThinkstockPhoto/89908712/iStockPhoto
Copyright © ThinkstockPhoto/87609731/PhotoObjects.net/Hemera Technologies
Copyright © ThinkstockPhoto/82152604/GoodShot/Jupiter Images
Copyright © ThinkstockPhoto/78618526/Fuse
Copyright © ThinkstockPhoto/147084639/iStockPhoto
Copyright © ThinkstockPhoto/137088827/iStockPhoto
Copyright © ThinkstockPhoto/136338650/iStockPhoto
Copyright © ThinkstockPhoto/106546676/iStockPhoto
Copyright © ThinkstockPhoto/101495952/Hemera

Published by Telemachus Press, LLC
http://www.telemachuspress.com

Visit the author website:
http://www.jldoty.com

Follow the author on Twitter:
http://www.twitter.com/@JL_Doty

ISBN: 978–1–938135–88–0 (eBook)
ISBN: 978–1–953757–01–2 (paperback)
ISBN: 978-1-953757-09-8 (hardcover)

Version 2022.11.16

KEpuz!po!KJNEFTLUPQ:
Formatted using eTools for Writers 3.8.8, Nov 29 2022, 20:37:36
Copyright © 2013-2016 by J. L. Doty

Printed in the United States of America

10 9 8 7 6 5 4 3 2 1

Child of the Sword

Book 1 of *The Gods Within*

Prologue:
Thrice and Thrice of a Benesh'ere Blade

Forge the steel thrice in the fires of hell.
Quench the steel thrice in the waters of heaven.
Blood the steel thrice in the agonies of death.
For thrice and thrice must a blade be born.

1

The Thief

RAT EYED THE purse and followed its owner as he meandered through the market square. It was a fat purse tied to an even fatter waist, and the hunger in his gut demanded he make it his. The hunger in his soul demanded so much more than simply a purse and food, but he tried not to think about that. Rat darted out of his shadow, scurried the short distance to a fruit vendor's stall and hid behind it, keeping his good eye focused on the purse.

One of his many flea bites demanded his attention. He moved slowly—quick movements drew attention—slipped a hand through a rent in his muddy cloak of rags and scratched at it, his eye following the purse.

Fatpurse wandered aimlessly, eyeing the vendors' goods. Rat was too short to see over the stall, which was only waste-high for big people, so he leaned out of his shadow and peered around the edge to follow the fat man's progress.

"Away with ye, scum!" the fruit vendor shouted, hurling a spoiled apple at him.

Rat sidestepped the throw and caught the apple, pleased he'd acquired a bit of food without resorting to theft. He scurried between the market booths and disappeared into another shadow. With mud and horse manure squishing between his toes, he ate the rotten apple while his eye tracked the purse through the market. His stomach grumbled with satisfaction, then growled a demand for more.

Heavy rains the night before had turned the dirt streets into a quagmire. The crowds in the market were thin, and the vendors looked nervous and edgy. They'd drive off anything that turned customers away—especially someone like Rat. He knew he must understand these things to survive.

Something drizzled down his left cheek. He reached up and wiped it away, a smear of puss on his fingertips. The boil next to his left eye had opened; he hoped the swelling would lessen and allow him to see again, though by then new eruptions would form, so he didn't expect much relief.

He reached into his rags and retrieved an object the size of the tip of his littlest finger: *gesh*. He placed the hard, woody substance on his tongue and began chewing. It mixed with saliva to form a fibrous mass that tasted both bitter and sweet. He let some of the juice trickle down his throat, and it immediately lessened the throbbing in his eye.

Somehow gesh made the cold nights of winter warmer, and it softened the filthy straw of his bed. Rat had learned that gesh was good, and the lack of it bad. The last of his supply had dwindled to no more than a taste or two hidden away in his den, so he needed that purse, needed it badly.

A rock smashed painfully into his cheek, sent him sprawling into the mud. "It's Rat," a young boy shouted. "Get him."

Rat jumped to his feet and ran a zigzag pattern to the nearest shadow. He paused there, then changed shadows as another rock sailed his way. He skipped randomly from shadow to shadow, hoping to confuse anyone tracking him, then froze into still-ness and waited.

There were three of them, boys not much larger than him, searching the shadows and seeking a little sport. If there had been more he would have feared them, for when they banded together in large numbers it became difficult to elude them, and often he must hide in his lair until they lost interest. But this time there were too few, and they'd chosen the wrong shadows to search. They had surprised him only because he was too absorbed in his pursuit of the fat purse. And he'd let the pleasure of the gesh distract him.

With his tormentors searching elsewhere, he changed shadows again and moved away, seeking the fat purse. He'd lost sight of it, but he found it again because the fat belly beneath which it hung was easy to spot as it jiggled and swayed through the ev-er-thickening crowd. Rat eyed the purse and squatted in a shadow, chewing his gesh and biding his time.

"Not here, Rat," another vendor said. "You'll not be a'scarin' away me customers with yer stench."

Rat changed shadows.

Fatpurse meandered toward the center of the market so Rat followed, skipping from shadow to shadow, counting on the thicker crowds there to confuse pursuit at the moment of truth.

Rat stopped in a shadow at the edge of Mathal's fruit stand. She'd seen him ap-proach, but turned her head and pretended not to notice. She frequently did that, al-lowing him to steal a piece of fruit, and in return he was never greedy, took only one. Often, in the dark of night, he left her a gift in return: a pretty stone polished by the weather, a half-eaten mouse or rat, or a small pile of grubs. He knew she appreciated the gifts, for in the morning she always took them in without scorn or distaste.

Rat lost sight of Fatpurse, then spotted him again where he'd stopped to watch a juggling act. The jugglers were good, and a dense crowd had gathered. Rat scanned the throng, making sure that no one looked his way—his moment had come.

He stayed close to the stalls, picking his shadows with care, choosing each so it brought him closer to that purse. He loved dancing in the world of shadows.

He paused in the last shadow, reached into his rags and withdrew a wicked little knife. Then he broke from his shadow, sprinted the short distance through daylight to the fat purse, gripped it and sliced out with the knife. But the cut was not smooth. Fatpurse must have felt a slight tug as the blade bit into the purse strings, and when Rat turned to flee he slipped in the mud, landed in a puddle with a splash.

"Stop," Fatpurse yelled. "Thief."

Rat jumped up and ran.

"What?" someone shouted.

"That scum, there," Fatpurse shouted. "He stole my purse. A reward to anyone who catches him."

"It's Rat. Get him."

Rat had miscalculated. The mud was too thick and the crowd not enough so. Everyone saw him easily and many reached out for him as he shot past. A hand caught hold of his shoulder; he turned on it, bit it hard and it let go.

"Ahhh! I'll get you, you little shit."

Rat dodged in and out of shadow and barely made it out of the market square. But the crowd quickly coalesced into a mob to give chase, and leading it were the boys who had hunted him earlier, as knowledgeable as he in the ways of the streets.

"Cut off the thief's hand," someone shouted.

Rat ran, heedless of direction, his fear pushing him, the mob close on his heels. He had no time for stealth or cunning, no time to find a shadow. He turned down a street, up an alley, down another street, conscious only of the mud splashing beneath his feet and the mob behind him. He turned into another alley, raced down its length, skidded madly through a hard turn, and there found featureless stone walls on all sides, no windows, no doorways, a blind alley with no escape. The mob would catch him; they'd cut off his hand, and with that realization the fear consumed him. It forced him to his knees in the mud, and without tears or sound, unable to move, he awaited his fate.

The mob rounded the turn in the alley only an instant behind him, a wave of angry people that knocked him into the mud, then washed over him and past him, slamming hard into the wall that marked the end of the alley. He heard several of them grunt or cry out in pain when those in the lead found themselves smashed between the hard stone ahead and their companions following close behind. Many were slow to rise.

"Where is he?" someone shouted.

Rat lay in the mud somewhat trampled but basically unhurt, while the mob milled about, surrounding him and paying him not the least bit of attention. Some scratched their heads and looked directly at him, but didn't seem to see him.

Fatpurse lumbered up the alley, lurching from side-to-side. He stopped two paces from Rat, put his fat hands on his hips and said, "Well. Where is he? Where is the little bastard? I can smell him"—he grimaced—"and he has my purse. Fifty coppers—No, a hundred coppers to whoever catches him."

Garbage and litter lined the edges of the alley. The mob focused on that, overturning anything that might hide a small thief, leaving Rat standing alone in the center, unhidden and yet ignored by all. He looked at his hands and arms; they were still there, stained brown by mud and horse shit. He looked at his legs and they too remained visible and unchanged.

Rat knew better than to question his good fortune. If these maniacs wanted to ignore him when he was there for the taking, so be it.

The mob had focused on the clutter that lined the alley, so Rat chose a path down the center. He moved slowly, careful lest he bump someone who stepped back from their search. But as he neared the mouth of the alley a tall man stood blocking his path, legs spread, fists on hips, elbows out. He wore a hip length leather jerkin over a fine linen shirt, and the sleeves of the shirt glistened in the sun, an immaculate white unstained by the mud of the streets.

"Well, well!" the man said, smiling and looking directly at Rat. "That's an impressive trick, young fellow."

Rat edged experimentally to one side, hoping that, like the others, the man was looking through him and not at him. But the man's eyes followed him unerringly.

The mob had turned quiet. Fatpurse approached the tall stranger and bowed from the waist. "Lord Roland," Fatpurse said. "You do us honor."

Lord! Rat thought. This stranger was a clan witchman come to carry Rat away to the hell-pits of Kathbeyanne.

"What goes here?" the witchman demanded.

Fatpurse bowed again. "We seek a cutpurse, Your Lordship. A disgusting, filthy, little thing."

The witchman took two steps and towered over Rat, who froze, his heart pounding uncontrollably. The witchman stuck out his hand. "Give me the purse, boy."

Fear flooded through Rat's soul, threatening to consume him. He could not move to hand the witchman the purse, though he lost control of his bladder and he felt warm urine streaming down his leg.

"Stop that," the witchman said.

Rat tried desperately to control his bladder.

The witchman grimaced and put a hand to his temple. He groaned and said, "Stop that, I said. Too much fear!" He struck out with his hand. Rat ended up sitting in the mud with a fiery red welt on his cheek and his head spinning.

"Stop that or I'll slap you again even harder."

Rat prayed to the gods to help him control his bladder.

"I see him," someone said. "He was invisible." The crowd came alive, turned again into a mob.

The witchman retrieved the purse from the mud. He handed it to Fatpurse. "Here's your purse. Now clear this mob out of here."

"But, my lord," the fat merchant pleaded. "I have no control over these people."

"Chop off the thief's hand," someone shouted.

"Take off his head."

The witchman raised both hands above his head and cried, "Silence."

All became still in an instant.

"There'll be no chopping of hands or heads this day," the witchman said. "At least not here and now. Now be gone. Clear this alley, or face my wrath."

The mob obeyed without question. They shuffled out of the alley, grumbling some, but no one questioned the witchman's authority. They left behind Fatpurse, Rat, and the witchman, and their passive compliance with the witchman's orders meant he must be a truly powerful wizard.

"Lord Roland," Fatpurse squealed, pointing at Rat. "Look. He's disappearing again."

The witchman's head snapped around to look at Rat with those terrible eyes. "Just remember you this, boy. I can see you. I can always see you."

He turned back to Fatpurse. "You've got your purse now so leave."

"But Lord. What about punishment for the thief?"

The witchman smiled. "I'll see to that personally, Raffin. And you, thief," he said, turning on Rat. "You're coming with me."

Rat simply fainted.

••••

As the witchman stepped out of the alley, followed by a servant carrying the unconscious, young thief, a rat scurried out of the rubbish, a small finger-length bone in its mouth. It lay the bone down in the mud and nudged it with its nose as if its exact position held some meaning. Another rat scurried past it carrying another bone, laid it down next to the first. More rats appeared, each carrying a small bone and placing it in the mud. The pattern they formed took on the shape of a man, but since none of the bones were human, the man-shape was an undersized, twisted and deformed skeleton of bird, cat, dog and rat bones. The rats placed the last bones in the shape of a crown about the little skeleton-man's head, then they retreated to the rubbish and disappeared beneath it.

The air about the skeleton-king shimmered, and the bones of one hand moved. Then the skeleton-king's chest heaved a sigh and he sat up. He climbed carefully to his feet, stood no taller than the small thief. And while deformed and misshapen, he strode to the mouth of the alley as a king might walk among commoners.

He caught a fleeting glimpse of the wizard, accompanied by a servant carrying the young thief. He stayed hidden in the shadows of the alley and watched as they weaved their way through the crowds in the street. He sighed, the empty sockets of his skeleton eyes focused on the young thief, and he whispered, "Now it begins, my child, and there's no turning back. Can you forgive me for setting you on this course?"

The skeleton king lowered his head, the bones tumbled to the ground and lay in a shapeless heap. The rats reappeared and quickly scattered them.

••••

Rat awoke in someone's arms. He kept his eyes closed and remained motionless, and he listened.

"Forgive me for saying so, my lord, but the stench is terrible." That voice belonged to the one carrying him.

"You're quite right, Avis," the witchman said. "He does stink, doesn't he? Place him on the table here."

"On the table, my lord? Might the Lady Olivia object?"

The witchman hesitated. "Yes, one should never anger my mother. Best place him on the floor then."

The arms laid Rat gently on a stone floor. He took care not to move, and he continued to listen.

"Will that be all, my lord?"

"Yes. Thank you, Avis. You may go. But summon the Lady AnnaRail, please."

"Certainly, my lord."

Rat heard feet walk across the floor, then a door closed and the room grew silent. He waited for several seconds, and when he heard nothing more he opened his good eye the tiniest bit. Across the room the witchman sat in a chair, his elbow resting on a table, his legs sprawled out before him, his ankles crossed. And he looked directly at Rat.

Rat snapped his eye shut.

"Come, child. I know you're awake. Open your eyes and stand up."

Rat kept his eye shut. After a pause he heard more footsteps, then the toe of a boot nudged him gently in the ribs. "Do as I say, boy. I don't have the time to put up with your games. Now stand up."

The boot nudged him less gently. Rat still didn't understand, but he realized he could no longer play dead. When the boot nudged him again, he reached out and grabbed it, pulled it to his mouth and bit it.

"Ahhh! Damn you," the witchman shouted, twisting his foot free. "That's a new pair of boots. You'd better not have marked the leather." The witchman examined the boot carefully.

Rat squirmed to his feet, hissed and spit at the witchman, who stood near the only door. Rat put his back to a wall and slid to the nearest corner.

The witchman ignored Rat, returned to the table and sat down. "I'm not going to hurt you, boy, so calm down."

Rat scanned the room, looking for hidden traps. But at that moment he sensed another presence, something he could feel but not see or hear. It was not in the room but was conscious of him, and coming for him. It was angry at him, with an evil, terrible hatred, and it was going to punish him. He fought back tears as his legs gave out and he slumped to the floor. He crammed several fingers in his mouth to silence the sobs, curled into a fetal position and couldn't take his eyes from that single, closed door.

The door burst open to reveal a wrinkled, old, demon witchwoman in long, flowing, black robes with the fires of magic burning about her. Her face was a mask of wrinkled fury as she pointed at Rat with a shaking finger and demanded, "And what, in the name of the Unnamed King, is that filth?"

In that instant Rat simultaneously fainted, winked into invisibility, and lost control of his bowels.

••••

Roland watched his mother's fury dissipate and turn into curiosity. Still standing in the doorway, her finger stopped shaking and she paused. "Well now!" she said. "What do we have here?" She crossed the room to stand over Rat and answered her own question. "A young magician it seems. Now I understand. I sensed his power—raw and uncontrolled, but power nevertheless—and I assumed something had invaded our household. Are you responsible for this, Roland?"

He nodded. "Yes, mother."

At that moment his wife appeared in the doorway. "Husband. Mother," she greeted them formally. "Avis said you wished to see me."

Roland looked at her and frowned. "Don't you see him, AnnaRail?"

"See whom?" the younger woman asked.

"A boy child," the old woman answered, "at my feet. An urchin of the streets, it appears. And, unlike us, apparently you cannot see through his invisibility." The old woman nudged Rat with the tip of a slipper.

"Don't stand too close, mother," Roland said. "He bites, and your soft slippers won't protect you."

The old woman stepped back.

"And it's not invisibility," he said. "Just a shadow. He makes his own shadows and hides within them."

AnnaRail frowned. "But the lights in here are too soft." She bent over Rat.

Roland shook his head. "He needs no light to make the shadows he makes."

"I'm impressed," AnnaRail said, reaching out like a blind man to find the child she could not see.

Standing over her the old woman said, "Not a powerful spell but a subtle one. Who is he? And where did you find him?"

Roland gave a summary of the morning's incident. "I questioned several of the merchants. No one seems to know who his parents were, or when he was born, or where he came from. They call him Rat, and he seems to have been living somewhere near the market. A fruit monger remembers him as far back as two years ago. He appears to be about six or seven years old, though that might be due to malnutrition. She said he steals an occasional piece of fruit, but thinks he lives mostly on garbage and dead animals and worms and the like. Incredible as it seems, he's apparently survived on his own. But I don't think it could have lasted much longer. Look at his teeth. They're so stained by gesh I doubt he's eaten anything else for some time now."

"I can't see his teeth," AnnaRail said. She frowned and her attention seemed to shift elsewhere. She sat down on the floor unceremoniously and looked up at the old woman. "Something's wrong here. Will you ward me?"

"Certainly," Olivia said. She stood over AnnaRail and began chanting words in a hushed voice, words incomprehensible to Roland whose own magic was so limited.

After several heartbeats Olivia stopped chanting, and AnnaRail's eyes lost that faraway look. "It's hopeless," the younger woman said. "He's gone into some sort of recession. Very severe. So much fear! What could cause such fear in one so small, I wonder. It will kill him, I think. Soon his soul will be beyond our reach."

Something deep within Roland told him he could not allow that. "Then we must act quickly."

"Hold," Olivia said. "Why should we act at all?"

"But we must."

Olivia's eyes narrowed. "Really? He is nothing to us; let him die."

"No," Roland said.

The old woman stared at him and Roland felt naked under that gaze. "What has come over you? Has this bundle of filth enchanted you? It is definitely a thing of magic; that I sense, even if you cannot. Have you lost your senses? Are you enspelled?"

Roland tried to calm himself. "No," he said. "I'm not enspelled. I'm answering to my instincts. To let this child die, I think . . . would be a grave mistake. To save it . . . to save it will somehow benefit House Elhiyne, though how I cannot say."

Olivia nodded. "Very well. You are not enspelled. And I know the power of your intuition, even if you doubt its magic. But what you suggest will require powerful and dangerous spells. Besides we here, only Marjinell and MichaelOff are available. And MichaelOff is only just of age, and far too inexperienced. I'll not endanger him so."

"We must do something," Roland said.

Olivia looked down at AnnaRail. "What say you?"

AnnaRail looked at Roland as if she could see into his soul. "I sense strange forces at work here, subtle forces. This child is strongly tied to the arcane in some fashion I cannot fathom, and I trust my husband's instincts. We can take precautions to protect MichaelOff. I say we at least try."

Olivia did not reply immediately, but looked at each of them, measuring them. "Are the two of you prepared to accept responsibility for this . . . this guttersnipe?"

Roland nodded instantly. AnnaRail hesitated, then said, "Yes, I suppose we must."

"Very well," the old woman said. "AnnaRail, prepare the child. Roland, summon Marjinell and MichaelOff to the sanctum. I'll go there directly and set the Wards."

••••

Olivia turned her back on them, left the room so quickly they had no time to react. She enjoyed such dramatic exits; it kept her offspring on their toes. Out in the halls the servants rushed aside as she strode past them. They feared her, she knew, and they avoided her when they could, which was right, for she was a woman to be feared.

Avis, the chief steward of the household, stood outside the sanctum waiting for her. It was not the first time he had anticipated her with almost clairvoyant accuracy, and it was not the first time she wondered if there wasn't some small talent hidden within his soul.

She paused before entering the sanctum, though she kept her eyes straight ahead looking at the power within. "You know the procedure."

"Yes, madam. I'll seal the chamber and post guards."

She nodded, then stepped forth into the sanctum, the servant gone from her mind. This room, and others like it, always struck her as odd, even after all these years. She turned about, taking in all twelve walls and twelve corners. Almost round, but not quite. The servants would never enter such a room, not even in fear of their mortal lives.

For a moment she stood without moving, looking at the ceiling, concentrating and focusing her power. Then she chose the corner designated for the first Ward, though there was nothing to distinguish it from the rest. She approached it, stood motionless before it, and concentrated with every ounce of her will on the words of power she had learned as a younger witch.

She spoke the words from memory, by rote, for as always they carried no meaning at first, as if they were not meant to be understood by a mere mortal such as she. But then slowly the power within them filled her soul with meaning, and the air about her began to shimmer without luminance, a wavering of the senses only there at the edge of vision. Then, as if something beyond her own will controlled her actions, her hand thrust upward. Her sleeve billowed about a leathery old wrist quivering with tension, and she cried out in a voice strengthened by the power at her command: "*Primus*," she called, "I bid you come."

Pain shot through her arm as a spark of radiance flared within her upraised hand, and light that was not meant for mortal eyes splashed across the room. She wanted to look away, wanted to wince at the pain that burned a hole into her soul, but she dare not show such weakness to the life she had called forth from the nether reaches.

She stood for a long, motionless moment. And when certain she had achieved control, she lowered her hand slowly to the floor, left behind a pillar of such intensity that it forced her to look away. To her eyes it was a rod of golden light no wider than a finger, but to her soul it was power, the First Dominant Ward of Power, vibrating with a sound that hurt her ears, blistering her hand with heat, and torturing her soul with a life beyond what she could ever hope to comprehend.

She turned away, could not resist the urge to glance at her hand. There were no burns to mark the skin.

She walked to the next corner, raised her hand again and cried, "*Secundus.* I bid you come," and there she drew forth another Ward. But where the first had been gold, the second flared violet, and it sang a note higher and more shrill. "*Tertius*," she cried at the third corner, and brought forth the white Ward. *Quartus* answered her summons at the fourth, and *Quintus* at the fifth. When *Sextus* finally occupied the sixth corner she paused and wiped sweat from her brow with her sleeve.

She passed the next two corners without filling them, for between them stood the only entrance to the room, a heavy stone door hanging on iron hinges. At the ninth corner she called upon *Nonus*, and at the tenth *Decimus*, then *Undecimus*, and *Duodecimus*. She completed the circuit of the room, and turned to look upon her work: ten Wards in ten corners, each flaring its own color, sounding a note harsh and demanding.

Roland entered the room, carrying Rat and glancing her way nervously. Still unconscious, the urchin had been stripped naked, his grime and filth washed away. AnnaRail walked into the room, followed by Marjinell, her other daughter-in-law, and young MichaelOff, Marjinell's oldest son. Roland placed the naked child on the stone floor at the center of the chamber, then turned and left the sanctum without a word. About them all the air shimmered with power.

Olivia's eyes were drawn to the child's face where one eye had swollen shut with some malady. Next to that were three puckered scars, previously hidden by the filth and grime. They were ugly pocks, probably caused by some sort of infectious eruption, and poorly healed. It struck her that the child could have grown up a handsome young man, but not with such unpleasant disfigurement.

Olivia turned to MichaelOff. "Come, grandson, I need your strong back."

She'd trained him herself, so he knew what was required; he stepped to the heavy stone door and put a shoulder to it. It swung silently on its hinges and closed with a thud to form the twelfth wall. He threw the bolt, sealed the chamber, and except for the hinges, handle, and locking bolt of the door, the twelve walls were now featureless stone. The boy joined the two younger women at the center of the room.

Olivia stepped up to the empty seventh corner, and without hesitating she reached upward and cried, "*Septimus.* I bid you come." And in her lowering hand she brought forth the Ward of the Benesh'ere, the seventh tribe of the Shahot, exiled to the Great Munjarro Waste for their ancient crimes. It stood black and silent, unique in its lack of color or sound.

She stepped to the last corner, the only one not filled with the infinite power of a Ward. The eighth Ward was hers to command, and calling it forth always made her feel as if the vitality of youth flowed through her veins once more. She straightened her back, thrust her chin out, and could almost believe that her sagging old breasts stood out pertly like those of a young schoolgirl. She felt strength in her movements, and knew that her eyes glowed with godfire, for the room appeared as if viewed through blood-tinted water. "*Octavus*," she commanded, "Ward of the power of the eighth tribe, Keeper of the House of Elhiyne, I command you . . . attend me."

Instantly the eighth Ward flared, red, angry, and powerful. She admired it for a moment, then turned her back on it, showing it her contempt. "The circle is complete," she said. "None may enter. None may leave."

She joined the others at the center of the chamber and added her hands to the living circle they now formed about Rat. She looked at each of them, judging them. She stood wrapped within her power and knew that to the others, the godfire in her eyes gave her the appearance of near madness. They would see her as dark, arrogant, and dangerous.

She lifted her face to the gods and spoke. "We, of House Elhiyne, of Clan Elhiyne, of the eighth tribe of the Shahot, are here assembled in arcane rite. Let those whose magic is not ours . . . *Be gone.*"

••••

Rat snapped awake, careful not to move, eyes closed and listening. Only when certain he had heard every sound the room would yield did he open his good eye. He lay naked and alone, beneath a blanket on a cot in an otherwise empty room: a bare stone cell with an open doorway. The gesh pulled at him and he hungered for it, knew that soon the lack of it would grow into a painful need. And there were witches all about him. He could sense them, especially the wrinkled, old, evil one. He had to get out, get away from her and find his gesh.

He tossed the cover aside, swung his legs off the cot and crossed the room. He found no one in the hallway beyond, but to his delight he discovered many shadows. It took much searching to find his way in such strange surroundings, for often he had to hide in a convenient shadow while witches passed. And then there was the stairway, a long winding path of steps down which he crept with no help from shadow. But once below he easily found the courtyard. From there it was a simple matter to find the front gate, to slip through the iron bars and lose himself in the shadows of the city.

It took all afternoon to cross the city to his den, where he scrabbled among the straw of his bed to find his gesh. To his great relief it remained undisturbed. But as he placed a pinch of the root on his tongue it seemed to catch fire, his eyes felt as if they would burst from his head, and the contents of his stomach came boiling forth to splatter all over the filthy straw of his bed. The convulsions continued without mercy until he fainted.

Twice more he awoke in the bare stone cell, naked and alone, and twice more he escaped from the witch's den to the city. Each time he returned to his lair to taste the gesh, and each time convulsions twisted his body until he fainted.

A fourth time he awoke, naked and alone. And a fourth time he made his way to the courtyard, but this time an invisible something filled the gaps between the bars of the gate. He could feel it, but not see it, and it prevented him from slipping through. He tried the wall, but it was too high and he found no purchase for climbing. He spent the entire day working his way around the compound, seeking some means of escape, and found every path blocked.

Late that afternoon he returned to the front gate, desperate, exhausted, the cramps in his stomach demanding more gesh. In his frustration he chewed on the lock and rattled its mechanism.

"You're a stubborn one, aren't you?"

At the sound of the voice Rat dove for the nearest shadow and froze. One of the witchwomen approached, stopped a short distance from him and smiled. "Don't be afraid, Rat. I won't hurt you. I'm AnnaRail, and I'm here to teach you, for you have much to learn, and the first thing you must learn is your new name. From this moment on you will be called 'Morgin', and no one will ever again call you 'Rat.' "

She finished speaking by passing her hand before her as if to emphasize her words, though for an instant Morgin thought he saw a faint, red flash dance along her fingertips.

"Now that is the second thing you must learn, Morgin. I have placed a spell upon you. You will not again leave this compound without my permission."

"Gesh," he croaked.

"And that is the third thing you must learn." Her voice surprised Morgin, for he heard sadness in it. "You have sampled the pleasures of gesh, and now you must pay a price for that, and I'm afraid you will find that lesson harsh in the extreme.

"Never again will you enjoy gesh, for I have placed another spell upon you, a spell that will remain until you are old enough to remove it yourself. And that will not be for a very long time. You will suffer in the learning of this lesson, but I'll be by your side, and I'll help you as much as I can."

She held out her hand. "Come with me now, Morgin. It's time for you to begin a new life."

He hissed at her like a snake, "Sssssssssss!"

Her eyes saddened. "Won't you be my friend? Come. Take my hand."

Morgin was tempted—this witch seemed kind. He considered her for a moment, then slowly he emerged from his shadow, and wondering all the while if some trap awaited him, he edged closer, step by step, until he could lean forward and sniff the outstretched hand.

It was sweet, and soft, and gentle.

He scanned the courtyard, ensuring that no other witches lurked nearby. Then he reached out and placed his hand in hers, and began a journey from which there could be no return.

2

In the Witch's Den

MORGIN SPENT THREE days in bed, his hunger for gesh a constant ache. With his hands shaking, his knees trembling, it was not until the morning of the fourth day that he could stand on his own, and then only for short periods.

On the morning of the fifth day an old man shook him awake at dawn. "Come, boy."

He bundled Morgin into a blanket and lifted him carefully, then carried him down to a courtyard filled with people, horses, wagons and a carriage, placed him on a seat in the carriage, and they left the city.

Morgin drifted in and out of sleep for most of that day, and finally awoke at dusk when the witches stopped to set up camp for the night. His stomach no longer cramped, and as a warm and comfortable darkness settled over the land, he felt strong enough to escape. He waited until no one was looking, then slipped into the shadows surrounding the camp. But he encountered that invisible wall of something, the same thing that had blocked the gate in the city. And as he circled the entire camp, he found no gap or breach through which to escape. He'd have to bide his time.

After three days and two nights on the road they arrived at a large stone building they called Castle Elhiyne. He looked about as the carriage rolled through the main entrance, and realized he could never find his way back to the city.

The next six months were hard. They forced him to learn numbers and letters, and the pretty witch AnnaRail tried to teach him the witch magic. She insisted it had something to do with the shadows he loved, but he knew better; shadows were just shadows. At least he managed to avoid crossing paths with the evil, old witch Olivia. And he did find a special place to hide, a little den that no one else knew about, though, oddly enough, it moved around, and was never in the same place when he went looking for it.

The first six months were hard.

••••

AnnaRail had been summoned to Olivia's audience chamber to discuss the child Morgin, and while Olivia spoke in subdued tones with her oldest son Malka, Marjinell, his wife, sat beside them, obviously bored. She had openly expressed her opinion that it had been a mistake to adopt Morgin into the clan, and AnnaRail hoped she would not interfere when the topic turned to the child.

Olivia's audience chamber could accommodate only a few selected guests. There were two couches, a small table, and a hearth for heat during winter, a warm and comfortable room that contrasted sharply with the old woman's cold nature. Olivia preferred to conduct important business here, reserving the Hall of Wills for ceremonial occasions and large crowds.

"AnnaRail," Olivia said. "Attend me."

AnnaRail stepped forward and curtsied.

Olivia patted the spot next to her on the couch. "Sit beside me and tell me of the child Morgin. Roland. Malka. Marjinell. Pay attention. I'm sure we're all interested in AnnaRail's report."

Report? AnnaRail thought. Time for a report on the piece of property named Morgin.

"Does he still act like an untamed animal?" Marjinell asked.

The silence that followed her outburst clearly embarrassed Malka. The big warrior tried to end it quickly. "You were to conduct a seeking. What did you find?"

AnnaRail hesitated for a moment, and when she did speak, she couldn't hide a slight tremble in her voice. "I . . . attempted one."

"You *attempted* a seeking?" Malka asked.

"Yes."

"And?" Olivia prompted.

"I . . . failed."

The room grew silent. "Explain yourself," Olivia said.

AnnaRail hesitated, but it was no use trying to hide her own fear of the ordeal. "Based upon a survey of the child's contact with the netherworld, I placed several minor wards, and summoned a demon under geas, whose continued existence was dependent upon my safety. I entered the child's soul and found much pain, sorrow and unhappiness, and no joy. And fear. I found fear above all else."

While Olivia, Malka, and Roland listened, Marjinell seemed preoccupied with a mirror.

"Between birth," AnnaRail continued, "and an undefined time several years ago—probably his entry into life in the market in Anistigh—there is a large period that is ruled absolutely by fear. When I investigated it I found myself ensnared, almost consumed, and when I tried to leave, I could not; the fear trapped me as if it were a living thing. The demon pulled me from that existence screaming in terror. I freed the demon, released the wards, and have not returned to that place since."

"Kill it," Marjinell said. "Kill the little monster before it harms someone."

"Silence," Olivia said. "I will not rule out killing a being if it becomes a threat to this family. But at this time, that would be premature."

Marjinell scanned their faces then stood in a huff. "Well, if that's all you think of my word—"

"Sit down, daughter," Olivia said. "Your opinion is always valued here. But we all are sometimes wrong."

Marjinell sat down slowly.

Olivia turned to AnnaRail. "How long did this period of fear last?"

Now was not the time to be timid, so AnnaRail looked the old women in the eyes. "My sense of the time scale confused me; I got the impression he'd lived with such fear for centuries, but we know that cannot be, so I failed to learn anything of value."

Olivia's eyes bored into her, and she could not have looked away had she tried. The old woman said, "You may go now—all of you. I wish to be alone to ponder this Morgin child."

••••

Morgin's first two years with the witches were lonely, more so than living alone on the streets of Anistigh. In the city no one punished him for not knowing his letters or numbers or magic, and Mathal had always had a gentle smile for him. But among the witches no one looked upon him kindly. Well . . . there was AnnaRail. When she punished him, he sensed she took no joy in it. And her youngest daughter little NickoLot; Nicki was all smiles and happiness, a tiny bundle of energy with big, round eyes.

The other boys his age were his biggest problem, especially JohnEngine, Anna-Rail's second son. When the older boys weren't about, JohnEngine and his followers could be quite cruel.

In his third year with the witches the situation came to a head. Morgin had just finished a lesson with AnnaRail, and was taking a shortcut through the cook's garden, when he found his path blocked by several boys. He turned to flee, but they encircled him completely.

JohnEngine swaggered out from among them to face him. "It's Rat," he said, "the thief. I bet we'll find everything that's gone missing hidden beneath your cot."

Morgin was too terrified to speak.

JohnEngine shoved him hard, forcing him to stumble backwards. Morgin cringed as JohnEngine stepped forward and raised his fist to deliver a painful blow. But at that moment the shadow of a hawk, coasting on a thermal, drifted lazily between them.

Morgin had had enough, and instinctively he stepped into the shadow, danced within it for a pace or two, then stopped in a dark shadow in the lee of a stone wall.

JohnEngine shouted, "Where'd he go."

Watching for an opportunity to slip away, Morgin remained motionless in his shadow as the boys searched about. He would have left it at that, but JohnEngine's efforts to find him slowly brought him closer. So he waited until JohnEngine was within arm's reach, and he struck out from his shadow, hitting him squarely in the nose.

JohnEngine staggered backward, blood pouring over his upper lip, so Morgin stepped forward, bringing his shadow with him, and kicked him in the shin.

Surprisingly, Morgin found shadows just where he needed them. So he danced among them and gave JohnEngine a sound beating.

••••

AnnaRail stifled a sigh as Olivia stormed through the door into her chambers, demanding, "How is JohnEngine? I hear Morgin beat him rather badly. I swear I'll personally tear that little guttersnipe apart with my bare hands."

AnnaRail did not want the old woman to take a keen interest in Morgin. "Calm down, mother," she said. "JohnEngine has some bruises and minor cuts that will heal quickly, and he will hopefully learn something about picking fights. Besides, how much damage can two eight year old boys do to one another?"

Olivia hesitated. "You say JohnEngine picked the fight?"

AnnaRail nodded. "And Morgin gave him a sound thrashing. Unfortunately, he used his shadows to do it and he's been punished for that, and JohnEngine has been punished for starting the fight."

"I don't understand. You sound pleased."

"In a way, I am. I hear JohnEngine has been picking on Morgin regularly, acting the bully and inciting the other boys against him; a cowardly thing, but a very boyish thing.

"Apparently, JohnEngine was up to his usual tricks, and Morgin vanished into a shadow. Instead of going someplace to hide, he turned on JohnEngine and beat him mercilessly. I'm afraid JohnEngine was utterly helpless against an opponent that was virtually invisible." AnnaRail chuckled.

"What better way can JohnEngine learn the reward for cowardly violence than to be punished by his intended victim? I hope JohnEngine learned something today.

"And look at Morgin. He finally faced up to someone he's afraid of. I've been waiting to see this for two years. He didn't run, he stood up to his fears."

Olivia nodded, and her frown disappeared. "I begin to understand," she said. "But this Morgin child is an odd one, what with these shadows. I doubt I've actually seen him more than a few times since he came to us, though I can sense him. He hides from me, you know. I'll round a corner, or step out of a room, and catch a fleeting glimpse of him as he slips away."

"He's afraid of you."

Olivia shrugged. "He should be. But my curiosity is aroused. I would like to speak with him. Where is he?"

"Actually, I don't know."

"You don't know?"

"No. He seems to have found a hiding place with a certain enchantment to it, for I can detect him neither here nor in the netherworld."

"That is serious, daughter."

AnnaRail shook her head. "Not really. He's used it before, but never for more than an hour or two, and only when he felt badly hurt. We all need a place to be alone at times, and he has his. I'll begin to worry only if he's gone over long."

AnnaRail felt relieved when Olivia said, "Very well. We'll allow the brat his private hole, as long as he doesn't abuse the privilege."

Olivia turned and left, and was gone as quickly as she'd come.

••••

Morgin was on his way to AnnaRail's chambers when he sensed the wrinkled, old witch behind him coming his way, her anger roiling like the thunderheads of a violent storm. He stopped in the middle of the corridor, glancing about desperately for a place to hide, but the hall was long and straight, with no doors at hand. Then the wall beside him shimmered, and the opening to his special alcove appeared where no room should be. He stepped into it and pressed his back against a wall. He knew that where he saw an entrance to a recessed alcove, everyone else saw featureless stone blocks. Still, he cringed as Olivia thundered past him, her robes billowing out behind her.

He heard her throw open the door to AnnaRail's chambers and demand, "How is JohnEngine? I hear Morgin beat him rather badly." Then the door closed and he could hear no more.

Trembling, he sat down on the floor with his back to the wall and tucked his knees up tightly to his chest. He was sitting like that when the old witch left AnnaRail and marched back down the hall. Eventually the trembling ceased and he drifted off into a restless sleep.

DaNoel and MichaelOff's voices woke him with a start. They'd stopped in the hall just outside the alcove.

"Any sign of him?" MichaelOff asked.

"No," said DaNoel. He leaned against what to him was solid stone wall, but to Morgin was the entrance to the alcove. From within he saw the flesh of DaNoel's hand flatten as it pressed against a wall that wasn't there.

"Why do we have to waste our time looking for him?" DaNoel asked.

"Because grandmother wants to find him," MichaelOff said, "and is angry that she can't. Your mother says to look for a short while then don't bother any longer. She said she'll take care of grandmother."

DaNoel shook his head, pulled his hand away from the wall, and he and MichaelOff walked away.

Morgin had been standing with his nose only inches from DaNoel's hand, marveling at how the older boy could lean against nothing. He had always known the alcove was a magical place, for no one could find him when he hid there. He'd gone looking for it a hundred times and it was never where it should be, nor anywhere else for that matter. But when he desperately needed a place where the wizards and witches could not find him, it would appear in the oddest of places; an alcove several paces deep often set in a wall only a hand-span thick.

His stomach growled. Perhaps he could sneak into the kitchen, steal some food, and return before they caught him. He stepped out into the hall, then realized his mistake. He spun about to confront a featureless stone wall. The alcove had disappeared, and he knew from experience that he would not see it again until *it* was ready.

3

To Glimpse the Wizard

MORGIN STOOD MOTIONLESS as the other boys closed in; JohnEngine wanted revenge for the beating. With no escape at hand Morgin made a run for it, charging into their midst with all the speed and force he could muster. Badly outnumbered, he ended up face down in the dirt with several of them on top of him; they pinned his arms behind his back then lifted him back to his feet with their combined strength. He struggled as they twisted his arms painfully. He tried to cry out, but they crammed an old rag into his mouth.

JohnEngine swaggered forward. He looked Morgin over, then spoke. "It seems we have captured some vermin here," he said, his fists resting on his hips. "Now what is to be done with Rat? Any ideas?"

"Throw him in the river," someone said.

JohnEngine shook his head. "No. The river's too far, too much trouble."

"The pig wallow?"

Again JohnEngine shook his head. "No. The pig wallow will only make him homesick. And it might insult the pigs."

They all laughed.

"No," JohnEngine said. "We have to teach this pest a lesson." He thought for a moment, then his eyes lit up. He reached into his tunic and pulled out a short, stubby candle.

The other boys snickered.

"Let's go," JohnEngine said, and they dragged him away.

He was half carried, half pushed, to a dank, musty, subterranean storage room deep within the bowels of the castle, an old room filled with abandoned casks and pots and chests. While three of them held him, the rest dismantled a pile of refuse that had been stacked in one corner, exposing a large and jagged hole in the wall, with complete darkness beyond.

"What's that?" Morgin asked.

JohnEngine said, "Elhiyne goes far deeper into the earth than most people know. The old castle was built almost entirely underground, though most of it has been walled off. And you, vermin, are going to join us while we do some exploring."

They pulled him through the jagged hole, laughing at him. Inside they paused only to light a candle, then dragged him off into the darkness.

Morgin saw that these were not crude caves but smooth, stone walls with ceilings and floors. And while he could see little in the flickering shadows of the candle's light, he found that in the ways of Rat he knew the darkness as his captors never would. A calm descended upon him as he realized that he need only bide his time.

At each intersection of the ancient corridors the boys paused to examine chalk marks on the walls. Apparently they had placed some code there during earlier explorations. Morgin began to understand that the corridors of the old castle were a labyrinth.

Eventually they pulled him into a narrow side passage, with walls and ceiling so close the flickering shadows of the candle hovered just overhead. They stopped at a small wooden door, pulled it open and hurled him into the room beyond. He tumbled across the dusty floor of a small cell of unknown purpose. JohnEngine and his followers entered behind him.

"We're going to leave you now, Rat," JohnEngine said. "I would advise you not to strike out on your own. Without a candle you stand no chance, and even with one you'd not understand our markings. And if you're foolish enough to become hopelessly lost, you'll rot here for the rest of your days."

"Will you come back for me?" Morgin asked.

JohnEngine thought about that for a moment. "I suppose so," he said, "in a day or two, when we have time." He spun about and left; the rest followed, closing the small door with a loud thud.

Morgin jumped up immediately and pressed his ear against it. He heard their voices receding slowly, laughing at his expense. He waited until certain they'd not hear him, then he lifted the latch on the old door and leaned against it. It creaked slowly open, and he sighed with relief that it had no lock. The fools had expected the darkness to hold him.

He stepped through the door, closed it and moved silently in their wake. There was never a question about the direction he should choose, for he was in darkness, and darkness was like shadow, and in shadow he always knew his way.

He caught up with them quickly, then held back, following just beyond the limit of the candle's light, dancing among the shadows.

"Are you really going to leave him there for two days?" one of the boys asked.

"No," JohnEngine said, laughing loudly. "If he's missing through the night mother'll find out and have my hide. We'll just let him stew in the dark for a couple of hours. By that time he should be a whimpering mess."

The other boys laughed, and Morgin chose that instant to act. He picked a shadow he knew would pass close to JohnEngine and melted into it, and as JohnEngine's candle came within reach, Morgin gave a light puff of breath and blew it out. Darkness descended.

"What happened?"

"Stay calm," JohnEngine said. "It'll only take a second or two to relight the candle."

Morgin stood calmly among them and watched JohnEngine fumble in his tunic for a striker and flint. Before coming to the witches he'd thought everyone could see in the dark, but slowly, through hints and clues, he'd learned his ability was quite unique. He didn't know if he actually saw JohnEngine with his eyes, or if he just sensed him and pictured it in his mind's eye. In any case, it was just one more thing that would make him different from the other boys—make him not normal—so he'd always kept his night-vision a secret.

Once JohnEngine had retrieved his striker and flint, he knelt and placed the candle on the floor next to some tinder. Morgin reached out, picked up the candle and stepped back a pace. When JohnEngine struck the first spark, the flash of light briefly illuminated the floor. "Where's the candle?" he demanded.

"I don't know," someone said. "You're the one who had it."

"I must have knocked it aside with my boot. Does anyone have a spare?"

"I do," a boy named Dannasul said, reaching into his tunic. He fumbled for a moment, then held his candle blindly out in JohnEngine's direction. "Here," he said.

Morgin reached out and took the candle, and Dannasul relaxed, assuming JohnEngine had taken it.

JohnEngine groped forward in the darkness, pushing Morgin aside to grasp Dannasul by the shoulders. "Where is it?"

"Where is what?" Dannasul asked.

"The damn candle."

"I just gave it to you."

"No you didn't."

"Yes I did."

"You must have dropped it."

"Well it can't have rolled far. Both candles must be here at our feet."

"All right," JohnEngine said. "Everyone down on their hands and knees. Let's find those candles."

Morgin stepped back several paces to watch. He enjoyed watching them grope about, grabbing at one another, pouncing upon the slightest bit of debris, hoping it was one of the missing candles. They grew more frantic; their voices rising in pitch as they realized the candles were nowhere to be found. Their efforts raised a cloud of dust from the floor, and several of them began to cough and panic.

Morgin considered leaving them there in the darkness. He would have no trouble finding his way back, though he realized how unfair that would be. JohnEngine had intended, no matter how cruelly, that Morgin's capture should last no more than a few hours.

Morgin decided to return same for same, and as JohnEngine had said, he would ". . . let them stew in the dark for a couple of hours."

"Everyone calm down," JohnEngine said. "We have to stay together. We mustn't get separated. Let's grasp hands, and no one let go."

"But how do we find our way?"

"I think I can remember it," JohnEngine said. "I've been over it often enough. We take a left at the next corridor, then skip three, and right after that it should be a straight walk from there."

Morgin stifled a laugh as they started out, for JohnEngine's first mistake was to start in the wrong direction. As their course took them deeper into the old castle, Morgin followed.

It took them almost an hour to realize they were lost, another to see that it was hopeless, and a third for them to decide their predicament was all JohnEngine's fault. They collapsed in the middle of a corridor, berating him, some crying, some swearing, all of them radiating the fear that Morgin knew so well.

He sat down next to JohnEngine, who sat with his knees tucked up close to his chest.

"Here," Morgin said, holding out a candle. But then he realized that JohnEngine could not see in the blackness that surrounded them. Morgin pressed the candle into JohnEngine's hand.

JohnEngine started, groping at the familiar feel of the wax, pressing the candle close to his face as if he could see it in the dark. "Where did you find it?"

Morgin didn't answer him.

"I've got a candle," JohnEngine said, leaping to his feet.

They all jumped to their feet, listening while JohnEngine brought out his striker and flint and a small bit of tinder. After several tries the tinder caught, and light flared in the hallway.

They shouted and cheered, hugging each other and slapping JohnEngine on the back. But when they realized they stood in a hall they had never explored, their joy died. They sat down silently, once again lost.

Morgin, standing at the edge of the candle's light, stepped calmly in among them.

"Where did you come from?" JohnEngine asked.

Morgin saw the fear in JohnEngine's eyes. "I followed you."

"Then you're lost too."

"No," Morgin said. "I know the way."

JohnEngine jumped to his feet in an instant. "Have you been marking our back-trail?"

"No. I just know the way."

JohnEngine sat down. "You're a lying fool."

"Or maybe you're a fool," Morgin said. He held out the other candle.

"Where did you get that?"

"I took it from Dannasul, as I took yours from you."

JohnEngine stood slowly, unexcitedly. "Then lead the way," he said, his voice lacking conviction.

"I can't," Morgin said. "Not until you blow out your candle. I don't know the way in the light. I know it only in the dark."

The other boys looked at him oddly. Morgin saw no revulsion in JohnEngine's eyes, just indecision and perhaps some understanding. JohnEngine stared at him for a long, silent moment. Then he said, "Blow out that candle."

••••

After the incident in the ruins of the old castle, JohnEngine stopped tormenting Morgin. An easy peace settled between them and they grew to be friends. And during the year that followed Morgin came to accept his place among the wizards and witches of the clan.

His schooling continued, though the only lessons he found of interest were the stories of the Benesh'ere: fierce desert tribesmen who lived in the Great Munjarro Waste. They were said to have pale, bone-white skin and coal-black hair. The shortest of them stood a head taller than the tallest clansman and they were ferocious warriors. They'd done something evil in the far past and were exiled to the Waste.

The lessons in inter-clan relationships were dry and academic. But near the end of his fourth year with the witches, as winter receded and spring began to blossom, an emissary from the Greater Council arrived with a considerable retinue. And Morgin had the opportunity to observe first-hand the anger that smoldered beneath the surface of every Lesser Clansman's pride.

Dannasul, a boy Morgin's age, hissed conspiratorially, "Come. Let's go watch the action."

Dannasul led him to the Hall of Wills, a cavernous room with a dais and high throne at the far end. As the crowd grew Morgin realized every clansman present had gathered to watch the emissary face House Elhiyne. Standing with the other lesser clansmen, he and Dannasul were politely nudged toward the back, their view blocked by the adults. But Dannasul showed him a narrow staircase that opened onto a high gallery where a dozen other boys his own age were huddled behind a rail, peering between its balusters at the main floor below.

Nothing happened for the longest time, but then a hush descended on the crowd, and moments later Roland and AnnaRail appeared below, walking toward the dais at the far end of the hall. They were followed by their children: Annaline, DaNoel and JohnEngine; NickoLot was too young to attend such an event. Once they had taken their positions on the left-hand side of the dais, Malka, Roland's older brother, and Marjinell, his wife, followed with their sons MichaelOff and Brandon, and they stood to the right. They were making their appearance in inverse order of clan rank. Malka, as Olivia's heir, had come after Roland, and the old witch, as head of the clan, would come last. Morgin had to laugh: the clan had Olivia at its head, and Morgin at its tail.

But where was Tulellcoe, the only son of Olivia's dead sister Hellis? Morgin disliked and feared Tulellcoe, though not in the way he feared Olivia, for the old woman was hot fury, while Tulellcoe was a cold madness stalking silently at the edge of one's senses.

JohnEngine said that Tulellcoe's mother, Hellis, Olivia's sister, had been raped by Clan Decouix during the last clan war; that Hellis hated the child that had been conceived within her, and shortly after Tulellcoe's birth, had taken her own life. She'd tried to take the child Tulellcoe with her, but Olivia had stopped her and raised him as one of her own. JohnEngine said that the man Tulellcoe had inherited his mother's madness, and most feared him for that.

Morgin finally spotted Tulellcoe standing among the lesser clansmen.

When Olivia made her entrance, something seemed to tickle Morgin's spine, and he realized she had come cloaked in her power. Dressed in black robes, a veil of black lace draped over her gray-black hair, she walked the length of the hall unhurriedly, then climbed the steps of the dais, turned and scanned the crowd. Morgin thought her gaze paused on him, and he had trouble breathing for an instant.

Standing at the top of the dais, Olivia sat down on the throne. The enormous chair reminded Morgin that the Greater Clans forbade the Lesser Clans from crowning kings or queens, so it was a throne only in appearance. Olivia paused, then spoke very softly, but her voice carried to them all, "Bring him forth."

Movement near the entrance to the hall drew Morgin's attention. The crowd parted and a herald stepped forward wearing foreign livery. The herald carried a long staff, and thumped it loudly on the stone of the floor. "His Grace, Thandin et Decouix, advisor to and voice of His Majesty, Illalla, High King of the twelve tribes of the Shahot."

The tickle at the back of Morgin's spine turned chill, and he shivered.

Dannasul whispered, "Cold, are you?" Morgin realized the other boys did not sense Olivia's power as he did.

The herald stepped aside. Nothing happened for a few heartbeats, then a man dressed in incredible finery stepped forward. He wore a hat with a giant, feather plume, and clothing covered with embroidery the like of which Morgin had never seen. The man marched forward confidently, and with each step the icy depths of Olivia's power chilled further. He paused about ten paces from the dais, doffed his hat and bowed with a flourish. "Olivia," he said. "My king sends his regards. And I have come for the yearly tithe."

Morgin had known that some animosity existed between the Greater and Lesser Clans. But now he sensed the enmity that radiated from every clansman in the room, he saw the anger in their eyes and now understood the depth of hatred that colored Olivia's power. He tried to listen to the words that Olivia traded with this Decouix lord, but he found it difficult to breathe.

Finally, after trading barbs with the man, Olivia stood and said, "I have arranged rooms for you, Thandin. You may go."

Thandin bowed with a flourish, turned and departed, striding proudly out of the hall.

In his absence Olivia, Malka, Roland, AnnaRail and Tulellcoe huddled in a small group at the base of the dais. Morgin waited patiently as the other boys funneled into the staircase that led down to the main floor. But that itch at the base of his spine wouldn't ease up, and when he glanced toward Olivia, he noticed that while she spoke in hushed tones with the others, her eyes were lifted toward him, and they followed him as he left the balcony.

••••

Two more years passed and the friendship between Morgin and JohnEngine grew. Morgin was daydreaming through a lesson on the planes of existence[1] when Marjinell shouted, "JohnEngine, Dannasul, pay attention."

Morgin flinched at Marjinell's words, even though they were not directed at him.

He felt the draw of power just as a switch materialized in her hand. She pointed it at the two boys. "If you don't behave, I'll show your backsides the edge of this switch." Morgin knew that threat well.

JohnEngine and Dannasul straightened, though when Marjinell turned her back on them JohnEngine winked at Morgin.

"As I was saying," she continued. "There are three planes of existence—Celestial, Mortal and Nether—divided into twelve levels. The nine hells of the Nether Plane occupy the lowest nine levels, and the seven heavens of the Celestial Plane occupy the highest seven. They overlap on levels six through nine, and that is the Mortal Plane . . ."

Morgin drifted off, thinking about the crossed broadswords above the mantle in Roland's study. He and JohnEngine were about to reach their twelfth birthday, and would be allowed to practice with real, steel swords. They were both quite excited about it. They wanted—

The crack of the switch slapping the table in front of Morgin startled him and he jumped. The other boys chortled as Marjinell waved the switch in front of Morgin's nose. "I just asked a question," she demanded, "so you can answer it."

Morgin knew better than to try a lie. "I'm sorry, I didn't hear the question."

"Daydreaming again, were you?"

"Yes."

"I asked what is most significant about the Mortal Plane?"

AnnaRail had coached Morgin carefully on this subject, so he spoke confidently. "Gods cannot walk beyond the Celestial Plane, and nether beings cannot walk beyond the Nether Plane, so it is only on the Mortal Plane where gods, mortals and nether beings can all meet."

He waited for her to find something wrong with his answer, but she frowned, disappointed he could be right.

---

[1] See The Levels and Planes of Existence at the end of this story.

"Well enough. And what is most significant about we mortals?" She wanted him to be wrong.

He spoke carefully. "We are the only beings that can walk all twelve levels, though it takes great power to go beyond the Mortal Plane."

She stood there, staring at him, slapping the switch into the palm of her hand with enough force that it had hurt a bit. She was about to say something, when the door to the room opened and MichaelOff leaned in. "Mother, the boys are late."

She smiled at MichaelOff warmly. "I'm sorry son. I lost track of the time."

4

To Glimpse the Man

"HURRY, MORGIN," JOHNENGINE called. "We mustn't be late."

"I'm hurrying," Morgin said, frantically tying the laces of his jerkin. "Go on without me."

"I'll wait," JohnEngine said. "But hurry." He stood over Morgin waiting.

With his jerkin laced, Morgin sat on his cot to pull on his new boots. He was proud of them: working boots, steel shod, with heavy soles and thick leather about the toes. Roland had paid a high price for such craftsmanship, and presented them to Morgin on his twelfth birthday only the month before. Actually, it had been JohnEngine's birthday, but since no one knew Morgin's birthday, and the two boys were of an age and inseparable, they were treated as twins. JohnEngine had received an identical pair of boots.

Morgin jumped to his feet. "I'm ready. Let's go."

They rushed out of the dormitory, down a long flight of stairs and onto the main floor of the castle. They cut through the kitchen, out a side entrance, then through a narrow gap between two buildings. Bursting into the main castle yard, they crossed it at a sprint and joined a small cluster of boys seated on the ground there.

Breathless, and seated among their fellows, JohnEngine leaned toward one and asked, "Are we late, Dannasul?"

"No," Dannasul said. "What kept you?"

Morgin answered. "Mother kept me at my lessons."

Dannasul gave a knowing nod. Everyone knew that the Lady AnnaRail gave Morgin special tutoring. It was no secret Morgin could barely read and write, so they all assumed he was slow. They didn't know the training had included lessons in magic; training that didn't normally begin until a boy attained manhood at the age of twelve. To Morgin, the earlier lessons were just one more thing that made him different from the other boys, like an illness or deformity, so he was not going to be the one to enlighten them.

"Hush," someone said. "Here they come."

Old Beckett, the weapons master, approached from across the practice yard. He was followed by MichaelOff, Brandon, DaNoel, a tall stranger, and many of the older boys. The weapons master stopped several paces away and said, "Stand. And form a straight line in front of me here."

The younger boys rushed to comply. Beckett grumbled a bit then continued, "Now. You boys are here because you have reached, or will soon reach, your manhood. As men . . ." he looked aside with a sly grin, letting it be known that he considered them men only by clan law, ". . . you'll no longer practice with wooden swords. This year you'll use steel, dull and pointless, but steel nevertheless. Take care when you strike a blow, because a dull steel edge can still cut.

"Now. This man here . . ." Beckett turned, indicating the tall stranger, who stepped forward, ". . . is Lord Hwatok Tulalane, a *twoname*. He is a clansman, and a guest of Elhiyne. Furthermore, he is an accomplished swordsman and has entered into service with House Elhiyne. If you disobey him, you disobey me."

Morgin sized up the stranger: a big man, with a hawk face and deep set eyes. Not as old as old Beckett, but older than twenty-two year old MichaelOff, his face was weathered and lined. A scar bisected his left cheek, not a scar like the three pocks on Morgin's face, but a clean sharp line put there by some weapon. It was the stranger's eyes, though, that were his most distinct feature; piercing and hard, they left Morgin with the impression the man knew nothing of compassion or kindness. But then he realized those eyes were looking at him, probing him as if they could see to the layers beneath the outer skin, and he looked away.

"Pay attention, master Morgin," Beckett bellowed. The other boys chuckled; Morgin was always the one to be caught daydreaming. "Watch closely, all of you. Lord Hwatok and Lord MichaelOff are going to give a demonstration. Now clear out of the way and give them room."

The boys moved to the edge of the practice yard. MichaelOff and the stranger removed their sword belts and other items that might hinder them, then unsheathed their swords and began warming up.

While the two men prepared for their mock combat, Morgin asked JohnEngine, "What's a twoname?"

"He's a clansman by right of his magic," JohnEngine said, "but a twoname claims allegiance to no one clan. They usually wander about, often selling their services to a clan where they have some ties."

"They're mercenary wizards then?" Morgin asked.

"Some," JohnEngine whispered. "Most are more particular than mercenaries about who they sell their services to. And the services they sell aren't necessarily the sword and battle. They're supposed to be good advisers."

"If he bears no allegiance, can he be trusted?"

JohnEngine shrugged. "Grandmother must think so. He's . . ."

"JohnEngine," Beckett hollered. "Pay attention. And Morgin. Stop bothering your brother."

MichaelOff and the Tulalane bowed, then squared off in the center of the yard. Each used a lightweight rapier with a simple cross-hilt, the preferred weapon among the clans, and without ceremony they began trading blows sword against sword, testing each other's defenses.

The ring of steel came slowly at first, in an almost dance-like cadence. Morgin could not look away; the men struck at each other again and again, beads of sweat forming on their faces. They were blurs of motion in the swirling dust of the yard, the rhythm of the battle unchanging, each ring of steel deliberate, controlled. Then the blows came faster—slash, parry, strike, repeat. Magic hung in the air; the shimmer of power was palpable. The two swordsmen moved with inhuman swiftness, almost vanishing from one spot to appear instantly in another. Then, abruptly, the contest ended.

MichaelOff made a slash, which the twoname did not oppose. Instead, he backstepped, avoiding the blow, sliding his own sword behind MichaelOff's, adding to the momentum of the slash. MichaelOff over-swung his stroke, and to maintain balance was forced to expose his side to the Tulalane. The twoname slammed his forearm into the back of MichaelOff's shoulders, sending him sprawling face down in the dust of the yard.

There was a moment when both men appeared disoriented as they came out of their magics. And then the Tulalane helped MichaelOff to his feet, both of them laughing and brushing dust from the younger man.

"You'll have to teach me that one, Hwatok," MichaelOff said.

"Gladly, Lord MichaelOff," the twoname said as they walked off the field.

"All right, boys," Beckett hollered, "Line up again."

They rushed to obey.

"Now what you've just seen is a combination of skilled swordsmanship and magic. To use the two together, you must be skilled in each individually, and it will be years before you'll be proficient in either. So until you are, you'll never use the two together. Is that clear?"

They all nodded quietly.

"Good. Others will teach you magic, but I will teach you the sword."

Old Beckett turned away from them and walked slowly to the edge of the yard, retrieved a large bundle and returned to the line of boys. He opened the bundle, spilling several steel rapiers on the ground.

"Each of you pick a sword, and a partner, and we'll review the lessons you've supposedly learned in the past two years. But remember, you're using steel now, not wood."

Morgin and JohnEngine were practice partners, as they were partners in almost everything, including mischief. Most of the afternoon was spent getting used to the feel of the heavier steel blades, with Beckett moving among them offering advice and correcting errors. Later in the day he had them trade partners, even using some of the older boys as combined opponents and instructors.

The day was almost over when Morgin paired off with DaNoel, JohnEngine's older brother. And without prelude the older boy began with a rain of blows that Morgin was hard pressed to deflect. When DaNoel's steel hissed menacingly past Morgin's ear he realized this was no lesson, but a venting of some anger that might leave him maimed or crippled, or even dead. In desperation he fought back with what little strength and skill he could command, but his arm tired quickly, and DaNoel used that to advantage, stepping beneath his guard and batting him to the ground with the hilt of his sword. "Defend yourself, peasant," he said, then attacked.

Morgin scrambled to his feet as DaNoel struck at his face, then ducked quickly beneath a stroke that could have taken off his head, dull edge or not. "What are you doing?" he pleaded.

DaNoel's face reddened with anger. He gave no answer, gripped his sword with both hands, and brought it down with all his might.

Morgin threw his own blade clumsily in the way. It met DaNoel's with a clash that rang painfully through his arm and shoulder. He fell to the ground, tried to roll over quickly to avoid DaNoel's sword as it bit into the dirt near his face. DaNoel stood over him, his sword clutched in both hands and raised high over his head, his face a mask of hatred. Morgin rolled over quickly as DaNoel's sword cut a furrow in the earth where his head had been. Morgin rolled again, then stumbled to his feet.

DaNoel's rapier hissed past Morgin's nose as he back-stepped blindly. The older boy raised his sword for another lethal strike, but JohnEngine plowed into him with a full body block. The two of them sprawled into the dirt of the yard, raising a cloud of dust. They separated and jumped to their feet, facing one another.

"What are you doing?" JohnEngine demanded.

Beckett interrupted, bellowing, "What's going on here?" He elbowed his way through the crowd of boys that had gathered about them. "Here, here! What's this? Are you fighting again, Morgin?"

"No," JohnEngine said. "It wasn't him. It was DaNoel."

DaNoel ignored JohnEngine and Beckett, looked at Morgin and said, "Don't you ever call her mother again. She's not your mother. She's mine. You have no right, whoreson." Then he spun about and stormed off the practice field.

"All right, boys," Beckett yelled. "Break it up. Practice is over today. Go clean up for dinner."

••••

"Morgin," Annaline called. "Morgin."

Morgin held his breath, hoping to stay hidden. If he were lucky she'd not climb the stairs to the top of the battlements where he lay idling in the sun. Today was a holiday, and he would do as he pleased.

"Morgin. Are you up there?"

He held his silence. Maybe she would think he had gone down to the festival in the village market. There was always something going on there on the monthly holiday.

"You come down here, Morgin. I know you're up there somewhere."

He sighed and scanned the horizon. It was a beautifully clear day with Attunhigh dominating the skyline, a monolith of rock and snow standing guard over the valley of Elhiyne. The mountain range called the Worshippers of Attun extended the length of the horizon.

"If you don't come down I'll send the ShadowLord after you."

Didn't she realize he was too old to believe in mythical demon netherlords? That was as stupid as believing in fairies and angels. He swung his legs off the battlement and dropped to the parapet. If he'd been smart he would have made himself absent from the castle long ago. "I'm coming," he hollered as he started down the stairs.

He met Annaline on her way up. She looked him over quickly and said, "Good. You're not dirty. We won't have to waste time cleaning you up."

"For what?"

"Grandmother wants to see you. Better hurry or you'll make her angry."

Morgin shut his mouth and followed her. The old woman wanted to see *him*! He shivered.

In the years he'd been at the castle he hadn't personally faced the old witch. Of course he'd seen her many times, but always from a distance, and he could count the number of times she'd actually spoken to him on the six fingers of one hand. There was something powerful and frightening about her that he didn't like.

Annaline took Morgin to the old witch's suite of rooms—a part of the castle he'd always avoided—and outside of the Olivia's haunt they met AnnaRail waiting for them. "The Lady Olivia wants to examine you to determine the extent of your power," she said. "So be on your best behavior." She fussed at his tunic for a moment, then swept his hair back out of his eyes. "There. You look like a fine young man."

Annaline seemed to sense his unease. She leaned down and whispered, "Don't worry. Grandmother just likes to make you think she's mean and nasty. Inside she's really just a sweet old lady."

Annaline's words did little to reassure him as he stepped into the audience chamber. He halted just inside, carefully surveyed the room. AnnaRail joined Roland and they both stood beside the old woman. Olivia was seated in cushioned elegance near a large hearth; she commanded the room entirely.

"Come, child," she said. "Stand before me."

Morgin could not have disobeyed even had he wanted to. He walked across the small room unable to take his eyes off her. He'd seen her from afar many times, marching through the castle corridors. This close, it was impossible not to stare at the old witch's face: a field of wrinkles surrounding black-pupiled eyes. Her hair was black, with flashing streaks of gray that radiated outward from her face. It was pulled back to the top of her head where it lay knotted and fastened with combs and braids, and studded with tiny jewels.

"Am I that fascinating, child?"

Morgin remembered his manners, closed his mouth and diverted his eyes. "I'm sorry."

"Don't apologize, boy. If you wish to look at me, then do so."

Morgin chose to look at the floor.

"Come, child. Raise your head. Look at me when I speak."

He looked again at that wrinkled face and those cold, black eyes. "Yes, milady."

"That's better. Now you sound like a proper clansman. You're here because I want to test your power, though I must admit I feel remiss at not doing so earlier. I want to know how much of a witch you are. Do you understand that?"

"Yes, milady."

"Good. Now listen to me carefully. I am going to cast certain spells, and while I am doing so you must relax and remain absolutely still. You may experience certain sensations, some of them not altogether pleasant. If so, do not resist, for if you do, you will be the one that is harmed, not I. Is that clear?"

"Yes, milady."

"Excellent. Now, I must have absolute silence."

The castle walls were thick, and not even the bustle of the busy yard could penetrate. Morgin sensed something building within the close confines of the room, and he had a sudden desire to be away from there. It was akin to what AnnaRail did when she performed a seeking, but where that something was kind and soft, this was cold, hard, and powerful.

Olivia's lips began to move almost imperceptibly, and Morgin caught the hiss of a faint whisper at the edge of his hearing. The words she spoke sent a shiver up his spine, words of power; he concentrated on them carefully as AnnaRail had taught him to do. He could hear each syllable clearly, and yet when he tried to put them together into a word, the final product eluded him. Power! This was no subtle spell or incantation; the old women was calling forth raw power.

Morgin watched Olivia build something indefinable within her, and then she built something similar within him, and he realized she was not merely calling forth her own power, but his as well. He felt violated, but he remembered her words and fought the desire to resist her, though he felt he was being squeezed between her power and his own. He staggered under the suffocating weight. As he struggled to breathe he instinctively pushed back, though he didn't really understand what he did, or how he did it. But Olivia gasped, stood, slapped him, and shouted, "Monster!"

The slap snatched him back to the moment, staggering, his face stinging. He watched helplessly as the old woman raised her arm to strike again, but now her hand glowed with streaks of power dancing up and down her wrist. The room was electrified with a sense of unreality, and all Morgin could see was the old woman's eyes: black and angry.

"Mother, no," Roland said. "You'll kill him."

The old witch hesitated, though her magic swirled about her and demanded to be used.

AnnaRail quickly filled the silence. "He didn't know what he was doing. It wasn't his fault. I warned you to move carefully. His power is extensive, and he has too little training to control it properly."

Olivia lowered her hand and the room became still. She looked at Morgin like a bug she might squash, and her eyes glowed with malevolence. He saw a hint of pleasure in her face, and a faint, greedy smile. She looked at AnnaRail and spoke through clenched teeth. "You are right, daughter. You did warn me, and I should have heeded you."

Then she looked again at Morgin and he cringed. "You are forgiven this time because of your ignorance. But never, ever, strike me again."

Morgin, staring at the floor and thinking he'd struck no one, decided he'd best keep his mouth shut.

"And stop staring at the floor"

Morgin looked up, and Olivia surprised him by smiling openly as she said to AnnaRail, "You were also right about his power. It is extensive. Certainly more than anyone else his age."

Her eyes narrowed, and for a long silent moment she appeared to think carefully. Morgin had no doubt that whatever she might be considering bode ill for him. "I have come to a decision," she announced. "Such power should reside within House Elhiyne."

She looked pointedly at AnnaRail and Roland. "So the child will be legally adopted into House Elhiyne as your son, and we will have a Naming. Between now and that time you will give him as much training in the arcane as he can absorb, and if need be, he will be excused from his other lessons. You will teach him control, for he will never again be allowed to do what he has done this day. And someday, he will prove useful to us."

She looked at each of them for a moment, especially at Morgin. "I have spoken. It shall be so. Now leave me. I wish to be alone."

Without a word Roland and AnnaRail bowed and backed out of the room. Morgin did the same.

5

A Wizard's Name

THE MORNING AFTER Olivia tested Morgin he learned he was not to have any food that day; a Naming required fasting by all directly involved. Early that morning they executed the formal adoption papers and he became a member of House Elhiyne. After the brief ceremony AnnaRail said, "You are no longer a simple clansman; you are now part of the family that rules the clan that rules the eighth tribe of the Shahot. As a mere clansman, you would have been expected to grow up and serve House Elhiyne. But as a member of this family, you will be expected to lead those who serve us."

"But what is the Naming for?" he asked.

"The Naming," she said, "is a ceremony by which a proper name will be chosen for you."

"But I already have a name."

"Yes, and it is a good name. But I chose it for its sound, not for its power or for its relation to you. It is an arbitrary name, no more than a label, a peasant's name. Many live their entire lives with such a name, and there is no shame in doing so. But you have been chosen for a Naming, and that is a high honor."

"But *Morgin* is good enough for me."

She smiled and laid a hand gently on his shoulder. "Then you may use it always, if you wish. Come. Don't be so fearful. The Naming won't be difficult, and from it you will receive a name that will give you power and tell us much about you."

"The Naming will do all that?"

She shook her head. "No. The name will. The Naming is merely a ceremony to help us determine that name. It is not an easy ceremony, for much magic and power is required, and so it is reserved only for those of high caste."

"What's going to happen during the Naming?"

"You will see firsthand the ranking of power within the clan."

Morgin had learned that a hierarchy of power existed within the clan having nothing to do with one's lineage. At its bottom were those like Roland; Morgin was embarrassed for him since he ranked below some of the children.

"All those present will stand before you, one at a time, in ascending order of power, beginning with lesser witches and finishing with Malka, then Olivia. We are trying to call forth ElkenSkul, a very special demon, and each wizard and witch will take their turn adding to the power needed to bring it forth."

"A demon?" Morgin asked, unable to hide his fear.

"Don't worry. Malka will remain close at hand, and should something untoward happen with one of the lesser witches, he'll intervene to ensure no one is harmed. And I'll be close by to help you if you need it."

Olivia scheduled the Naming for midnight, and everyone in the castle hastened to make the arrangements. Morgin had little to do to prepare for the ceremony, for he was the "new born infant," the passive object of the preparations. The women of the house bathed him carefully—he was thoroughly embarrassed to have to sit naked in a tub while AnnaRail and Annaline scrubbed him down. Then, with charcoal from a fire twelve days cold, they wrote runes on his body.

Morgin feared he'd have to appear naked in front of half the clan, but AnnaRail gave him a simple loin cloth. Late that evening they led him to the Hall of Wills—known to the villagers as The Wizard's Hall—and sat him on the cold stone floor in the middle of the Hall. He sat stiffly upright, his legs tucked beneath him, his hands at his sides. Before him a young witch sprinkled a circle of fine black sand in a thin layer on the gray stone of the floor.

Slowly, clanfolk high and low filled the Hall, almost everyone who lived in the near vicinity of Elhiyne. The members of House Elhiyne were the last to arrive, though Olivia was notably absent until she made a grand entrance, walking slowly and carefully. Oddly enough, her black robes billowed out behind her, even though the air in the Hall remained still.

She stopped opposite Morgin, standing on the other side of the circle of black sand and towering over him. She raised her arms, looked to the heavens and declared, "Let the Naming begin."

Olivia stepped aside, was replaced by the young witch who'd sprinkled the circle of sand. The girl paused, then began a long incantation. He heard other witches in the crowd join in. When she finished she stepped aside and a young man took her place.

Hours passed as one witch after another stepped forth. Morgin was not supposed to move so his joints grew stiff and sore, and his stomach growled for food. He longed for the ceremony to end, but knew it was only just beginning.

A gasp ran through the assembled throng as a demon from the netherhells of his own nightmares materialized in front of him. Fangs and claws appeared first, then a tail with a barbed point dripping venom, the body of an ogre and the head of a goat, and it looked at him hungrily with fiery eyes. Then it advanced, saliva spilling from its muzzle in anticipation of a meal.

Morgin had never seen a demon before, wanted to bolt and run from the Hall, but Malka intervened, stepping in its way. It struck Malka with its claws. He staggered, but withstood the blow. Then, wielding his own power like a sword, he cried out in the godtongue and struck back. The demon whimpered sorrowfully. Malka struck again, lashing his power like a whip until the demon screamed an agonized, inhuman cry. Malka raised his power to strike again, but the demon vanished, gone, dematerialized. A cry of anger and pain echoed back from the netherworld, then all was silent.

Morgin shivered, and wondered how many more demons might come to investigate.

A young and pretty witch stepped forward to stand on the other side of the circle of black sand. She cast spells, tracing runes in the air with her fingertip as she chanted more of the words that always eluded him. He'd asked AnnaRail about this, was told the words would take on meaning when he was older.

The young witch finished her incantation. But as she turned and melted into the shadows, the runes she'd traced in the air remained, visible by some magic of their own, then slowly faded. Morgin grew tense with the new power he sensed in the room.

He cast a spell AnnaRail had taught him for protection, then another to banish fear. He wished now that he could have mastered more of her teachings, for the young and pretty witch was obviously the first of the truly powerful. He tried the spell of confidence, but as usual he failed.

AnnaRail had warned him that a gap existed between those of little power and those of great. She had cautioned him not to be frightened when the first of the truly powerful stood before him, but her warning meant nothing as he sat there with power dancing up and down his spine. He tried to think of other things, of other times, but his thoughts would not leave the present and the magic that surrounded him.

A train of wizards and witches followed, including Annaline and many of his newly adopted brothers and sisters and cousins, with MichaelOff the last and most powerful. The next to stand before him was Tulellcoe, whose strange eyes darted about like a caged animal. He was a silent, angry man, with seething hatred hidden just beneath his demeanor.

Tulellcoe finished his magic and AnnaRail stepped forth to begin hers. Like the others, she stood opposite him, the circle of black sand between them undisturbed, and she spoke words that Morgin could not understand. But where Tulellcoe's magic was an angry thing, and Olivia's was fearful, AnnaRail's was warm and soft and loving. Morgin felt it wash over him, calming him, as it added to the power building in the Hall.

Malka stepped forth next in his glory and strength. He shouted words of power that echoed off the walls of the Hall. The air of the room answered back with a rumble that Morgin felt in his spine. Malka the powerful warrior, whom all knew would inherit the clan at Olivia's death. Malka the strong, whom none dare anger.

Malka finished and the room fell silent, Morgin alone at its center. The air was charged with power, all directed at him, waves of it crawling up his skin. He felt the small, blond hairs on his arms and legs stand on end. Here and there a strand of his hair, freshly washed, fluttered before his eyes waving in whatever motion the air possessed.

Olivia stepped forth slowly to stand before him, motionless and unspeaking. She stood with her arms folded within her billowing sleeves, uttered no spells, cast no incantations. Morgin knew that however motionless she might seem, her power was building, and his power could do nothing but follow. Terrified, he tried to retreat, to cease the rise of a strange force that threatened to consume him. He concentrated on the spell of confidence, for Olivia's power would allow no faltering or withdrawal. For a moment he felt as if he stood on the brink of a fearful abyss, then he calmed as nearby AnnaRail cast a spell to aid him. He concentrated on the spell of confidence, felt it wash over him, comfortable and refreshingly cool. He opened his eyes and looked up to meet Olivia's gaze. She nodded reluctant approval, then continued exercising her power.

Morgin felt a presence at hand, something having no place in this world of mortals. It hovered at eye level over the black sand, and though he saw nothing there, he sensed it was angry at being summoned.

"Demon ElkenSkul," Olivia cried. "You have come at my bidding, soul taker. Giver of names, yield unto the newborn his power."

There came no answer. Morgin stared at Olivia, holding his breath. If ElkenSkul gave him no name, he would live his life in disgrace, bearing only his earthly name and relegated to the most menial, servile tasks. His newfound status would be gone, erased by an instant of silence. It would have been better had he never been granted the honor of a Naming.

An invisible claw broke the silence as it scratched a small circle in the sand. It hesitated for several seconds before scratching a small line; just that, a simple line pointing outward from the circle, then another and another and another, a grouping of lines around the circle all radiating outward, like a child's drawing of the sun in the sky. It finished with one, long line slanting through the middle of the circle.

Morgin had no idea what it meant, but Olivia leaned forward and hissed, sucking air between her teeth as if the symbol held some special meaning. "The sunset king? Aethon? Aethon what?" she demanded. "Complete the name, demon. Complete it now. I command you."

Pausing momentarily, the invisible claw scratched again, slowly adding two crossed lines beneath the symbol.

"Aethon's Law!" the old witch cried to the heavens. She looked down at Morgin with purest greed in her eyes. "You are the Law of Aethon, my grandson. Rise AethonLaw." Olivia crowed, "He is AethonLaw."

Morgin started to climb to his feet, his eyes still on the symbol scratched in the sand. Olivia didn't see it, but the claw quickly scratched two more small lines, bisecting each of the two crossed lines beneath the sun symbol. The two new lines were like cross-guards on swords, making the lines beneath the sunset symbol appear like two crossed swords. "But . . ." Morgin said, pointing at the sand.

Olivia sliced her hand through the air where the demon had been. "Be gone, demon. Leave us, ElkenSkul."

The demon cried out, and the circle of sand scattered across the floor, obliterating the marks in it. Morgin said, "But the marks in the sand—"

Olivia glared down at him angrily, a clear message he was not to speak.

The demon paused before obeying Olivia's command, as if reluctant to do so. Then apparently resigned to Olivia's power, it winked out of existence, and with it went the power that had accumulated in the Hall.

Olivia took a deep breath and exhaled slowly. She looked down at Morgin, proud, willful, her eyes alight with the fires of magic. Morgin felt like a mouse, prey to the cat Olivia.

"Arise," she said. "Stand, AethonLaw et Elhiyne. Embrace the clan, for you are named."

••••

In the days that followed the Naming Morgin's change in status unsettled him. No longer was he *boy*, or *child*, or merely *Morgin*, he was now Lord Morgin, or Lord AethonLaw. In the small village near the castle people nodded their heads as he passed. Even other clansmen took note of him, greeting him warmly in passing or inviting him to join them.

What bothered him most was a barely noticeable change in the attitude of the other boys, a subtle difference that he wasn't sure even existed. Only JohnEngine treated him the same, and one day Morgin asked him about it.

"You're crazy," JohnEngine said. "Nobody treats you any different than me."

Something to think about: treated no different than JohnEngine.

That explained the boys his age, it did not explain the old witch Olivia. She now demanded that he see her regularly, and she quizzed him on his lessons, paying particular attention to the magic he had learned, or failed to learn. Some of those sessions were quite grueling.

One day, after a particularly difficult audience with the old woman, who, as usual, found him wanting, he sought out AnnaRail to ask her why the Naming had changed so many things.

"Things?" she asked patiently. "I think you're really concerned about your grandmother, and her increased attention. Correct?"

Morgin nodded silently.

AnnaRail smiled. "Clan law recognizes no difference between adoption and birth, and so by that law you are now a son of the House of Elhiyne. Your grandmother is concerned that you represent us well. Overly concerned, perhaps. But nevertheless, concerned."

Morgin couldn't conceal a frown. "There's more to it than that."

"That's very perceptive of you. Do you remember when we spoke of names, and I told you that the clansman reflects the name and the name reflects the clansman?"

"Yes."

"Well, AethonLaw," she said, placing emphasis on his new name. "You bear a name of power, a king's name, which tells us that you may someday control much of the arcane."

"A king's name?" Morgin asked wonderingly.

AnnaRail nodded. "Aethon was the last of the true Shahotma kings. The Benesh'ere betrayed him centuries ago in the Great Clan Wars, but he was the last to rule the Sword. To bear such a name is a great honor—for you, for our clan, and for House Elhiyne—for Aethon was also of the eighth tribe."

"But I can't be all that," Morgin said.

"Ah, but you can," she said. She took his hands gently in hers. "Someday you may be a great wizard, perhaps even greater than Malka or Olivia. Then again, you may not, and there is no shame in that. Grow strong and healthy, and be just and kind to others, and serve Elhiyne faithfully, and you will bring us honor. We can ask for no more than that."

"Grandmother wants more."

"Indeed! Sometimes she does expect too much, especially from a young boy who'd rather be out getting in trouble with his brother JohnEngine, eh?" AnnaRail winked. "Your grandmother is excited for you, Morgin, and proud that you should receive such a name. So be patient with her, and I'll speak to her about her demands."

Morgin had intended to tell AnnaRail about the extra slashes ElkenSkul had added at the last moment, the extra slashes that no one but he had seen. But he realized that doing so might bring more attention from Olivia, so he resolved then to never mention them again.

••••

"Damn women!" Malka cursed as he stepped off the stairs at the top of the parapets. It was well past sunset, and Morgin, who'd been seated in the lee of the battlements, jumped to his feet, startled by the warrior's unheralded arrival.

"Sorry, boy. Didn't mean to scare ya. But that grandmother of yours can be damnable at times."

Morgin wanted to step into a convenient shadow, but to do so would be an open insult. The warrior was a big and powerful man. Few men would face him squarely, especially when, as now, anger clouded his features.

"Give me a battle to fight, an enemy to kill, but the gods save me from the sharp tongues of those damn women. Blast and be damned! By the name of the Unnamed King I wish they'd give me peace. I'd rather face the Queen of Thieves herself."

Malka spit and cursed as he stormed the length of the dark parapet. He could be heard more than seen, for the night was moonless and gray. He reached the end of the walkway, turned and came thundering back. Morgin stood directly in his path, trembling, wondering if the great warrior might choose to vent his anger on a helpless boy. But before reaching Morgin the big man stopped, threw his arms up in disgust, then sat down on the walk with his back to the wall. He pulled his knees up to his chest and sat almost exactly where Morgin had been a moment before. "Damn!" he whispered. "Damn!"

For some odd reason Morgin felt pity for the big man. "What's wrong, uncle?" he asked.

"Ahhh!" Malka said. "Women! They're what's wrong. Your grandmother wants a king to unite the Lesser Clans, and all I can give her is a warrior. I'd be happy to——"

Malka stopped his rant and looked about, as if realizing for the first time where his feet had taken him in his blind anger. "What are you doing up here at this time of night?"

"I uh . . ." Morgin shrugged noncommittally and shuffled his feet. "Just thinking."

"Come up here for a little peace, did you boy?"

Morgin nodded.

"I came up here for the same reason. Looks like instead of finding my own peace I disturbed yours. Sorry about that."

Morgin shuffled his feet again. "That's all right."

"Spend much time up here, do ya?"

Morgin shrugged. "Sometimes, after seeing grandmother."

Malka laughed quietly. "Well, Morgin, she's my mother, and I've been coming up here for more'n thirty years. It's a good place for thinking, isn't it?"

"Yes, uncle."

"Well you watch out, boy. She's got her eyes on you. You've got power, lad, more'n your share. She's got a nose for power, that one. I expect you'll be spending many a night up here. And when you do come, and you're all alone, think a thought for your old uncle Malka, eh? Because I'll likely be with your grandmother wishing I was up here enjoying the quiet."

As the years passed and Morgin grew, Olivia's scrutiny never slackened. Even as he became a young man on the threshold of adulthood, he always remembered that night on the parapets with Malka, and he never forgot the big warrior's words: *She's got her eyes on you. You've got power, lad, more'n your share.*

6

The Man

ANNARAIL CRINGED AS Olivia demanded, "Why has he not progressed? He showed so much promise, yet after ten years he's still far behind. He's sixteen years of age and should have advanced much farther."

"He fears his own magic," Roland said.

"Or perhaps . . ." Marjinell inserted smugly, ". . . other than a few simple spells, he has no magic?"

"No," Malka said, shaking his head thoughtfully. "The boy has magic aplenty, no doubt of that."

"Exactly," Olivia said. She looked at AnnaRail. "So why has he not begun to live up to his name?"

AnnaRail paused to allow Olivia's irritation to subside. It was difficult enough to handle the old woman without her temper getting in the way. "Roland was right when he said Morgin fears his own magic. And we unknowingly reinforced that by punishing him when he used it to hide in shadow. He is progressing steadily toward control, though for a sixteen-year-old he is a bit backward. But control is less dramatic than his early spontaneous use of magic, and that's all that's happening."

"That's not good enough," Olivia said. Her eyes narrowed as if considering the situation carefully, but AnnaRail sensed that the old woman was up to something. "I want visible progress. Perhaps the boy should be pushed."

"No," AnnaRail snapped. "That would only worsen the situation." She shut her mouth quickly, realizing she'd yielded a point.

"Very well," Olivia said happily. "His training will remain in your hands. But I demand regular progress, or that situation will change."

AnnaRail nodded, knowing better than to speak further.

"Good," Olivia continued. "Now what's this about his scars? You want them removed?"

"He's quite self-conscious about the scars on his face. If we could do something about that, it would be one less thing that separates him from the rest of the boys."

Marjinell said, "I've heard what separates him is he's aloof, or maybe he's just stupid and slow witted."

"That's enough, Marjinell," AnnaRail said. "You always seek to malign him. I'll not stand for—"

"Be still." Olivia snapped. "You're bickering like maidens. AnnaRail is right, Marjinell. You're much too harsh with Morgin. We know he's not stupid, so I'll hear no more of that. And you," she said, turning upon AnnaRail, "are much too quick to defend him. As for his scars, I see no reason why we shouldn't treat them."

"It will take much magic," Marjinell said.

"For a member of this family, we have much magic to give. But he will not be allowed to remain separate. He will participate in all activities of this family, and that is final."

AnnaRail nodded. "We are in total agreement there." That took them all by surprise. "But your actions must match your words."

Olivia frowned. "What do you mean?"

AnnaRail had gained a point. "Correct me if I am wrong, but had you not planned that the entire family, with the one exception of Morgin, would accompany us next month to Anistigh for Annaline's wedding?"

Olivia nodded and her eyes narrowed.

"Then we cannot blame the boy . . ." AnnaRail continued, ". . . if he interprets that to mean that he is separate, and not equal."

Olivia's brow remained wrinkled, but with indecision, not anger. "But the boy cannot be trusted in the city, not with gesh easily available there."

"I think he can; he left that addiction behind ten years ago. And in any case he'll have to be trusted, unless you wish him to become even more of a loner."

Olivia had trapped herself, but recovered quickly. "Very well. He'll go to Anistigh. But he'll attend each and every function before, during, and after the wedding. With no time to himself, there'll be no time for temptation."

••••

Anistigh was a leisurely three day journey from Elhiyne. Morgin and his brothers and cousins could have ridden it easily in two, but no one felt the need to hurry. Besides, there were women along, and carriages were slow, and even those like Annaline— who had chosen to ride horseback—were hindered by the petticoats and skirts that Olivia demanded they wear. "My granddaughter . . ." she had proclaimed, ". . . will not ride to her own wedding dressed in the breeches of a man."

Annaline didn't seem to mind. They were on holiday and they made the trip in comfort, though little eight-year-old NickoLot was not at all happy about the situation. She wanted to ride with her brothers, but AnnaRail would have none of that.

They followed the river Bohl; it passed close to Elhiyne and through the middle of Anistigh. Late in the evenings Morgin and his brothers fished its banks, hoping to catch something tasty for breakfast.

They came to Anistigh late on a warm sunny day, though it was not what Morgin had expected. What few memories he could still recall were of muddy streets, cold, stone walls, gray alleys, and dark hovels. But his first sight of the city was a stretch of outlying farms, with Anistigh itself a jagged edge on the horizon. The farms were neat and well kept, and the people that greeted them as they passed were strong and healthy.

The city grew slowly out of the landscape, a maze of buildings without a clear-cut boundary. Morgin had expected something more sharply defined; a stone wall perhaps, with city on one side and country on the other. He chided himself for being so naive.

A grouping of large estates formed the heart of the city, with the Elhiyne compound at its center. It was walled, heavily fortified and guarded, for the clan was Elhiyne, and Elhiyne was the clan.

They arrived with a flurry of servants and retainers, and spent some time moving in. Once settled Morgin wanted to do a little sightseeing. There were a few hours left before dinner so he found JohnEngine, and as the two prepared to leave Olivia intercepted them and intervened. "Two teenage boys," she said, "alone, in the city? Never. You'd find trouble where none existed."

The logical choice for a chaperone was MichaelOff, who was reluctant but allowed himself to be persuaded. Accompanied by an adult ten years their senior, Olivia had no choice but to give them leave. The two boys set off with their older cousin in tow, talking incessantly of the discoveries they would make.

They headed straight for the market square, hoping to see jugglers and acrobats, mimes, puppet shows, acting companies, and all forms of diversion. There were vendors with sweets and delicious foods, wine and ale, though, as JohnEngine put it, the most important treats were the girls. But as they approached the market Morgin had a set of memories far different from his brother's. It had been ten years since he'd seen these streets, and though much had changed, he recognized them easily. While his memories were not clear, they rekindled long forgotten, unhappy emotions. They were memories best left unrecalled.

The market square itself remained almost totally unchanged. Ramshackle stalls filled it completely; each separated by narrow dirt pathways and operated by vendors loudly crying their wares. Those with the greatest seniority were near the outskirts where they could accost potential customers as soon as they arrived. And of course, the most valuable properties were the permanent shops that formed the outer perimeter of the square. The noise and excitement were overwhelming.

MichaelOff decided they should first tour the perimeter, strolling down the aisle between the permanent shops and the outermost stalls. And as they walked Morgin became progressively uncomfortable, for everyone bowed deeply to the three of them. The stall owners held samples high for easy viewing, but they never shouted prices at the three young men as they passed. Morgin slowly came to realize that he and his kinsmen were the center of attention here. With that, and the familiarity of the market square, he found himself looking for a convenient shadow.

A hand touched his shoulder. He jumped with a start. It was MichaelOff.

"Morgin. Why so jumpy? What's wrong?"

Morgin tried to look in all directions at once. "They're all staring at us."

MichaelOff scanned the crowd casually. "Yes they are, aren't they?" He smiled, looked back at Morgin and shook his head sadly. "You're going to have to get used to that. You are an Elhiyne. You are of the ruling house of the foremost clan of this city, and wherever you go people will stare. So get used to it and learn to ignore it." MichaelOff turned to a nearby stall. "Come. Let's spoil our appetites a little. I'm buying."

Morgin found he couldn't ignore the staring eyes. No one was rude enough to stare directly into his face, but if he turned quickly, he caught several of them watching him. At one point a young boy of eight or nine ran across his path, stumbled, and fell into the dirt. Without giving it a thought Morgin reached down to help the lad to his feet. Once up, the boy turned to see who had helped him and froze. His eyes grew wide and he hissed "Witchman!"

Morgin looked at the boy carefully, and thought that maybe he saw a bit of Rat in the child. He almost envied the boy; life in the streets had to be far simpler than his own newfound status.

An old woman, as filthy as the boy, stepped out of the crowd and grabbed him by an ear. She gave the ear a twist. "I've told ya not to bother the gentlemen," she shouted.

She gave the ear another twist and turned to Morgin. "Fergive me boy, yer worshipfulness. He's a brute, he is. I'll punish him rightly."

"Oh no!" Morgin said. "No. Don't. He did nothing wrong. He just stumbled in front of me."

"Well," she said. "If ya say so, yer wizardness. I'll let him go this time." She turned back to the boy and gave the ear one final twist. "And you be more careful." Then she released him; in an instant he disappeared into the crowd.

Most of that afternoon was a strange kaleidoscope of images and events that faded into an overall impression of a lot of poor people, surviving through this day and into the next, though there was one incident that Morgin would remember well. He was browsing through the stalls at the center of the square, thinking he might find some little trinket for Annaline with the few pennies he had. He stopped at one stall to look at some small amulets. He could sense the stall's owner hovering nearby in anticipation of a sale. He looked into the man's face to ask his prices, and was struck by terror, for he was looking at a face that would always make Rat's heart jump, a man whom he remembered as the cruelest of the vendors, with a sharp throwing rock always at hand.

Rat back-stepped quickly, eyes wide, looking for the safety of a nearby shadow.

"Is something wrong, Your Lordship?" the man asked.

Rat, still back-stepping, stumbled over someone. They both fell to the ground in a tangled heap. Rat stood, ready to run, but found instead poor Mathal sprawled at his feet.

She looked up fearfully. "Forgive me, you worship. I didn't see you coming. Stupid me! Stupid me!" Then she began picking up the fruit he'd knocked from her hands.

"Out of his lordship's way, old hag," the man snarled. "You made him stumble. Be gone."

The vendor lifted a hand to strike her, and in that instant something crawled up the back of Morgin's spine, something alive and deadly. "Hold," Morgin shouted angrily, feeling the power of magic sparking among his fingertips as he raised his own hand high.

The vendor froze. "It was I who made her stumble," Morgin said. He looked into the man's eyes. "And if you strike her—" He borrowed an expression from the first time he'd ever seen Roland in these same streets. "—you'll face my wrath."

The man bowed meekly. "Yes, Your Lordship," he said, then disappeared into the crowd.

Morgin was stunned by how quickly he'd been obeyed, and how all nearby activity had ceased. He and Mathal were at the center of a circle of silence and fear, everyone waiting for him to make the next move. Mathal stood like a statue, half way through the motion of picking up a piece of fruit.

With an effort he suppressed his magic, crouched down beside her to help her. "Forgive me for knocking you down, Mathal. Is any of the fruit damaged?"

The incident was over. The crowd returned to its business and Mathal returned to picking up fruit. "No, your worship. It's just fine, sir. It wasn't that good to begin with."

And it wasn't. What Mathal had been hawking was, at best, the day-old stuff from another vendor. Clearly, her fortunes had declined. Not knowing what else to do, Morgin bought all her fruit. She seemed thankful for the few pennies he had. To her it was probably a small fortune.

On their way back to the Elhiyne compound he gave the fruit away to some beggars. JohnEngine teased him unmercifully for wasting his money on groceries. MichaelOff said nothing. He just looked at Morgin queerly, as if he understood there was something more to the incident than he and JohnEngine knew.

••••

"She was kind to you?" AnnaRail asked.

"Oh yes," Morgin said. "She always let me steal fruit. She pretended not to see but I know she did."

"And now you say she has fallen on hard times?"

"It must be that," Morgin said. "She's a walking vendor with no stall, selling in the center of the square. That's the worst that can happen to a vendor. The others look down on the walkers and treat them badly. Can't we do something for her?"

AnnaRail, busy with some preparation for Annaline's wedding, looked up from her work thoughtfully. "She was kind to one of my sons when he was in need. Therefore, I must be the same with her. Let this be a lesson to you. The obligations of a single clansman are the obligations of the entire clan. If she is willing to enter into our service, I'm sure we can find something for her. And if she works hard, and proves herself trustworthy, she will prosper."

"Oh thank you, mother," Morgin said. "But she must never know that I was once Rat. Never."

"Very well, son. Now run along. I have work to do."

The next morning Morgin found a pouch containing a considerable sum of money tied to one of the posts of his bed. Attached to it was a note that read:

> Son:
>
> Your mother says you gave your money in a kind-
> ness. Here is some to replace it. It may seem a great
> deal, but it must last you while we are in Anistigh.
> I'm proud of you. But remember, there is such a
> thing as too much kindness.
>
> Roland.

Morgin found far more money in the pouch than he'd spent on Mathal's fruit. He tucked it away and felt proud, but he quickly learned he wouldn't have an opportunity to spend any of it. Avis told him he was to dress in his best and attend Olivia immediately.

It was a group interview with Brandon, DaNoel, JohnEngine, NickoLot, and himself. MichaelOff was too old, and Annaline too busy preparing for her wedding, but the rest had to endure a morning-long quiz in the details of inter-clan relationships.

Olivia focused on the representatives of the other clans that would be attending the wedding. Since Annaline's future husband was an Inetka, they were heavily represented. The other Lesser Clans—Houses Tosk and Penda—had sent only a half dozen emissaries as a courtesy.

The Greater Council had sent only Valso, prince of House Decouix and heir to the throne of King Illalla. Valso traveled with a retinue of twelve twelves, and for protection had brought along as many Kullish armsmen, led by the infamous Captain

Salula. The Kulls were known for their loyalty to House Decouix, their fighting ability, and their cruelty. And Salula surpassed them all in these qualities.

All of this Morgin had learned long ago, then forgotten as quickly as possible. Olivia's grilling served its purpose, reminding them of the inter-clan relationships, and emphasizing that now they would need to put that knowledge to use.

At the end of the interview Olivia dismissed everyone but Morgin. She demanded he join her at luncheon, where he met several guests from Clan Inetka, among them SandoFall and the clan's leader Wylow, a large, boisterous, bearded man whom Morgin rather liked. Olivia chose to call Morgin by his formal, family name, AethonLaw. Clearly, she gained some edge by doing so, though Morgin wasn't exactly sure what. The whole affair bored him terribly, and he had trouble staying awake. Following that he attended a banquet that evening at the Inetka compound, where he met the Penda and Tosk contingents. Later that evening he had to be content with JohnEngine's account of his afternoon adventures.

The next morning he awoke early, hoping to be gone before Olivia found something to detain him. But Avis met him with a message to attend Malka. They met with BlakeDown, High Lord of Clan Penda, and between BlakeDown and Olivia, Morgin sensed subtle, constant sparring, as if they were at odds in some way. He spent the morning entertaining BlakeDown's youngest daughter, a girl about his own age who was quite pretty, but had a tendency to giggle and twitter. And then one of Olivia's interviews filled the rest of the afternoon, and another banquet filled the evening. Again Morgin had to be content with JohnEngine's stories.

The third day saw another morning-long quizzing by Olivia, and the afternoon filled by a meeting with Valso et Decouix. The Decouix prince was a young man, only a few years older than MichaelOff. He was handsome, with dark, delicate features, though Morgin noted that his tunic did not lack muscle to fill it, and his eyes were as hard as the edge of a sword. Oddly, for the first time, Olivia chose to call Morgin "Morgin," with no mention of the name AethonLaw. And once introduced, she ignored him completely.

He returned to the family compound that evening and learned there was another banquet scheduled. After further inquiry he found it would be attended exclusively by the elders and him, with none of his brothers or cousins present. He spoke with Avis and learned that his time for the next two days would be fully occupied, with all arrangements made by Olivia, and he began to realize she had some ulterior motive.

He sought out Olivia. He was feeling the first touches of anger, though he was determined that it would not show. Expecting nothing, but curious to hear her response, he asked if he might be excused from the banquet that evening.

"I'm sorry, child," she said. "But that's impossible. PaulStaff, leader of the Tosks, wishes to meet you."

"PaulStaff met me two days ago," Morgin said.

She wasn't ready for that. "So he did. So he did. But I wish you to be there. The younger generation of House Elhiyne must be properly represented."

It sounded hollow and Morgin recognized it for the lie it was. "But it's someone else's turn tonight."

She put on a show of tolerant displeasure. "I require you, and not someone else."

"You've required me day and night for three days now. It's not fair."

"Of course it's not fair. What does fairness have to do with it? I require your presence. You will be there."

"But I want some time of my own. I want to see the city."

She leaned forward menacingly, staring at him without blinking. "And why would you wish to see the city? It is a city, nothing more."

"But you're wrong," he said. "There are a hundred things to see and do, a thousand. Everyone else gets to. And you're not being honest with me."

She rose angrily from her seat, and he realized then that he'd gone too far. "How dare you?" she said. "You accuse me of lying when you no doubt have nothing on your mind but gesh."

Morgin started, and thought he hadn't heard her properly. But then he played her words back in his thoughts and he understood. He realized that there could never be any trust for *Rat the bastard whoreson*, and felt a flood of hot anger. "Gesh?" he asked. He barely remembered the gesh, couldn't recall any great pleasure, only the need and the pain that came without it. But the want and the desire had long ago vanished, and all that remained now was shame.

"Gesh?" he asked again. "You think I want gesh? You think I'll head straight for the gesh? Why . . . I haven't thought about gesh in . . . I don't know . . . how many years. And you think I'll lie and deceive to get it now? You have so little faith in me?"

For the first time in memory her face showed indecision and she hesitated. In that instant he silently turned his back on her, and moving at a carefully measured pace, he walked out of the room.

"Come back here," she demanded. "You haven't been dismissed."

His shame did not allow him to turn back, though he could hear her calling him. The twists and turns of the hallways in the Elhiyne compound quickly muffled the sounds of her anger, but not his humiliation.

The stranger kicked the body aside, pulled Morgin to his feet and slapped him in the face. "Snap out of it, boy. We don't want armsmen finding us here." Then he turned and ran.

Morgin hesitated for only an instant, then followed.

As they approached the market square the streets were lit by an occasional torch or the open door of a saloon. The stranger peered into several inns before stopping at one and muttering, "Good. This'll do."

He examined Morgin carefully in the light of the inn's open door, then pulled off his own cloak and threw it over Morgin's shoulders. "Until we get that blood washed off, keep your tunic covered with this." The stranger held out his hand. "Now give me yer purse."

For the first time Morgin looked at the man carefully. Tall, golden, blond hair hanging to his shoulders, a large mustache resting on the upper lip of a handsome face, a felt cap tilted rakishly on his head. He had no reason to trust this tall, blond stranger, but if the man chose to steal his money, it was a small price to pay in return for his life. Morgin gave him the purse reluctantly.

"Good. Now follow me, laddie-boy, and keep your mouth shut."

A few minutes later they were in a private room on the second floor of the inn. The stranger had returned the purse after paying for the room, and while Morgin cleaned the blood from the front of his jerkin, the stranger cleaned his sword, and his long moustache wagged as he filled the air with talk. "Well, laddie-me-boy. Looks like we'll get away with this one. Those bodies'll be stripped by morning. And if the clan armsmen come asking questions . . . Well, even if anyone saw the blood on you, these people don't talk much."

"But I killed him in self-defense," Morgin said.

"Yah, boy," the stranger said. "I know. And I killed two meself for the same reason. But sometimes them clan witches don't see it the same way as you an' me. So it's best to keep your mouth shut and stay clean."

But Morgin didn't feel clean. "Who are you?" he demanded. "And why did you help me? And why are you helping me now?"

"Who am I?" the stranger asked. He grinned and sighted down the length of his sword. "Why! I'm France, the swordsman." He hefted the blade as if to test its balance. "In fact, boy, I'm the best swordsman I've ever met. Better than any clansman, I'll wager."

"But you're a brawler," Morgin said. "Swordsmen fight by rules."

"Rules!" France said. He took a swipe with his sword and laughed loudly. "Ha! I court a fine lady by rules, boy. Otherwise she'd scorn me favors. I kill only men who need killin', and steal what ain't mine hardly never. So I live much of me life by rules, boy. When I fight for pleasure or practice, I usually fight by rules. But when I fight for me life, boy . . ." His expression hardened. "Well . . . any man who fights for his life by rules is a fool. And soon to be a dead fool at that."

Morgin considered that for a moment. "I guess that's fair. But why did you help me?"

"Well, laddie boy. I comes out of a particular drinking place near here and sees you stomping down the middle of the street like you owned the place. And behind you is gathering a pack of wolves to steal your money. So I followed to see what would happen."

"But how did they know I have money?"

"Boy, when you walk down these streets at night, you make sure your money don't chink in your purse, especially loud enough for others to hear."

"Oh!" Morgin said, feeling quite foolish. "I guess that's just common sense."

"Yup. And you seem to be a little short of that. What's yer name, boy?"

"Morgin," he said. "But you haven't told me why you helped me."

"That's simple enough, Morgin. I hate to see a fine, young lad like yourself get hurt."

Morgin shook his head. "I'm not that stupid."

France shrugged. "And I expects to be rewarded properly for me trouble by your parents."

"How do you know my parents?"

"I don't," the swordsmen said. With the tip of his sword he touched a newly acquired tear in Morgin's sleeve. "But look at your clothes. Till an hour ago there wasn't a tear in them. And you, a young lad with money jingling in your purse."

Morgin became acutely aware of the worn and tattered condition of France's own clothing.

"Tell me, boy. Why was you walking these streets at night?"

"I had an argument with my grandmother," Morgin said, and that was all he cared to tell this vagabond.

"So you stomped out of the house and went to the Thieves' Quarter." The swordsman shook his head sadly. "Didn't you know you'd get in trouble?"

"But I've been here before."

"Yah. Sure. During the day, no doubt. Damn it, boy. They don't call this the good-fellows' quarter. It's thieves and murderers here, and don't you forget it."

Morgin didn't tell him he'd come here because this was where his life had begun. He just sat silently, trying to understand why he'd done what he'd done. He also thought of the man he'd killed.

"Well, boy. You fought bravely, if not skillfully, and that's good enough for any-one."

"Not for my grandmother," Morgin said.

France laughed. "She's a mean old witch, eh?"

"How did you know?"

"Know what?"

"That she's a witch."

France's face, worn with experience, took on a dangerous look. He peered intently at Morgin. "Are you a clansman, boy?"

Morgin answered hesitantly. "Yes."

"Which clan?" France demanded.

"Elhiyne."

"Which house?"

"Elhiyne."

"And the name of this grandmother of yours?"

"Olivia."

Without warning the swordsman grabbed Morgin by his tunic, nearly lifted him off his feet and slammed him against a wall. "The Lady Olivia has no grandson named Morgin. And I don't like liars."

"My given name is AethonLaw, but I go by Morgin."

The swordsman whistled, released him and dropped into a chair. "I got a prince on me hands."

"I'm no prince," Morgin said.

"Maybe not," France said. "But you're close enough." He shook his head. "I'll be damned! Come on, lad. Sit down. You're making me nervous standing there like that."

There were only two pieces of furniture in the room, a simple chair and a musty, old bed. France sat in the chair, so Morgin sat on the edge of the bed. "What are you going to do with me?"

The swordsman leaned forward and became serious. "You listen to me, boy. I'll not be doing a thing with you. You're your own man. If I forced you to do anything, I'd have your grandmother after me. And there ain't a man alive who wants her on his trail."

"Then what should I do?"

"Well now," France said. "If it's advice you're asking for, I got plenty of that. The bad advice is free. The good advice'll cost you. But let me ask you. What do *you* want to do?"

"I don't know," Morgin said. "I just don't want to go back to the compound. At least not yet."

"Well then why don't you stay here, lad? I'm sure it's not as good as you're used to . . . ." France drew a finger through the dust on a bed post, ". . . but the owner takes pride in the fact that none of his customers gets robbed or murdered in their sleep. And there ain't no bedbugs, and the food ain't bad neither."

Morgin considered it. If he went back to the compound, every time he saw Olivia he'd just be reminded of his past. And if the mere sight of her didn't remind him, she'd be sure to bring it up.

"And," the swordsman said slyly, "for some wine, a little food, and a wee small fee, I'd be happy to be your guide and show you a bit of the city."

••••

It was a good bargain. They shared the room's only bed, sleeping in their clothes on top of the covers, for the sheets were too musty.

Morgin fell to sleep quickly. But it was a restless sleep, filled with dreams of strange people walking some unknown street, and all of them had eyes that reflected death in the moonlight. At one point he dreamed he was making love to a beautiful, young girl, but while lying face to face on top of her she turned into the man he'd killed. He awoke shivering in a cold sweat.

As he lay there, trying to sleep again but afraid he would dream the same dream, France spoke very softly in the dark. "Morgin, me lad. Whenever you think back to the first man you killed, just remember that it was him or you, and that was one man that deserved killing."

The following day they toured the Thieves' Quarter. They visited people and places that Morgin could never have seen in the company of clansmen. They stopped frequently in dark, forbidding saloons where France spoke with men whose eyes seemed never to rest, and who looked at Morgin with open distrust. France had warned him earlier, "Keep your mouth shut and tell no one you're a clansman, boy." Unfortunately, keeping his mouth shut allowed his thoughts to drift back to his last conversation—argument—with Olivia.

There were other places more festive, where pinching a barmaid was clearly part of the fare, and the drink flowed freely, though never for free. Morgin paid for it all gladly, and had the time of his life doing so, and it cost him only a pittance. Evidently, what was to Roland some spending money for one of his sons, was a small fortune to these people.

They also browsed through several weapons shops; France said he was always on the lookout for a good blade. In one shop France turned to Morgin and said, "There's some good steel here, lad. Pick one out for yourself."

"A sword?" Morgin asked. "For me?"

"Sure. You're of a proper age, and sword trained, you say."

"A sword of my very own? But I don't have enough money for a sword."

The swordsman winked and whispered, "You have more than you think. And you have to know how to talk prices down, boy. Just pick one out and leave the rest to me."

Morgin looked about while France spoke to the shop's owner. He'd been in weapons shops before, but the kind the clan frequented offered a better cut of merchandise than this place. He searched carefully, and finally found one of the few nice looking blades. He hefted it to try its balance.

"Not that one," France said. "It's too pretty. Killing steel shouldn't be pretty. And it's too expensive. And it ain't that good a blade."

Morgin began again, looking this time for steel, and weight, and balance. As he picked up each blade he closed his eyes and tried to judge it on its own merits, and not its looks, but the blade he chose, the one that felt most natural in his hand, was a crude, ugly thing that had seen many a battle in its day. He returned it to the rack and walked away.

He tried several more, again closing his eyes as he tested each, until he found another blade that felt right. He opened his eyes and discovered that again he'd chosen the ugly blade.

"What you got there, lad?"

Morgin handed the blade to France. "It's probably not a very good blade," he said, "but it seems to feel right."

France looked at the blade casually. Then his eyes lit up and he looked again. He handed the blade back to Morgin and whispered, "Buy it. Don't argue. Just buy it."

France argued with the shop's owner and managed to bring the price down by a few coins, but Morgin could see that his heart wasn't in it, though he did get the owner to throw in a proper sheath. He was in a hurry to be away.

Once out of the shop he scouted several alleys until he found one that was roomy and well lit by the sun. He pulled Morgin into it then asked to see the sword again. Morgin handed it to him.

France examined the blade in minute detail, and as he did so, his eyes gleamed with delight. "This is a rare find, lad. It's a Benesh'ere blade, an old one, and them crazy desert men make the best blades in all the tribes. It's got a few nicks, and the hilt needs to be remounted properly, but it's damn good steel. Ah, lad! I'll bet there's some stories in this blade."

"If it's such a good sword," Morgin said, "then you should have it."

France shook his head. "It was your hand that found it, lad. It's your blade. It would be unlucky for me to take it now."

France's eye's stayed on the blade for a long moment. Then he reluctantly returned it.

"I'm such a poor swordsman," Morgin blurted out. "Sometimes they even make me practice with the younger boys. Could you teach me how to fight? Please."

France shook his head. "You fought just fine in that alley last night."

"I was scared."

"That's the best way to fight, lad. Good and scared. But it ain't fighting you're talking about. It's dueling. The fancy stuff. And that ain't for you, boy. You're a fighter, not a duelist."

Morgin shook his head. "Grandmother says clansmen only duel. That it isn't gentlemanly to fight."

"The old witch ain't never had to swing a sword for her life, has she? Well you remember something, boy. When you're in the thick of it, and your life's on the line, use the point to stab, the flat of your blade to slap, the edge to cut, the guard as a steel fist, the hilt as a club. Use your elbows, your knees, your claws, your teeth. You just remember that, boy, and you'll live a lot longer. But I ain't got time to teach you to duel. And besides, it ain't in you."

They spent the rest of the afternoon sightseeing. But as the day drew to a close France led them back to one of the dark, forbidding saloons they'd visited that morning, and an unfriendly man that Morgin remembered well. France and the man spoke for a time privately while Morgin waited nearby. Then France left with the man, saying he had urgent business and would meet Morgin back at the inn after dinner.

Morgin returned to the inn, had a quiet dinner of simple fare, and was happy to see France arrive shortly thereafter. The swordsman wasted no time but said quickly, "Morgin, me lad. I've got to be leaving you. I've got business elsewhere that'll take some days so I'll be saying me good-byes."

"Won't I ever see you again?" Morgin asked.

"Maybe," the swordsman said. "Then again, maybe not."

"But what about a reward for saving my life?"

"Ah, lad! There ain't time. I've got to be moving on. And I learned long ago not to ask for things from witches. It's too dangerous. Just put in a good word for me."

Moments later the swordsman was gone. Morgin envied him, leaving on a moment's notice, travelling to far lands on some strange adventure. Alone now, Morgin chose a place at an empty table in a corner of the common room. He sipped his wine, tried to imagine where France might have gone, and for the most part was ignored by the inn's patrons. The bar maid, as a matter of course, propositioned him, though she seemed relieved when he turned her down. Perhaps it was the shadows that hovered about him. He felt safe in those shadows.

Sitting there alone with his thoughts, he recalled the many times he'd been slighted by clansmen. People casually referred to him as *whoreson*, even to his face, did it so easily and callously that they couldn't understand what it meant to him, how it angered him and shamed him all with the same word.

The evening progressed and the room began to fill with more patrons. Some were noisy and loud, laughing, drinking. Some sat quietly and spoke in soft tones. They were of all shapes and sizes, both male and female. The only thing they had in common was the obvious condition of their financial status: poor.

His thoughts turned to Olivia. He was thinking of their argument when the laughing and noise died, the clinking of glasses and the clank of mugs disappeared, and all eyes turned to the entrance and the clansmen that stood there. Being on the fringe, this inn was accustomed to the occasional highborn who wanted to do a little slumming. The crowd looked quickly away. The din of their pleasure returned.

Morgin didn't look away because these clansmen were his cousins and brothers. He watched closely as they removed their cloaks and scanned the room. His first thought was that somehow they'd discovered his whereabouts and come to fetch him, but that thought vanished as they located an empty table and sat down to enjoy themselves.

Hidden within his shadows he watched them, curious as to why they'd come to this inn. They ordered ale and wine, laughing and joking among themselves. JohnEngine was there, with DaNoel, Brandon, and MichaelOff. Morgin recognized SandoFall, soon to be Annaline's husband, and several more Inetkas whose names he could not remember. They made a few toasts, loud and raucous, some quite crude, and he realized they were celebrating the end of SandoFall's bachelor days. Morgin looked on with envy, wishing he and DaNoel had gotten along better so that he too could join in the fun.

Then, too soon to be coincidence, the room again fell silent. But this time the silence lasted, for standing within the doorway were two Kullish guardsmen.

Morgin had heard much of the Kulls. They were men who had no magic of their own, but desirous of power, had pledged their service, and their souls, to House Decouix. In return, the Decouixs located minor demons who wished for contact with the Mortal Plane. Then, with the consent of both parties, the demon and the man were melded into one. The result was irreversible: a man to all outward appearances, a cruel, demon, fighting machine within, forever obedient to Decouix command.

The two Kulls looked the room over. Satisfied, they signaled to others outside. Moments later Valso and three of his kinsmen entered, surrounded by a dozen Kulls. They walked to a table that was occupied, one not far from Morgin's kinsmen, and stood there waiting. The table's occupants did not at first realize what was required of them, but when they did, they stood quickly and left. The room remained silent.

Once seated Valso nodded, and the captain of the Kulls announced loudly, "Innkeeper. Drinks for all. The prince of House Decouix wishes all to enjoy his generosity."

The barmaid began hurriedly filling mugs, though the room held to its silence, yielding only to the clatter of the maid's activities.

One of Valso's kinsmen, a fop by all standards, turned to the prince and spoke just loud enough for all to hear. "Your Highness, I smell something unpleasant in here."

JohnEngine's tankard of ale spilled. A stifled curse could be heard. Again the room was still.

Another of Valso's kinsmen spoke, again just loud enough for all to hear. "You're right, Degla. There is a stench here, and I've smelled it before." He sniffed the air experimentally. "I believe it's the smell of swine." Again the room was still.

None of Morgin's kinsmen spoke, though all could see the anger building.

The third of Valso's kinsmen spoke. "No, GeorgeAll. That's not swine. What you're smelling is the stench of a swineherd, I believe, though the two are quite the same."

JohnEngine swore and started to rise. MichaelOff quickly put a hand on his shoulder and forced him back down. "No, cousin," he said. The silence of the room was heavy with fear.

Valso leaned backward so that the two forelegs of his chair rose from the floor. Preparing to speak, he took a slow, deep breath, then exhaled loudly. "I do believe you're right, Andra. Definitely the smell of a swineherd."

He paused, nodding his head. Then peering about the room as if seeking someone, he asked, "I wonder. Are there any Elhiynes about?"

JohnEngine jumped to his feet and shouted, "Decouix scum!"

Everyone moved, and Morgin moved with them. The room filled with the deadly sound of steel escaping sheaths. Lines were drawn, positions taken. Then all movement ceased, though Morgin continued to work his way along the shadows that lined the edge of the room.

JohnEngine stood in the center of the room, his hand on the dagger at his side. His kinsmen were behind him, ready to back him. In front of him Valso stood at sword's length, also backed by his kinsmen. Surrounding them all stood a ring of Kulls facing inward, their backs to the outer periphery of the room where Morgin danced in the shadows.

Morgin's kinsmen were lightly armed and outnumbered by the more heavily armed Kulls. If a fight began it would be a slaughter, for Kulls gave no quarter.

Morgin moved among his shadows, stepping lightly from one to the next. He had no idea what he could do. There was no time to make a plan, only to react. Then one of the Kulls looked his way and he froze into stillness, pressed his back tightly against the wall and held his breath. The Kull looked away.

MichaelOff spoke. "Valso. We've already walked away from your taunts once this evening. If you continue you'll leave us no choice. Please stop this deadly game, cousin, before there is no return."

While MichaelOff spoke, Morgin moved again, using the noise of MichaelOff's words to mask any noise he might make. He took a position to the side of JohnEngine and Valso. He was still against the wall, about three long paces from them, but with a direct line of sight between two Kulls, their backs toward him. There were no chairs or tables to block his path, and so he froze and held his breath, for the room again grew silent.

Valso spoke. "You call me cousin?" he asked, and laughed in the asking of it.

Morgin prepared to move. "Well now," Valso said. "I claim no kinship with one whose mother sleeps with pigs."

Everyone moved at once; Morgin pulled power and charged. He surprised the two Kulls, knocked them aside as he burst between them, used his power to drag his body at lightning speed through what felt like a sea of honey. As he crossed the distance to JohnEngine and Valso, he watched Valso's sword rising toward his brother's throat, even as he drew his own sword, swinging it up in an arc toward Valso's throat. His intention was to stop the tip just short of the skin there, but with his limited skill as a swordsman he overshot. The tip of his sword barely touched Valso's neck, and everyone froze into statues as all motion ceased.

JohnEngine had drawn his short dagger and was held at bay by Valso's sword. The tip of Morgin's sword hovered just under Valso's chin, and while Valso's arm was fully extended, Morgin's was cocked and ready to thrust, to drive the blade up through the neck and into the prince's brain. If blood were spilled, none there questioned that Valso would be the first to die.

Slowly the prince's face turned red, then blue. His lower lip began to quiver and his breath came in a stuttered gasp. Then the fit of rage passed, receding slowly like the ocean's tide. Valso glared malevolently at Morgin. His eyes held a hate that was frightening. And again the room was still.

Morgin waited for someone to move, to say or do something. But then he realized they were waiting on him. The next move was his, but there hadn't been time to think his moves through, only to act. He forced himself to pause, to think.

No one had yet been killed, or even seriously wounded. A small drop of blood dripped down Valso's throat where his sword had touched the prince, but that was all, more like the nick of a razor than that of a sword. Morgin held that in mind as he spoke, though he was unable to hide the tremble in his voice. "Your Highness," he said carefully. "My kinsmen and I wish to go . . . May we have your leave?"

Valso's eyes were black, hard stones of hatred. "You'll pay for this, Elhiyne. You'll pay."

Morgin tried to think of some witty remark, but none came to mind. "I asked for your leave, Your Highness," he said, and for emphasis he touched the flat of his blade to Valso's throat, smearing the drop of blood there.

Valso's face twisted into a mask of rage. "Go."

Morgin nodded to MichaelOff. The Inetkas and Elhiynes backed slowly out of the room, ever conscious of the Kulls with their drawn blades. But JohnEngine stopped beside Morgin and whispered, "We don't leave without you, brother."

Again the action had caught up with Morgin's plans. Again he didn't know what to do, and during his moment of indecision Valso smiled sweetly. "Well, Elhiyne. What will you do now? The instant you take your blade from my throat, you'll die." The Kulls muttered expectantly, like a pack of dogs given the scent of their prey.

"Then I won't take my blade from your throat," Morgin said. "As a common courtesy, you'll accompany us to the door, won't you, Your Highness?"

The rage and the hatred returned to Valso's face.

Morgin used the tip of his blade to force Valso's chin toward the ceiling, until his back arched uncomfortably. "Let us walk carefully," Morgin said.

They moved slowly, JohnEngine leading the way, Morgin back-stepping behind him, the prince following with his chin forced high in the air. The Kulls closed in behind Valso, ready to take advantage of any chance misstep.

When they reached the door Morgin paused, his back to the street. He had to think of some way to exit quickly, and so without warning he raised his boot and kicked Valso in the chest, using the momentum of the kick to push himself out into the street. JohnEngine slammed the door in front of him, and the last thing Morgin saw was Valso sprawling into the waiting arms of his Kulls.

They ran, he and JohnEngine and the others, following MichaelOff, dodging through alleys and back streets. At first they could hear Valso shouting at his Kulls to catch them, but soon his cries were lost in the distance and the night.

Morgin rounded a corner at full speed and plowed headlong into someone. He went sprawling into the street, rolled quickly to one side and came up sword drawn. At his feet lay SandoFall. About them both stood their kinsmen, breathing heavily and listening silently. And but for the sounds of a nearby inn, the night was still. No Valso. No Kulls.

"We've lost them," MichaelOff said.

SandoFall stood, brushing dust from his clothes. "I'm not sure which is more dangerous, Valso and his Kulls, or this charging bull of a cousin of yours." He nodded to Morgin.

MichaelOff laughed. "But you owe him your skin. The least you can do is let him knock you down a few times."

JohnEngine laughed uncontrollably. "We all owe him our skins."

"Right you are," someone said and slapped Morgin on the back. Suddenly they were all laughing, shaking his hand and congratulating him for so deftly humiliating the Decouix. Even DaNoel was for once friendly.

"Hah!" JohnEngine said. "The evening is still young. Morgin can join us."

"Aye," SandoFall yelled. "And he'll not buy his own drinks."

They swept Morgin along as they moved to another inn in the Clan's Quarter where there'd be less likelihood of trouble. He had become one of them, he realized, a witchman. Perhaps he would always be something of an outsider, but he understood now that he was a clansman. He could not have abandoned them in that inn any more than they could have abandoned him. They were his kin, even if not by blood; his family, even if not by birth. He would have to trust them, whether Olivia trusted him or not.

Olivia! Morgin had a horrible thought. He grabbed MichaelOff's sleeve and pulled him close. "What's grandmother going to say?"

MichaelOff looked as if his drink had just gone sour in his mouth. "Oh Morgin! Let's not think of unpleasant things tonight. We'll face grandmother when the time comes."

••••

"You put steel to the Decouix?" Olivia demanded, her voice rising with each word.

Morgin, kneeling with his brothers and cousins at her feet, decided to assume that she meant the collective you. She hadn't specifically addressed him, and MichaelOff had done all of the talking so far, so let him answer

"Morgin. I'm speaking to you. Answer me."

"Yes, grandmother."

"Do you mean, 'Yes you put steel to the Decouix'?"

"Yes, grandmother. But I—"

"You drew his blood, and then you asked his permission to leave?"

Morgin cringed. "Yes, grandmother." He knew the symptoms well. The old witch was building to a monumental explosion.

"Ah ha!" Olivia cawed, throwing her head back and laughing like a young girl at a dance. "How exquisite! How utterly exquisite! Such irony I had never hoped to see. The Decouix, publicly humbled, and by his own foolishness."

Morgin glanced up to sneak a quick look at the old woman. She literally shook with mirth, but it died as quickly as it was born, and her gaze returned to him.

"How came you to be in that inn?"

"I was staying there, grandmother."

"So! You find their accommodations better than ours?"

"No, grandmother. I just needed a place to be alone and think."

"And what made you choose that particular inn?"

"I didn't choose it. France did."

"And who is this France?"

"A swordsman, grandmother. He saved my life."

"He saved your life, eh?"

"Yes, grandmother."

She pondered that for a moment. "It seems you have a story to tell. But first I think you owe me an apology."

"I'm sorry, grandmother."

"That's better," she said, softening a little. "You are forgiven this time. Especially since you redeemed yourself by humbling the Decouix. But don't ever walk out on me like that again."

"Yes, grandmother."

"Good." She was all smiles as she sat down on her couch. "Come, grandson. Sit beside me and tell me of this adventure of yours. Leave nothing out."

She was positively merry as Morgin told his story, laughing at times like a young girl. He told her of France and the fight in the street. When he told her of the man he had killed she said, "So, you're a blooded warrior now."

JohnEngine and DaNoel both looked envious, and AnnaRail looked sad. He left out France's comments about witches, and there was no need to mention things like the barmaid who propositioned him. When he told of buying the sword she asked to see it. She looked it over mechanically, commenting only that it appeared rather crude. But when Malka examined it he pronounced it ". . . functional, well balanced; a good weapon. This France fellow knows his steel." Morgin didn't tell them it was a Benesh'ere blade.

The story ended almost festively, with all of the young men contributing bits and pieces to the final scene in the inn with Valso. Olivia hung on every word, asking for embellishments on this and that, especially concerning Valso's red and angry face. When she dismissed them it was with smiles and compliments for all.

Morgin wasted no time cornering MichaelOff in his room. "Why was grandmother so happy Valso was humiliated?"

MichaelOff sighed, clearly not interested in telling a long tale. He sat down and leaned back in his chair, then spoke almost mechanically. "Olivia's parents, Bertak and Hillel, had no male offspring, so when she married Karlane he became consort and Elhiyne. She bore three sons and a daughter, the youngest of which was Malka."

Morgin asked, "But why have I never heard this?"

"Because your grandmother does not like it spoken of. Now back then the seat of Elhiyne was located in Yestmark and we grew strong, so Decouix attacked. They murdered Bertak, Hillell, Karlane, and Malka's older brothers and sister. Illalla, Valso's father, was then a young prince of House Decouix. He raped Hellis, Olivia's younger sister, and Tulellcoe was conceived. With Roland growing in her belly, your grandmother escaped with Malka and Hellis, and they hid for months among the other Lesser Clans. Eglahan rules in Yestmark now, and is our first defense against Decouix attack."

"But what about Olivia and Hellis?" Morgin asked.

"Be patient," MichaelOff said. "They remained in hiding while Roland and Tulellcoe were born. But by that time Hellis had gone mad. She took her own life, though Olivia stopped her from killing Tulellcoe as well. When Olivia came out of hiding she rebuilt Elhiyne where it now stands, on top of the ancient ruins of Elhiyne. You know them well, I'm sure, since you explore them regularly."

Morgin started to protest.

"Don't bother to deny it," MichaelOff said. "I explored those same ruins myself. And before me I'm quite sure that Malka, Roland, and Tulellcoe did the same.

"So our grandmother survived the Decouix attack. And since then she has lived for two things: to rebuild House Elhiyne, and to hate Decouix. She dare not defy them openly, but every move she makes is calculated to strengthen us against them."

"Will there someday be war?" Morgin asked.

MichaelOff shrugged. "Probably. But all there is now is hate. And you, cousin, have stepped unknowingly into the middle of that. You've made a mortal enemy this night. Valso is known for his vindictiveness, and I fear that someday he will strike back at you. Beware of him, Morgin. It is said he murdered his own brothers to eliminate any rivals for the Decouix throne. He will not forget that you made him look foolish in a public inn."

8

Hero's Walk

"HURRY UP, MORGIN," JohnEngine said. "The wedding's about to begin."

"Go on without me," Morgin said, struggling into his breeches.

"If you're late," JohnEngine said over his shoulder as he ran out of the room, "Grandmother'll be mad as netherhell."

Morgin scrambled into his tunic, pulled on his boots, and tied the laces frantically. Then he jumped to his feet and shot out of his room into the upstairs hall, tucking his tunic into his breeches as he ran. But Annaline called out as he ran past her suite and he screeched to a halt.

"I have to hurry," he said, turning toward her. "If I'm late, grandmother'll . . ." But when he saw her, words escaped him.

She stood in the doorway to her room, dressed in Elhiyne red, smiling happily and radiating gladness like a bright lamp in the night, her eyes filled with joy. "They won't start the wedding without me, little brother."

For the first time Morgin saw more than just a bothersome older sister. "Annaline," he said. "You're beautiful. And you look so happy."

"I am happy because of you, Morgin."

"Me? What did I do?"

"I'm told you rescued SandoFall."

"Oh!" Morgin said. "You mean Valso. But that was nothing."

"You prevented him from turning this into a day of sorrow instead of joy." She leaned forward, kissed him on the cheek. Then she curtsied to him as if he were a great lord. "I thank you, my brother, my lord. Today you are my hero."

••••

The wedding ceremony was long and tedious, but it did not bore Morgin in the least. Once, when Annaline and SandoFall turned to face the audience, her eyes met Morgin's, she smiled and winked. He winked back, and his pride swelled.

He tried to seek her out during the grand ball that followed, but was intercepted almost immediately by a Penda dowager. She chattered incessantly, while pushing her daughter on him and insisting they dance.

JohnEngine had warned him, "Be careful. You're not just any Elhiyne. You're one of *the* Elhiynes, and there's not a mother in the Lesser Clans who wouldn't bed with demons to see her daughter married to you."

The daughter was a miniature copy of her mother. She even chattered like her mother, when she wasn't giggling. There wasn't a moment during which her lips weren't making some sort of noise.

Why me? Morgin thought. But he was polite. And when the dance ended, he even dallied for a few moments to avoid being obvious. Then he returned the girl to her mother and retreated quickly.

But no sooner had the next dance begun when another mother accosted him with another daughter. Again he danced with the girl and was polite. At least this one didn't giggle, and she laughed knowingly when he said something witty. In fact, she laughed at everything he said, even when, as an experiment, he mumbled incoherent babble.

The next dance saw another mother-daughter team, and the one after that another. It became so ridiculous that Morgin no longer even bothered to talk, and each daughter, having been thoroughly instructed by her mother to display her utmost charms, filled the vacuum with polite, but uninteresting, conversation.

Morgin quickly tired of this foolish charade. Mothers and daughters! He couldn't even remember the name of the girl with whom he was dancing at the moment, though he was certain she was an Inetka. At least she, realizing that his patience for hollow conversation was exhausted, had ceased prattling.

She suddenly stopped dancing and Morgin stepped on her foot.

"Ouch," she said. She stepped back from him, put her fists on her hips, looked at him with a storm growing behind her eyes. "Your brother said you're a gentleman, and that if you're quiet, it's only because you're a little shy. But I find you boorish. And you're also a clumsy oaf."

"I'm sorry," Morgin said. "It's just that these mothers keep forcing their daughters on me."

Her eyes darkened further. Green eyes, Morgin noticed. Pretty eyes. "So I was forced on you, was I?"

"I didn't mean it that way."

"Your meaning was quite clear. And what makes you think that you weren't forced on me as well?"

"I . . . Well I . . ."

"At least I had the courtesy to be civil in what was a mutually uncomfortable situation."

With that, she turned her back on him and walked away, leaving Morgin in the middle of the dance floor. He moved quickly to avoid any mothers with daughters.

He steered straight for JohnEngine, who stood among a cluster of young men, including DaNoel, Brandon and several others.

"What in netherhell's going on?" he demanded.

JohnEngine grinned. "Difficulties, brother. I wish I had such troubles."

"Too many ladies for you?" Dannasul asked.

"Yes," Morgin said angrily. "No. Too many mothers pushing too many daughters on me. What's going on?"

"Shall we tell him?" JohnEngine asked Dannasul.

"Tell me what?"

Dannasul ignored Morgin. "I don't know, John. As usual his head's up in the clouds and he hasn't the vaguest idea."

"Idea about what?" Morgin demanded.

"You're right," JohnEngine said. "Perhaps he should find out for himself."

"Damn it!" Morgin said. "Find out what?"

Brandon elbowed his way between JohnEngine and Dannasul. "Your reputation is spreading."

"What reputation?"

Brandon shrugged. "No one likes the Decouix, and you humbled him badly."

"How did they find out about that?"

"It's all over the city," Dannasul said. "You can't keep a duel like that quiet. Especially when it involves the Decouix."

"But there was no duel," Morgin said.

Brandon shook his head as if Morgin were a slow-witted child. "The story that's going about the city is that Valso was ready to let his Kulls murder us all. You challenged him. He could not refuse without seeming cowardly, but he demanded that it be a duel to the death. The two of you fought, and by superior swordsmanship you overcame him. But you were merciful and granted him his life on the condition that we be allowed to leave unharmed."

"That's preposterous," Morgin said.

Brandon agreed. "I know."

With a sneer on his face, DaNoel leaned forward and said, "Yes, it is preposterous."

"But Brandon tells the story so poorly," JohnEngine complained. "Oh he's got the facts straight, but in the streets it's told with so much more embellishment: a blow by blow description of two master swordsmen battling their way from one end of the city to the other. It sounds so much better that way, don't you think?"

DaNoel raised his mug of ale. Already a bit drunk, swaying slightly as he spoke, he said, "To mighty Morgin. The greatest swordsman in all the land."

He drank deeply, as did the others. They all laughed, but DaNoel's sounded forced. He staggered into Morgin, and under the guise of catching his balance, hissed in his ear, "You don't fool me, whoreson."

JohnEngine's eyes brightened. "Ah, Rhianne!" he said, looking over Morgin's shoulder.

Morgin turned about, found himself facing the young Inetka girl on whose toes he had stepped.

JohnEngine swooped around him and took her hand, kissed it with a flourish. "Rhianne. This is a pleasant surprise. I hadn't expected to see you free so easily."

"Good evening, JohnEngine," she said pleasantly. "I tire of dancing, and of oafish dancers who step on my toes." Her eyes passed quickly over Morgin.

"Then what besides dancing would you like?" JohnEngine asked.

"A small goblet of wine and some pleasant conversation."

Dannasul fetched the wine while JohnEngine hovered jealously about her.

She said, "I don't believe I've met everyone here."

JohnEngine frowned. "You don't want to know these ruffians."

She sipped her wine. "You just want to keep me for yourself."

"Ah Rhianne," he said. "You know me too well. Nevertheless." He shrugged and turned to the rest of them, introduced those she didn't know and finished with Morgin. "And the one here with his mouth open is my brother AethonLaw et Elhiyne, who goes by the name of Morgin."

She looked at Morgin, turned one brow upward and offered her hand. Morgin took it, bowed, kissed it much like JohnEngine, but without the flourish, hoping he was doing it properly.

"So you're the great swordsman," she said. "It's a pity you can't dance as well."

Morgin shrugged.

JohnEngine frowned. "Do you two know each other?"

Rhianne smiled an unfriendly smile. "We're acquainted."

Morgin wished he knew a spell of invisibility. "I'm the oafish dancer who stepped on her toes."

DaNoel's teeth shined in the middle of a broad grin. Brandon shook his head. Dannasul choked back a laugh. JohnEngine let one out. "Oh brother-of-mine. That's precious."

"AethonLaw," a woman called. "AethonLaw is that you?"

Morgin cringed inwardly. He recognized her: a Penda woman with more than one daughter, one of whom she literally dragged across the dance floor now.

"AethonLaw. You must meet my other daughter Anja. Anja. Meet AethonLaw et Elhiyne."

The girl was all of twelve years old. She looked at him and wrinkled her nose.

Morgin summoned every ounce of courtesy he could find. He bowed. "I am honored, milady."

"Anja's been wanting to meet you all evening, AethonLaw. Haven't you, Anja?"

The little girl wrinkled her nose again.

Dannasul snickered.

"You two run along and dance now," Anja's mother said.

"I don't want to dance," Anja said.

JohnEngine spluttered and coughed, spilling ale and slapping himself on the chest. "Sorry," he said. "Took a little ale down the wrong pipe."

Morgin wanted to get this over with as soon as possible. "Would you care to dance?" he asked Anja politely.

"No," she said.

JohnEngine turned away, fighting back open laughter. "Think I'll get more ale."

"Now, Anja," her mother said. "Don't be rude. Dance with AethonLaw."

After a little cajoling Anja finally condescended to dance with Morgin, though she was none too happy about it. Morgin took care not to step on her toes, though she walked all over his. When the music ended he escorted her back to her mother then snuck out into the gardens where he hoped to find refuge from mothers and daughters.

The night air was still and pleasing. He found a stone bench to one side of the terrace and sat down alone. Below him lay the city, a dark skyline of buildings with small, lighted pockets of activity.

"Morgin," Rhianne said. "Are you out here?"

He stiffened, remained quiet, hoping she'd pass him by unnoticed. Then he heard the soft rustle of her skirts behind him. "That was terribly humiliating, wasn't it?"

"If you mean Anja?" he asked, trying to sound unconcerned. "It really didn't bother me."

"Yes it did," she said softly. "And you were very polite about the whole thing, as you are trying to be polite now."

He shrugged.

"May I join you?"

"Sure," he said. "Sit down."

She did so, and again he heard the soft rustle of her skirts. Her perfume drifted about him, carried by a gentle breeze. Like Rhianne herself, the scent she wore was soft, and while he desperately wanted to, he refused to look her way. He felt like a clumsy fool.

"I'm sorry I stepped on your toes," he said.

She laughed a little. "You hurt my pride more than my toes."

"Well I'm sorry about that too."

He wanted to say something more, to be witty and charming like JohnEngine, but he knew if he tried he'd make a mess of it.

"Morgin," she said tentatively. "When my mother introduced me to you, was she anything like Anja's? And be honest with me. Don't be polite again."

"To tell you the truth," he said. "I really don't know. I don't even remember being introduced. By that time I'd stopped paying attention and was just going through the motions."

"How many times has that happened this evening?"

"I don't know that either," he said. "I lost count long ago."

"You must have had a thoroughly wretched evening. Surely it can't all be because you humbled Valso."

Morgin shrugged. He'd been thinking about that himself. "There's more. Of course my brothers and cousins don't see it that way, but they're not adopted either."

"What does that have to do with it?" she asked. "Clan law recognizes no difference between adoption and birth."

"You're being naive." He turned to face her, to truly look at her for the first time. A small lock of hair had fought its way loose from the elaborate tangle on top of her head, and he realized he could lose himself in that face. Her curiosity was honest, but remembering a lifetime of subtly unintended insults and unknowing slights, he wondered if she could ever understand.

"Don't you see?" he said. "Clan law is enforced by men and women who are as fallible as you and I. In gross matters I am of House Elhiyne, and none dare say otherwise. But in the fine points, the little things that are ruled by people's prejudices, I am still the adopted whoreson, as I shall always be."

In the moonlight he saw her brow wrinkle; even frowning, she was beautiful. "But what does that have to do with dances and mothers with marriageable daughters?"

Morgin said, "Every one of those daughters, including you, and I mean no insult, but every one of them was the daughter of a minor lord. A daughter of one of the major houses may expect to marry high within one of the clans. And while by adoption and law I am of the highest caste, I am still the whoreson and that makes me just a little more accessible than my brothers and cousins. Your mother, and the others, thought that their daughters, who ordinarily could never expect to marry into one of the great houses, might still have a chance with me, the whoreson."

Rhianne nodded slowly. "And the incident with Valso?" she asked.

"That's what opened up all the possibilities in those mothers' minds. Since I am the hero of the moment, the mothers have hopes that their daughters will resist them less when they propose marriage with me."

Rhianne reached out and took his hands in hers. "You don't seem at all bitter about this."

Morgin could feel the bitterness in his gut like sour ale, but this was not the night to admit it. "Why should I be bitter?" There were many facets of his life in which he could find joy. "My life is much better with the clan than it was before. I love my brothers and sisters and cousins. And they love me"—he thought momentarily of DaNoel—"for the most part. And there has never been any question that I am deeply loved by my mother and father. So what do a few slights matter?"

Her brow wrinkled and she spoke in a more subdued tone. "I do understand, you know. Perhaps better than you think. I am the fourth of four daughters, of a—as you pointed out—rather minor lord. My prospects of a good marriage are poor. But my mother tells me I shouldn't let that get in my way. She's told me I can set my sights higher, and marry well, and I intend to."

She looked at him oddly. "I like you, Morgin." She stood, still holding his hands. "Come. Let's dance again. But this time we'll dance because we want to. And I'll bet we can both set our sights higher. I'll help you find someone, and you can help me."

Morgin only danced when forced to by circumstance, or required courtesy, and at that moment dancing was the last thing he wanted to do. But for Rhianne, he would have done anything. He escorted her out onto the dance floor, smiling outwardly, but terrified. For once, he was grateful Olivia had forced dance lessons upon them all.

The music began. He managed to stay with it, concentrating intently, moving with utmost care. And then he realized that Rhianne had asked him something, and he hadn't heard a word she'd said.

"What?" he asked.

"I asked if you are as good a swordsman as they say."

"Who me? Who says I'm a good swordsman?"

"The story I've been told is that you're a master."

Oh no! Morgin thought, but without hesitation he confessed. "It's all false. I've been trained with the sword, but I'm an exceedingly poor student."

"But how did you overcome Valso?" she asked. "He is a master."

Morgin laughed uneasily, knowing he had no choice but to tell her the truth. He told her of the incident in the inn as he remembered it. "So you see. I came out of nowhere. I had surprise with me. Were it not for that, I could never have succeeded."

Her lips turned upward as he spoke, and when he was done she threw her head back and laughed heartily. "Oh that's funny, Morgin. That's so terribly funny."

Humiliation washed through him, but then she saw the look on his face and stopped laughing. "Oh not you, Morgin. I'm not laughing at you. Don't you see? The joke is on them. What you did still took great courage, and yet they don't realize it."

"I didn't feel courageous at the time."

She said, "My father says brave men never feel brave while they're being brave."

The dance ended then and Morgin escorted her off the floor. She was very popular, and much in demand by all the young men who were far more handsome than he. But he wanted to dance with her again, and hoping beyond hope he dallied for a moment.

The music began again, and sure enough a young Penda lord approached. He was tall and handsome, and Morgin could see her face light up as he requested the next dance. But instead of accepting she said, "I am honored Lord ErrinCastle, but alas I've promised the next dance to Lord AethonLaw here."

Morgin had heard of ErrinCastle. He was BlakeDown's son, and the heir to Penda. He smiled politely at Rhianne, managed to avoid acknowledging Morgin's presence. "Perhaps the next dance?" he asked.

She nodded politely and agreed. "The next dance."

Once she and Morgin were again out on the dance floor, she whispered in his ear, "I've been hoping he'd ask me to dance."

"Then why didn't you accept?"

"Oh, you wouldn't understand these things," she said, then proceeded to spend the rest of the dance talking about ErrinCastle, and how he was so handsome and brave and strong. By the end of the dance Morgin had developed a healthy dislike for the young Penda lord.

Morgin surrendered her to ErrinCastle, rejoined his brothers and cousins and tried not to spend the rest of the evening watching her from afar, but he did nevertheless. He was talking to JohnEngine about girls, looking over his brother's shoulder, watching Rhianne dance with ErrinCastle again, when he heard Valso speak behind him. "Elhiyne."

Morgin jumped, spun quickly about, faced Valso squarely. A ripple passed through the crowd and the music stopped.

But Valso stood casually, not menacingly, and holding onto his arm, almost clutching it desperately, was a beautiful woman about AnnaRail's age. But her face bore the sharp lines and characteristics of House Decouix; her beauty was something dark and cold, and her eyes were touched by a hint of sad madness.

"Jumpy," Valso said, "aren't we?"

Morgin shook his head. Something was muddling his senses, as if the woman at Valso's side had enthralled him with a spell, as if reality were slipping away from him. When he spoke he could not hide the tension in his voice. "Good evening, Lord Valso."

"Is it?" Valso asked. The corners of his mouth held the hint of a sneer. "May I introduce my older sister?" he said. He looked at the woman at his side. "Haleen et Decouix. This is the Elhiyne pup I told you about."

Haleen looked at Morgin strangely, not with malice, but with the look of one stricken by some great sorrow. She reached out wonderingly and touched his cheek with a soft, gentle caress, as if she were drawn to him by some invisible thread. Her reaction surprised them all.

Again Morgin felt himself sliding into a thrall. It scared him. He flinched away from her touch, and that, more than anything, seemed to hurt her.

Valso tugged viciously on her arm and cursed. "What are you doing?"

She ignored him, continued to reach out to Morgin. "Don't fear me, child," she said. "Please don't fear me."

Valso slapped her face. "Would you dally with an Elhiyne again?"

He raised the hand to strike again, but Tulellcoe appeared out of nowhere, knocked the hand aside, then struck Valso in the face and sent him sprawling onto the floor.

Valso jumped to his feet, blood trickling from his lip, anger and hate flashing across his face.

Morgin had never before seen Tulellcoe show anger. He snarled at Valso through clenched teeth, "We Elhiynes treat our women with respect, Decouix."

Valso flicked his wrist, and a little dagger appeared in his hand.

The women nearby gasped and stepped back. But Morgin stepped forward to stand supportively beside Tulellcoe. And then Elhiyne clansmen made themselves visible everywhere.

Malka stepped in front of Valso. "If I were you, Decouix, I'd think again before using that knife on anything but a plate of food."

Valso scanned the crowd of Elhiyne clansmen. He flicked his wrist and the knife disappeared.

"And if I see you strike that woman again," Malka continued, "I'll wring your disgusting little neck."

Valso gave Morgin one, last hateful look, then turned and stalked from the room. Haleen followed not far behind, constantly glancing over her shoulder at Morgin.

"That was interesting," Rhianne said.

Morgin hadn't realized she was standing beside him. "Haleen did seem a bit strange."

Rhianne nodded thoughtfully. "Oh, rumor has it she's quite mad. Apparently she had a rather torrid affair with one of your kinsmen, but neither House would condone such a union. And years of grief over her lost love have unhinged her, so they say. Valso was quite furious at her behavior, dubbed her the *mad whore* for dallying with an Elhiyne."

Morgin wanted to forget the incident, but he couldn't put out of his mind the look on Haleen's face as she left the room. He asked Rhianne to dance again, but she declined, pleading tired feet. Yet a few moments later when ErrinCastle joined them and asked her to dance, she accepted without hesitation.

••••

During the week that followed there were no formal events that required Morgin's attendance. The entire city slowed down as life returned to normal, and while that was the time during which the great houses conducted most of the serious interclan business, it was done in small informal groups that Morgin had little trouble avoiding. In fact, the only event he was required to attend, accompanied by Roland, was a small banquet at the Inetka compound.

Upon arriving he found to his pleasure that Rhianne was there with her parents Edtoall and Matill, and her three older sisters whose names he could never keep straight. He was also pleased to find that the seating arrangements put him next to Rhianne. But his pleasure ended quickly, for all she cared to talk about was riding in the country that afternoon with ErrinCastle.

After dinner Edtoall and Roland separately approached him, both interested in what he thought of Rhianne. He shrugged their questions off, managed to get excused from the rest of the evening and left early. Olivia intended to leave the city at dawn the next morning, so he thought he'd get a head-start on packing. Roland stayed a bit longer to discuss some issues with Edtoall.

In the Clan's Quarter the streets were well lit and frequently patrolled, but his walk was a solitary one, for the place seemed deserted. Everyone else must also be busy preparing to leave in the morning. He walked carelessly down the middle of a street, thinking of Rhianne and trying to devise a plan to get her to pay more attention to him the next time they met, though it was unlikely such an opportunity would come for a season or two.

"Kinsman," a voice said sweetly.

Morgin froze, recognizing Valso's voice. It had come from the shadow of a nearby alley.

He scanned the street quickly, checking his backside before turning to face the alley. It was dark and unlit, filled only with black shadow, and he could see nothing within for whoever hid there had cast some sort of spell that obscured his shadow-sight. The alley could hide any number of Kulls, and Morgin was unarmed, but then he thought of France's advice about feet and knees and elbows and fists and claws and teeth.

"Kinsman," the voice said again.

That voice! The timber was actually quite different from Valso's. He approached the alley slowly, stopping well out of reach of any swordsman that might be hiding there. He stood in a crouch with the full width of a well-lit street behind him. He would not be surprised from the rear.

"Kinsman," the voice said again. "Why do you fear me?"

Morgin answered carefully. "Step into the light so I can see who is speaking."

Haleen, not Valso, stepped out of the alley. Morgin relaxed, realizing he had mistaken her voice for her brother's. She stood just within the light thrown by the street lamps, the darkened shadow of the alley immediately behind her. "Do you distrust me?" she asked.

"Should I?" He scanned the street again, checking either side, listening for any noise that might signal an attack from the rear.

Haleen sighed unhappily. "You certainly have no reason to trust me, do you? But then I am not my brother, kinsman."

Valso had supposedly left the city that morning. "I thought you'd already left?" Morgin asked.

"My brother has," she said. "But I stayed behind with a small escort."

"Why?"

Her demeanor broke. "I wanted to see you again."

She raised her hand toward his face and stepped further into the street, and again Morgin felt drawn to her, enspelled in a way that muddled his senses. He backstepped, shook his head to clear it. "Stay away from me."

She stopped. Her hands dropped to her sides. A tear rolled down her cheek. "Very well. I'll not bother you again."

Her shoulders slumped. She turned toward the alley. "Come, Salula," she said. "Let us go."

That name struck fear in Morgin's heart, and he back-stepped into the street. Salula, senior captain of all Kulls, a halfman of whom Morgin had heard but never met. The stories of his brutality, and the pleasure he derived from it, were known to all.

There was no movement in the alley. Morgin squinted, hoping to catch a hint of from where Salula might strike, for there was no doubt that Salula would strike. Morgin back-stepped further, trying to put distance between him and the alley, wishing he could see something within the shadows there, but it remained black, still, silent and deadly.

He stepped back again, then heard something behind him, and in that instant realized he'd played into their hands. He ducked instinctively and turned, saw the blow coming, a blunt object appearing out of the night. He sidestepped it, but then the mad whore's spell took him, a wave of terror and fear and sorrow that pulled at him, slowing him, defeating him.

••••

Cold fire splashed across his face and shoulders, dripping to the ground where he lay. He gasped, sucking in air as the icy water cascaded off his bare chest.

"Ah! Good," a nearby voice growled, a voice filled only with hatred. "He's conscious. Call the prince." The voice was harsh, a voice Morgin had never before heard. All about him other voices responded to the first, and even through the pain Morgin could sense a touch of fear in their replies.

"Bring him to his knees," Valso said.

"Aye, lord," the voice said.

Cruel hands lifted Morgin by the arms his body had forgotten, arms tied behind his back, and now gone completely numb. His shoulders ached, sending flashes of agony down to his elbows. Beneath that, his forearms and wrists were lifeless.

The cruel hands set him down on his knees, then a fist knocked his head back and a rush of flashing lights burst through his mind. The hands prevented him from falling back, pushing him forward with such force that it drove him back to the ground where his face slammed into the dirt. The toe of a boot crashed into his ribs; a heel into his back.

"Don't hurt him. Please." Morgin recognized Haleen's voice.

"Get the whore out of here." That was Valso. "And restrain her."

Hands gripped him by his shoulders and lifted him back to his knees. A hand tore at his hair, pulling his head back, his chin up. Salula leaned down to stare nose-to-nose into Morgin's eyes. The cruelty and hatred Morgin saw there frightened him. "His Highness is going to speak, fool, and you will listen."

The halfman raised a fist, but Valso stopped him. "Now Salula, not yet. I want him conscious for a while. A slap will do."

The slap brought the flashing lights again as it echoed through the night and took Morgin to the brink of consciousness. Then a fist knocked him forward into the dirt again.

"That's better, Captain," Valso encouraged. "Now. A bit more water."

This time Morgin braced for the icy cascade that engulfed him, though he still gasped and coughed. He opened his eyes, conscious only of a throb at the back of his skull.

They were in a small clearing, obviously far from Anistigh, his hands tied behind his back, his cheek pressed into the dirt. To one side an open fire crackled loudly, close enough for him to feel its heat. All about him stood Kulls, gray black shadows in the night, and in front of him stood a pair of shiny black boots, covered by a layer of soft, brown dust.

Morgin raised his head slowly. Above the boots were a pair of knees, then hips, then chest, and finally the face of Valso et Decouix.

Kullish hands picked him up and set him back on his knees.

"Well," Valso said sweetly. "Lord AethonLaw. You've decided to join us, I see. How kind of you. But I don't believe you've met Captain Salula yet."

Morgin looked into the empty face next to Valso's, a face devoid of humanity. "Your Lordship," it greeted, nodding its head slightly.

Valso said, "I know you've heard of the good captain, haven't you?"

Morgin moved his focus back to Valso. The effort caused his head to swim.

"Captain," Valso said.

Morgin's head rocked back with another slap. He held onto consciousness only by an effort of will, but his ears rang long afterward.

Salula spoke. "Answer His Lordship's question, fool."

Morgin opened his eyes and nodded. He tried to croak a "yes" past split and cracked lips.

"That's better, Elhiyne," Valso said. "The captain is known for his cruelty, is he not?"

Morgin was careful to at least nod this time.

"But remember this, Elhiyne. Salula is only as cruel as I allow him to be. And tonight, I, through the good captain, am going to teach you what happens when you touch a Decouix. Prepare him, Salula."

Morgin became acutely conscious of his elbows. They were tied painfully behind his back, forcing him to hold his chest out. The cruel hands grabbed him by his upper arms and half dragged him to a nearby boulder, then slammed him face down in the dirt nearby.

For a moment his arms were free, but numb below the elbows it was impossible to use them. Just as they were beginning to feel the prickly fire of returning circulation cruel hands grabbed each of his four limbs, hoisted him atop the boulder, held him face down on its surface. They attached a rope to each limb, then tied it to a stake in the ground. His shirt had already been torn away, and the cruel hands now did likewise to his breeches.

His cheek rested on the boulder. Valso stepped into his field of view, holding a long saddle strap about the length of a grown man, a common piece of harness equipment, only a little wider than thick.

Valso leaned close enough for Morgin to smell stale wine on his breath. "I'm going to enjoy this, Elhiyne. I'm going to enjoy this immensely."

Morgin didn't answer.

Valso stepped back and handed the strap to Salula. "You may begin now, Captain. But remember. I don't want him to lose consciousness. Not for a long, long time."

Salula took the strap casually and folded it in two, holding both ends in one hand. He stepped to the side of the boulder, and his face held the first hint of expression that Morgin had seen: a hateful smile.

Morgin watched as Salula raised the strap slowly above his head, and resolved not to cry out, not to give them the satisfaction. The strap paused for a long moment, then, with lightning speed it came down.

Fire laced Morgin's buttocks. He screamed. The world about him faded from sight, then the pain receded and his vision returned.

Valso stood there smiling. Salula stood next to him grinning. The prince said, "Learn your lesson well, Elhiyne." Then, to Salula, he said, "Again, Captain."

The lash struck again, across Morgin's back, and again he screamed. His vision failed in a fiery agony of pain, then returned to the hell that had become his night. Salula paused before the next strike, while Valso made some witty comment. And then the lash fell again. And again the prince paused and commented. Sometimes the pause was long, and sometimes short, but always the lash returned.

After a time Morgin could no longer scream, no longer cry out at the pain that was now a constant burn from shoulders to knees. He lost consciousness several times, only to be reawakened by a flood of icy water across the back of his head. And while it shamed him to do so, he begged for mercy. Valso merely laughed.

Later he remembered only two things: the pain, and Salula's face, a hard face, weathered with hate, a face that grinned after each stroke of the lash, and smiled in anticipation of the next. When Morgin could no longer cry out he lay there, silent, watching that face. When the lash was raised high Salula's face twisted with the effort to strike with all his might. The muscles of his jaw clenched, his lips curled back to expose white teeth locked in a grin that only death could break, his nostrils flared, his eyes closed to mere slits, and as the lash came down he grimaced with pleasure.

Morgin would always remember that grimace, a grimace etched on the back of his mind by the white hot fire of the lash, a grimace that remained with him as he drifted slowly toward a place where not even the icy water could revive him.

••••

Morgin awoke and cried out.

"Easy, brother," JohnEngine said softly. "Easy now. Don't move. We have to untie you."

Morgin laid his cheek back down on the boulder. Gentle hands worked at the knots at his wrists and ankles. The sun stood high in the sky, a warm dry day. He wondered if that added to the slow burn that ran from the back of his neck to his knees.

His face rested on his right cheek, and all he could see was his left shoulder and arm where the lash had deposited bloody welts and bruises all the way down to his wrist. There was dried blood and scab there too, for the rope had bitten deep during his struggles. Brandon worked at the knot there, his fingers moving with great care. There were tears in his eyes.

"The Decouix left you for us to find," he said. "He will pay for this." And in Brandon's eyes Morgin saw hate mixed with the tears. It was almost unbelievable that kind, quiet Brandon could hate so.

Morgin lifted his head slowly and laid it down on the other cheek. JohnEngine worked at the knot at his right wrist, and tried to hide the tears in his eyes.

Morgin resolved not to move again. The blood on his back and neck had dried in the warm sun, then split and cracked with fiery awareness as he'd moved his head. But moments later his resolve meant nothing as his brothers and cousins gently hoisted him off the boulder, carried him to one side, placed him face down on some blankets. At least he did not shame himself by crying out as the wounds on his back split into hundreds of fiery lines, each distinguishable from the next.

"Don't move, cousin," he heard MichaelOff say from a place far away. "DaNoel is going to put salve on your back. It should ease the pain."

Sometime later, hours it seemed, Morgin felt coherent again. The salve had cooled the fire some, and his mind came slowly out of the fog where it had hidden. He replayed the events of the previous evening: Salula using the lash with such vigorous joy, Valso looking on with pleasure. At the memory of Valso's smiling face a wave of murderous hate washed through him.

Nearby he could hear his cousins and brothers speaking softly, making plans to spend the night. They were concerned that it might be some time before he could ride again.

Morgin lifted himself up onto his elbows, the motion bringing considerable pain to his burning back and thighs. He scanned the clearing, seeing no one present but his four kinsmen. When he spoke, the words came out in a croak: "How did you find me?"

All four heads turned toward him; MichaelOff spoke first. "Ah! You've decided to rejoin the living. We thought you might sleep the day through." MichealOff's voice had a tight, restrained timbre to it, as if he struggled to speak casually.

They stood, crossed the clearing, gathered around him. "How did you find me?" he asked again.

MichaelOff said, "When you failed to return we searched the city for you, and finding no sign of you we knew the Decouix must be involved."

DaNoel said, "The four of us rode out with an escort following the Decouix trail while mother and father continued searching the city."

"With the help of a few spells we found you here," Brandon said, "And sent the escort back to tell them you're all right. They'll be returning home soon, and we'll follow in a day or two, when you're rested."

Brandon hadn't said it, but Morgin could see it in their eyes. They'd sent the escort back to save him shame and humiliation. "I can ride now," he said, anger clutching at his gut.

"That's not necessary," MichaelOff said. "We'll rest here a few days, give your back a chance to heal, conjure a few spells to help it along."

Morgin shook his head. "Did you bring my sword?"

Brandon nodded. "Yes."

"Then I will ride now, after the Decouix."

They started at that. MichaelOff said a flat "No." DaNoel shook his head. JohnEngine looked worried, undecided. Brandon, without word or expression, stood and walked toward the horses.

MichaelOff spoke carefully. "Valso has an escort of twelve twelves of Kulls. That would be suicide."

"I want Valso's blood," Morgin said. He could feel tears forming in his eyes. "So I ride after him now, while the trail is fresh."

DaNoel shook his head angrily. "You're in no shape to ride, let alone fight."

At that moment Brandon returned from the horses carrying a sheathed sword. He knelt down nearby, unsheathed it, and Morgin recognized it as his own. Brandon reversed the blade, placed the hilt in Morgin's hand, and curled his fingers about it. "If you ride after the Decouix, cousin, then I ride with you, gladly."

"And I ride too," JohnEngine said with much bravado.

DaNoel hesitated, but then said, "And I."

They all turned to MichaelOff, the oldest and wisest. Morgin could see that the others wanted the older man's support, while all he wanted was blood. Valso's blood. Salula's blood. As he thought of the Decouix and the halfman, a wave of murderous hate washed over him again, leaving tears in his eyes, and as he looked at his kinsmen he realized they were all tied together in some odd way. Not by blood or family, but by love and friendship. And he realized they could all feel his hate, his shame.

When MichaelOff spoke, he too had tears in his eyes. "It appears I cannot dissuade you from this suicidal revenge. Don't you know that you will all die?"

The tears started to pour openly down his face as they answered him with silence. "Well then. If you choose to ride foolishly to your deaths, then I must ride with you."

He looked at Morgin, sadly defeated. "We will all die together, Morgin, if that is what you choose."

That was the key. It was Morgin's choice. But there was no choice. He wanted Valso's blood and he wanted it now. He would ride after the Decouix and he would fight, fight until they killed him. What was death when he could die killing the Decouix? But he wouldn't kill the Decouix, he realized. He'd just die.

He had a vision of AnnaRail, weeping, crying over the deaths of her sons and nephews. That was followed by a vision of JohnEngine's decaying body. And Brandon's. And DaNoel's. And MichaelOff's. His brothers and cousins all, dead and rotting in the sun. Dead because they were loyal to him and followed him in his foolish revenge. Uselessly, senselessly dead.

He shook his head, said simply, "We'll wait here a day or two, then ride back to Elhiyne."

9

The Swordmaster

MORGIN'S THOUGHTS OCCASIONALLY drifted to France, the vagabond swordsman, and he would recall their little adventure with fondness. But after two years he concluded he would probably never see the man again.

He saw Rhianne several times at one clan event or another. She always greeted him warmly, but showed no interest beyond simple friendship.

"All right now, yer lordships," the smith said, pulling Morgin out of his reverie. "We're ready fer a pour. But take care. I just want me this line. No more."

With sweat beading on his forehead the smith bent down and used the edge of his hand to make a finger wide impression in the dry sand. As he did so Morgin watched a drop of sweat hang momentarily from the tip of his nose, then fall into the sand and leave its own impression there. Even in winter the foundry was a miserably hot place to be.

Morgin wiped a coarse rag across his face then tossed it to JohnEngine. At the age of eighteen both boys had filled out nicely, and Morgin took a little pride in the muscle he'd gained, though he'd outpaced JohnEngine in height and stood a good hand-span taller than him. JohnEngine wiped his face with the rag and leaned forward conspiratorially. "Next time I'll know better than to volunteer for this hellhouse."

"We didn't exactly volunteer," Morgin said.

"But next time I'll not come so easily. I thought this would be better than freezing in the fields."

"You'll come next time. Olivia wants us to learn about smithing."

"All I'm learning is how to sweat."

"Quit your gabbin', boys," the smith said, "and pour."

Morgin and JohnEngine pulled on heavy leather gloves, then bent to the task of lifting the small crucible out of its cradle. It was back breaking work, and as they edged toward the sand in short, jerky steps, the heat of the furnace, now fully exposed, washed the room in an eerie, orange glow.

"All right, boys. Remember. Ya don't pour fast, just smooth and steady."

Morgin nodded to JohnEngine, his arms aching under the weight of the load. They tilted the pot forward slowly, until the molten steel within slipped easily over its lip, splashed into the line the smith had cut in the sand, and made its way smoothly to the end of its journey.

"Not bad," the smith said. "Not good. Ya still got a lot to learn."

Morgin and JohnEngine edged their way back to the furnace where they replaced the crucible in its cradle. The smith crouched over the line of steel they'd poured in the sand. "We'll quench 'er perty soon, then see what kind of edge she'll hold, and how strong she be."

They'd been through this procedure several times already. The smith's two brawny apprentices would fill the crucible. Morgin and JohnEngine would then pour a line in the sand—a sample only, so the smith could judge the quality of the steel in the furnace. If it was not right, he would do something to the melt to change it, the nature of which he revealed only to his apprentices. Then they'd test the steel again, and if the smith was satisfied, the apprentices would take the crucible for the important pours, while the two boys stood by to assist when called for.

After days of improving the melt, the steel was approaching sword quality. During the first days of the melt they'd poured belt buckles and light harness hardware, items that required little strength. As the days passed and the melt improved they'd produced items for heavy equipment and hard use; finally, two days ago, they'd finished by pouring two plowshares. Since then, they'd done nothing but improve what remained of the melt. "Fer blades," the smith had said, "we don't need much steel, but it has to be the highest quality. Only the best. And we don't pour blades, lads. We let the steel cool some, then we work it; two, maybe three days. Hard work that. Harder'n this. You boys'll be swinging hammers and pounding hot steel, good steel."

"A message fer Lord Morgin."

They all looked toward the strange voice: the apprentices from their furnace; Morgin and JohnEngine from their crucible; the smith from his cooling sample of steel. The one-eyed lame beggar from the village stood fearfully in the entrance to the foundry.

"What ya be wanting here?" the smith demanded.

"Begging your fergiveness, master, but I gots a message fer young Lord Morgin."

"Well give it and be gone with you."

"I was told to give it to him in private."

"Very well," the smith grumbled, turning to Morgin. "Talk to him outside, lad."

Morgin walked quickly. This was the smith's domain and intruders were not welcome.

Morgin's boots crunched in the snow outside. Bare from the waist up, soaked with sweat, the harsh winter air bit at him mercilessly. "Make it fast," he said. "It's cold out here."

"There's a man wants to see you, milord."

"What man? Where?"

"He's outside the village, milord. Didn't give no name. Told me to give ya this. Wants you to come an' see 'im."

The beggar handed Morgin a fine linen handkerchief. It was dirty and crumpled, had seen better days, and while it was obviously supposed to carry some hidden meaning, Morgin at first drew a blank. But then he remembered it had once been his, though the last time he'd seen it had been almost two years ago in Anistigh. France had taken a liking to it, and the scoundrel must have stolen it.

"Wait here," Morgin said, spun on his heels and reentered the foundry. He excused himself, claiming urgent family business, though JohnEngine looked at him narrowly as he threw a cloak over his shoulders.

The beggar led Morgin to the small woodland that separated castle Elhiyne from the nearby village. He found France waiting there and greeted him gladly.

"Keep your voice down, lad," France hissed. He tried to conceal the fear written plainly on his face, and he eyed the beggar with distrust. Morgin noticed that France's horse was badly lathered. "I promised the man a reward, and I got nothing of me own to pay 'im with."

Morgin dug into his pockets, found a few pennies and paid the beggar. The man eyed his reward happily and turned to leave. Morgin gripped his shoulder, halting him. "There is enough there to pay for your silence too. Be certain you give me my due."

"Aye, lord, I will."

"You have earned my good favor," Morgin added. "Take care that you do not lose it."

The man nodded uneasily. He knew that any clansman could make the life of a beggar miserable if he chose.

Morgin released his shoulder. "Away with you now."

The man scurried away quickly.

When they were alone Morgin asked, "What's wrong, France? Are you in trouble?"

"Me, lad?" France said innocently. "In trouble? Nay, not I."

"Then why all this secrecy?"

"Ah, you know me, lad. Just me normal precautions. Not one for being seen much in public."

"Come on, France. There's more to it than that."

France opened his mouth to protest, but just then there came the sound of many riders thundering down the road. The swordsman's eyes lit up with fear. "I need a place to hide me and me horse, lad, and fast. I'm asking you to return the favor of a life saved, boy."

Morgin looked quickly about. He and France were not far off the road; the trees of the forest were winter bare and they'd be quite visible to any riders passing by, so instinctively he reached for shadow. France gasped as it enveloped him, his horse, and

Morgin. To anyone looking their way, they'd appear to be dim gray shadows in a white landscape of naked trees and snow. Morgin hissed, "Keep yourself and your horse still."

The riders rounded a bend in the road: a posse of Penda border marshals riding angry and hard. They passed going toward the castle, where they would undoubtedly request shelter for the night. Morgin waited to be sure there were no stragglers, then released the shadow spell.

France staggered. "A cute trick, that," he said. "I can't stay here long, though. They know I'm in the neighborhood and will be searching the area soon enough."

Morgin looked up the road. "Give me your horse. And wait here. I won't be long."

He jumped on the animal's back. It shied beneath him, but he held it tightly in control as he pulled it out onto the road and headed for the village, slapping its rump, digging his heels into its flanks.

He found the beggar still hobbling along the road. Morgin pulled up beside him. "I would ask another favor of you, beggar, and in payment I will give you a warm set of clothes for what's left of the winter."

The beggar's good eye lit up. "Gladly, milord."

"Follow me then."

Morgin led the beggar back to France and ordered them both to strip.

"What?" France demanded.

"I said strip. And exchange clothes."

"Put on them filthy rags," France said. "Never."

"Then I'm sorry, friend," Morgin said. "I cannot help you."

"By the Unnamed King!" France cursed, throwing off his cloak and working at his tunic.

Morgin had trouble concealing a smile.

"And don't you be enjoying this, boy."

When the two had completed their exchange, Morgin told the beggar, "And give him your eye patch, and your walking stick."

"I'll give him me cane," the beggar said, "in exchange for his sword."

France unsheathed his sword, crouched, said, "Not the sword, beggar, not unless you want it point first."

The beggar cringed. Morgin stepped between them. "Don't be greedy, beggar. Yield up your cane and the eye patch for good measure. Even then this day has been a highly profitable one for you."

The beggar gave up his cane and eye patch, then departed, walking cockily down the center of the road. In his new clothes he bore himself with a dignity Morgin would not have thought possible. But then France called after him, "I'd stay out of sight if I was you. In them clothes the Pendas just might mistake you for me. And I know you won't like the way they show their displeasure."

The beggar hesitated, thought better of the bargain he'd made, slipped off the road and disappeared with practiced ease.

"Come," Morgin said. "I'll ride your horse and you walk in front of me. We'll enter the castle together."

"The castle! You're crazy, lad."

"What better place to hide?" Morgin asked. "It's big and spread out all over the place. They'll never think to look for you there. And that's the only place I can think of to stable your horse where there'll be no questions asked. Now hide your sword in those rags you're wearing, and hobble on that cane like the beggar you're supposed to be."

France cursed and spit all the way up the road, though when they entered the castle yard, which was full of angry Pendas, he became unhappily silent.

Morgin quickly found Erlin, the stable boy. They were friends, of a sort, and Erlin readily agreed to hide France in the stables.

"What about me horse, boy?"

"I'll stable him with the Penda horses," Erlin said. "Gorguh—he's the stable master—he won't notice one more among all the rest."

"Morgin," DaNoel shouted from out in the yard. "Blast you. Where are you?"

"I'd better go," Morgin whispered. "With clansmen about claiming guestright, grandmother'll want the whole family to put on our manners and entertain."

"Blast you, Morgin. Where are you? Answer me."

"Go on, lad," France said. "Erlin and me can handle it from here. And thanks."

••••

The leader of the Pendas was a large angry man who wanted to find the vagabond swordsman and ". . . hang his balls in my trophy room." He claimed that France had raped his wife, and was a most evil scoundrel.

Later that evening, when Morgin could slip away, he questioned France on the matter. According to the swordsman, any raping done had been quite mutual, and he hadn't known the woman was married until after the fact. Knowing France, Morgin was inclined to believe the former, but not the latter.

The Pendas left Elhiyne early the next morning, their leader confident they would soon catch the fugitive swordsman. With them gone, Morgin started for the stables to tell France the danger was past, but DaNoel intercepted him in the castle yard.

"Grandmother wants to see you," DaNoel said smugly. "Now. In the Hall of Wills."

That didn't sound good, and as Morgin stepped through the great double doors of the Hall his worst fears were realized. He found all of House Elhiyne waiting for him there. Gorguh and Erlin were there too; the stable master had hold of one of the stable boy's ears, and gave it a good twist now and then. The beggar knelt before

Olivia, dressed in his fine new clothes and trembling with fear. To one side stood a cluster of armed clansmen. France, still dressed in the beggar's rags, knelt before them, his hands tied behind his back.

"Well now," Olivia said to Morgin. "Here we have the leader of this little conspiracy. So good of you to join us, grandson."

DaNoel snickered behind Morgin's back. "It'll be interesting to see you talk your way out of this one, whoreson."

Morgin scanned the faces in the Hall. Most of the men there were trying to conceal an embarrassed frown. No clansman liked to be reprimanded in public, nor see another treated so.

What would Olivia do if she were in my shoes? Morgin thought, and realized she would take the offensive. He held his chin high, walked boldly forward, not to the open space before Olivia as expected; instead he approached France. He put a hand on the kneeling swordsman's shoulder and said, "Forgive us, friend. You have been ill-treated." Then he turned upon the armsmen guarding France. "Release this man," he ordered. "Immediately."

"What?" Olivia cried.

Morgin turned carefully toward her. "This man is under Elhiyne guestright."

"By whose word?" she demanded.

"By my word."

"He is a common criminal."

"According to the word of a Penda," Morgin said. "And I do not know that the Penda speaks truly. I do know that I owe this swordsman my life."

"You deceived us."

"There was no time to consult you."

"Perhaps not at first," the old witch said. "But there was more than enough time after the fact."

Roland, close at hand, whispered in Morgin's ear, "Don't anger her further, son."

Morgin nodded, cast his eyes downward, conceding Olivia the point. "I make no excuses for my own actions. But your displeasure should be with me, and not this innocent swordsman. The fact remains that he is under the protection of Elhiyne guestright, granted to him freely by me, and each moment he is held in bondage, dishonors not only me, but all of House Elhiyne."

Olivia sat on her throne staring at him, her eyes narrow and pinched, the godlight sparkling in their depths, her anger strongly aroused. Morgin could feel it, sense it, a thing to fear.

Suddenly it disappeared, and she smiled at him warmly. She turned to the armsmen guarding France. "My grandson's point is well taken. Release the swordsman."

A clansman stepped forward, displaying a small knife. He cut France's bonds and helped him to his feet. The swordsman bowed deeply and somehow, even in a beggar's rags, faced the old woman with quiet dignity. "Thank you, milady," he said, with no trace of his usual accent.

"You must forgive us, swordsman," Olivia said. "Had my grandson bothered to inform us of his actions, you would not have been detained. As it was . . ." She nodded, indicating the rags he wore. "Under the circumstances I'm sure you'll understand our misgivings."

France bowed again. "Of course, madam."

"As for the beggar and the stable boy." Olivia eyed them narrowly. "It appears they were only obeying my grandson's instructions. Is that so, Morgin?"

Morgin nodded; now was the time for silence.

"The fault, then, lies with my grandson. Release the beggar and the stable boy unpunished. We will condemn no man for merely obeying the House of Elhiyne. And give the beggar a hot meal to send him on his way."

The beggar stood and bowed immediately. "Ah thank ye, milady," he said, bowing as he backed out of the room. "Ah thanks ye, me does."

The Tulalane leaned aside to whisper something in Olivia's ear. Olivia looked France over carefully. "I am told you are a master of weapons, swordsman."

"Not all weapons, madam," France said, still with no trace of a common accent. "Merely the sword, milady, and its accompaniments."

"Truly a swordsman then?" she asked.

He nodded politely.

"Well then, vagabond. How good of a swordsman are you?"

France spoke without hesitation. "The best, madam."

"You claim to be the best among all commoners?"

France shook his head. "I make no qualifications, madam. I am merely the best. No more. No less."

Olivia raised an eyebrow. "You claim, then, to be the best swordsman among all men, commoner and clansmen alike?"

"As I said, I am the best."

Morgin was not alone in his astonishment. For one to speak to the Lady Olivia in such a cavalier fashion was rank stupidity.

Her eyes narrowed. "I cannot believe that."

France shrugged, bowing slightly. "As you wish, madam. But do not confuse magic with swordsmanship. A clansman may win a duel using his magic, but that does not mean he is the better swordsman, merely the better wizard."

To Morgin's utter surprise, Olivia smiled. "A point well taken, swordsman. But if you are so skillful, and not merely arrogant, why did you allow yourself to be taken by my armsmen?"

France held his hands out, palms upward, and cocked his head slightly. "I thought you might forgive a little arrogance, milady. But killing your armsmen . . ."

"Indeed! And do you think you could have succeeded?"

"In killing armsmen, madam?"

"In that. Or in whatever else you might have chosen to do."

France shrugged. "One never knows."

Olivia's brows shot up. "There is some doubt? The best of all swordsmen doubts his own ability?"

"No, madam. You misunderstand me. I doubt my ability not in the least, but nothing is ever certain. Chance is always waiting in the wings to lend a hand, or create a misstep. Sometimes it is wiser to place your trust in others, and since I have committed no crime here, I felt I could trust your justice."

"You felt you had a better chance with my justice."

"Perhaps," he answered, the hint of a smile on his lips. "Even making that decision is a chancy thing at best, milady."

"And if you thought my justice might be too harsh for your tastes?"

"Then, madam, I suppose I might seek justice elsewhere." He finished with a polite nod of the head, and a deep bow.

Olivia laughed. "Well, swordsman, you were right. Arrogance I can forgive, but of course, not murder. Would you care to demonstrate this great skill of yours?"

"If that is your wish, madam, it would be my pleasure."

"Very well," she said, standing. "You shall fight our best swordsman: the Tulalane."

The Tulalane grinned a wide, toothy smile, and Morgin had no doubt the twoname had whispered that thought in the old witch's ear.

A servant was sent to bring France a pair of breeches, so he could be rid of the beggar's rags. Others were sent to spread the word that a contest of swordsmanship would take place shortly in the practice yard, and that Olivia would begrudge no one a short break from a busy day's work. The entire castle turned out to see the arrogant swordsman taught a lesson.

The practice yard, a large open square just within the main gate of the castle, was bordered on one side by the stone wall containing the gate, and on the other three by various buildings in the compound. Spectators crowded several deep along all four sides of the yard. They overfilled the parapets that lined the battlements high on the wall, and in the castle proper windows high and low were jammed to capacity with faces, all anticipating a few moments of respite from the drudgeries of the workday. It was a fine, sunny, winter afternoon. The air had warmed. The snow had melted. The ground was dry.

France and the Tulalane limbered up carefully. Olivia gave them a few moments, then stepped out into the middle of the yard and all fell silent. The old witch was always one for a show, and warmed up to a good audience. After an appropriately dramatic pause, she said, "This is not a duel in anger, or revenge. He who draws the other's blood first, will lose. The purpose of this duel is for each of you to demonstrate his skill with the sword. You will attempt to bring the tip of your sword as close to the other as possible, without drawing blood. No other weapon will be allowed, and you may not make bodily contact. The match will end on my command, or at first blood."

The crowd gave a short round of applause in recognition of her shrewd choice of rules. The two men would be taxed to the utmost, forced to use their skills to the limit.

The applause died. Olivia looked at the two swordsmen. "Are there any questions?"

Hwatok Tulalane's hawk face stretched into a broad grin, the scar on his left cheek puckering visibly. "I have no questions," he said.

"None here, milady," France said. He bowed.

"Then begin," Olivia cried, and walked from the yard with a flourish.

The two contestants bowed formally to each other, stepped back and raised their swords, then touched the two blades one to the other lightly. They paused for a motionless second, waiting, each silently daring the other to strike the first blow, and then the Tulalane moved. He cut low with lightning speed, then thrust high toward France's face. But France, having moved with even greater speed, was no longer there.

France took the offensive then, testing the Tulalane's reflexes, thrusting and slashing within inches of his skin. And while the magician parried each stroke, backing across the yard, yielding ground slowly, grudgingly, it became obvious to all that France would not be the easy prey they had thought.

Both men were stripped to the waist, and as they danced about the yard playing their deadly game the Tulalane's bulky muscles made him seem larger than life, yet at the same time trim and agile.

France, on the other hand, was a lean, wiry strap of leather, sun baked, tough and gristly. Earlier he had stood casually in front of Olivia; now each muscle seemed to hum like the string of a bow after an arrow has been struck on its way.

The Tulalane took the offensive, changing the tempo of the match, backing France into the center of the yard. Their swords rang out as France appeared to be weakening. The Tulalane sensed victory; his eyes flashed greedily, but without warning France quickened his back-step. The Tulalane charged forward to keep pace. France halted rock still, locked swords with the overbalanced magician and thrust against his weight. The larger man stumbled awkwardly. France's sword leapt to within a hair's breadth of his neck then sliced across his throat. The spectators gasped, thinking a death stroke had been delivered in a mere contest of skill. But as the two men separated, all could see that the Tulalane was untouched, bloodless. The audience gave France a rousing round of applause.

The Tulalane's face turned an angry red. The two swordsmen reengaged, but now the Tulalane seemed just the slightest bit quicker, and all there who understood magic knew that the wizard had called upon his for speed. Then moments later the flavor of the match changed as he brought his sword through a long, flat arc aimed at removing

France's head. France ducked beneath it and the crowd murmured. The Tulalane attacked again, his eyes on fire with hate, the air about him glowing with magic. Morgin
tried to catch Olivia's eye, to stop what was about to become an execution, but she
ignored him, looking delightedly on.

A gasp from the crowd brought Morgin's attention back to the two contestants,
locked chest to chest in combat. France fell backwards, the larger man falling on top
of him, but France turned the fall into a roll, used his knees to throw the Tulalane
over him and into the dust. And as both jumped to their feet, France stepped lightly
beneath the Tulalane's guard and cut him on the cheek.

Olivia cried out, "The contest is done."

Even more angry than before, the Tulalane ignored her, steam rising from his
sweat-soaked shoulders. He thrust at France again, and their swords rang out once
more.

"Halt I said," Olivia cried. "I command it," and all fell silent, for when she used
that voice, not even the Tulalane dare disobey her.

The two swordsmen separated, and it appeared that the Tulalane's old scar was
bleeding on its own. Breathing heavily, still angry and almost in a rage, he looked at
the old witch as if he might actually defy her.

In the silence that followed she said calmly, "By the rules, Lord Hwatok has won
this match."

The Tulalane realized that according to the twisted rules laid down earlier, he had
won. He grinned in triumph, while France bowed deeply in acknowledgement. The
audience broke into cheers and applause, the men whistling and stomping their feet.
France had clearly demonstrated he was the better swordsman.

Olivia led France and Morgin to her small audience chamber. "Swordsman," she
said. "Your actions bear you out. In my lifetime I have seen none better, though I will
not insult the Tulalane by acknowledging that in his presence. Would you consider
taking service with House Elhiyne?"

France's eyes narrowed thoughtfully. "Perhaps. But I must know what my duties
will be before committing myself."

"To serve as one of our lieutenants in battle."

"Battle?" France asked. "But there has been no war for many years, madam."

"And let us hope there will be none in the future," Olivia said. "But there are always border skirmishes, and bandit holdings to clean out. And in between you might
give lessons in the art of the sword."

France started, scandalized. "I am no man to be teaching young boys how to fight
with wooden blades."

Olivia shook her head. "We have a weapons master for that. What I had in
mind was one specific student." She nodded toward Morgin. "My grandson here is
sorely in need of a tutor. And his lack of skill is such that I fear only a master will
do."

France looked at Morgin, eyeing him as if he were a piece of steel whose quality must be judged. Morgin looked back, tried to say with his eyes, 'Please. Would you?'

France bowed politely. "Very well, madam. I would accept such a responsibility. But before doing so we must discuss the price of my services."

10

The Fool

"NO. NO. NO. No. No," France shouted. "I'm not teaching you how to duel; I'm teaching you how to fight."

Morgin lifted his face out of the dirt of the practice yard and let France's words sink in. After two years of the swordsman's instruction, Morgin was still a poor student. Just when he thought he was getting the hang of it, the hilt of France's sword had come crashing out of nowhere into the side of his head.

"Come on, lad," France said more kindly. "Up with you now. Let's try 'er again."

Morgin stumbled to his feet, though the ground swayed beneath him. He thought back to the day France had first come to Elhiyne two years ago, and how he'd so wanted the swordsman as a tutor. He raised his sword, but couldn't hold it steady.

"Ahhh!" France said. "Ferget the damn rules, your almighty lordship." He reached out, put his finger on the tip of Morgin's sword and pulled the point down. "Lower your guard some. And square off your shoulders more. This ain't no duel and we ain't fighting by no rules. If ya get the chance, kick me in the balls, 'er punch out me eye."

Morgin shook his head. France's image rippled and swayed in the hot spring sun.

France peered at Morgin. His brow wrinkled, then he casually brushed Morgin's sword aside and stepped in close. He reached out, pushed one of Morgin's eyelids back and looked closely into his eye. Then he felt along the side of Morgin's head.

"Ah! A nice bump there, lad." France held his hand up in front of Morgin's face, his fingers spread wide. "How many fingers you see?"

Morgin looked at the swordsman's hand, and instead of the usual six fingers he saw seven, then eight, then seven again. He closed his eyes, shook his head, groaned miserably.

"That's what I thought," France said. He slid his sword back into its sheath. "Put your sword away, lad. You're in no shape for any more fighting today."

France turned toward the porch. "Come on. Let's get out of this sun." He sat down in the shade near a leather bucket of water; Morgin sat down beside him. France drew a ladle of water from the bucket, sipped some and splashed the rest on his face. He dipped another ladle and handed it to Morgin. "You see your mother a little later about that head of yours. I don't think you're hurt much, but she's best to judge that."

"I'm sorry," Morgin said. "Rhianne's coming today. I guess my mind's just not on swords."

"Well now, lad, that's the most encouraging thing I've heard you say. The ladies is as good a reason as any for not thinking about fighting. Then again, sometimes it's the ladies we do our fighting about, ain't it?"

Morgin nodded. "Do you know why she's coming?"

"Sure, lad. Everyone knows. The whole castle's abuzz with it. You an' the little lady are gonna get married, eh?"

"Yes," Morgin said. "But not now. Father says we'll sign the marriage contracts today. The wedding will be in the fall."

"You don't sound too awful excited about it, lad. I thought you liked that pretty little thing."

Morgin shrugged. "I do. But I'm not sure she really likes me, not that way, though father says most marriages of high caste are political, and have nothing to do with what the bride and groom want."

France dipped another ladle of water and sipped at it. "Is that how it is with you and the little lady?"

Morgin thought of the last time he'd seen Rhianne. She was always kind to him, and friendly, and polite, but her feelings for him ended there. She often sought him out, but to her he was just a friend whose company she enjoyed. She told him she'd much rather talk with him than with her gossipy girlfriends, and then she might proceed to tell him of her latest true love, her latest conquest: usually some handsome young lord born to one of the great houses of the Lesser Clans. So Morgin was careful to keep his feelings to himself, because every time he saw her he could think of no one else for days. She might laugh at him if he ever told her he was infatuated with her.

Morgin sighed, shrugged. He wasn't about to admit to France or anyone else that he cared for only her. "We're friends, but not in that way. And besides, I didn't even know about it until last month. I never really thought about marriage."

France had a faraway look in his eyes. "There was this lady once. Got it in her head that we was gonna get married, her an' me. Sure took me by surprise."

"And you got out of it?"

"Yah," France said. "I got out of it. Is that what you want? To get out of it?"

France hadn't understood Morgin's question. He wanted advice on how to make Rhianne feel about him as he did about her. "Well . . . no, not really. I just . . . maybe . . . wish she thought of me like those other fellows."

"Tell me, how old are you?"

"Twenty."

"And the little lady?"

"Eighteen."

"Well now. Seems to me your parents done you right. From what I seen of the little lady she's awful pretty, and she's got a smart head on her shoulders too."

"I know," Morgin said. "Mother says that's one of the reasons she consented to this marriage."

"Well, lad. Remember that being part of the family you're part of, you'd have to get married sometime anyway. Better her than someone else, eh?"

Morgin nodded.

"And look at your brother. When they come up with a bride for ol' JohnEngine, bet she'll be some old crone of a she-bat, twice his age and with a tongue like fire. But she'll have money, or land, or soldiers, or something your grandmother wants. You can bet on that."

"But it's all happening so fast."

"That's part of being a prince, lad."

"I ain't no prince."

"No. You ain't no prince. And you ain't much of a swordsman neither. But that don't mean you can start talking like me. Your mother'll have me hide if you do."

"But what am I going to do?"

France shrugged. "Well lad. Let's see what your options are. One: you can flat refuse to marry the little lady. That'd shame her, her family too. And it probably wouldn't work anyway."

Morgin shook his head. "I could never do that."

"Two: you could just run away. Give up everything you got here. And if you feel that strongly about it, I'll go with ya, lad."

Morgin shook his head again.

"Okay. Three: I suppose you could insult the little lady's father, or even Wylow. That's it! Insult the great Lord Wylow, leader of clan and head of House Inetka, make 'im so pissed-off they won't sign no marriage contract. But you'd likely end up challenged to a duel. And I'd hate to lose you, lad."

"Seems to me I have to marry her." He'd almost said, *I want to marry her.*

France shook his head. "You got the wrong attitude. You don't have to do nothing. If you're really set against it, go talk to yer parents. They're soft touches. They'll smooth things over so you don't have to marry the poor girl and nobody's feelings are hurt."

"I can't do that."

"No. You can't, can you? Cause you want to marry her, but you're worried about how she feels." Morgin realized then that France had just been teasing him. "Well you remember this: you're a son of the greatest house of the greatest of the Lesser Clans. She'll be real happy about that. And I'm sure she knows her place when it comes to marriage. She'll come around."

Just then one of the kitchen maids walked by, a shapely young woman who seemed to have an eye for France. Morgin had been watching her pursue him for some days now, though the swordsman obviously thought he was doing the pursuing.

France's head turned slowly as she walked past, his eyes locked to the sway of her hips. He stood. "Well lad. You best run along now. Get cleaned up for your ladylove. All this sword practicing has made me a mite hungry. Think I'll head over to the kitchen and see if I can't get me a bite to eat."

He walked away quickly, his attention now fully on the charms of the kitchen maid.

Morgin watched France go and thought carefully about Rhianne. Rhianne had always been more of a fantasy than a reality, until Roland had told him about the negotiated marriage. He and AnnaRail and Olivia had been negotiating with Rhianne's parents for some time now, and neither she nor Morgin had been informed of the situation until the negotiations were complete. Morgin had always known he'd have no say in the choice of his wife, but now that the situation was upon him . . .

The Inetkas arrived later that afternoon. Not merely Rhianne and her family, but also Wylow, Annaline and her husband SandoFall, and a large retinue that threw all of Elhiyne into a panic. Morgin tried to get Rhianne alone, but other than a short greeting when she first arrived, at which she seemed ill at ease, he had little chance to see or speak to her. And then Olivia had some tasks for him so he didn't see Rhianne again until the banquet that evening, where the formality of the occasion came between them.

Olivia and Wylow sat at the center of the long banquet table, with Morgin and Rhianne to either side of them. They were separated by only a few feet, but with the leaders of the two clans between them it might as well have been the entire length of the hall. Dinner lasted an eternity, with a short ceremony that followed. Several times Rhianne flashed him a friendly smile, though the twinkle in her eyes was gone.

The betrothal ceremony began with Olivia and Wylow; each stood and gave a short speech then signed both copies of the contract. Then the parents of both betrothed stepped forth and signed, smiling and happy, congratulating one another for making such an excellent match. Olivia handed the pen to Morgin and simply said, "Sign, grandson."

Morgin did so quietly, saying nothing, glad to speed the ceremony in any way possible. Then it was Rhianne's turn, and she too signed quickly.

The festivities were short lived since most of the Inetkas were tired from their long journey. A few clansmen wanted to celebrate all night, JohnEngine among them. He quickly got drunk, then went off with the others to do some wenching in the village.

When the banquet finally came to an end Morgin and Rhianne were left to their own devices. "We have to talk," he said. "Alone."

Her smile seemed forced, and there was a shyness in her that he'd never seen before. "Yes," she said.

He led her to Roland's study, took some moments to light a lamp, was glad for the time it gave them both to think without an uncomfortable silence stretching out between them. When the lamp was lit he closed the door.

She walked past him and pretended to look at the scrolls that lined the walls. The uncomfortable silence he'd hoped to avoid filled the room. When he could take it no longer, he said, "I'll be a good husband. I promise."

She turned to face him. "I know you will. You're a good man, Morgin. And I'll make you a good wife. I . . ." The thought died on her lips. She closed her mouth, lowered her eyes.

All he could think about in that moment was how she was so incredibly beautiful, and so sad. "Does the thought of marriage to me bother you so much?"

"Oh no," she said, but she turned away from him to look at the scrolls again. "No. It's not that."

"Then what is it? It's been on your face all evening."

The room stood quiet and still for a long moment. He heard her sniffle, but with her back to him he could not be sure she was crying. He watched the back of her shoulders rise as she took a deep breath. They were bare shoulders that were soft, smooth, and quite fair.

She turned to face him, her eyes puffy and red. "My mother and I had such plans," she said. "She taught me that beauty is easily had, and just as easily lost. That if I ever hoped to marry into power and position, I must improve my prospects by improving my mind. She taught me to read and write, to manage a large household, to keep accounts and tally goods. I've learned much, so that some lord might find me useful beyond the bedroom."

She buried her face in her hands. "Oh what am I saying? It's done. The contracts are signed and the marriage will be." She took a deep breath and sighed. "I will make you a good wife. I promise. But all my life I have been prepared for marriage as a piece of property is prepared for sale. And when your family petitioned for a marriage contract, my father saw it as a stroke of incredibly good fortune. An Elhiyne! He couldn't have hoped for more, even though . . ." She hesitated for a moment, as if reluctant to voice some thought. Her voice trailed away into nothingness. It left a painful, lonely stillness. "I had hoped to marry a great lord," she whispered into that stillness.

"But I can be a great lord," he said. "I am an Elhiyne. I may never be one of the clan's leaders, but I am an Elhiyne."

She turned away from him then, as if she couldn't say what followed to his face. "But you're not."

He didn't understand. "I'm not . . . I'm not . . ."

She turned back to him. "My mother was born into one of the oldest families in Inetka. When she married my father she was forced to marry into blood not as pure as hers."

"Not as pure," he said. "I . . . I don't understand."

She shook her head. "I bear the heritage of the clan in my blood. But you—"
And there she stopped, unable to say more.

It took him a moment to realize the implication in her words, but still he refused
to believe she could be so callous. "But I do not?" he asked.

"It's just that . . ." she stuttered.

"That what?" he said. He grabbed her by the shoulders. "Say it."

She turned her head away, couldn't look him in the eyes. "I . . ."

Anger crawled up his throat. "Say it, dammit."

"I . . . can't."

"I'm the bastard whoreson. That's what bothers you so much, that the sweet, pure
blood of your almighty family will be contaminated by a mongrel from the streets."

"No, Morgin," she sobbed. "I didn't mean that. Not that."

"Liar," he shouted. "I thought you were different from the rest, but you're no
better than any of them." He gripped her shoulders so tightly she winced, and he
pulled her face close to his. "Damn you!" he said. "If you don't want me, then I'll not
have you." He pushed her away, saw her fall to the floor in a flurry of petticoats. He
turned away from her and rushed out of the room.

Morgin's eyes were filled with glimpses of servants scurrying out of his way as he
stormed through the halls of Elhiyne. At first he paid no heed to direction, just let his
anger guide him, and it took him to Olivia's audience chamber. She would be there,
with Malka and Marjinell and his parents, entertaining Wylow and Rhianne's parents.

Avis wanted to announce him, but Morgin brushed him aside and burst into the
chamber. They all turned toward him, but he was conscious only of Olivia, and her
eyes. Before any of them could speak he said, "She doesn't want to marry me."

"What?" Wylow asked.

Morgin turned to the Inetka leader. "She doesn't want to marry a bastard whoreson."

Edtoall turned to Matill. "This is your doing, woman. You've been filling her head
with those fantasies of yours again."

He looked at Morgin. "Pay no attention to her, lad. She will marry you."

Morgin turned his anger on Edtoall, and his voice sounded like the growl of an
angry beast. "But I'll not have her. If she thinks her blood is too good for me she can
damn well marry whomever she pleases."

"Morgin," Olivia said. "Be still."

Morgin looked at the old witch defiantly. "Since she does not want me, I'll not
have her."

Olivia dismissed him with a slash of her hand. "The choice is not yours."

"Nor hers," Wylow added.

"Morgin," AnnaRail said softly. "You're having a lover's quarrel. Such quarrels
end as quickly as they began."

"We're not lovers," he snarled, surprised that he could raise his voice even to AnnaRail. "And I'll not marry her."

"Enough of this," Olivia said. "Edtoall. Matill. I suggest you speak with your daughter. And I shall have words with my grandson."

She looked like a statue of ice as she said, "Come, AethonLaw. We will speak in the Hall of Wills."

Roland spoke quickly, "I'll come too."

"No," the old witch said flatly. "My grandson and I will discuss this matter alone."

Morgin followed her through a small door that gave private access to the great council hall. It was an enormous room, the largest in the castle. Olivia climbed the six steps to her seat of power, and sat down facing him.

Morgin stopped a good distance away in the center of the hall. If he approached her closely, the added height of the dais and throne would allow her to tower over him. "She doesn't want to marry me. And I'll not have her if she is forced."

Olivia shook her head as if, for once, she honestly wanted to understand. "But why? She's a woman. She knows her place when it comes to marriage. Is it you? Have you done something?"

"I've done nothing. It's her. She says her blood has been in the clans for centuries, and it's beneath her to marry a whoreson."

"Foolish young girl!" Olivia said. "Stupid! Idiotic! Ahhh! Children! Both of you. The contracts are signed. You will be wed, and that is the end of it. I command it."

Morgin spoke only one word: "No."

Olivia froze, her stillness so complete she could have been formed of stone. Morgin saw the anger building in her eyes, and from them godlight flashed.

"Too much depends upon this marriage," she said. "The Inetkas need our influence and we need their support. We could do without this marriage, because ordinarily you and the girl are of little import. But to default on signed contracts would make Inetka our enemy. It would split the Lesser Council, and BlakeDown would love that, for he has always sought to take my place, to lead the Lesser Clans. And since that dog PaulStaff will, as always, support him, he could succeed this time. No, grandson. You will marry your foolish young girl. You will marry her whether you choose to or not."

Again, Morgin said, "No."

Olivia's eyes widened. "We have given you much, Rat. You owe this to Elhiyne."

Her cruel words fueled his resolve to resist her. "No."

Her magic pulsed about her. "Do not defy me. You cannot win."

Morgin watched the air about her begin to glow with radiance. He could see her power building, encompassing her. She seemed to grow, to expand. The Great Hall felt reduced, and it became difficult to breathe. Sweat dripped down his brow. She was suffocating him with her power.

Morgin would not have believed such power was possible had he not felt it in his own soul. He felt small, puny, a thing to be brushed aside before that which stood over him. Her magic enclosed him, shrank in upon him. He knew terror, and for just an instant he stood back in the market square, Rat the thief, running blindly, harried on all sides. But he was no longer Rat, no longer the scurrying, terrorized guttersnipe. He was a wizard. He could withstand Olivia's magic. He did not know how, but he knew he could hold it back, prevent her from forcing her will on him.

He summoned all of his strength and power, felt it coalesce within him, then released it, letting it swell outward. It pushed the old woman's will back, forced her to retreat.

"AARRUUGGHHHH!" she screamed. She threw her hand high in the air, and it glowed, for the fires of magic were cupped within her palm. Giddy with his own success he no longer feared her. Never again could she harm him, so he struck, advanced against her retreat.

"You impudent whelp," she cried, and hurled the raw power in her hand directly at him. It arced across the room, aimed at his soul. He stood in his newfound confidence, prepared to withstand it, an orb of flaming, crackling energy he knew he could defeat.

His magic came fully upon him. He stepped beyond the universe of mortal men, and his own universe narrowed to that single, monstrous spark of Olivia's power. But it did not halt or slow when he commanded, and he knew fear again. Rat's terror struck, and as Olivia's power splashed across his soul, he knew defeat.

••••

Roland burst into the Hall of Wills to find utter chaos. The tapestries on the walls were in flames, debris scattered about the floor, the ceiling high above blackened and charred. Morgin lay lifeless and still in the center of the floor, his head thrown back at an odd angle, his back arched and rigid, with his eyes wide and unseeing. Beyond Olivia's dais, the only place in the room that remained un-scorched was a small, gray oval of stone floor surrounding Morgin.

AnnaRail brushed past Roland and ran to Morgin. Roland moved to help Olivia. The old woman sat upon her throne, stunned but conscious, staring blankly at Morgin's lifeless body. Roland reached her an instant before Malka and Marjinell. The Hall filled quickly with servants who moved to extinguish the flaming tapestries.

With Malka and Marjinell caring for Olivia, Roland was free to look to Morgin. He stepped off the dais and stopped beside AnnaRail, who sat on the floor with Morgin's head in her lap. Her head hung, and he knew she was deep in trance seeking her son's soul.

Wylow and Edtoall stormed into the room. Wylow demanded of Olivia, "What have you done?"

Olivia moved for the first time, and looking at Roland her eyes returned from a great distance. Her voice trembled as she spoke. "He . . . became unyielding. I tried to . . . control him with my power, but he struck me, and I . . . I lost control."

Roland's heart went cold. "And you struck him back?"

She swallowed. "Yes."

Roland looked down at AnnaRail's bowed head. "Wife?"

After a long pause her head moved and she looked up. He had to look away from the strange depths of the nether reaches he saw in her eyes.

She spoke in a flat monotone. "He lives, just barely. He's sorely wounded but he'll recover . . . no permanent damage."

She closed her eyes then, and bowed her head.

He looked back at Olivia. "Thank the gods you had the presence of mind not to kill him, to at least hold something back."

Olivia continued to stare at Morgin. "But I didn't," she whispered.

"What?" Malka asked.

"When he struck me . . ." the old woman said, ". . . I lost control. For the first time in my life I . . . completely lost control. I threw everything I had at him . . . I completely lost control."

"Impossible," Wylow said, but his face held an odd, greedy look. "There isn't a man in the lesser tribes that can survive the full force of your power."

The Hall was still as everyone waited for Olivia to speak. Her gaze did not leave Morgin's lifeless form as her lips curved upward into a greedy smile that mimicked Wylow's look. Her voice came out in a tiny, distant whisper, but silence hung so heavily in the Hall everyone there heard each word. "There is now."

Roland said, "This marriage must be stopped."

"No," Edtoall said, his eyes alight with the same greedy look as his kinsman. "The contracts are signed. What care we if children choose to act like children? The contracts were made in good faith on both sides. You cannot fault us that your AethonLaw turned out to be more than you thought, nor that our Rhianne turned out to be less."

He pointed at Olivia and finished. "The contracts were made in honor. And in honor you cannot break them."

Wylow turned to Roland and said, "I must back my kinsman in this. And if you choose to default, that could mean clan war."

Olivia stood with a flourish. "Very well. The wedding will take place. But now, not later. As soon as Morgin is conscious. We must not give these children the opportunity to fail us."

Edtoall nodded his agreement. "Aye. When the boy is conscious, the girl will be ready."

••••

When Morgin awoke he learned he'd been unconscious for three days. Roland, with the help of several servants, quickly dressed him in his finest. Immersed in a sea of confusion, he did what they told him. When they finished, Roland held him at arm's length and looked him over sadly. "I'm sorry, son. But we'll make this work out somehow."

They led him down to the Hall of Wills in a blur of disconnected, incomprehensible sights. His family and Rhianne's were all waiting there. For some reason the hall was devoid of the tapestries that normally covered its walls, and much of the stone was blackened by fire.

He stood there concentrating on staying upright. An oppressive pall hung over the place as Rhianne's mother escorted her into the hall. She moved like a doll dancing on invisible strings of magic. Matill held on to her tightly as she crossed the room, releasing her only when she stood beside him. He lost track of time for a heartbeat, or perhaps many heartbeats. Olivia was saying something, and while she spoke he turned his gaze upon Rhianne. She turned to look at him, and when their eyes met, she blinked rapidly and looked about in confusion. She took in her surroundings as if only now realizing where she stood. Then she spun about and ran from the hall in tears.

Rhianne's mother and father traded angry words, then followed her in a rush.

That lone act of looking upon him, then running from him, had condemned him to forever be Rat the whoreson.

Again Morgin lost track of time, returned to the present only when Edtoall and Matill returned with Rhianne supported between them. She could barely stand, and would have crumpled to the floor in a heap had they not supported her.

Olivia read the marriage vows, requiring from Morgin and Rhianne a simple *Yes*, though Rhianne could barely manage even that one word. It came out slurred, and he realized she'd been heavily spelled and drugged.

When the ceremony ended, the last thing he remembered was the look in JohnEngine's eyes, a sad look, a sorrowful look, as if his brother mourned him.

He awoke in the night, still dressed in his wedding finery. He had the most demanding erection he could remember. And Rhianne lay beside him, sweet and soft, and now she was his wife.

He pulled back the covers to discover that they had made her ready for him. She had been undressed, and wrapped in a filmy, gauzy thing that he could tear off with his fingers if he chose. He could see her soft skin beneath it, with the nipples of her small breasts standing out. And in the moonlight that splashed through the window he could even see the dark shadow where her legs met. There lay his desire, his want, his need.

At the last moment, barely an instant before he ripped her nightgown to shreds, only then did he realize he was operating under one of Olivia's spells. How like her, using her magic to ensure that he consummated the marriage, even with Rhianne drugged to unconsciousness, and him no more than a mindless, rutting animal.

It took every bit of will he had to replace the covers, walk across the room, and sit in a chair to masturbate, to relieve the tension of the old woman's spell. And after that he refused to return to bed for fear that she might cast another. If he could defy her in no other way, he would do so in this.

His head slowly cleared as the night passed, and at some point he stood and walked to the room's only window. Below him lay the castle yard, enveloped in the swirling mists of early morning, and with the sun just beginning to rise over the distant mountains he watched as the Inetkas mounted up and began their long journey home. As the caravan snaked its way out of the compound, he realized he'd spent no time with Annaline. And it would be a long time before he'd have the chance again.

He watched, and he waited, and finally, hearing a gasp from behind him and the rustle of covers, he turned to his wife. Awake now, she sat up in bed, pulled the sheets high about her neck. Her eyes widened as she took in her surroundings. To her unasked question he answered, "Good morning, wife."

She gasped. Then, realizing where she lay, she ran one hand quickly over her body to discover its nakedness, while the other hand still held the sheets tight about her neck. The fear on her face and her frantic actions were the final insult.

"Don't worry, wife," he said. "You are untouched, unsoiled. You needn't fear bearing the seed of the whoreson. I'll touch no woman if she is unwilling." His was surprised that his voice came out so flat and lifeless. "And since my mere presence seems to repulse you so, I'll be taking apartments elsewhere in the castle. We are wed, you and I, and I cannot change that. But from this day on, the less our paths cross, the better."

He walked to the door, opened it, and paused at the threshold. "Oh! One more thing. You may take lovers if you wish. I fully intend to myself. But be discreet, and don't ever humiliate me like that again."

He could see in her face that she understood the depth of his anger, his hatred. She would heed his warning, for she feared him now. It tore at his heart. He had never expected to see her face turned to him in fear. He almost relented, then he recalled her running from their marriage vows, running from him.

He looked at her one last time and let her see the anger. Then he closed the door softly and left.

11

The Magic of Power

FOR THE NEXT two years Morgin lived with the single men in the bachelors' barracks. At play he became their leader: he drank, whored and fought more than all of them. His life consisted of one long blur of work and play, punctuated by the daily practice at arms. Of course Olivia disapproved of it all. Their disagreements had almost become a daily ritual, though he'd learned his lesson that night in the Hall of Wills and never again touched her with his magic.

He had one secret that not even she knew, a secret that he might someday reveal to her, just to irritate her. It was a matter of pride with him that she disapproved of his rowdy conduct, and that she continue to disapprove.

At first, his anger and humiliation drove him to carouse in earnest. But the whores soon lost their appeal and the ale no longer washed away the bad memories. And it hurt like netherhell when the innkeeper bashed his head in the midst of a brawl he'd started.

He still spent most of his free time at the village inn, but two out of every three cups of ale were carefully transferred to the mugs of others, a trick of magic that he found almost trivial. He also splashed most of that third cup down the front of his own tunic in a show of drunken sloppiness. He'd finally learned the art of deceit, and most evenings he staggered back to the castle where he might fake the noises of vomiting in the privy, then pass out on his bunk. But when Olivia's spies were about he drank in earnest, and took care to pick a fight, often with one of them. Occasionally he managed to start a real brawl, usually managed to get Olivia's lackeys embroiled in the midst of it. Certainly the news always got back to the old witch, and hopefully to Rhianne too.

Rhianne! Shortly after their wedding they met in passing in a hallway, one of the few times they found themselves alone together. His fury was still a raw, open wound. At his anger she froze, and seeing the fear in her eyes he was torn between sorrow and joy.

"Morgin," she said, and he could see she wanted him to forgive her.

He wanted to, wanted so many things, but a strange evil part of him made him turn and walk away without a word.

Shortly after that the ladies put on a small party for her birthday, and Olivia ordered Morgin to attend. He showed up late, and honestly drunk. He stumbled in,
staggered about the room, sat down next to Rhianne and glared at everyone there,
especially her. He poured more wine; drank some, splashed some on his tunic, the rest
on those about him. Rhianne, who'd been happily opening presents when he'd arrived, ended up in quiet tears. It took all of the fun out of it for him.

JohnEngine angrily told him to leave, but Morgin was so drunk they had to help him
from the room. And as DaNoel and Brandon supported him on either side, he caught a
glimpse of AnnaRail just before he passed through the door. There were tears in her eyes,
and he saw shame in her face. She'd loved him and spanked him, held him close when
he'd needed her, been angry with him when he was bad, but never before had she been
ashamed of him. Never had she given even the slightest hint that he was anything less
than she could hope for in a son. That day Morgin learned the true meaning of shame.

As time passed he and Rhianne were forced to interact regularly at family func-
tions, but any interplay between them was always stiff and proper. They'd sit or stand
next to each other, silent, husband and wife, an impenetrable wall of formality between them. More than once he'd considered trying to breach that wall. At one banquet more than a year after their wedding he looked her way, saw her toying with her
food, and said, "Rhianne."

She stiffened, then slowly turned her face toward him, her eyes cold and hard.
When she spoke, her voice mirrored the look in her eyes. "Yes, husband."

He realized then that she'd reject any overtures he might make, so he shook his
head and said, "Nothing . . . nothing."

They avoided one another as much as possible, and two years passed in an uneasy
truce of formality.

••••

France waited patiently outside Olivia's audience chamber. She had summoned him,
which, in the four years he'd been tutoring Morgin, was a rare occurrence. As usual
the old witch made him wait, sitting patiently, hoping the audience would not last
long. He had no doubt she did so intentionally, a not so subtle reminder of who she
was, and who he wasn't.

He saw her three or four times a year this way, and each time they played the same
game. She'd want to know every detail of Morgin's training. France would tell her what
he could, sometimes making a recommendation or two, and then she'd finish by asking
for details of the lad's private life, about which France would feign ignorance.

"The Lady Olivia will see you now."

Avis's words brought France out of his reverie. He stood, and as Avis opened
the door he stepped into Olivia's sanctum, and realized this time would be different.

The old witch sat among cushions on her couch wearing a hooded, floor-length gown with billowing sleeves and simple lines. As always she had chosen a dark color, today a green almost black. She reclined, one arm resting casually on the back of the couch, the hood thrown back over her shoulders. Hwatok Tulalane stood behind her, and in front, to one side, stood old Beckett.

France took a place beside the old weapons master. He bowed deeply. "You wish to see me, milady?"

"Yes, France," she said pleasantly. "And you no doubt are aware of what I wish to discuss."

"I assume you wish to speak of Lord Morgin, milady."

"Exactly, swordsman. How does his training progress?"

"Slowly, madam. But steadily. He improves regularly now. No miracles, mind you, but each week he is a little better than the week before."

"Is he finally becoming a swordsman then?"

"Yes, madam, in the sense that he can fight and defend himself he is becoming quite proficient. At that, he is an excellent pupil. But let me caution you that he is not a duelist, and never will be. It's not in him to think like one."

"Then how does he think?"

France considered that carefully before answering. "I would say he thinks in terms of survival."

"His only concern then is for his own skin? He is a coward?"

"No, Your Ladyship. He is as brave as the next man. And the survival he chooses might be yours, at the cost of his own life. But where his brother JohnEngine will almost foolishly seek honor, Morgin avoids conflict to begin with."

The Tulalane spoke. "Sounds like a coward to me."

France was careful to hide his dislike for the wizard. "Forgive me for disagreeing, Lord Hwatok, but Morgin is no coward. He merely thinks first of defense. He is a survivor."

Olivia's lips tightened. "Does he never take the offensive?"

"Occasionally, madam, when forced."

"And do you ever force him?"

"I have, madam. One must see both sides of a coin."

The Tulalane leaned forward. "And how do you force him?"

France looked at the wizard. Their eyes met, and while they said nothing openly, their dislike was clearly mutual. France chose not to answer the wizard.

Olivia said, "Answer the Tulalane, swordsman."

France spoke carefully. "If he is challenged, prodded into doing so, then he will take the offensive. But it must be done carefully. He must not attack in anger. Combat should be a decision, not an emotion."

"But if you wanted to," she asked, "could you make him attack in anger?"

France shook his head and lied. "No, madam. I could not." He could see that she knew it for a lie.

Old Beckett spoke for the first time. "My lady. I must agree with France."

"Thank you, Beckett," she said. "Your opinion is valued here. But it is I who must decide what is best for my grandson. And I would like to see how he performs when on the offensive. Can you arrange such a demonstration, swordsman?"

"With all due respect, Your Ladyship, I'll not goad him into anger."

Olivia brushed his words aside impatiently. "I did not ask you to."

"Very well, madam. Tomorrow, after the class workout, I'll be tutoring him privately. If you observe from the sidelines you'll see what you wish. But it must be done carefully, and I must not be rushed."

"As you wish." She dismissed him with a wave of her hand. "You may go now." She looked at Beckett. "You too."

••••

Once they were alone the Tulalane said softly, "I don't like that man."

Olivia said, "And it's obvious he doesn't like you."

"He's rude and disrespectful."

"Yes he is. But I have use for him, and my grandson needs him, so you stay away from him. If I ever want him dead, you'll be the first to know, but for now leave him alone. Is that clear?"

"Aye, milady."

"Good. I'm still concerned about Morgin. It's been two years since he and Rhianne were wed, and he has yet to come around. He's surly and uncivil. He does nothing but brood. The winter has been long and his temper short. Is it true he lives with the young bachelors and has never slept with Rhianne?"

"Aye, milady. Since the first morning after the wedding."

"And is it true that he now spends most of his free time in the village, drinking and wenching?"

"Aye, milady."

"Blast and damnation!" she cursed. "And he still shows no magic. Will that boy never do as I wish?"

"He does show magic," the Tulalane said.

"I know he does. The shadows. And his defense against my power. But that's all passive magic. I wonder if Roland is right, if perhaps that is the boy's limitation, that his magic is purely defensive."

"Perhaps," the Tulalane said. "Then again, perhaps the boy is simply a coward."

"I hope you're wrong," she said. "But I fear you may be right. Blast! I would give anything to see that boy go on the offensive. I must know what we have in him. But how?"

The Tulalane grinned. "I think I can come up with something."

••••

As Morgin reported for sword practice his magic climbed up into his gut, and it took a conscious effort to suppress it. The day had progressed as many others: a day of work and now sword practice in late afternoon, but his magic had pushed at its bounds throughout the day, as if it had a will of its own. Morgin assembled with the other young men in the castle yard.

Old Beckett bellowed, "The Lady Olivia requires Master France's presence, so he'll not be helping today." France usually condescended to act as old Beckett's assistant for the advanced class.

"I'll fill in for the swordsmen."

Morgin turned to see the Tulalane marching across the practice yard. As the man passed him their eyes met, and Morgin saw something there that made him wary.

"Thank you, Lord Hwatok," Beckett said.

The lesson began in the usual fashion, the young men pairing off with partners of roughly the same skill. Old Beckett and the Tulalane walked among them, offering advice, and occasionally, a demonstration. But then the Tulalane paused to watch Morgin and his partner sparring. "No," he said, interrupting their exercise.

To Morgin he said, "You're doing that all wrong. Here, let me demonstrate." He drew his sword and faced Morgin.

Morgin dropped into a crouch, wary of the twoname. The Tulalane grinned, then struck. He lunged, and Morgin parried the stroke, their swords ringing. The twoname spun and brought his sword around in a flat arc. Morgin back-stepped and let the stroke swing past his face, then lunged in, catching the Tulalane off guard. The twoname side-stepped Morgin's stroke, then back-handed Morgin in the side of the head with the hilt of his sword. Morgin hit the ground hard and almost lost consciousness.

It had been an unfair strike. In these lessons they were supposed to avoid bodily contact and practice only sword skills.

The Tulalane grabbed Morgin by the collar and lifted him to his feet. "You're a clumsy one," he said, and some of the other students laughed.

That set the tone for the rest of the lesson. The Tulalane focused on Morgin as a subject for his demonstrations, and Morgin was no match for the wizard swordsman. Each time he was made to appear more stupid, foolish, and inept. The demonstrations frequently ended with Morgin face down in the dirt, his head spinning, the Tulalane standing over him with a boot buried in the small of his back, making some witty comment that brought chuckles from his friends. The Tulalane even cut him several times, shallow cuts that produced only a drop or two of blood, then dried quickly in the mixed dirt and sweat on Morgin's chest and arms. It required great skill to make such cuts with the tip of a sword, and not cut deeply, and Morgin had no doubt the Tulalane had done it intentionally. But with his relative lack of skill he was powerless to defend himself against the wizard, powerless, frustrated, and angry; an anger that grew with each cut, each bruise, each insult, jibe, and witty remark.

When the lesson ended Morgin sat in the shade of the porch watching the Tulalane's back recede as he walked casually across the practice yard. For just a moment he wished he had the nerve to bury his sword in that back and watch the bastard slump to the ground. But then the twoname would probably hear him approaching and it would be Morgin who died.

Morgin's head thundered painfully. His stomach churned. Even sitting still he felt ill. He'd spent the previous night in the village pretending to drink, but not really drinking that much.

"Well, slacker," France called as he walked across the yard. "How goes it?"

Morgin looked up, said nothing.

"Come on, lad," France said. "Up with you. We have some practicing to do."

"I don't feel like practicing," Morgin said. Nevertheless he picked himself up off the porch.

"Ah, lad! Paying the price of your evil ways, eh? Well you'll not use that as an excuse for getting out of your lessons."

Morgin stood reluctantly, followed the swordsman to the center of the yard, trying desperately to hold down his anger as well as the contents of his stomach.

France pointed with the tip of his sword. "I see you've already been in the dust a few times."

"I always end up in the dust," Morgin said.

France's eyebrows lifted. "You're sure in a sweet mood today, lad. Come on. No more of your growling. Up with your sword and let's get on with this."

They crossed swords, then without hesitation France attacked. Morgin was already exhausted and he defended himself clumsily. It seemed he was always on the defensive; against the Tulalane and now against France. He backed up slowly, barely able to stay ahead of the swordsman's strokes. He was tired, hungry and sore, and with each step more dirt ground into the Tulalane's cuts, and France allowed no slacking, no yield, no rest.

Morgin, preoccupied with his own thoughts and trying at the same time to avoid one of France's strokes, missed a step and faltered. A fist caught him between the shoulder blades, knocking the wind out of him, driving him face down in the dirt again. He lay there and gasped for air.

"By the gods, Morgin! This is the clumsiest I've seen you in the years I've been teaching ya."

Morgin shot to his feet. "Taunts I don't need," he shouted. "I've had more than my share this day." He slashed out angrily with his sword.

The swordsman danced away from the slash easily and his eyes narrowed. "What's wrong, lad?"

Something pulled at Morgin painfully. It told him even beyond his own reasoning that this fool was his enemy. It drove him, fed his anger, made him strike out at the swordsman. Like a madman he slashed and struck, again and again, and like a mocking demon the swordsman parried the blows easily, dancing among Morgin's strokes with ease.

Morgin screamed, lashing out again with his sword. He twisted within the mad grip of magical hatred, for this impudent commoner of a swordsman had no right to mock him so. Not he, not an Elhiyne: a clansman, a wielder of magic and power, magic that flowed through him now as it was meant to, power in its infinite glory. He felt it guide his arm, his hand, his sword. It ruled his mind and his soul. It fed him. It devoured him. And from a far distant place he looked on as it swept France's sword aside with ease. He sensed the fear in France's heart, and was horrified that a piece of him reveled in it.

He fought his magic as it sought to consume him in an orgy of blood. But it would not yield. It gripped his sword in both hands, crashed the hilt into the side of France's head. Morgin looked on powerlessly as his boot lifted of its own accord and slammed into France's crotch. The swordsman grunted, doubled over, then fell to the ground at Morgin's feet. Morgin's sword lifted in a nightmare that would not end, his control completely gone, his hands little more than passengers on its hilt.

Something hit him hard, slammed into his side, knocked him sprawling into the dust of the yard, rolling in a tangled heap with a new opponent. He broke free, rolled to one side, came up swinging.

Tulellcoe dropped below his first stroke, jumped over the next. He danced just out of range of the tip of Morgin's sword. He back-stepped hard, drew his own blade, and as he met Morgin's next stroke, steel rang loud and demanding in the castle yard.

Tulellcoe disengaged, back stepped and said, "If it's a fight you want, fight me." He gripped his sword with both hands, called forth his power in an instant, and attacked.

Morgin retreated on the defensive again, for Tulellcoe's power was no small thing. Morgin could feel it, smell it, hear it, see it. One part of him rejoiced, tried to falter, to stumble, to give Tulellcoe an opening so that this mad orgy of power could end as it should. But his own power, now fully in control of him, would not allow it. It was that part of him that finally understood why it was called power. He felt its strength, and sensed that Tulellcoe's power was nothing against his own.

It became easy to back Tulellcoe across the yard, to swat him about playfully, to toy with him for the sheer pleasure that came with such a nightmare of power. He caught Tulellcoe hard beneath the chin with the hilt of his sword, then brought the blade around in a long flat arc. It bit into Tulellcoe's neck, passed through him without stopping, took off a piece of the opposite shoulder as it exited. Tulellcoe's head actually jumped upward before falling. Then it tumbled to the ground, bounced once with a sickening thud, and came to rest in the dirt of the yard.

Morgin staggered backward. His sword and hands were soaked with Tulellcoe's blood. He staggered again as his magic left him. The world around him slowed, came to a grinding stop. The eyes in Tulellcoe's head, glassed over in death, stared at him without forgiveness, and Tulellcoe's headless body, still standing for a horrifying moment, finally toppled forward into Morgin's arms, twitching uncontrollably.

Tulellcoe? Morgin thought. *Dead? Murdered by my own hands?* Morgin dropped his sword. "No," he pleaded. "No." He lowered Tulellcoe gently to the ground, trying to understand what had happened, to comprehend the magnitude of what he'd done. He'd murdered his uncle.

"Tulellcoe," he whispered. Tulellcoe's headless neck poured forth a deep red stream that soaked Morgin's trousers then spilled to the ground, and in the fine, dry dust it formed little round beads and puddles that coalesced into a large red stain around the two of them.

"Uncle," Morgin whispered. "What have I done?"

"You lost control," Tulellcoe said.

Morgin snapped his head up to look in the direction of the voice. Tulellcoe stood over him, his sword still in his hand. He stood in the shade of the porch leaning casually against a support column, and in a cold, angry voice he said, "You have much to learn about power, Morgin."

Morgin looked down into his lap. No blood soaked his trousers. No body lay at his feet, no head. The dust blew dry and brown in the hot summer breeze. He looked back at Tulellcoe.

"Most of us are not deserving of your hatred, nephew," Tulellcoe said. He stepped away from the column, sheathed his sword, turned his back and walked away.

Morgin looked back at his hands, his trousers, his sword, the dirt about him. Nothing.

A shadow crossed the ground before him. Olivia stood over him, with the Tulalane at her side.

"Well," the Tulalane said with a smirk. "He's no coward."

"Perhaps," Olivia half agreed. "But he's a magician with no control. And that may be even worse."

She looked at Morgin, her eyes pinched with anger. "Well, young man. What do you have to say for yourself?"

Morgin looked again at his bloodless lap, then back at Olivia. He could think of nothing to say, and into the silence the Tulalane said, "As usual he has little or nothing to say. I think he's just daft."

Bile rose in Morgin's throat. He stood. His fists clenched. His knuckles whitened. He trembled as he stepped up to the twoname and stood facing him.

The Tulalane grinned. "Touch me, boy, and I'll squash you."

"Go inside, Morgin," Olivia commanded. "This is over."

Morgin's fists remained clenched as he turned toward the castle gate and began walking.

"What do you think you're doing?" Olivia demanded.

He clenched his teeth as tightly as his fists, refusing to speak, and marched toward the castle gates. As he approached the guard there he heard Olivia command, "Stop him. Seize him."

The guard took one step toward him, indecision written on his face. AnnaRail saved the poor fellow from being forced to assault a member of House Elhiyne. "No," she said sharply. "Let him go."

Morgin did not look back and walked silently out of the castle. Behind him he heard AnnaRail and Olivia arguing heatedly. As he walked down the road that led from Elhiyne the distance slowly muffled the sounds of their argument until he could hear no more.

12

Prelude to War

THE TULALANE TOOK great care to appear normal as he stepped out of the hot sun and into the darkened interior of the village inn. He resisted the urge to look over his shoulder like some fugitive thief. He was Hwatok Tulalane, a man above suspicion.

The common room possessed an odd quiet in the middle of the day, with only a few patrons present. The messenger from Yestmark sat in the far corner.

The Tulalane stopped at the bar to order a mug of ale, then crossed the room casually and sat down at the table with the messenger. He spoke softly. "You wanted to see me?"

The messenger eyed him uneasily. "Yes, my lord. I have a message for you."

"Eglahan sends me messages?"

"No, my lord. The message I have for you is from His Highness, Prince Valso et Decouix."

The Tulalane leaned forward and hissed, "Silence. Keep your voice low when you speak that name here. Better yet, don't speak it at all."

The messenger cast his eyes down fearfully. "Yes, my lord."

"Good. Now what is this message?"

The messenger looked carefully about the room. "I am to inform you that the time to act is now."

The Tulalane couldn't suppress a grin. "At last! Now we can crush these upstart Elhiynes. I assume there is more?"

"Yes, my lord. Tomorrow you are to ride east out of Elhiyne with six twelves of armed men to Sa'umbra Gap, your purpose being to patrol for bandits in the mountains. And since I am leaving for Yestmark tomorrow, I will ride with you. When we get to Sa'umbra you and I will poison the Elhiyne armsmen so they die in their sleep. His Highness will meet us there with a like number of Kulls. They will strip the Elhiyne dead, put on their livery and ride their horses. Then, with you in the lead, we will all return to Elhiyne.

"While we are gone, a messenger will come from Penda Court to tell the Elhiynes that Valso's father, Illalla, crossed the Worshipers far to the north at Methula. The messenger will tell them he's riding at the head of an army and marching down the western side of the Worshipers, sacking and plundering Penda and Tosk lands on his way to Elhiyne. Malka will rally the local armsmen and ride to the west to defend Elhiyne lands. When we return from Sa'umbra in the east, Elhiyne should be all but deserted, protected by no more than women and old men. And since we ourselves will appear to be Elhiyne, we should gain easy access."

The Tulalane shook his head. "And what then do I do with seventy odd Kulls and a castle full of women?"

"His Highness instructed me to emphasize that timing is critical. At this moment King Illalla is marshaling his army north of Yestmark. In truth, while the Elhiyne armsmen are riding up the western side of the Worshipers, he will march down the eastern side, cross at Sa'umbra, then assault Elhiyne directly. The messenger from Penda will arrive here in two days, just as Illalla begins his assault on SavinCourt. You must be gone by then so that you will not be obligated to ride with Malka. And you must return within six days to take the castle. We must stay ahead of any word from Yestmark."

The Tulalane thought carefully. "So I take the castle in six days, and Illalla cannot have his army here in under twelve. What of Malka? Surely he will discover the ruse and return before then to retake Elhiyne?"

"You will have six twelves of Kulls to guard all entrances to the castle. You will have the Elhiyne women as hostages, and Prince Valso's considerable magic to help you discover any plots they or their men attempt to hatch. The Elhiyne men will consider any move carefully before making it, and Illalla's army will catch them in the open, without their castle walls to protect them. It will save him the trouble of an extended siege."

"Brilliant," he said, thinking of how he would take great pleasure in seeing Olivia humbled. "I have waited years for this."

He held up his mug of ale. "To Elhiyne," he whispered softly, "and its downfall."

••••

Seated by a small fire, Morgin watched the sun rise peacefully over his little mountain campsite, while far below JohnEngine worked his way carefully up the mountainside, allowing his horse to choose its own path. Since walking out of the castle four days ago his magic had grown erratic. Sometimes it flowed strong and demanding, and at other times it merely trickled out of him, like water in a babbling brook.

Twice now, feeling the need to attempt some form of control, he had tried to stem the flow when at its weakest. But that had been like trying to dam the water in a stream. The water flows relentlessly, and eventually overflows the dam. He had learned to yield to its whims, a reluctant prisoner of his own magic, and it lay dormant now within him, a sleeping beast waiting to wake upon the next tide of power.

JohnEngine topped the last rise and spurred his horse into the campsite, SarahGirl following close behind him. Morgin stood as JohnEngine looked down at him, his eyes mirroring the apprehension in his soul.

Morgin made an effort to smile. "Brother," he said. "It's good to see you."

Morgin saw JohnEngine's apprehension ease somewhat. He dismounted. "How have you been?"

Morgin shrugged. "Hungry. Cold. Tired." He decided not to mention that he had gone without sleep since leaving the castle.

JohnEngine turned about and reached into his saddlebags. He retrieved a lump of journeycake and tossed it to Morgin. "Chew on that."

Morgin dug his teeth into the hard, sweet cake. He had thought it crude and tasteless, but now he delighted in it. "Thank you," he said. "Here, let me help you with the horses."

He took SarahGirl's reins, led her to the edge of the campsite, careful to stay well clear of the teeth that had nipped him so often. He expected her to begin quivering now that he was near, to see her nostrils flare, her eyes widen with fear, but instead, she raised her muzzle to his face. He ducked to avoid a nasty bite on his cheek. Her head followed him down, and she licked him sloppily on the back of his neck. He lifted his head, looked in her big, round, brown eyes. Her tongue lashed out, slurping a big kiss across his cheek.

He shook his head. "You've changed," he said.

"No," JohnEngine said. "It's you who have changed."

Morgin nodded. "Yes. I believe I have."

Morgin tied SarahGirl's reins to the branches of a nearby bush, then joined JohnEngine at the campfire. They both sat in the dirt with their legs crossed.

"How is France?" Morgin asked.

JohnEngine shrugged and wrinkled his nose. "He's all right. He's a tough bird. Bruised a little. Nothing more."

"I'm sorry," Morgin said.

"You have nothing to be sorry about. You were merely the dupe in one of grandmother's conniving schemes, something she hatched with the Tulalane."

Morgin shrugged. "I know. Once I calmed down, got out of the valley and away from their influence, I could feel the difference. It seemed clear they'd done something, though it's good to have it confirmed. I know what she did, I just don't know why."

"Because she's an evil old woman."

Morgin grinned. "None of us have ever doubted that."

JohnEngine laughed, shook his head in disgust. "She'll never learn, will she? You know even Marjinell was on your side for once. And mother was positively livid when she found out. I've never heard anyone speak that way to grandmother before. It was quite an ear full."

"I'm sorry if I hurt mother," Morgin said.

JohnEngine nodded. "That you did."

JohnEngine hesitated, and Morgin sensed that his brother had something difficult to say.

"Mother sends you her love," JohnEngine said. "And father too. Mother also had me bring your sword, and your sheath, and your cloak, and two sets of clothing, your horse, your saddle, and your saddlebags packed with twelve days of trail rations, a hunting bow, a belt knife, a game knife, and a purse of gold coins."

A lump formed in the pit of Morgin's stomach. "Grandmother exiled me?"

"Oh no!" JohnEngine said. "Not that. She doesn't even know I'm here. She keeps demanding that we send out search parties to hunt you down and bring you back. But mother and father said you're a grown man and can take care of yourself, that you'll come back if and when you choose. And mother sends you a message. She says . . ." JohnEngine had difficulty speaking. "She says that you have every right to hate the witches of Elhiyne. That we have treated you poorly. That you would be fully justified if you chose to ride away and never see us again. She has given you what she can so that, at the very least, you may leave us with more than when you came. And I am to tell you that it is your choice, that no one binds you to Elhiyne, that if you choose to go, you go with her love always, and father's love . . . and my love too."

JohnEngine's gaze burrowed into the embers of the fire.

"How can I hate the witches of Elhiyne," Morgin asked, "when I am one myself."

JohnEngine's eyes came up to meet his. Morgin said, "I can deny that no more than I can deny the power that has always been a part of me. I know that now."

JohnEngine said, "Then you'll come back?"

"Certainly I'll come back."

JohnEngine's eyes returned to the fire. "I'm glad. Will you come back with me now? Mother asked me not to dally; she's anxious to know your decision."

"Then go and tell her I'll return, but not immediately. I need more time alone. I have a lot of thinking to do."

"When will you come back then?"

"Tell her I'll take no more than the twelve days allowed by the trail rations, and probably a lot less."

••••

JohnEngine shielded his eyes against the late afternoon sun as his horse took its first steps into the valley of his home. He had an odd sensation of something amiss, a tension that hung in the air like fog.

The fields in the distance were empty. There were no field hands taking advantage of the last rays of sun. The wheat sat motionless in the calm of sunset. The entire valley lay blanketed by an unnatural quiet that set his heart to pounding.

He spurred his horse on, his mind racing through a hundred catastrophes that could have befallen those he loved. Fear drove him to push the animal to its limit, to charge across the valley to Elhiyne.

The village near the castle was a soundless cluster of small buildings and huts that sped past his vision as he raced through it. Only when past it and well into the small woodland that separated the village and the castle, only then did he hear the first real sounds of life: the ring of steel hammers, men shouting hurried orders, horses neighing and spluttering.

The castle loomed before him, a dark shadow against the now sunless horizon. He charged through its open gates, found in the yard a confusing mass of armed men and horses. Some of the men were already mounted, some just mounting up. They ignored him.

Someone shouted an order. Someone else shouted another. And then, like bees abandoning a hive, they spilled out through the gates and rode off into the night. In a few heartbeats they were just a muffled rumble of charging horses in the distance.

JohnEngine hit the ground at a run, leaving his horse untethered. In the settling darkness he stumbled up the steps of the main building, sprinting toward the light cast by the open doors there. Within he hoped to find sanity, reason, calm. But he ran head-long into DaNoel, and they both tumbled to the floor in a crash of arms and legs.

JohnEngine picked himself up quickly. "What's happening, brother?"

DaNoel, weighted down by sword and mail, rose slowly. "Where in netherhell have you been?"

"I've been out of the valley running errands for mother. What's wrong here?"

DaNoel looked at him suspiciously. "Errands, eh? How is the coward?"

"He's no coward, Da. He's your brother."

"He's no brother of mine. He's a fatherless peasant, a whoreson."

JohnEngine's anger rose; he threw his forearm up, caught DaNoel beneath the chin and pressed him hard against the cold stone wall. He spoke slowly through gritted teeth. "Tell me what is happening here."

DaNoel gripped JohnEngine's forearm, struggled silently against it. They were evenly matched, and could have struggled all night, but both realized the futility of such a battle and they came to an unspoken compromise. They separated. DaNoel straightened his tunic.

JohnEngine fought to contain his anger. "What's going on here? Where were those armsmen going?"

"We have war," DaNoel said as if he found some pleasure in that fact. "Illalla has assembled an army, and crossed the Worshipers at Methula. A messenger came this morning from Penda. Illalla has already taken Tosk, and burned Drapolis. He is marching now on Penda, and they ask for our aid, for we will be next. Malka is assembling our armsmen and expects to have six hundred when we ride out tomorrow. I assume you'll ride with us."

"Of course."

"Then come with me now. I'm to report to Malka."

JohnEngine shook his head. "I have to see mother first. Tell him I'll be there shortly."

••••

Morgin's saddle shifted dangerously as SarahGirl cantered beneath him. He would have fallen had they been riding hard, but instead he tugged lightly on the reins and brought her to a stop. "Let's see what's wrong here, girl," he said, dismounting and patting her flank. He flipped the stirrup up over her saddle, found a loose cinch and tightened it. He walked forward and scratched her between the ears, and in reply she licked his ear, then gave him a big sloppy kiss on the cheek.

He wiped his face with his sleeve, then reached into his pocket and brought out a small square of hard, sweet journeycake. She gobbled at it greedily.

He raised a hand to shade his eyes from the bright, midday sun. He should have no difficulty making it home before dark, though he was tempted to take his time just to put off the inevitable confrontation with Olivia. He scratched SarahGirl between the ears. "I'm not looking forward to that meeting."

SarahGirl nuzzled his ear, begging for more journeycake. He scratched her between the ears again, climbed back into the saddle and spurred her forward into a trot. He was anxious to find France and apologize for trying to kill him. Then he must do the same with Tulellcoe, and after Tulellcoe, Rhianne. Thinking of her his heart filled with sadness and shame.

It was time to make peace with Rhianne, to mend what little remained of their marriage, perhaps start anew, though now she would have just cause to spit in his face and curse him.

At that moment the road crested a small hill, and the valley he knew as home stretched before him, twilight approaching, a thin crescent moon rising in the darkening sky. He halted SarahGirl, gauged the sun on the horizon, estimated he could be home by nightfall, though he'd have to push it a bit.

The impression that something was amiss grew upon him slowly as he rode SarahGirl down into the valley. He and SarahGirl crossed the no-man's-land outside the castle walls, stood at the castle gates themselves before he realized they were actually closed.

That explained it. Roland and Malka were on some errand out of the valley with most of the men.

"Hello," he cried out. "Let me in. It's me. Morgin."

He waited. Nothing happened at first, then a shadowy head leaned out over the battlements and muttered something like, "Aye, lord."

Morgin waited longer. Then, creaking loudly the gates began to open. He waited until they had swung a good distance on their hinges before riding through. He spurred SarahGirl forward, and immediately his magic told him to beware. He looked about carefully as he rode into the yard, noting that all appeared as it should. But just as he approached the main building a figure stepped from the doorway, and even standing in the shadow of the overhanging balcony, his face hidden from view, Morgin recognized the Tulalane, grinning in that unholy way of his.

"Well, boy," the wizard said. "You're back."

Morgin gave no answer. He waited, stomach churning, heart pounding, unsure of what to expect.

NickoLot's voice startled them both as she shouted from somewhere high in the castle, "Run, Morgin. It's a trap. They're going to kill you."

The gates began to creak shut. At the same moment Valso stepped into view and said calmly, "She's right, Elhiyne. We are going to kill you, slowly."

Morgin pulled viciously on SarahGirl's reins, dug his spurs in and brought her about. He bent low in the saddle, charged for the closing gate, heard an arrow hiss past his ear. Another sliced through the air in front of him, a third thudded into his saddlebag as he shot through the gates and into the clear. He charged down the road, zigzagging from side to side as arrows rained down about him. In the distance he could hear Valso shouting, "Kill him. Kill him. Don't let him get away. Kill him, damn you. Kill him."

Morgin's only chance lay in the cover of the small woodland, but he must first cross the cleared no-man's-land that formed part of the castle's defenses, and there he was an open target.

The first trees seemed just within reach, approaching with nightmare slowness, when SarahGirl screamed and collapsed beneath him at full charge. They both hit the road rolling and bouncing, and Morgin barely missed being crushed by SarahGirl's body.

Morgin came up running, dove into the brush filled ditch at the side of the road. Arrows hissed and thudded into the dirt all about him. He crawled, hoping the darkness would give him some protection. He stumbled up the ditch on his hands and knees, stopping in the brush to one side of where SarahGirl lay whimpering in the middle of the road.

An arrow protruded from her back, two from her side, another from her hip. While he watched another buried itself in her shoulder. Blood poured from her nostrils. She lay there coughing and whimpering, wheezing on the blood filling her lungs, looking at Morgin with big, round, brown eyes. She could not understand why he didn't help her, why he did nothing about the pain. There were tears in her eyes, and tears in his, as he thought of the one thing he could do, the only thing left to him.

His sword was still sheathed and strapped to her saddle. He could see it now, the hilt protruding from beneath her. He stood, ran into the middle of the road and grasped it with both hands. He tugged on it, but pinned beneath her weight it didn't move.

The rain of arrows began anew. He pulled harder, lunged against it, and it came free with a jerk. Then, in one continuous motion, he raised it high over his head, pulled power, fed it into the blade and brought it down with all his might on the back of SarahGirl's neck. It bit into her spine, partially severed her head, and she died painlessly then and there. And Morgin, sobbing like a child, sprinted into the woods carrying nothing more than his bloodied sword.

13

The Magic of Kings

AS ARROWS RAINED down about him, Morgin charged deeper into the woodland, branches slapping at his face and arms. Twice he tripped and tumbled to the ground, almost impaling himself on his own sword. He stopped when the trees were dense enough to shield him from the arrows, leaned over, put his hands on his knees and sucked air into his lungs.

He heard shouting, couldn't see any real detail through the trees but spotted a flicker of torch light. He crept toward the castle, stopping behind a tree well inside the woodland just short of the no-man's-land. Valso had sent two twelves of Kulls out to hunt him down, one moving out double-time to his left, the other to his right. Clearly, they intended to flank him on both sides, then work their way toward him, squeezing him between them.

Morgin had no choice; he pulled a shadow, got down on his belly and crawled out into the no-man's-land. He hoped that to anyone's eyes he would appear to be just a blotch of shadow on the rough ground, one among many. The crescent moon helped, ensuring that he and all the shadows about him were poorly defined. He'd crawled about ten paces out of the woodland when he heard the Kulls calling out to one another; he froze.

"Anything?"

"Nothing so far."

He spotted a Kull moving along the edge of the wood, carrying a torch, pausing at any clump of bush large enough to hide Morgin and stabbing it with his sword. The Kull approached slowly, keeping pace with his comrades deeper in the wood. Morgin could do nothing but remain still and hope.

The Kull glanced Morgin's way, but he must have been looking for a man, not a shadow. He looked back toward the woodland and called out something to his comrades, then moved on. Morgin inched farther into the no-man's-land.

••••

BlakeDown et Penda, leader of Clan Penda, stood at the battlements of his castle and looked fearfully upon Malka and the Elhiyne armsmen. He would never acknowledge fear; as the head of the clan he must always appear strong. Clan Elhiyne was a force to reckon with, and if they sought war with Penda, a force to be feared.

War? No. Certainly BlakeDown and Olivia were opponents in almost all facets of the Lesser Council, and he made no secret of the fact that he sought to usurp her position. But war, open and unchecked? No. BlakeDown could not believe Olivia would be stupid enough to choose war.

In the distance the Elhiyne force came slowly into full view. As BlakeDown's scouts had reported they were not the largest numbers Elhiyne could muster, and they brought with them no siege engines. But they were a force of armed men violating Penda land.

The Elhiynes halted well out of range of any bow-shot from the castle walls. BlakeDown had two of his scouts waiting on horseback just outside the castle with a flag of truce. He nodded to them, and they rode out to the Elhiyne force. The fact that they were not cut down immediately was a good sign. They spoke briefly with Malka, then returned at a quick trot.

"My lord," the head scout said. "Lord Malka agrees to your terms of parley. He will meet you alone, unarmed, half way between here and his own forces."

When Malka rode out to the intended rendezvous BlakeDown marveled at the girth of the warrior. Even at such a distance he was an imposing man, and BlakeDown knew he would feel small beside him.

"Your horse is ready, my lord."

BlakeDown decided it would do Malka good to stew a while, to contemplate the folly of an attack on Penda. Only when Malka seemed on the verge of leaving did BlakeDown climb down from Penda's battlements, mount his horse, and ride slowly out to the rendezvous.

"What is this?" Malka demanded. "You treat an ally as an enemy."

BlakeDown showed no emotion. "I treat an ally as an honored guest. But I must know first that he is truly an ally, and not some enemy in disguise."

Malka grew visibly livid. "An enemy in disguise—what game do you play, Penda? You ask our aid, then scorn us when we come?"

BlakeDown shook his head. "I did not ask for your aid."

Malka's brows furrowed and his eyes turned coal black. "Did not ask—what lies are these? You sent a messenger, with a tale of Decouix attack."

BlakeDown tried not to show any interest in Malka's unfolding story. "I sent no messenger."

"But he bore the seal of Penda inscribed with magic upon the palm of his hand."

BlakeDown shrugged. "Then the seal was forged, the messenger an impostor."

"But who?" Malka demanded. "Why?"

BlakeDown took great pleasure in his next words. "If I were you, Elhiyne, I would look to my rear."

BlakeDown watched comprehension dawn on Malka's face. "By the gods!" he swore softly. He spun his horse about and charged back to his men. He shouted at them, and soon they were racing back toward Elhiyne.

Poor Elhiynes, thought BlakeDown. Foolish Elhiynes. They would be no match for the Decouix machinations. The Decouixs were subtle, sophisticated, like BlakeDown himself, subtlety that would see them victorious over Elhiyne.

With Elhiyne out of the way Penda would become ascendant in the Lesser Council. BlakeDown would finally have the opportunity to show the Decouixs how worthy an opponent he could be. Yes. They would learn to respect Penda, and its leader.

It occurred to him that the coming conflict between Decouix and Elhiyne would be bloody in the extreme. It might be wise to bolster his border troops, perhaps even to close the borders entirely. Otherwise the bloodletting might spill over into Penda lands, and that would not do.

••••

A cock crowed in some yard somewhere. A dog barked in reply. The wind gusted cold through the stubby growth of the newly planted wheat fields below. Morgin had spent the night wrapped in shadow and crawling on his belly across the no-man's-land, and he shivered in the morning air. He had no cloak to keep him warm as he huddled tightly within the shadow of the castle's man-gate, waiting. The sun would soon rise and the shadows, for a short while, would be long and deep.

Clearly Valso was waiting for something. He had seventy or eighty Kulls. Not enough to take and hold the countryside, but enough to hold the castle for a short while. With NickoLot and the Elhiyne women as hostages, the returning Elhiyne men, dare not try to retake the castle by frontal assault. Morgin reasoned that stealth might yield some gain where force would reap only blood.

It had taken most of the night to reach the castle's man-gate, a heavy wooden door recessed into the outer wall. Its dimensions had been carefully chosen: too narrow for two armed men to walk through shoulder to shoulder, but large enough for a single man leading an un-mounted horse. Morgin would have to pick his moment carefully, and do it right the first time.

A gust of wind swirled through the gate's recess. His jaw muscles tightened as he tried to control his shivering. He'd stood there waiting for hours, and wondered now if his chilled muscles would be too stiff to act when the time came.

The sun peered over the eastern lip of the valley. The shadow in which he hid deepened, its edges sharply defined. He needed shadow, for he dare not cast spells that Valso might sense. He waited until the sun rose, deepening the shadows further, then he began forming a simple wind spell, something he'd never tried before and wasn't sure would work. He built it slowly, carefully, lest he use too much power and alert those within. He waited, holding his spell in check, allowing it to gust the wind just a little here and there so it wouldn't grow beyond control.

He heard a shout from within, then boot steps marching across the castle yard. He tensed at the sound of muffled voices behind the thick planking of the man-gate, then the bolt shot back with a sharp crack.

Morgin moved. He brought his shadow with him as he stepped out of the recess and pressed his back tightly against the outer wall. If one of the guards at the battlements above happened to lean out and look down, he had little hope that his shadow magic would be sufficient.

The gate slammed outward. He heard voices and boot steps. A cloaked Kull walked past him, without looking back. Morgin watched the halfman's back as he stomped his feet and blew breath into his cupped hands. It made a cloud of steam in the cold morning air. Another Kull joined the first, then another, then a large group, all looking outward to the woodland with their backs to Morgin.

"It's bloody cold," one of them cursed.

"No colder than the tits on that old witch Olivia, I'll wager you," one of his fellows said.

More of their ilk joined them. "I'll be glad when this spring is done," one said, "and summer's here to warm my bones."

"I'd like to warm my bones on that witch AnnaRail," another said.

One of them laughed. "If Lord Valso is pleased with us, you may get your chance."

Morgin waited, shivering. He counted twenty-three Kull backs now. There'd be one more, then a few words of instruction, and the gate would close. He deepened his shadow, tensed for action, waited.

The last Kull stepped out. The Kull gatekeeper followed, but stopped, one hand on the half open gate. As he made some crude joke about the Elhiyne women Morgin released the wind spell, praying that it would work. It gusted, blew the gate momentarily free of the gatekeeper's hand. Morgin slipped behind him, past him, through the gate and into the castle yard, then pressed his back tightly against the inner wall near the gate.

The gatekeeper cursed, grabbed the gate and held it securely. Morgin didn't have long to wait; the Kull patrol that had just been relieved marched through the gate, past him and into the castle yard without looking back. Two twelves of Kulls, then the gatekeeper swung the gate shut and threw the bolt. He walked away swearing about Elhiyne winds, and did not look back. Morgin slipped into the inner recess of the gate and the dark shadow that lurked there. He huddled against its inner side, waiting, biding his time.

He had no delusions about the limitations of his shadowmagic in broad daylight. By the time the castle fully awoke he'd have to be well concealed elsewhere. So he waited only long enough to be certain the yard was empty, then moved quickly, just another shadow among the many beneath the parapets.

A commotion at the entrance to the main building drew Morgin's attention, so he ducked into the relative safety of the stables. Valso and the Tulalane stepped into view. The Decouix prince strode to the man-gate. "I tell you something is wrong here. I can sense it."

Several Kulls accompanied Valso and the Tulalane. Their commander said, "But, Your Highness, our guard has been meticulous."

As the Tulalane scanned the courtyard, Morgin ducked back into a deep shadow, holding his breath. Valso stood within the recess of the man-gate and sniffed about like a hound on the scent. He turned to the Kull commander angrily. "He's been here. Inside. I can smell his magic."

"But that's impossible, Your Highness," the Kull said. "This gate is rarely opened. And then only under the eyes of two twelves of my men."

"Don't argue with me, Verk," Valso said. "He's been here. And not long ago."

"He's right," the Tulalane said, still scanning the courtyard. His head moved slowly from side to side like a snake preparing to strike.

Morgin watched and waited, trying not to let the twoname spook him. The Tulalane scanned the yard once more, then his head froze, looking in Morgin's direction. His lips curled slowly into a satisfied grin. He raised his arm, pointed at Morgin. "He's there, Verk. Take him. Now."

The Kull peered intently, shook his head. "I see nothing, my lord."

Morgin waited no longer. The stables were a trap with only one exit. He put all the power he could muster into the strongest shadow spell he could make, then sprinted out of the stables and across the yard. The cry rose immediately, for gray-black shadows do not run by themselves in the light of day.

Morgin dove into a narrow gap between two buildings, a back route he'd taken hundreds of times as a boy and knew well. He burst into a small garden, hurdled one row of flowers and trampled another. He turned right, then left, then cut into the kitchen and ran head-on into two Kulls. All three of them sprawled into a tumble of pots and pans.

Morgin scrambled to his feet, was the first up. He kicked one Kull in the side of the head, then spun about and brought his sword down blindly on the other Kull. It bit deeply into the halfman's shoulder. He spun back to the first Kull, kicked him in the face, then sprinted out of the kitchen and into the main building.

This was home ground. He knew it well, but the Kull pursuit was close on his heels so he cut a random path through the ground floor halls. Shouts and cries followed behind him and all around him. There was no time to think ahead, just to the next room or corridor, often only one step ahead of his enemies. There came a moment when he thought they would catch him, but then the pursuit thinned out as they split up to search the castle. For the first time he had hope of losing them.

Elated that he might be free to move about at will, adrenaline surging through his veins, he turned into a wide corridor and met two Kulls face-to-face. One reacted quickly and swung his sword out. Morgin's magic surged as he parried the strike, swept the halfman's sword aside. With the next stroke he took off most of the Kull's head.

The other Kull, armed with a crossbow, was slower to react. Morgin turned on him, brought his sword down in an arc just as the halfman raised his weapon. He felt his blade bite into the Kull's skull as he heard the twang of the crossbow. The bolt slammed into his chest, lifted him off his feet, passed straight through him and out his back. He landed in the center of the corridor.

He coughed, struggled for air, tried to cry out but no sound came. His mouth filled with blood. He spit it out. More blood pulsed from the hole in his chest. He tried to breathe, but a white hot lance of pain shot through his chest. His mind blinked, and for an instant he lay in an odd world of painless tranquility, then it blinked again and he returned to a world of agony. The corridor tilted and swayed crazily. His mouth filled again with blood, and he understood then that his wound was mortal. He had come to life's end, and curiously, his only fear was that his family would not know he was dead.

As his mind roiled in pain he rolled onto his side to die. His vision blurred, narrowed, then his eyes locked onto an indistinct shimmer of light that caressed the wall before him. It sparkled, fluttered like an ethereal flame fed by some unknown power. Then it disappeared, and he saw the alcove he remembered as a child, his enchanted place of hiding. It had not appeared to him in years, but now old memories flooded back as he used his last agonized moments of life to drag himself across the floor.

The pain seemed almost distant as he crawled into the alcove and struggled to the far end. He rolled onto his back, lay with his head resting against the wall. Now he could die, the Kulls wouldn't find him, Valso wouldn't know his fate, and perhaps the prince of the Decouixs would always wonder at his return.

Just outside the alcove a lone Kull stepped into view. He glanced down at the bodies of his two dead comrades, and looked cautiously up and down the corridor. He looked back the way he'd come. "This way," he said. "He come this way."

The corridor filled quickly with Kulls, the black pits of their eyes eager for blood. "Where is he?" one demanded.

"Don't know," the first said, squatting down to examine one of the dead. "He's a fighter, this one is. Not easy to kill."

"I like 'em not easy to kill," another growled. "Makes for more sport."

Their leader eyed the scene, then reached down and picked up Morgin's sword. "He must be bad wounded to leave his blade behind."

Another pointed to the crossbow bolt half buried in the wall. "Look! Here's Mook's bolt. It's blooded."

The Kull leader looked the scene over one more time, as if trying to reconstruct what had happened. He examined Morgin's trail of blood, a jagged smear. Morgin knew that, to the Kull's eyes, it disappeared strangely beneath a solid stone wall. The Kull inspected the wall, probably seeking a crack or fissure. It looked as though the Kull was inspecting thin air.

The Kull leader shook his head and turned away. "Enough of this. He can't be far, and if we don't find him soon the prince'll have our balls."

Morgin watched the Kulls move down the corridor, his mind flickering in and out of consciousness, his soul fluttering between life and death. The blood stopped pulsing from the hole in his chest. His ears filled with a distant roar and he tried to scream, but only managed a gurgled croak. His grip on consciousness began to fail and he drifted toward the darkness that awaited him.

As death approached, he had a vision that the alcove opened into a much larger chamber, a room cluttered with swords, shields and ceremonial armor. A jewel glinted in the hilt of a sword, another in the face of a shield, although the metal lacked luster, dulled by the dust of ages. The tapestries on the walls hung in moth-eaten tatters, and cobwebs filled the corners.

A throne sat at the center of the chamber, surrounded by dust-covered riches, and on it sat a king, though like the tapestries he too was decayed. He was no more than a framework of bones and tufts of hair, one skeletal arm resting casually on an armrest, the other on the hilt of a great sword.

Morgin recognized the skeleton king of his dreams.

Morgin's eyes were drawn to the sword, for it was a thing of craftsmanship beyond that produced in any land known to man. Gems and stones of incredible value studded the hilt, and etched along the blade were runes of vast power. It rested tip down in the dust of the floor, its upper weight balanced by no more than the skeleton's hand.

The skeleton's hand! It seemed oddly indistinct, as if the bleached white bones of the fingers were changing, fleshing out. Morgin's eyes moved to the crowned skull, a grinning white mask of death framing eye sockets of black shadow. The skeleton moved, its head turned, the eyeless pits looked upon Morgin and there came a moment of clear, crisp thought in which he seemed to understand all, then a sea of pain washed it away and the darkness consumed him.

••••

The flesh continued to form on the skeleton; the face filled out: a young face, strong, handsome, the eyes pools of sorrow. The king was once again hale and vigorous, seated upon his throne dressed in a suit of golden mail, glimmering silk and rich leather. Once again the tapestries shown with brilliant colors, and the assorted trappings of arms and armor were clean and bright. But there was one feature that marred the beauty; at the king's feet lay the skeleton of a simple warrior. He had died wearing common clothing and he remained in decay. He appeared to have entered the chamber sometime long after the king's passing; mortally wounded, he'd died at the feet of his long dead king. And still clutched in the bones of the warrior's hand was a plain and unadorned sword, the only weapon in the tomb that did not sparkle with inlaid jewels and precious stones.

The king turned to look first upon the decayed body of the warrior at his feet, and then upon Morgin, and his eyes held a sadness beyond time itself. About him there hung a scent of unreality, as if he clung life by a thread of ancient magic. He gripped the great sword in a powerful hand, stood, and strode across the room.

He knelt over Morgin, his face a mask of sorrow. He reached out and placed a hand on the wound in Morgin's chest. He placed the great sword on the floor and with both hands lifted Morgin's lifeless form, holding him tightly against his own breast. The young king looked old and sad, closed his eyes and bowed his head. He whispered softly, "Forgive me, mortal, for what I must do."

Much later he returned Morgin gently to the dust covered floor. The wound in Morgin's chest had disappeared, though the blood stains on his tunic remained. The king stood as if tired and old beyond imagining; the sorrow had not left his face. He turned, and carrying the great sword he walked back to his throne. But he paused and looked back as if something remained undone. He stared at Morgin's still form for a moment, and then at the skeleton of the warrior who had died at the foot of his throne. He bent down over the warrior and removed the simple sword from his grasp, then returned to where Morgin lay. He placed the sword's hilt in Morgin's hand and curled Morgin's fingers around it. "You will need this, Lord Mortal," he said. "May it stand you in good stead."

He returned to his throne, sat down, resting one arm casually on an armrest and the other on the hilt of the great sword. The tapestries lost their brilliance and the weaponry lost its shine. And the king, powerful and majestic in life, was once more a skeleton of brittle bone and rotted flesh.

14

The Magic of Shadow

MORGIN SNAPPED AWAKE and sat up instantly, feeling his chest for a non-existent death wound. His mind filled with glimpses of a strange dream: a throne room in decay and a long dead king. He shook his head, trying to make sense of the fragmentary images, but just when the dream seemed real and whole, it disappeared.

His hand touched something at his side: his sword. He picked it up, looked at it closely. It was his sword; he was certain of that. He knew every nick and scratch on the blade. But he remembered dropping it in the corridor when hit by the crossbow bolt. The crossbow bolt! Again he examined his chest, shaking his head with wonder. But he didn't have time to ponder such mysteries; he had to do something about Nicki, Rhianne and AnnaRail, and the rest of Valso's hostages.

Before leaving the alcove he peered into the corridor beyond. The carnage there lay untouched; the Kulls had not bothered to remove the bodies of their dead comrades. They appeared to have been laying there for some time. He must have been unconscious through the night and into the following day. He shook his head. More hallucinations, he decided.

Morgin called on his shadows then stepped into the corridor.

He turned back to the alcove and was not surprised to find it no longer there, just bare stone wall. He stripped the dark gray cloak off one of the dead Kulls; it would do well with his shadows. Sword in hand, he turned and slipped from shadow to shadow down the corridor.

••••

The torch on the wall flickered slowly, sending shadows skittering about the room. Morgin stepped into one and followed it for a few paces. The Kull guard leaned on his lance by the door to Olivia's audience chamber, unmoving, unknowing. Morgin chose another shadow. He moved again, striving for that fluidity of motion that would make him indistinguishable from the flickering gray-black shadows.

The Kull yawned. Morgin moved again, edging his way along the tapestried wall, knowing that if he erred his only escape was back the way he'd come. The door near which the Kull stood led directly into the audience chamber, while opposite that was the doorway leading back into the castle proper, where another Kull stood guard. Morgin chose another shadow, and with each step moved closer to the audience chamber.

He had awakened in the alcove in late afternoon. With Kulls marching up and down every hallway in the castle, he'd hidden in the ancient corridors of the old castle to wait out the last few hours of daylight. It had taken great patience to wait so, for his first impulse had been to hunt Valso down without delay. But he needed the darkness and its shadows if he had any hope of succeeding.

Valso stayed hidden in one of the upstairs suites, ringed by Kulls. The Tulalane had all but taken up residence in Olivia's audience chamber, with Kulls reporting to him there. Morgin was within a sword's length of its entrance when he heard boot steps approaching from the castle proper. The guard lost his slouch and straightened. Morgin pressed his back tightly against the wall, wrapped the cloak about his shoulders and concentrated on his shadow spell.

Valso emerged from the hallway followed by a retinue of Kulls. He stomped past the guard and stormed into the audience chamber.

"He's alive," Valso said. "I can sense him lurking about."

"If the coward lives," Morgin heard the Tulalane say, "then he's crawled into some hole to hide."

Morgin heard the Tulalane's scorn as he said, "Do you fear him, my prince?"

"No. Never. I just want to be certain he doesn't spoil my plans. Have you kept up the search?"

"Yes," the Tulalane said. He made no effort to hide his contempt for the Decouix prince. "We haven't been able to find him, but don't concern yourself with the gutter-snipe. His fear will keep him hidden until this is done."

Morgin changed shadows, found one that allowed him a slanting view of Valso standing in the audience chamber.

"Of course it will," Valso said. He eyed the inside of the room. "I like your blasphemous choice of a command post. You and I will do well together."

"I take a certain amount of pleasure in having the old witch attend me here, our situations reversed. And I do not care how well you do, Your Highness. My only concern is for myself, and I intend to do well indeed by this."

Valso smiled. "Just remember that you will do only as well as me."

Morgin waited for a reply from the Tulalane, but all he heard was the rustle of papers. Valso continued speaking, "Have you learned anything from the Elhiyne lord-ling?"

Morgin stiffened, held his breath.

"No, Your Highness. He is stubborn. But we'll break him."

"What of the girl?" Valso asked.

"Why don't you just take her at your pleasure?"

"Because I want her willing cooperation in this. Far more humiliating for her husband, don't you think?"

The Tulalane shrugged. "I dropped a hint or two and she seems willing to cooperate."

"Then have her sent to my rooms immediately. I want to see how far her desire to please goes."

"I do not arrange for your bed chamber entertainments."

"You will do as I say, twoname. Or my Kulls will turn you out to deal with the Elhiynes yourself." Without waiting for a reply, Valso turned and left the room.

Morgin watched him march through the antechamber. Moments later the Tulalane cried, "Guard."

The guard turned, rushed into the audience chamber. Morgin heard the Tulalane say, "Bring the girl." The guard rushed back out and disappeared into the castle proper.

Morgin decided to wait. He was curious to see who "the girl" might be.

The guard returned quickly, followed by Rhianne and several of his fellows. The Kulls waited in the antechamber with Morgin while Rhianne joined the Tulalane in the audience chamber.

"You called for me?" she asked coldly.

"Play no games with me, girl," the Tulalane said. "I know your mind. You have no reason to love the Elhiynes, every reason to hate them."

Morgin realized where this was going, but could not believe for a second that Rhianne would betray him so.

Rhianne spoke cautiously. "I will admit that my husband hasn't been the most attentive of spouses. What do you want of me? You've dropped veiled hints. It's time to speak plainly."

The Tulalane continued. "Prince Valso wishes you to attend him in his private apartments."

"I am no plaything of Valso's."

The Tulalane laughed. "I care not whose plaything you are, woman. But you must choose: the Decouixs, or the Elhiynes. You will attend Valso willingly, and please him however he chooses, or you will die with the rest."

"And what will I get from this? If you think I will go down this path merely to save my life, you are a fool."

"Make Prince Valso happy and you can probably get whatever you want."

Morgin heard Rhianne sigh. "Very well. But tell His Highness I wish to freshen up first. I will attend him within the hour."

With those words Morgin's heart dropped down into his gut. He heard Rhianne's petticoats swirl as she turned. A moment later she emerged from the audience chamber, but the Tulalane stopped her by calling, "Girl."

Morgin watched her turn slowly to face the Tulalane. He could have easily reached her with his sword, and as sorrow and rage boiled up within him it was all he could do not to cut her down then and there.

The Tulalane's voice filled the silence. "You have made the right decision, woman."

Rhianne gave no answer. She turned slowly to leave, but as her eyes passed Morgin she hesitated for an instant as if looking directly at him. He tensed, thinking he was discovered, determined that the traitorous bitch would be the first to die. But if she saw something she must have dismissed it as just another shadow, for she completed her turn and left the room without another word.

Morgin waited a dozen heartbeats, then melted into the shadowy night.

••••

Rhianne concentrated on taming her racing heart. She had managed to control it so far, but she knew if she relaxed for an instant it would run away from her. It would climb up into her throat, pounding like a drum, and destroy what little composure she'd managed to achieve. Her breasts, already chilled by the low cut gown and the damp castle air, would chill even further as her chest muscles tightened with fear. If only she could speak with the other women. If only Valso didn't keep them isolated, alone.

Morgin came to mind. She had seen him hiding in the shadows near the audience chamber, though not with her eyes, but with her heart, her soul, her magic. She'd felt a murderous hate radiating from him like the heat from a white hot hearth. It had come upon her with such intensely she'd almost cried out, but she'd held her silence, and she wondered if he would ever forgive her for rejecting him so long ago.

He'd wanted to, she knew. She'd seen the forgiveness and love in his eyes time and again, but something else always appeared there too: hate, fear, pride; she could never be certain, and it stood between them now, a wall whose making she could blame on no one but herself. If only he would come to her, she would beg his forgiveness. She would prove to him that she was no longer the stupid young girl who'd let her pride mirror her mother's ambitions.

He'd certainly overheard her conversation with the Tulalane, and his hate must have blossomed a thousand-fold. She briefly toyed with the idea of somehow getting a message to him, but that was nothing more than an impossible flight of fancy. In any case, her actions this night would show him where her true allegiance lay.

The door to her apartments opened. The Kull Captain Verk entered, bowed deeply from the waist. "His Highness will see you now, Your Ladyship."

A chill ran down Rhianne's spine. It was said the Kulls were half man and demon, but nothing human hid behind those eyes, only cruelty and desire. She had chosen her gown for effect. It squeezed her small breasts upward, produced a slight but provocatively enticing bit of cleavage meant to please Valso, but it appeared to have the same effect on the Kull.

She stood, walked past Verk whispering small spells quietly to herself. She walked rapidly down the hall, allowing no one to lead her to Valso's suite, forcing them to follow. Verk caught up with her only when she stopped at Valso's door.

The Kull knocked politely. From within there came a grumbled "Enter." Verk opened the door, stepped into the room and closed it, while Rhianne waited in the hall. She cast quiet spells to hide her thoughts, emotions and fears.

The door opened. Verk reappeared, his eyes settling on her breasts as he spoke. "You may enter."

Fear threatened to overwhelm her, to sweep away the confidence she'd struggled to maintain. Her nerves taught, her emotions raw and barely in check, she took a deep breath, swallowed, and stepped through the open door.

Valso stood and bowed. "Welcome, Lady Rhianne," he said. "You must forgive the setting . . ." He spread his arms, indicating the room about them, ". . . but Elhiyne hospitality is crude at best."

She smiled and nodded. "There is no need to apologize, my lord. I myself have had to bear with them for some time now."

Valso seemed pleased at her response. He looked at the Kull. "You may go, Verk."

"Aye, my lord," the halfman said. He bowed at the waist, turned and left.

Valso stood near a small table upon which rested a crystal decanter and two crystal goblets. "Would you care for some brandy?"

"Only if you will join me, my lord."

He poured an amber liquid into the two goblets and handed one to Rhianne, then raised his to eye level. "To the rightful ascendancy of the Decouix rule."

Rhianne raised her glass and took a small sip. The drink burned as it trickled down her throat.

Valso seemed pleased at her response. He raised his glass a second time. "To the fall of House Elhiyne."

Rhianne hesitated and Valso's eyes narrowed. She forced herself not to blurt out a quick excuse. "I cannot drink to that, my lord. I am of Elhiyne, and as such would be toasting my own destruction."

Valso's eyes slitted with curiosity. "And what if your destiny were not tied to that of Elhiyne?"

Rhianne raised her glass. "Well then, my lord . . ." She finished by touching the brandy to her lips.

Valso relaxed. His eyes settled hungrily on her breasts. She saw no difference between his desire and Verk's, but sensing that her moment had come, she said, "Am I right when I assume that you are interested in coming to some sort of mutually beneficial accommodation?"

Valso looked away from her breasts. "I have . . . many appetites," he said, "appetites that will be satisfied. I have an appetite for power, and a desire to see these upstart Elhiynes humbled. I will consume them."

Valso's eyes caressed the length of her. He approached her, stood within inches of her. She could smell the brandy on his breath, and the cologne that he wore too much of. "I also have an appetite for things of beauty, and a beautiful woman such as you could please me greatly."

Rhianne drew upon her magic, trying to enspell him with desire, but she knew in her heart that her success was due to her womanhood, and not some otherworldly power. "To please you, my lord, would please me."

Valso's breathing quickened. Holding his drink with one hand, he placed the other about her waist. He pulled her forward and kissed her. She bit his tongue to tease him, her arms at her sides, the drink still held in one hand.

Valso released her, took the drink from her, walked to the small table and placed the goblets on it. Returning, he made an obvious effort not to rush. He took her in his arms and kissed her again. This time, with her hands free, she wrapped both arms around his neck and pulled him tightly against her, pressing her body against his.

Valso became almost frantic. One hand grasped at her breasts; his pelvis pressed against hers. She teased him, did everything possible to excite him, to thrill him, and while he responded, her left hand crept slowly up her right sleeve until she felt the head of the needle she'd concealed within the folds. She withdrew it slowly, taking great care lest the point touch her own skin. The poison she had chosen was lethal in the most minute quantity, and would take her own life as quickly as his. And that was how it must ultimately serve her, for once their master was dead, she dare not live to face the Kulls.

Under the guise of passionately rubbing the back of Valso's neck, her right hand located a spot at the base of his skull. In her left hand she backed the needle away, lining it up to thrust it deep within his neck. Death would come so quickly he'd be unable even to cry out. She tensed for the thrust, ready for Valso to stiffen then slump in her arms. But at the moment of truth she found herself unable to move, frozen into the immobility of a statue.

Valso withdrew his tongue from her mouth and bit her painfully on the lip, drawing blood. She tried desperately to move, to jab the needle into the back of his head. She struggled to remove her arms from around his neck, but could not move in the slightest. Her body stood locked within a spell of his making, trapped within his control.

He drew his head slowly downward out of the circle of her arms. She stood frozen as if she were caressing some phantom, her arms still held high, the needle still poised to kill. She could not see his actions, but she felt the pain as he bit her cruelly on one breast. In a last desperate attempt, she tried to stab the needle into her own face, but Valso's magic prevented even that.

He reappeared within the range of her vision, grinning. "You are a fool like your husband."

He reached forward and pinched one of her breasts. "I told you I have many appetites." He reached down, groped at her crotch, snarled like an animal. "I'm glad you chose this path, for I think I'll find your resistance even more pleasurable."

He snapped his fingers. The needle vanished. "I could do the same with your gown," he said, "but I'll enjoy it much more if I tear it from your body. I'm going to enjoy you, Rhianne esk et Elhiyne, and when I'm done, we'll see how much pleasure you can bring to Verk and his halfmen. I think I'll save you as a special prize for the most diligent of them. Lend you out every now and then when one of them pleases me most. And if one of them goes a bit too far, I'll see to it you're healed so you'll always be around to pleasure my Kulls."

He stepped back and looked at her. "I'm going to make sure you have a very long and unpleasant life."

••••

Morgin wanted to know the identity of the Elhiyne lordling Valso and the Tulalane had spoken of. Perhaps he was a brother, or cousin, left behind for some reason. Or he might be the son of the lord of one of the outlying holdings, captured before the castle was taken. In any case he would be kept in the dungeon. Morgin knew the place well; he'd spent several days there after one of his drunken brawls, locked in a cell by Olivia's command. She had meant it to be a lesson, but he had learned only that the cells were cold, dark and damp.

The dungeon was guarded by a single Kull seated at a wooden table far below. He passed the time by rolling bone dice and mumbling to himself, the only access to his level a series of stone steps directly in front of him. The room was well lit; Morgin had to depend solely upon his shadowmagic. He wrapped himself deep in shadow and stepped out onto the open stairs.

The Kull's attention remained on his dice, though Morgin knew it could shift to the shadows at the edge of the room at any moment. He tried to blend with the shadows as they danced about the walls, to become part of them. It demanded all of his skill, and for an instant he felt made of shadow. He danced among them as if shadows were his substance, his essence, and a heartbeat later he stood safely at the bottom of the stairway.

He hugged the wall tightly, worked his way slowly about the edge of the room. When he reached a point just behind the Kull he stopped, reinforced his shadowmagic, stepped quietly away from the wall, and laid the flat of his sword softly on the Kull's shoulder. The halfman started with surprise and froze, his hand poised motionless above the dice.

"Do not turn," Morgin said. "If you value your life, remain seated and place your hands flat on the table."

The Kull did so, without speaking.

Morgin asked, "Where is the Elhiyne lordling?"

The Kull said, "I do not value my life that much."

Morgin had no answer to that. The Kulls were infamous for their lack of fear. What inducement could he offer the Kull, what threat? Threats were reputedly the only thing a Kull understood, but if you couldn't threaten his life, what could you threaten?

Morgin concentrated on his magic. This had to be done carefully or he might alert Valso to his whereabouts. He devoted every thought to control, allowing a hint of power to pass from his fingers into his sword. The power glowed an eerie red as it traveled down the blade; it passed the Kull's shoulder, made the hairs on the back of his neck stand on end, then sparkled to extinction on the tip of the sword just within the Kull's view.

Morgin whispered, "And how much do you value your eternal soul, halfman?"

The guard sat silent for a long moment, then spoke. "The Elhiyne is in the second cell from this end."

"And the key?" Morgin asked.

"Hanging near the door."

Morgin lifted his blade and smashed the hilt of the sword into the back of the halfman's head. The Kull slumped forward on the table.

Morgin shot across the room, pulled the key off the wall, unlocked the heavy wooden door and threw it open. He stepped into the darkened cell; the stench of human waste and decay assaulted his nose. He peered blindly into the darkness, but before he could speak, a charging body tackled him from the side and threw him hard against a wall. Rough hands closed about his throat in a viselike grip and tightened. "Filthy Decouix!" MichaelOff snarled.

Morgin fought to speak, managed to squeak out, "Cousin."

The hands released him and he could breathe again. In the black darkness of the cell they touched his face, feeling for recognition. "Morgin. Is that you?"

"It's me."

"Ah Morgin!" MichaelOff said. "Thank the gods you've come. I'd given up hope."

"We have to get out of here," Morgin said, "and quickly." He stepped out of MichaelOff's grasp, charged out of the cell to the unconscious Kull still slumped at the table. "Help me with this Kull," he hissed as he gripped the halfman under the armpits. He intended to tie and gag the fellow and lock him in a cell.

MichaelOff didn't follow immediately and Morgin turned back to him angrily. There, stumbling out of the open cell, a blind man felt his way uncertainly along the wall. Where there had once been eyes there were now horribly scarred pits, the result of a red-hot poker.

"Morgin," the blind man said in MichaelOff's voice. "You must guide me. I cannot see."

"Cousin," Morgin cried, turning back and gripping MichaelOff by the shoulders. "What have they done to you?"

MichaelOff said, "Valso had his pleasure with me, and someday I hope to return the favor. But for now, you will be my guide, and I'll do as you say. What is our destination?"

Morgin looked into the not-eyes of MichaelOff-the-strong. "The old castle. Where we used to play as boys."

"An excellent choice. Let's go."

MichaelOff strangled the Kull guard, and they stuffed his body into an empty cell. They closed and locked the cell, then hung the keys back in their proper place. Hopefully, they'd have a little time before the Kulls discovered MichaelOff's escape.

••••

As they worked their way slowly through the castle, Morgin detoured once to steal MichaelOff a cloak. Like his own it was some Kull's: gray-black, heavy, warm. At one point, as they passed Roland's study, MichaelOff grabbed Morgin's shoulders and said frantically, "Cousin. Do you remember the two crossed broadswords above the mantle in your father's study?"

"Yes," Morgin said.

"Get one for me. Please."

"But you can't—" Morgin closed his mouth, embarrassed.

MichaelOff smiled without eyes. "I can't fight, you were about to say. And blind as I am, you're right. But with all these Kulls about, a sword in my hands would give me comfort."

Morgin retrieved the sword. They continued, and throughout that slow journey MichaelOff held it tightly to his breast, clutching it as if he was a small child with a toy that might be taken from him at any moment. Morgin wanted to comfort him, but no words or deeds would bring back his eyes, and short of a miracle, anything else seemed hollow and meaningless.

The hideout Morgin had chosen was adequate: a small room located deep within the old castle. A thick layer of dust covered the floor, muffling their footsteps. Morgin suspected that millennia had passed since these halls had seen light of any kind. He had chosen the hideout not for its size, or for its comfort, but for its great distance from the nearest lighted hall.

He and MichaelOff sat cross-legged in the dust to rest. MichaelOff held the broadsword in both hands with its tip on the floor before him. He sat unmoving, unspeaking, lost in his own thoughts. Morgin too chose silence.

MichaelOff startled him when he spoke. "Are we in the dark, cousin?"

"I can make light if you want," Morgin said.

MichaelOff shook his head. "Don't bother. You like the dark, while the rest of us fear it. Why is that?"

"I don't know," Morgin said. He felt a tear roll down his cheek, and he tried to hide the quiver in his voice. "When I was Rat the dark was my home. It protected me from the people in the streets. I was in danger only when they could catch me, and they needed light for that."

MichaelOff laughed. "You love the dark. And like others I fear it. And here I sit, condemned to my fear for eternity."

"Why did they do this to you?" Morgin asked.

"The Decouix tortured me for his own pleasure."

MichaelOff sat up straight. "Promise me something, cousin."

"Anything."

"If you ever hold Valso's life in your hands . . . take it. Not for me, but for those yet to feel the pain of his evil. Promise me this one thing, Morgin. Promise me."

"You have my word," Morgin said. "But how did you come into Valso's hands?"

"Sheer stupidity and pride. Oh cousin! I wish I had eyes to cry." MichaelOff buried his face in one hand, still clutching the sword with the other, sobbing in tearless pain. Morgin quietly shed the tears his cousin could not.

Slowly MichaelOff's sobs ended. He took a deep breath, ran a hand through his hair, then told Morgin of the false messenger, of Illalla's plans, of the Tulalane's treachery. "What fools we were! We were prepared for war, but we failed to anticipate treason, even by the twoname. And with the hostages Valso now holds we dare not storm the castle."

MichaelOff lowered his head, buried his face in the palm of his left hand. His right hand never left the hilt of the broadsword, as if it gave him comfort to clutch it so. He drifted off into his private thoughts and the room fell silent.

Morgin asked, "So you entered the castle to open the gates from within?"

"Aye," MichaelOff said. "We chose such a simple plan. Father, Roland and Tulellcoe helped me form a veil of illusion so I could go undetected. But Valso knew of it all along. He toyed with me, and when he was ready, he and his Kulls sprang their trap. So here I sit, a blind fool, and in the woodland outside father and six hundred men wait for gates that will never open."

Morgin considered the possibilities. Malka and the Elhiyne armsmen must have returned while he lay unconscious in the alcove. Morgin asked, "What of Illalla and his army?"

MichaelOff shook his head. "I don't know. He should already have driven Eglahan out of Yestmark, and be moving down the eastern side of the Worshipers now. He'll probably try to cross at Sa'umbra Gap, and that is where he must be stopped. And since I have failed, father is faced with a terrible dilemma: abandon the women to Valso's evil, or allow Illalla into our heartlands."

"What of the other Lesser Clans?" Morgin asked. "Will they help us?"

MichaelOff shrugged. "Inetka perhaps, though it is the least of the clans and can do little. Of course Penda thinks it can remain forever neutral, that it is our fight, ours alone. And as always the Tosks allow Penda to do their thinking for them. They both hope Decouix will be satisfied with only Elhiyne blood. No, cousin. We are alone in this."

Morgin thought carefully before speaking. "Perhaps you and I together might succeed where you alone failed."

MichaelOff's head snapped up. "What are you saying? Do you mean to open the gates? Valso's Kulls are everywhere."

"I can move us about without detection," Morgin hoped he spoke the truth. "In any case, if we fail, we lose nothing but our own lives. But if we succeed, how will Malka know to be ready?"

"He'll know," MichaelOff said, "from your father. Roland and I are tied by a spell of strong magic. He cannot discern details, only emotion. He won't know you are with me, but he will know of the gates."

"Good," Morgin said. "We'll open the gates, you and I. But we must act soon, before Valso discovers you're missing and triples the guard."

"Then our best chance will be at dawn."

"Very well," Morgin said. "Dawn it is."

15

The Traitor's Reward

"WHERE IS HE?" the Tulalane demanded. "He should be here by now."

Valso casually examined his fingernails. "I am not my father's keeper, twoname. When he does finally arrive you must ask him yourself why he is late."

The Tulalane grunted, then eyed Valso. "Is he late, I wonder, or were you early?"

Valso shrugged. "Perhaps I did move a bit hastily."

"Perhaps you moved a bit hastily," the Tulalane said. "Did you never consider our plans?"

Valso shrugged again. "I move according to my own plans, not those of some power hungry fool."

"That power hungry fool is your father, and your king."

"He will always be my father," Valso said unhappily. "That I cannot change. But when this is done I doubt he will be my king."

"Oh magnificent!" the Tulalane said. "I've waited for this moment for ten years, and you choose now to play your games. Couldn't you have waited another month?"

"I have my reasons for doing what I do," Valso said. "And beware how you speak to me, twoname."

The Tulalane mocked him. "Oh forgive me, my prince. Did I offend you?"

"You go too far, Tulalane." Valso's anger formed a halo about his shoulders and back. His lips curled into a snarl, and his power came upon him.

"Not here, you fool," the Tulalane hissed. "Not with six hundred Elhiyne armsmen waiting outside these walls. Put your petty magic away before it destroys us both."

Valso's confidence faltered and he allowed his magic to dissipate. "So you fear the Elhiynes, eh?"

"I fear nothing. But I know there is a time and place for everything. And I am patient."

Valso frowned. "Not terribly patient when it comes to your reward."

"Only a part of my reward," the Tulalane said, "and a very small part at that. You owe me much, and I demand partial payment now. Otherwise, I'll withdraw my services."

Valso changed the subject. "What have you done about the whoreson?"

"I've got your halfmen patrolling these corridors day and night. That'll force him to move slowly and carefully, and we'll be done with this before he can cause any harm."

"But he's here," Valso said uneasily, "in the castle. I can feel him. I can't locate him because he's using no magic."

"We'll deal with the whoreson when the time comes. For now, we were talking about my reward."

Valso eyed the Tulalane before speaking. "Very well. You will have what you request."

"Now," the Tulalane demanded.

Valso ignored him, turned with a flourish and walked to the door. He paused, looked back and grinned. "As you wish."

••••

Morgin, huddled in a shadow in the antechamber, watched him leave. The shadow in which he hid was much closer to the audience chamber than he'd intended, he'd become absorbed in their conversation and forgotten himself. Nervously he kept an eye on the three Kulls standing with their backs to him in the middle of the room. He decided to wait. There was time, several hours before dawn. It would be interesting to see what reward the Tulalane had chosen.

Earlier Morgin had moved MichaelOff to a spot closer to the occupied wings of the new castle, leaving him to reconnoiter the gates and gatehouse. He'd decided to make a short side trip, because there remained one question yet to be answered: Why had Illalla not arrived on schedule? He'd learned that Valso had acted prematurely. But again the question arose: Why?

Valso was no fool; bloodthirsty yes, and vicious, but not to the point where it clouded his judgment. Why would he risk so much to gain so little? Certainly the Tulalane believed him to be a blood-crazy fool, as did everyone. That bothered Morgin, for he suspected that was exactly what Valso wanted them to think.

Boot steps in the hallway brought Morgin's mind back to the present. He checked his shadowmagic and froze.

Verk and some of his Kullish bullies entered the antechamber escorting Nick-oLot. In her late teens she was a woman now, though she'd always been a small, tiny thing. She stood proudly, back straight, eyes forward, dressed in the finery of an Elhiyne lady. The effect was marred only by the silent tears that rolled down her cheeks, and the slight quiver that shook her chin.

The Kulls halted just outside the audience chamber and Verk turned upon them angrily. "Watch her. She may be small, but she's a witch just the same, and she has a nasty little sting."

He turned back and entered the audience chamber. "The girl is here, my lord."

"Then bring her in."

Verk reappeared, motioned for NickoLot to precede him. "After you, milady," he said. He followed her as she stepped through the portal.

On impulse Morgin stepped into Verk's shadow for an instant, followed him in, then stepped into a shadow against a wall. He changed shadows, moving away from the entrance, then froze.

The Tulalane eyed NickoLot as if looking at a meal. "Leave us, Verk. And close the door." The Kull obeyed.

The Tulalane looked upon NickoLot for a long, silent, hungry moment. She sniffed once, but said nothing.

"You are beautiful, milady," he said. He advanced slowly toward her.

She remained silent.

"I have been an admirer of yours for a long time now."

She frowned, sniffed back another tear.

He stood over her. "You have nothing to fear from me. I can protect you. Valso will not anger me by touching you, not without my permission. When this is done I will be very powerful, and you can share in that power."

Her eyes narrowed. "What do you want?"

"I want you, milady."

She squeaked, took one step back. "No."

The Tulalane stepped toward her. "My proposal is an honorable one, Nicki. I want you as my wife, not as a whore."

She stepped back again. "No. Never."

He advanced. "Think about it. You'll die with all the rest if you turn me down."

She tried to step back again, but found her back against a wall. "Never. I would rather die." She finished by spitting a single word in his face, "Traitor!"

"So!" he said, towering over her. "You would rather die, eh? Well that can be arranged. And believe me, little Elhiyne whore, the dying will not be easy. And like it or not, I will still have you anyway."

He reached toward her, but she ducked beneath his arm and raced for the door, tore it open and shot out of the room, eluding the grasp of the startled Kulls outside.

"Let her go," the Tulalane shouted. "I'll take care of this myself." He followed her, and Morgin followed him.

NickoLot ran through the castle proper, with the Tulalane casually following. His Kullish guards followed him; one of them spoke of enjoying some sport after the inactivity of the past days. Morgin followed in the shadows behind them.

When NickoLot turned toward the inner sanctum Morgin wanted to call to her that it was a dead end, but it was too late. The chase ended in the sanctum, NickoLot cornered, trying to close the heavy stone portal, while the Tulalane casually blocked it with the tip of his boot. "You won't escape me that easily, my little Elhiyne whore."

Morgin stopped in a shadow just outside the portal as the Tulalane gave it a shove, forcing it open and knocking NickoLot to the floor. He laughed, turned to his Kulls. "Wait here. I'm going to have some fun."

As the Tulalane turned and stepped into the sanctum, Morgin picked a shadow fluttering that way and followed, then stepped into a shadow at the edge of the room. The Tulalane turned, put his shoulder to the portal and closed it, sealing the sanctum, though he didn't throw the latch. Then he turned back to NickoLot, who huddled against the far wall. A single, dim brazier lit the twelve-sided room, casting flickering shadows everywhere.

Morgin was having trouble concentrating. The walls of the sanctum were more than a thousand years old, dug up from the ruins of the Great Clan Wars, the only thing left of the old Elhiyne magic. Something there pulled at him and it frightened him.

"Please," NickoLot pleaded as the Tulalane stood over her. She trembled uncontrollably as he reached down with a giant paw and gripped her chin. He bent down and brought his face close to hers. She tried to turn away, but Morgin saw the twoname's fingers press tighter into her jaw. His lips met hers, and at the same time his free hand groped at her small breasts.

Without warning sparks flashed between them. The Tulalane screamed and jumped back. "Elhiyne bitch!" he snarled, and he struck out. The room echoed with a slap that sent her sprawling to the floor in a heap of lace and petticoats. With one hand he grabbed her by the front of her dress and lifted her up. Snarling, he raised the other hand high to deliver another blow.

The power in the room had addled Morgin's thinking, but the fear on NickoLot's face jogged him out of his immobility. He stepped out of shadow, and in the same motion swung his sword through a high flat arc. It chopped through the wrist of the Tulalane's raised hand like a cleaver cutting through a shank of meat. The Tulalane's severed hand jumped high in the air. He screamed as it dropped to the floor, and as Morgin's momentum carried him past the Tulalane he grabbed a hand full of petticoats and swung NickoLot into a nearby shadow. He turned to face the wizard swordmaster.

The Tulalane grasped the stump of his sword arm with his left hand. It spurted blood as he shook with fury and pain, glaring at Morgin. But then his quivering shoulders calmed and the grimace left his face, replaced by a snarl that turned into an evil grin. He stood up straight, concentrated on the severed stump, and the spurting blood slowed, then ceased altogether. The stump glowed, at first faintly, but as the glow increased in strength and size, it took on shape. Detail came slowly, an eerie process that progressed until the glow disappeared and a phantom hand remained, visible by a vague, shimmering outline.

The Tulalane's grin broadened. He flexed the phantom fingers, then reached down with the unreal hand and drew his sword. It hissed with the scrape of steel as it slid from the sheath. His grin turned into a snarl of delight. "So the boy thinks he is a man," he said, then flashed his sword right and left to test his new hand. "This is going to be your last lesson, boy. We'll see how much of a man you are, then we'll see how well you die." The Tulalane growled, lowered into a crouch and advanced purposefully.

Morgin crouched also, holding his sword in front of him, facing the Tulalane and backing away. Not in his wildest dreams would he have considered facing the twoname, but when he'd seen the pain in NickoLot's face, and realized the rape that was intended, his sword had leapt in his hands as if it had a mind of its own.

The Tulalane struck his first blow, and again with a mind of its own Morgin's sword met it. Morgin gripped his sword with both hands as the two blades rang together. At the next stroke he felt the crash reverberate up his arms, numbing them to the elbows. Instinctively he deflected the next blow, then disengaged and stepped back several paces.

"You don't like that, do you boy?" the Tulalane said. He closed the gap between them in a single bound, swung his sword in a long sweeping arc.

Morgin ducked, barely able to elude the blade as it hissed past his nose. He met the next blow, the steel in his hands screamed and he felt the clash in his shoulders. He retreated desperately, back-stepping again, hoping to escape the wizard's bloodlust.

The Tulalane gripped his sword in both hands. Each blow Morgin met cost him dearly as he staggered under its impact. The Tulalane grinned and toyed with Morgin, played with him like a cat with a mouse. He batted Morgin's sword aside and raised his own well above his head for the kill. Morgin, his numbed hands barely able to hold his own sword, watched the Tulalane's blade descend in an agonizingly slow arc. In that instant lightning flashed from the other side of the sanctum, crackled and sizzled against the Tulalane's back. NickoLot had joined the battle.

The Tulalane stumbled. His blow faltered. Morgin seized the opportunity, ducked beneath it, turned, and melted into the shadows that lined the walls. He changed shadows, then froze. The air smelled of burnt flesh and singed hair.

The Tulalane raged, stood in the light cast by the single brazier and swung his sword blindly about. But then he stopped, scanned the room and his attention settled on the shadow where NickoLot hid. He slapped the only table in the room aside as if it were made of paper, then advanced.

Morgin moved quickly around the edge of the room, creating shadows as he moved and slipping into them.

The Tulalane stopped, stood over NickoLot's shadow while she uttered a childish whimper, then raised his sword. In that moment Morgin plowed into him at a full run, and as they both went down he made sure that his own weight landed full force on the magician. They hit the stone floor; the Tulalane grunted as Morgin bounced off him, and Morgin scrambled to his feet. He stepped into the security of the nearest shadow, changed shadows several times, then froze. The Tulalane groaned, and as he struggled to his feet the only sound that broke the silence was the scrape of his boot on the stone floor.

"Bastard Elhiyne!" he cursed, staggering about the room. "Stand out here and fight like a man. Whoreson. Coward."

Morgin held his breath, pressed his spine hard against the stone wall. His back tingled with power and he shivered at the thought there might be some magic waiting in the stone. He tasted it, realized it was everywhere, almost alive in its own right, menacing in its strength, permeating everything about the sanctum, waiting, watching, hoping.

Morgin changed shadows, tried not to think about power. The stone was tainted with it, and it called to him, a beckoning desire that he feared he could not withstand. It was his heritage as an Elhiyne, his ancestry as Shahot. It was more than a thousand years of the exercise of power, waiting to be used by whoever had the strength to contain it.

He reached out tentatively, touched it with his magic, picking at it, afraid to simply reach out and take it up. But it came unbound, falling forth in a cascade that overwhelmed him. He fought it, gasping for breath as it swept him away, power flooding through every thread of his soul. He barely had the presence of mind to duck as the Tulalane's sword hissed past his face. He staggered into the center of the room.

"Your family's power won't save you now, boy," the magician said, then lunged at him.

Morgin swung his sword outward. It met the magician's blade with a screaming flash of power and drove the twoname backwards. The Tulalane back-stepped, surprise on his face.

Morgin's first inclination was to retreat into shadow, but he'd gained some advantage and pressed it now by attacking. He swung his sword with both hands, backing the Tulalane across the room, their battle no longer a test of physical strength, but now of magical power.

The Tulalane halted, brought forth the last of his power in an effort to overwhelm him. Morgin staggered under the force of the attack and fell back, his own sword seeming to work against him. It pulled at his grip like a wild animal striving to break free. He stepped into a shadow, changed from one to the next, and came out at the Tulalane's side. He stopped fighting the sword and swung it with all the power at his command.

The magician, taken by surprise, parried the stroke clumsily. Morgin saw an opening and brought his sword viciously upward. It bucked in his hands, then bit into the Tulalane's side, cutting into the magician's chest, crunching ribs, stopping only when it came up against his spine.

The Tulalane froze with his sword high above his head, Morgin's sword buried to the hilt in his chest. They both stood there stunned, eyes wide in amazement, as the

Tulalane's half severed torso began to flow red with blood. The phantom hand disappeared; his sword clattered to the floor and the stump of his wrist again spurted blood.

The Tulalane looked down at his chest. He concentrated, and the blood welling from the mortal wound there slowed, then stopped altogether. His grin returned.

Morgin cried, "Noooooooooo!" He raised his boot, planted it squarely in the center of the wizard's chest, and gripping the hilt of his sword he pulled with all his might and kicked out.

The Tulalane staggered backward as the sword slid from his chest. His concentration broken, his magic slipped away. The blood flowed once more from his wrist and his chest, and with a look of surprise, the magician toppled forward like a great tree axed down in the forest. He landed on his face, bounced once, dust scattering in all directions. And with the passing of Lord Hwatok Tulalane, silence reigned in the twelve-sided room.

16

Sword Magic

MORGIN REELED WITH the Elhiyne power flooding through his soul, and stared dumbly at the dead Tulalane. A noise startled him. He spun to find Verk, the Kull commander, standing at the open portal, eyes wide with amazement. Morgin's sword leapt for the Kull's throat, but Verk moved quickly, ducked and backed out of the room, pulling desperately on the door. Morgin slammed into the portal, leaned heavily against it, heard Verk shout, "Get reinforcements. It's the Elhiyne wizard." The door closed with a heavy thud. Morgin pounded the latch in place with his fist, and again silence filled the room.

"Oh Morgin!" NickoLot cried tearfully. She jumped to her feet and ran to him, buried her face in his tunic, wrapped her arms around him and sobbed uncontrollably. "I was so afraid, Morgin. I was so afraid."

Morgin shook with power, barely kept it contained. He could do no more than pat the back of her head comfortingly. With a visible effort she stopped crying, pulled her face away from his chest and looked up, staring at him as if she now feared him.

He released her, crossed the room to the overturned table. "There's no time to explain," he said. "You must do as I say."

"Yes, Morgin," she said. She choked back her tears and frowned at him.

He slid the table up against a wall and stuffed her down behind it. "Hide here, curl up and be silent. I'm going to draw the Kulls away. If I can divert their attention they may forget about you."

"Are you going to die?" she asked.

"No. I won't die."

She looked at him and started crying again. "You're lying to me. I can hear it in your voice, and you've got the godlight in your eyes like grandmother. Oh Morgin, don't die. Please don't die."

Morgin pulled her tightly against his chest and let her cry. He muttered something reassuring, reaching back in his memory to find the words AnnaRail had used when he needed comforting. Her sobbing slowed, and finally she got control of herself.

He had to move quickly, before Verk returned with reinforcements. "Stay here," he said. "Curl up on the floor and hide behind the table."

"Yes, Morgin."

He left her there, stepped up to the massive stone door and eyed its simple iron handle. He cast spells to banish fear, to give him strength. The Elhiyne power that flooded his soul threatened to overwhelm him. He took a deep breath, cast a strong spell of shadow and tried not to think of death, though he knew it awaited him in the room beyond. But he must try, even if only to take a few of them with him to death's gate.

Shaking with fear, he reached up and quietly undid the latch that held the door. He held his sword in his right hand and clutched the door's handle with his left. He tensed his muscles, leaned far back and pulled with all his weight. The heavy stone door came toward him slowly, and as it did so he used its mass to propel him through the opening that appeared.

With no battle cry, he stepped among the Kulls silently, his sword gripped in both hands as he swung it through a hissing arc, a shadow dancing among his enemies. The first Kull went down before the rest even realized that death danced among them. The second fared no better, but as he turned upon the third the surprise ended and pandemonium exploded about him.

He chopped an arm, kicked a crotch, bashed a head with the hilt of his sword. He saw an opening, thrust into it with the point; saw another opening, cut down with the blade, and while he fought, France's words echoed through his head: "If you ever stand alone against many with no escape, stay in the thick of it. They will have to care for their fellows, but you can kill to your heart's content."

Morgin ducked beneath a stroke that hissed past his ear, saw an open knee and kicked at it. The room filled with cries of pain and anger. He stepped into a shadow, changed directions, stepped out again. His life narrowed to a world of slashing steel and hacking death, and slowly, inevitably, he weakened. But as his muscles grew weary his sword seemed strangely lighter, as if it swung with a will of its own.

Morgin saw a face, kicked it. He saw an arm, chopped it. He parried a stroke from a Kull saber, ducked beneath another as a heavy boot crashed into his ribs. He gasped, stumbled beneath a sword stroke, and parried the next one clumsily. He stepped away from it off balance, falling, knowing that once down he would not again rise. He watched helplessly as a Kull saber descended toward his face, knowing he was about to die. But then his own sword leapt to meet the Kull's, and Morgin, holding desperately to its hilt with both hands, was lifted miraculously to his feet.

He stood there for a moment in stunned disbelief, staring at the blade as it vibrated in his hands. It glowed and hummed with power, and moved with a strength of its own. It slashed out and deflected a Kull's saber with such force it knocked the half-man's sword from his hands, then it cut him in two. Morgin tried to control it, but the sword fought on, dragging him along helplessly behind it. He fought with all of his strength just to hold on, for it cut with a might far beyond his own. The battle became a rout. The few Kulls that remained retreated in confusion, but their only escape led back into the sanctum, and there they were cornered.

The sword pulled Morgin in after them, and he felt as if he were holding onto the tail of a wild animal mad with bloodlust. His arms ached, and he feared that if he lost hold of the sword, it would turn upon him and butcher him as readily as the halfmen. The Kulls fought back desperately, but the sword cut them to pieces, hacking, chopping, dismembering, throwing Morgin from side to side as if he were no more than a decorative tassel tied to its hilt. Then his grip failed, and for an instant he spun crazily through the air before he slammed up against a stone wall and lost consciousness.

••••

Morgin came to laying on something that felt like a dead Kull. He opened his eyes and saw red everywhere. As he lifted his weight off the halfman he realized it was just a piece of the Kull: head, neck, right shoulder and arm. Splatters of blood dripped from the walls and puddled on the floor.

A deep hum filled his ears, a vibration he felt in his bones. He raised a hand to shield his eyes from an intense red light in the center of the sanctum. He peered carefully through slitted fingers, saw his sword floating well above the floor, its point aimed toward the heavens. It hummed, vibrated, pulsed with power, waiting for him to move.

He moved slowly as he climbed to his feet. He had to choose his footing carefully to keep from slipping in blood, or tripping over parts of Kulls that littered the floor. He tried to work his way around the edge of the room toward the entrance, staying well clear of the sword and close to the wall. But as he approached the portal the sword moved, blocking his path. He tried moving around to the other side, and it did the same. It seemed not to threaten him; it merely floated in front of his face, waiting.

He could think of nothing better to do so he reached out and gingerly wrapped his fingers about the hilt. He stood for a moment, waiting for something to happen, but nothing did. He pulled on it, and it resisted. He pulled harder, and it resisted harder. He pulled with all his might, almost lifting his feet off the floor, and then whatever force held it up let go, sending him sprawling among the carnage.

He lay there for a moment in the flickering shadows cast by the brazier. The sword had gone silent and its light had vanished. In his hand it seemed now to be a steel sword and nothing more.

He heard Nicki gasp, saw her rising up from behind the table.

"Nicki, no," he cried, jumping to his feet. But he slipped in a pool of blood and landed on his butt.

He scrambled to his feet and rushed toward her, but she backed away from him and started screaming. He realized that he too was covered in blood, and must appear to be a monstrous specter from netherhell. Thankfully, she fainted and crumpled to the floor in a heap.

He couldn't allow her to wake up and start screaming again, so he cast a sleep spell on her, picked her up, enveloped them both in shadow, and left the sanctum.

As he stepped out of the sanctum's antechamber he heard boots thudding on the stone floor, the sound of a group of armsmen coming his way. He stepped into a shadow against the wall and froze. Verk and a twelve of his halfmen rushed past him.

It took every bit of shadow skill he had to get Nicki up to her bedroom. He stuffed her under her bed, reinforced the sleep spell, cast a separate shadow spell upon her, then headed for the old castle.

••••

"MichaelOff," Morgin hissed. "It's me. Morgin."

MichaelOff relaxed. He lowered the broadsword. "I heard the commotion and feared you'd been discovered."

"No," Morgin said. "I'm safe. But I had to kill the Tulalane and some Kulls. The gates can no longer wait for dawn. We must move now, while there's still confusion. Can you make my father aware?"

"I think so. I've been concentrating on Roland's image since I first heard cries from the castle proper, trying to convey a sense of urgency."

"Does he know, then?" Morgin asked. "Will they be ready with so little warning?"

"I can answer neither question. The magical bond that connects us is tenuous at best."

Morgin hesitated, tempted to abandon their quest and seek refuge in the old castle, perhaps open the gates at another time, but he realized that would be foolish. "We'll have to assume he understands." He took MichaelOff's hand and started for the gatehouse.

They moved through the castle night, aware that once the general confusion dissipated, there would be little chance of succeeding. MichaelOff stayed close, using his magic to anticipate Morgin's moves while Morgin tried to keep them both enveloped in shadow. They had decided upon two simple signals. If Morgin squeezed MichaelOff's hand with force, it was a sign to freeze in place and be still, to wait until the next squeeze before continuing. The other signal was less complicated. If they were discovered, surrounded by Kulls with no escape, Morgin would give the word, they would stand back to back, and die fighting together as kinsmen. Luckily that was never called for, though Morgin found it necessary to use the first signal several times before they reached the gatehouse.

There were three guards in the small room that housed the wheel that pulled the chains that opened the main gates. Two peered out a window while the third sat watching the entrance through which Morgin must pass. Shouts, cries and the sounds of pandemonium echoed up from the castle proper. One of the Kulls standing at the window said, "Wonder what all the ruckus is about?"

The other answered, "Bet one of them Elhiyne whores tried to kill Valso again."

The one seated said, "More likely the Tulalane tried to kill him. There's bad magic between those two."

The seated Kull looked toward the two at the window. Morgin took that opportunity to slip through the doorway and into a shadow within. "Aye," one of the two at the window said. "One of those two will kill the other before this is done."

Morgin worked his way along the wall to a point behind the seated Kull. It was a small room; he could easily reach all three with a step and swing of his sword. But he knew he couldn't kill them quickly enough to prevent an outcry. Standing there undecided, his sword made the decision for him. Without warning it leapt in his hand, left him no choice but to follow, and before he realized what had happened, all three lay dead at his feet.

He wasted no time pondering dead Kulls. He retrieved MichaelOff from the hallway, closed the door to the room, upturned a small table and wedged it tightly beneath the door handle. It would not hold against a determined effort, but it might buy them a few precious moments. MichaelOff, long familiar with the room, had found the gate wheel by touch and stood now with his hands upon it. Luckily, the portcullis was already up, so the gates were their only obstacle.

Morgin stepped up to the small window and peered out at the yard below. They were on the second floor just above the porch roof. The yard was empty. The only sounds were muffled cries coming from within the castle proper.

He climbed out onto the roof tiles, careful to make no sound since there might be a guard on the porch below. He held tightly to the windowsill and whispered to MichaelOff, "Wait one hundred beats of your heart, then open the gates as fast as you can."

MichaelOff left the wheel, groped his way to the window. He took Morgin's hand and placed it against his breast. "If your heart beats like mine this night, then the count of one hundred will come all too soon."

MichaelOff's heart pounded a staccato beat of adrenaline and fear against Morgin's hand. "Three hundred beats then," Morgin said.

MichaelOff held onto Morgin's hand tightly and for a moment would not release it. "Cousin," he said. He wrinkled his brow, turned his head as if to sense a distant sound beyond Morgin's hearing. "I think we'll not meet again, Morgin, not in this life, not in peace."

"Don't speak that way," Morgin hissed. "We'll protect each other."

"Yes," MichaelOff agreed. "We will defeat the Decouixs. And if I am lucky, I will die now, fighting like a man. I could not bear to spend the rest of my life led around like a blind pet on a leash, only half a man."

"Promise me you'll do nothing foolish."

MichaelOff said, "Don't worry, little cousin." He leaned forward and kissed Morgin gently on the cheek. "Fare you well, Morgin. And guard your back."

"Fare you well," Morgin said. He turned, tiptoed along the roof tiles, counting his own heart beats and wiping tears from his eyes. He reached the count of one hundred as he came to the end of the porch roof. He dropped to the ground below, stepped into a shadow and froze. There came no cry, no alarm, no call to arms.

He moved within the shadows at the edge of the yard, working his way slowly toward the main gates. All remained still and quiet. He reached the count of two hundred just as he stepped up to the gates. He scanned the castle yard cautiously, saw no one there. He stuck the tip of his sword in the dirt, grasped the pegs protruding from the heavy wooden beam that locked the gates, and pulled. It took all his strength, and he grunted with the effort, but the beam slid heavily to one side.

"You're so predictable," Valso said.

In one motion Morgin grabbed his sword and spun about. He and Valso stood facing one another surrounded by Kulls. Valso grinned. "So you would open the gates, would you?"

Morgin's heart climbed up into his throat. He'd lost count of its beats. There were at least twenty Kulls, far more than he'd fought in the sanctum. He waited to feel the vibration in the sword's hilt, to hear the hum of its power, but in his hands it remained no more than a piece of steel.

"Well," Valso said. "Now that you've unlocked the gates, you must gain the gatehouse. Or do you expect the gates to open themselves?"

At that moment the gates creaked loudly as they began to swing open. Valso spun and looked up toward the gatehouse; his Kulls turned to follow his gaze. Morgin seized the moment, raised his sword high, shouted at the top of his lungs, and with nowhere else to go, charged at Valso.

A Kull saber got in his way. He sidestepped, missed Valso completely, crashed into a Kull, ricocheted off the halfman and into another. He and several of them sprawled into the dust of the yard. He rolled out of the confusion, concentrated all of his power into a shadow spell, sprang to his feet and slipped into the shadows of the porch.

"Where is he?" a Kull cried.

"Forget him," Valso said. "To the gatehouse. And quickly."

The Kulls ran for the stairs that led to the parapets. Morgin moved through the shadows of the porch, got there an instant before them and cut down the first to arrive, then stepped back into another shadow. The next, only an instant behind, took Morgin's second thrust in the throat. Morgin changed shadows, but now warned, the third Kull stopped several paces short of any shadows near the stairs. He crouched low and looked carefully from side to side. Hidden within his shadows Morgin remained still.

Valso stood cockily in the center of the yard. He sniffed the air like a dog, turned around slowly until he faced Morgin's shadow, and Morgin realized he'd pushed too much power into his shadowmagic, had given himself away. Valso pointed a finger and lightning arced outward from his hand, struck Morgin squarely in the face. He staggered, almost lost consciousness, alive only by virtue of his own power. Valso's lightning struck again, and his world narrowed to a hazy vision of blurred shapes as he stumbled into the center of the yard swinging his sword blindly.

"Kill him quickly," Valso said, "and be done with him. Then to the gatehouse."

The Kulls closed in. Morgin back-stepped, bracing himself for the sword cut that would take his life. But MichaelOff's bloodcurdling cry stopped them all. "Decouix," he shouted from high above on the porch roof, having crawled out through the gatehouse window.

Morgin glanced over his shoulder, saw that MichaelOff had opened the gates wide enough to admit mounted riders.

MichaelOff cried, "Now you die, Decouix." He gripped the great broadsword with both hands and stood alight with power, his deathmagic glowing like a beacon in the night. He jumped from the roof, landed in the midst of the Kulls, his eyes glowing pits of power, the sword in his hands singing a song of death.

Morgin tried to fight his way toward him to help, but there were too many Kull sabers blocking his way. He side stepped a thrust, back-stepped, swung his sword through a flat arc, back-stepped again. MichaelOff fought without quarter, but little by little they cut him to pieces, and he died in the castle yard as he had chosen to die, while the battle forced Morgin slowly back through the open gates of Elhiyne and out onto the road.

He heard hoof beats on the road behind him. He side-stepped a Kull saber, turned, ducked beneath an Elhiyne saber wielded by a rider on a charging mount. He tried to shout that he was not some Kull, but the cries of battle were too loud. He dodged another Elhiyne saber, then straightened up in the path of a charging steed. He had one instant in which to realize it was not humanly possible to evade the animal, then the world disappeared in a blinding collision . . .

••••

A faint glow on the horizon hinted at the coming dawn as a lone figure moved cautiously through the darkness of the castle yard. He lurked in the shadows beneath the parapets, advancing steadily toward the castle's main gates. The triumphant cries of Elhiyne warriors pierced the night as they hunted down the last of the Kulls. In the yard the only sounds were the occasional moan of a wounded clansman, or a grunt as a disabled Kull was given the death stroke.

Valso moved hastily, conscious that he must be well away before the Elhiynes managed to restore order. He must get past the guard at the gates and into the open fields. At least the damaged gates and portcullis were open. MichaelOff, damn his soul, had done considerable damage to the mechanism that ruled their closing. They were open, and only a single guard stood in Valso's way.

Valso edged closer. He clutched his dagger in one hand and shielded it from view with the other, for it glowed in the dark with a magic more deadly than any earthly venom. His heart beat rapidly in anticipation of the kill, though the erection in his pants distracted him badly. He concentrated on the mechanics of killing the guard, tried not to think of the death itself, sweet, glorious death. As he thought of the kill his excitement grew, until he literally shook with murderous desire. He struggled against it, knowing that he must be swift; he denied himself the pleasure of tearing the guard limb from limb in an orgy of death.

The opportunity came and he moved. The knife flashed through the night and the guard died instantly. The magical poison Valso had conjured worked so swiftly the guard uttered not the slightest sound. Valso paused over the body, savoring the thrill of death, disappointed only by its swiftness. He struggled to look away, scanned the castle yard quickly to confirm that he remained undiscovered, then turned and vanished into the night.

17

The Question of Honor

THE SKELETON KING ambled up the road toward Castle Elhiyne like a frail, old man, using the magnificent, rune inlaid sword as a cane. About him scampered a small child, dressed in an array of filthy and torn rags. False dawn had arrived, the sun still hidden behind the mountains to the east, barely throwing enough light to illuminate the landscape. The ditch by the side of the road was filled with a thick mist that hid anything within it.

The skeleton king stopped at a certain spot and looked down at the mist-filled ditch. To no one in particular he said, "He's here."

He turned to the rag-draped child. "Rat, go find his sword."

The small child turned to one side, as if there was no question in his mind where to find the battered old blade. He disappeared into the mist, then reappeared a moment later, dragging the blade behind him across the road.

As he approached, the skeleton king reached down, lifted the sword by its hilt, then eased gingerly down into the mist of the ditch. He knelt and reached down into the mist, said, "Yes, he's here." He laid the sword down carefully.

He stood, turned to the small child. "Here, Rat, help an old man out of this ditch."

With the child's help, he climbed awkwardly out of the ditch. He paused over SarahGirl's carcass, still lying in the middle of the road and beginning to bloat. The skeleton king shook his head. "Come, Rat. We'll have to get him a new mount."

He turned to the castle, ambled toward its damaged gates. With the child scampering in his wake he said over his shoulder, "Yes, a new mount. A special mount. One equal to the ordeal that awaits him."

••••

Morgin became conscious first of a demanding throb in the back of his head, then of his arm, twisted painfully at an odd angle beneath him. He rolled off the arm and grimaced as a sharp pain shot through his elbow and shoulder. He gasped, lay on his back until the pain dissipated, and when it was bearable a quick examination by touch told him his arm wasn't broken.

He opened his eyes, could see only a strange, white mist surrounding him. He wondered for a moment if he had died and gone to some afterlife, but then he sat up and his head rose above the mist that filled the ditch. He saw the sun rising over the mountains and realized it was just after dawn. He scanned his surroundings carefully; dead Kulls were strewn about like broken dolls. He looked for his kinsmen among the dead, but the Elhiynes had had the advantage of charging cavalry against foot soldiers, and only Kulls littered the landscape.

He felt something lying hidden within the mist at his side, and even before he lifted it above the swirling gray haze his hand told him it was his sword. He clutched the hilt, climbed slowly to his feet, stood knee deep in mist, and swayed for a moment unsteadily. He didn't think he'd been unconscious for more than a few hours, but during that time the damp cold had worked its way deep into his bones. He looked down at himself, covered from head to foot in a brown layer of dried and caked blood, dusted with the dirt of the castle yard, splattered with mud from the ditch, all mingling with the mixed sweats of exertion and fear.

He climbed stiffly out of the ditch, up onto the dirt road. He backtracked up the road a short distance to poor SarahGirl's carcass, now stiff and lifeless. It took an effort to pull his sheath from beneath her weight, but he managed it. He wiped his sword on his sleeve, sheathed it, turned toward the castle and limped toward its open gates.

"Halt and identify yourself," someone called from the battlements above, "or die where you stand."

Morgin was careful not to move. "I am Morgin ye AethonLaw et Elhiyne, son of Roland and AnnaRail."

There was a muffled conference above. "Wait there," the voice on the parapets said. "And move not a muscle."

Morgin stood shivering in the cold dawn air. After a time the voice said, "All right. Come forward. But move slowly, and if you love life keep your hand away from the hilt of that sword."

Morgin did as he was told, careful not to make any quick movements as he walked through the gates. He was greeted by a dozen men armed with crossbows. More than a few of them shook with taut nerves and tired muscles.

Among them stood Avis. "It's Lord Morgin, all right," he said. He stepped forward and bowed slightly. The bowmen hesitated until he turned back to them. "There is no doubt. I've known him since he was a child."

The crowd of bowmen dissipated, leaving Morgin and Avis alone. Morgin saw more dead Kulls strewn about the castle yard, with an occasional corpse respectfully covered by a blanket and marked with a bit of Elhiyne red.

"Who are the strange bowmen?" Morgin asked.

"They're armsmen from the west," Avis said, "sent by March Lord Alcoa to aid us."

Nicki! Morgin thought. He spun toward Avis. "NickoLot?"

Avis eyes saddened. "We haven't found her, my lord. We fear the worst."

He gripped the servant by his shoulders. "She's under her bed, protected by a sleep spell and a shadow spell. Let's go there now."

Avis looked at him oddly, then shook his head. "The Lady Olivia commanded me to wait here for your arrival. She sends instructions that you are to join her immediately in the Hall of Wills. I'll tell Lady AnnaRail what you just told me, but I'll not be able to join the search for NickoLot myself."

The Hall of Wills was crowded beyond capacity. Many hovered anxiously in the surrounding corridors, mostly strangers among whom Morgin saw only a few familiar faces. He elbowed his way delicately past the crowd at the entrance, received several unhappy glances. He took a position against the wall just within the Hall, where he watched Olivia, seated on her throne, speaking to AnnaRail, who stood before her in the only clear spot in the room.

"You have been in contact with Eglahan?" the old witch asked.

"Yes, mother."

"And?"

"And," AnnaRail continued, "he reports that he can no longer delay Illalla and his army. He's done his best to harass him, to slow him, but Illalla moves ever south. Eglahan estimates they will battle for Yestmark as the sun rises tomorrow."

"And what are Eglahan's prospects for victory?"

AnnaRail shook her head. "Poor at best. He has six hundred men of his own, and he will soon have the six hundred we've sent him, and yet is still outnumbered ten to one. It is not a matter of winning or losing, merely of how long they can fight before they must yield."

"And how long can he hold?"

"One day of battle. Two if luck is with him."

Something drew Morgin's eyes to Malka, who sat woodenly beside Olivia, his left arm nothing but a bandaged stump, missing above the elbow. Then he looked more closely and realized that Malka's eyes were not focused, that his skin reflected a chalky white pallor.

"Grandson." Olivia's voice cut across the room like a knife. Morgin turned to her, found her now looking directly at him.

"So you have chosen to join us," she said. "Come. Step forward where I can see you better."

An aisle parted in the crowd before Morgin. He stepped forward warily, for he well knew that tone of voice, and it always bode ill.

She spoke sharply, almost spitting her words. "How was your stay in the forest?"

"It was restful," Morgin said, thinking of his days camping in the foothills of the Worshipers.

"Restful? With Kulls sniffing about at all hours? But then you always were good at hiding." For a moment he thought that was all she would say, but then as an afterthought she said, ". . . and running."

As always, her meaning eluded him. Morgin said, "There seems to be a misunderstanding—"

"Do you deny running from Valso?"

"No. I—"

"Do you deny hiding in the forest to save your precious hide?"

"No. But I—"

"Silence, coward," she said coldly. "You're not fit to call yourself of Elhiyne. If the Tulalane were alive I would not insult him by hanging the both of you from the same gallows."

"But it was I who killed the Tulalane. I—"

"And how could you have killed the Tulalane when you were hiding in that forest? MichaelOff killed the Tulalane. There was no one else here who could have done that."

"But MichaelOff and I—"

"MichaelOff died at the gates while you hid in the woodland to save your own life. Don't even speak his name. Don't you dare try to claim his victory as your own, coward."

Roland stepped out of the crowd. "Mother, please!"

She cut him off. "Silence. This time I will stand for no interference. I command it." Her power sparked, and no one dared disobey her. "For your cowardice I banish you from Elhiyne. You have the burning of one small candle to be gone from these walls and this valley. If you are not, I will order your death myself. And after that, any man who brings me your head will be handsomely rewarded. Now get out of my sight."

"But I—"

She pointed at two armsmen. "You and you. Escort him to the stables, get him on a horse and get him out of here. If he dallies or tries to go anywhere else, beat him into unconsciousness, then tie him in the saddle and send the horse on its way." She spit her final words in a staccato beat of rage. "It's time we rid ourselves of this whoreson."

Morgin staggered back a step. He'd always known that among many clansmen he would ever be the whoreson. But never had he thought to hear that word from someone who called herself family. Rhianne had certainly betrayed them all because of his tainted blood, a blemish she must feel would always hinder her ambitions. And now he saw how far that stain had blinded them all. He slowly looked about the throng assembled in the room, and in every eye he saw Rat reflected in one distasteful grimace after another. None of them would—could—hear anything he might say in his own defense.

The two armsmen marched across the hall and took positions on either side of him. Into the hush that filled the room he said, "I am no coward." Then he turned his back on the clan and walked from the hall.

Avis met him in the corridor. "My lord, I relayed your message about Lady Nick-oLot to Lady AnnaRail."

"Thank you."

The servant continued. "I was instructed to hold a horse ready for your departure. It's saddled and fully provisioned."

Morgin marched past him with the two armsmen in his wake, but the servant called out to him, "My lord?"

Morgin stopped, turned and demanded angrily, "Yes. What do you want?"

"I ah . . ." The old servant faltered. "I just wanted to tell you, my lord, that I don't believe you're a coward."

Morgin froze with an angry retort on his lips, and he remembered then that throughout his life the old servant had never borne him any malice, probably the only one who never thought of him as the whoreson. "Thank you, Avis. Thank you. It's good to know that."

But Avis's reassurances helped little as Morgin and his escorts made their way through the crowded castle. He had been branded a coward, publicly, by his own grandmother, and sentenced to death. Such news would travel throughout the clan almost instantly, and it would take only a little longer to pass every ear in the tribe. He was fair game for any man with the inclination to take him on.

Marjinell intercepted him in the castle yard. She stood with her fists on her hips and glared at him. He tried to step around her but she stepped to block his path and said, "Don't ignore me."

Morgin looked into her eyes. They were red from many tears, and sharp with anger. "That would be impossible," he said.

"You think you're witty, don't you?"

"No," Morgin said. "I'm just tired, and in a hurry."

"Hurrying to leave, no doubt."

"As a matter of fact, I am."

"Hurrying to slip away before you're discovered, before you pay the price for your cowardice."

"No," Morgin said again. "It seems I must always pay that price. Now what do you want?"

"You know what I want."

"I'm sorry. But I don't."

At that moment Brandon approached them. His face was pinched with concern for his mother, and his eyes had shed a few tears of their own.

"MichaelOff is dead," she spat.

"I know," Morgin said. "I grieve for him too."

Without warning she slapped him across the face and screamed, "Liar."

"Mother, please," Brandon begged.

Morgin tasted blood in his mouth. "What do you want?" he asked. "I can't bring him back."

Her lips curled into a snarl. Her eyes again filled with tears. "Why didn't you die instead?"

Morgin whispered, "I only wish I had."

She reached into her sleeve, pulled out a small stiletto and raised it high over her head. But Brandon reached up and gripped her wrist. "Mother, no."

As Brandon took the knife from her she started crying soft tears. Brandon tossed the knife to one of Morgin's escorts, then put his arms about his mother's shoulders and pulled her away, walking her toward the inner keep.

"The stables," one of Morgin's guards said. "Now. No more delays."

As Avis had said a provisioned horse awaited him in the stables, a coal black mare, lean and hard, a far cry from the likes of poor, dead SarahGirl. She stood motionless as he checked her carefully, a stillness unusual for such an animal in the presence of an unknown rider. When he tried to examine her teeth she nipped at him; she could have bitten him badly, but merely clicked her teeth near his ear as if to tell him he was irritating her.

He checked her hooves, then the saddle, then quickly rifled through the saddle bags, noting each item included in his provisions. Satisfied that nothing important had been missed, he closed the saddle bags, tossed them over the horse's back, and was about to mount up when Roland's voice stopped him, "Wait. Please."

He turned and Roland embraced him tightly. They stood that way for a long moment, and when Roland finally released him he stepped back and regarded Morgin carefully. He seemed to want to say something but couldn't get the words out.

Morgin asked, "Where is mother?"

"I don't know," Roland said. "Something to do with NickoLot."

One of the two men escorting Morgin said, "My lord, we have our orders. You must leave, now."

Morgin grasped the saddle horn and mounted up in one motion.

Roland grabbed his sleeve and asked, "What will you do?"

What would he do? There'd been no time to think ahead. After awaking in the ditch outside the castle, everything he'd done had been dictated by others. He said, "I don't know."

"Please," Roland pleaded. "You know my intuition, and I sense that death awaits you out there."

"Then so be it," Morgin said flatly. "How bad is Malka?"

"Not good. He lost a lot of blood with the arm. He should rest but he refuses to."

Because of the encounter in the castle yard, Morgin knew Brandon and Marjinell were well. "And what of my brothers and mother?"

"We can't find NickoLot, but other than her we're well and unharmed."

Morgin said, "Go find mother. If I'm right she will have found NickoLot by now."

One of the guards prompted him again. "My lord, you must go."

Morgin looked into Roland's eyes. "I love you, father."

"And I you, son. Fare you well."

Morgin pulled on the reins, turning the horse toward the stable entrance. The horse had taken only a few steps when Roland called out, "But you didn't ask after Rhianne?"

Morgin stopped the horse and twisted about in the saddle. "No. I didn't."

"She's hurt," Roland said. "But your mother is healing her."

Hurt? Rhianne! Perhaps in some way she was paying the price for her treachery.

"Father, I love you," he said, then turned away from Roland and spurred the horse forward. He didn't look back as he rode out of the stables, though he heard his father call after him, some sort of last farewell that was lost in the noise of the busy castle yard. He trotted the horse toward the main gates, tried not to cringe under the derisive stares of the clansmen on the parapets above. From somewhere JohnEngine cried out, "Morgin. Wait."

Morgin halted the horse as JohnEngine ran up to him breathlessly. "Don't leave without me. I'll ride with you."

"Are you sure you want to ride with a coward?"

JohnEngine sneered at him. "Don't insult me. You know I don't believe that."

Morgin looked at the sun. It seemed hours since he'd awakened in the ditch, but it was still just after sunrise. Morgin reached out to his brother, shook JohnEngine's hand. "I have to ride alone in this."

JohnEngine seemed to understand that. "But where will you go?"

Morgin shrugged. "I don't know."

JohnEngine hesitated, trying to think of something more to say.

Morgin said, "Fare you well," then spurred his mount through the gates and away from Elhiyne.

JohnEngine called after him, "Fare you well, brother."

Not far from the castle gates the road forked east and west. He could go west to Anistigh, then on to the port city of Aud and the sea. He'd never been to the sea before, and Aud was a city where he would apparently be free of clan law. There was nothing for him to the east, only the Worshipers, and Yestmark, and war. He hesitated for a moment, then turned east and rode toward the oncoming enemy.

••••

Valso watched the sun rise with smug satisfaction. He'd easily outwitted the stupid Elhiyne armsmen, had put a good deal of distance between him and them, and could now travel with less haste. He considered stealing a horse, but that might put them back on his trail so he rejected that idea. He was in good physical condition, trained in the lore of the land. It would not harm him to travel on foot for a day or two, and he felt extremely good. Everything had gone well, though not exactly as planned.

He decided to stop and rest through the morning. It had been a long night evading the fool Elhiynes, and some sleep would do him good. He scouted about and discovered an old, abandoned mill by a large stream. One wall had partially collapsed, but after a careful search he found a room completely intact. It would provide good shelter, and he could relax in relative comfort.

He cut some leafy branches from nearby trees to soften his bed, arranged them carefully on the stone floor, then lay down to sleep. *Yes*, he thought. The previous night had indeed gone well. His only regret was that he'd failed to kill the whoreson.

He dozed off quickly. In his dreams he moved toward a goal and sought a certain presence that he knew awaited him, a presence he had known for all his adult life. It was *that other* that was the source of much of his power, the existence that fed him, the magic that nourished him.

They met, he and *that other*, and tears of joy came to him, for in no other presence could he feel such awe, such magnificent wonder, such power. He was one of the most powerful wizards in all the clans, and he knew power as no other mortal could. He had stood before the greatest wizards and witches of the clans both Greater and Lesser, and they were as nothing compared to him. And yet, standing now in the presence of *that other*, he was as nothing compared to it.

"It is begun," he said respectfully. "The pieces of the game have been placed upon the board and set into motion. All has gone as you desired."

He sensed pleasure in the vastness of *that other*, and he sensed a question.

"No," he answered. "It was only a minor difficulty, merely an unanticipated incident that turned into a momentary setback, all caused by a rather bothersome mortal. He blundered into the midst of things, and I had to change my tactics for a short while. But in the end your desires were fulfilled. Your enemies believe themselves to be victorious, and they foolishly look to my stupid father as their primary source of danger. All has gone as planned. I have served you well, my lord."

He sensed pleasure in *that other* again. And then, his heart pounding rapidly in anticipation, he sensed that a reward was due. It came slowly at first, and then it came in a flood. *That other* brushed him with just the merest touch of the infinitely exquisite hatred that Valso so longed to caress, the wondrously malignant evil that would someday be his eternal reward, the power, the cruelty, the enmity that was *that other*, his master of masters, his lord, his king, his god. And Valso carried that touch joyously with him to his dreams.

18

The Magic of Dreams

MORGIN RODE HARD all that day. He followed the road out of the valley that led northeast to Kallun's gorge. He never paused, never rested, but drove himself to the limit of his endurance, trying to achieve a state of exhaustion that would wash away the anger and frustration of Olivia's public condemnation. His ride became a race. The news of his alleged cowardice was spreading somewhere ahead of him, travelling swiftly from ear to ear. He knew he could not rest until he caught up with it, and passed it; until then he would see nothing but disgust in the eyes of every clansman he met. Not until mid-afternoon did he realize he was chasing a phantom that could never be caught, and in the process, like a damn fool, he was riding his horse to death.

He halted then, stopped at a small mountain brook to water and rest the animal. He must be more careful, walk her for a while, alternate between walking and riding as a good horseman should on a long trail. But to his surprise he found the horse rather calm, and seemingly indifferent to the grueling pace he'd set. She was a coal-black mount, with no distinguishing marks. He looked into her eyes—they were even blacker than the animal's coat, if that was possible—and they stared back at him as if boring deeply into his soul. Morgin cringed under that gaze, as if there was an intelligence behind those eyes greater than that of any horse. He had the feeling he could set any pace for this horse, ride it for any length of time, and when he was done, she would still be ready to ride further.

He shook himself, looked away from the horse and the feeling passed. He was imagining things. She was just a horse, like any other horse in the Elhiyne stables, perhaps not as gentle as poor SarahGirl, but still just a horse.

He looked at her again, and again she looked back, and again that odd feeling came over him. A name came to mind: Mortiss, the DeathWalker. He said, "That's what I'll call you. Though I do wonder why I chose such a name for you."

She neighed, as if to say, *You didn't choose it.*

He shook himself again. He was letting his imagination get the best of him with foolish waking dreams of some strange horse with an odd name. "Just a horse," he mumbled as he mounted up and rode on.

He was high in the Worshipers on the trail to Kallun's gorge. The sun was getting lower on the horizon as darkness approached. Snow blanketed the landscape on either side of the trail. The air held a chill that cut through Morgin's tunic, and he was forced to bundle his cloak tightly about him. He wondered if the damn horse felt the cold as he did.

She snorted, as if to say, *Of course not, you fool.*

He'd never been this high in the pass before. He'd spent many a day in the Worshipers hunting and fishing with his brothers and cousins, but that had always been in the forests that carpeted the lower slopes. Never before had he been allowed to go higher, to ride above the tree line and attain the summit of the pass. Olivia hadn't trusted him sufficiently to allow him to cross the mountains, though he never understood why. It was another sore point between them. His brothers and cousins had all made the trip at least once, but Morgin had never been beyond the fields and valleys west of the mountains. For years he'd had to be content with stories of the vast forests to the east, and the Plains of Quam, and beyond that the Great Munjarro Waste.

He knew he'd probably not see them this time either. He rode now to war, though he had no idea what he would do when he got there. It was unfair, unjust, even more so since the traitorous slut Rhianne would probably go unpunished. Even if no one else knew of her treachery, he did, and he vowed now that if he ever returned she would pay with her life for going to Valso's bed.

"Halt," someone cried from the brush at the edge of the trail. Morgin pulled his horse to a stop and waited, careful to keep his hand away from the hilt of his sword. Directly in front of him a single man stepped into the trail. He held a sword in one hand and stood confidently blocking the trail. Morgin recognized him, though not by name; he was a sergeant-of-men that Morgin had seen about the castle occasionally.

The man peered carefully at Morgin's face, and after a moment his features relaxed and he said, "You're Lord Morgin, are you not?"

Morgin answered with a flat "Yes."

The man turned to the side of the trail and called out, "It's all right. He's Elhiyne. I recognize him." There came some rustling in the brush, then all was still again. The man stepped to one side of the trail and said, "You may pass."

Morgin hesitated. "You have the advantage of me."

The man bowed at the waist. "Forgive me, Your Lordship. I'm Abileen. May I ask if you bring word from Elhiyne?"

Morgin shook his head. "I bring no word. How much farther to the gorge?"

"Around the next bend in the trail, my lord. Do you intend to cross?"

Morgin nodded.

"There's a way-station on the other side." Abileen frowned, looked back down the trail and asked, "Where are your men, my lord?"

Morgin shrugged. "I'm alone. And I would prefer that you keep my identity to yourself."

"Certainly, my lord."

Morgin spurred his horse up the trail.

It was near sunset when, a few minutes later, he caught his first sight of Kallun's gorge, a deep slash in the earth cut directly across the trail. No more than a hundred paces wide, its depth was far beyond measure. It had supposedly been created during the last of the Great Clan Wars by the god Kallun. According to legend he had created it as a defensive barrier against the Benesh'ere. Morgin wondered about such a legend; if he was truly a god he had no need of a defense against mortals. He could merely have willed that the Benesh'ere no longer exist, and the war would have been done. Most legends had such holes in their credibility.

The gorge was impressive. Its walls were sheer, unmarked rock, as if sliced into the earth by a giant sword. It cut directly across the pass at its summit. The trail led straight to a massive stone bridge that was the only means of crossing the gorge. The bridge was barely wide enough for a single man or horse. The surface had been flattened by stone masons for surer footing, and rails had been added as protection against a chance misstep, but the bridge remained a fearful passage.

The bridge was considerably lower than the lip of the gorge. Morgin was forced to dismount and lead Mortiss down a steep and treacherous incline to reach the bridge. Out on the bridge itself he was infinitely grateful for the handrails on either side, for while the footing was sure, the path was narrow, and his imagination painted a vivid picture of what it would mean to fall.

On the other side he led Mortiss up another incline and paused at the lip, looking back on the bridge. With the handrails removed, a dozen archers could defend that bridge against an army. Any attacking force would be forced to run down one incline, across the bridge, and up another incline; all on foot and in single file. Now he understood why Illalla would not try to cross the Worshipers at Kallun's gorge, even though it was much closer to Elhiyne than Sa'umbra.

"Good even', traveler."

Morgin started, spun, found a grizzled old man facing him. The fellow seemed to have stepped out of nowhere. "You're headed the wrong direction," the old fellow said.

"Is there a place where I can rest?" Morgin asked. "And feed my horse?"

"Aye." The old man jerked his head to one side. "This way." He stepped off the trail into a dark shadow between two large boulders.

Morgin followed. In the gathering gloom he could see little in the shadows, but the sound of the old man's footsteps guided him. They emerged into a large level space, sheltered on all sides by rock walls and boulders. Masons had cut a shelf into the rock for seating, and three men huddled by a warm fire. Four more lay on the ground, rolled in their blankets and sleeping near another fire.

"I'll take care of your horse," the old man whispered. "Why don't you sit and warm yourself."

Morgin did just that, taking a spot by the three seated men. They acknowledged him with a nod, but said nothing out of courtesy for the men sleeping nearby.

The fire felt good. He found he could lean back against the rock wall and still feel its warmth. His muscles relaxed. The tension came out of his shoulders and he closed his eyes to rest for just a moment.

••••

Morgin sat upon a warhorse standing on a grassy field wearing the armor and clothing of a magnificent king. Before him the field sloped gently down to a massive battle in the distance. He heard swords clashing, men and horses crying out their agony as they died, though he could not have picked out a single voice, just the overall din of death on a scale beyond imagining. He could not take his eyes off that field of death, though it sickened him to see such carnage.

A single warrior stepped away from the battle and began walking slowly toward him, his pace almost casual. He carried no weapons and he stepped with an uneven gait, and as he came closer Morgin saw that he was drenched in blood. A horrible gash split his jaw, his left arm hung limply at his side where a sword had almost severed it, and the splinters of a broken war lance protruded from a horrendous wound in his thigh.

He stopped a few paces away, and bowed at the waist like a courtier. He had the face of a handsome, young man, a young king.

Morgin's right hand moved of its own accord, as if he were no more than a passenger in this body, and he realized he had no control over his own actions or words. He drew the sword slowly, and raised it to point at the apparition. "Name yourself, demon," he said.

The apparition nodded and spoke softly. "I am AethonDeath, my lord, and I have come for you."

Morgin's heart lurched as terror washed through his soul, and though fearful, this body he occupied remained calm. He spoke calmly, evenly, and said, "So be it."

Morgin awoke with a gasp, his heart pounding in his throat. He jumped to his feet, sword drawn, waves of terror washing over him. Directly in front of him the fire had dwindled to dull glowing embers. Gone were the men who had been seated next to him, also those who had been asleep. He peered into the darkness and prepared to defend himself against some unknown danger. But as his heart slowed and his breathing calmed, he realized it had all been only a dream.

The old man spoke from out of the darkness. "Would Your Lordship like some porridge?"

"No, thank you," Morgin said, trying to locate the voice in the gloom beyond the light of the fire, wondering if he should be angry at Abileen for telling the old man his identity.

"Are you sure, milord?" The old man stepped into the light and tossed another log onto the dying embers. Sparks erupted upward. "It's hot, milord, and thick. And what you don't eat I'm throwing into the gorge. No sense saving it for Decouix scum."

Morgin's stomach growled. He couldn't remember the last time he'd eaten, and the porridge sounded awfully good. "I think I will have some," he said. "But what's this you say about the Decouixs? They're coming here?"

"Aye, milord. About sunup. But we've got plenty of time before then. You just sit back. I'll get your porridge, and maybe we can find some sugar to go with it."

"Thank you," Morgin said, feeling better. "One more thing. Has there been any word from Elhiyne?"

"No, milord. None."

"How long ago did the sun set?"

"More than two hours, milord."

Morgin nodded as the old man left.

Later he learned that the old man's name was Durado. He and his only son Samull lived near the gorge where they maintained a way-station for travelers. Morgin remembered the depth of snow that still lay by the side of the trail, and thought that the old man and his son must lead a solitary and hard life.

Durado told him he'd received orders from Olivia to close the pass. They'd destroy any provisions on the east side, then remove the railings from the stone bridge and retreat westward. There, they'd station archers to stop anyone who might be foolish enough to attempt a crossing.

Salula was riding ahead of Illalla's army with twelve twelves of Kulls on short rations. He'd detach fifty or so to Kallun's gorge, then take the remainder south to Sa'umbra Gap. His intentions were obvious: to close both passes completely so that any Elhiyne resistance could not be supplied from the west. Salula and his halfmen would eat poorly for a few days, but Illalla and his army would not be far behind, and control of the passes would greatly speed his conquest.

Morgin listened to all of this, and wondered why he had chosen to ride into the face of that army. He noticed that the same question was written on the faces of the old man and his son, though they were too polite to speak it aloud.

Durado sent his son with Morgin as a guide. The trail down the eastern side of the pass was treacherous. With its twisting and turning ways it would have been impossible for Morgin alone, though even with Samull's leadership it was difficult and tiring. Morgin was thankful for the boy's company.

They passed through a number of small villages on the trail, strange little clusters of huts that clung precariously to the side of the mountain, always placed on what seemed the most inhospitable terrain. Morgin's imagination pictured them in daylight bustling with activity, peopled by a hearty race of mountain folk immune to the harsh winter in the Worshipers. But now they were silent, dark and deserted.

Well past midnight the trail leveled off some. Samull told Morgin the going would be easier then. No longer required to concentrate so on guiding Mortiss, Morgin relaxed his soul for the first time in days. His magic, now beyond his control, detected the scent of Kulls on a nether wind. They were not far below, and riding steadily up the trail.

He turned to Samull. "Go back. Now."

"But sir! The trail is still dangerous."

"The Kulls are approaching, and I'll not have you with me when they pass."

Samull's eyes widened. "The halfmen?"

"Go back. Now. I command it." Ironically, Morgin realized he sounded quite like Olivia.

"Aye, milord," Samull said. "May the gods protect you." The boy turned his horse and disappeared quietly up the trail.

Morgin backtracked up the trail, found a spot where he and Mortiss could step off into the trees. He dismounted and cast a spell to calm the beast and keep her still. But as the magic washed over her, she shook it off as if she needed not the aid of some mortal fool.

Only seconds later the first Kull rounded a turn in the trail, a dark apparition seated atop a black horse visible as a shadow in the moonlight. To Morgin's arcane senses the halfman emitted no humanness, no life.

More Kulls appeared behind the first. Their horses trudged slowly and methodically up the trail, and not a single Kull spoke. There was none of the chatter that would come from a troop of men, only the creak of saddle leather and the soft clop of hooves, an eerie sound that filled the moonlit night and raised the hairs on the back of Morgin's neck. He held his breath as they passed, and was thankful for the moonlight and the shadows in which he and Mortiss hid.

When the last Kull disappeared far up the trail, Morgin released his breath in a long, slow sigh. He stretched his tired muscles, and resisted the temptation to lay down to rest.

Sleep! With the exception of that short nap at the top of the pass he hadn't slept in days. It took great willpower to lead Mortiss back out onto the trail and mount up. Oddly, she seemed to know the trail even in the dark so he let her pick her own path. He would have to move with caution now; his enemies were both behind and in front of him.

Mortiss, without his urging, maintained a grueling pace. Even when he tried to slow her, to pace her carefully, she refused and pressed on, and by noon of the following day they had covered a good distance. The land about him was rocky and harsh, but green with a life of shrubs and ferns so thick he could not have cut a new trail through it. And above it all towered evergreens so high they were un-climbable, so dense that the sun seemed lost from the sky.

Morgin met no one on the trail that day. He passed by several small farms with no signs of life, and through three deserted villages. In the middle of the last a catch-pool collected water from a nearby stream, and he stopped to refill his water skin.

He desperately needed rest. He sat down at the edge of the pool and dropped Mortiss's reins, knowing somehow that she would not wander off. She walked casually to a nearby animal trough and bent her head to drink. The silence of the village was broken only by the slurping sound of Mortiss's lips in the water, and the rustle of leaves in a soft breeze. He thought he heard something else, almost masked by the other sounds, and Morgin was slow to recognize it: the pad of feet moving between two of the huts.

He jumped to his feet and drew his sword. Mortiss, sensitive to the tension in the air, stopped drinking. The silence descended again.

Morgin stood with his back to Mortiss and eyed the huts about him, then reached out with his magic to sense who might be lying in wait. It took but a moment for him to locate thirty or forty living beings scattered throughout the huts and the forest beyond, all more fearful of him than he of them.

"I am Elhiyne," he shouted. There came no reply. "You have nothing to fear from me. I am here to kill Decouixs, not peasants."

He waited several seconds and no one answered, so he sheathed his sword, mounted Mortiss, and rode out of the village.

Beyond the village the path widened enough for a small cart and the going eased somewhat. Mortiss kept up her pace as if she were in collusion with Olivia and wanted to be sure that no time would be wasted in delivering Morgin to his fate. Near nightfall they reached the Road of the Seventh Deed, often called the God's Road. Morgin remembered asking as a child what the strange names meant, but no one seemed to know, though quite a few were willing to make up stories.

The road led north to Yestmark, then into the Decouix lands. South, it led to Sa'umbra Gap, and beyond that to Castle Inetka. South was of no concern to Morgin. Illalla would use this road to bring his army down from the north to Sa'umbra Gap. And on this road Morgin would meet him. Morgin wondered what he would do when that time came, but he put those thoughts aside. He had reached the point of complete exhaustion, and it was time to rest.

He led Mortiss off the trail to a spot some distance into the forest, finding that the dense undergrowth was ribboned with small game trails. He tied the animal's reins to a nearby branch, then cleared a space to sleep. He summoned a minor demon and placed it under geas to watch over him and awaken him at the moon's rising, but Mortiss shooed it away with her own magic. She would watch over him, and she would wake him when the time was right.

I'm so tired I'm beginning to imagine things, he thought. He'd lost the demon through carelessness, and he was too weak to summon another. He shrugged, wrapped himself in his blanket, and without lighting a fire lay down to a restless and fitful sleep.

19

The Path of Power

TALL TREES LINED both sides of the God's Road, turning the night sky into a thin slit of sparkling stars. The light of a half-moon lit part of the road, while darkness obscured one side near the base of the trees. Morgin found it comforting to ride in the moon shadow there, feeling less exposed.

Mortiss had awakened him at the rise of the moon, and they'd begun their journey north. He was in no hurry to meet the oncoming army, so he kept her at a slow, steady pace. Shortly after they'd begun travelling he spotted a dark shadow ahead in the road. It appeared to be a crumpled heap of some sort, but not until he reached it did he realize it was the remains of some poor soul caught on the road by the Kulls and cut down without mercy. Farther on he discovered other bodies, and parts of bodies. The Kulls had butchered anyone they'd encountered on the God's Road.

Near sunrise he came to the river Augis. Just across the river the road passed through the center of a large village, and as he approached it he could smell death hanging on the air. The village had been burned and its population slaughtered. Bodies were strewn about everywhere; the lucky ones had been cut down quickly, the unlucky had been hacked slowly to pieces. He rode on, wishing he could look away from the carnage.

At the far edge of town his eye caught a brightly colored shape lying by the road. He dismounted to investigate, and found a small girl of no more than ten or twelve years. Her gaily-colored skirt had been pulled upward, then tied about her throat with a piece of rope to trap her arms within its folds. The Kulls had stopped for some pleasure, then finished by strangling her in the cloth of her own gown. He cursed them, then sobbing openly, he buried her in a shallow grave.

He rode out of that village at full gallop, spurring Mortiss unmercifully, demanding all the speed she could deliver. He rode through that day and into the next night, stopping only during the few hours between sunset and moonrise. He pushed himself and Mortiss constantly, tapping the power that now clung to him. The death he saw in the road goaded him into haste. It was never long between one crumpled form in the moonlight and the next, and as each appeared in the distance he felt drawn to it, rushing to confirm that it was more death, then rushing on to be away from it.

He now knew what he must do: end the killing. And without an army at his back there was only one way to do that: Illalla must die, even if Morgin died with him.

Mortiss never slackened her pace; perhaps she sensed the murderous rage that drove him. Again he sensed a strange intelligence within the animal, as if so much death touched her more than him. He tried to convince himself that his thoughts were pure fantasy, but he couldn't easily dismiss his suspicion that she was more than just a horse.

Shortly before sunrise of the second night Morgin came to the river Ulbb. The road plunged directly into a shallow and wide ford that varied from ankle to knee deep. The riverbed was solid, primarily pebbles and sand and small rocks. Morgin dismounted to drink, to rest, and to watch the sun rise. He allowed Mortiss free rein to graze, found a spot well off the road and sat down by the water's edge.

The ford was easily two hundred paces wide, and as the water rippled over the rocky bottom it produced a soft roar that obliterated all other sounds. He closed his eyes, but resisted the temptation to lie back, for he knew if he slept, he would not wake for hours. As he sat there, his eyelids brightened to a deep red and his face warmed as the sun splashed its first rays over the horizon.

He heard a voice in the distance and opened his eyes. On the other side of the ford, he saw three peasants walking his way: a very large and broad-shouldered man, a woman and a young boy. All three wore simple homespun, and carried bundles strapped to their backs.

The spot Morgin had chosen was far enough off the road that they clearly hadn't seen him yet. He waited until they'd splashed through the shallow water in the ford and crossed the river, then he stepped out onto the road and into view. They froze in their tracks and eyed him fearfully. The large fellow crouched into a defensive posture. The woman's eyes darted about desperately as she looked for a means of escape. The boy clutched her sleeve, his mouth open in a big round O.

Morgin extended his hands, palms up. "You have nothing to fear from me."

The big fellow said, "You're wearing a halfman's cloak."

Morgin glanced down at his clothing, then back at the peasants. "So I am. When I'm shivering in the cold I'm not too particular about the cloak I wear. I'm Morgin et Elhiyne, and I'm no Kull. In fact I've killed a few halfmen recently, and intend to kill a few more." Brave words, Morgin thought, and hoped he could live up to them.

The man and woman both dropped to their knees, muttering, "Yer Wizardness." The boy stood unmoving, his mouth still wide open. When Morgin approached them the woman grabbed his sleeve and begged, "Fergive us, Yer Wizardness. We be thinking ye was a black rider. They be all abouts, ye know."

Morgin said, "Stand up. And rest easy."

The woman's name was Gulk, the boy was Ikth, and the man Ott. The woman did most of the talking for the three. "We be fleeing the hordes from the north, hiding from the black riders whenever we sees 'em coming."

"You're from up north then? From Yestmark?"

"Aye, yer wizardship."

"Then you have news of the battle?"

"Aye. It went ill. Twas a slaughter, it was."

"And Eglahan?" Morgin asked. "What of him?"

"Only the gods know, yer wizardship. Likely he be dead like all the rest."

Morgin could not hide his disappointment.

"Do ya be going south, yer wizardship?"

Morgin shook his head. "No. I ride north."

"What for? There be nothing but death up there."

Morgin learned from her that the crossing on the Ulbb was called Gilguard's Ford. She had no idea why. He also obtained directions to Yestmark. "North of here the road forks, yer wizardshipness. Now I never rid no horse before, but it forks 'bout a day's walk from here. Take the left road, another day's walking, and you're there. Don't know how long it'll take ye ridin'."

Ott walked with a limp, and grimaced occasionally as if favoring some injury. When Morgin asked about it, Ott showed him a nasty gash in his calf that was beginning to fester. Gulk had treated it with a poultice of mud and leaves that added to the problem more than helping. AnnaRail had made sure his saddlebags carried a small amount of healing herbs. Morgin retrieved some redthorn, deadly poisonous if not properly prepared. He chewed the redthorn into a pulpy mass, careful not to swallow any. He shaped the mass into a poultice, then cast the appropriate spell to convert the poison into a healing potion. "Don't try to handle redthorn yourself," he warned them as he pressed the poultice into the wound. "You don't have the magic to prevent it from killing you."

Morgin showed Gulk how to make a proper poultice by boiling jagroot and thisk leaves, straining out the pulp, and using it to cover the wound. "Leave the redthorn poultice on for two days, then change to the jagroot and thisk leaf poultice."

He showed Ikth how to find ginberries and prepare them, then instructed them to clean Ott's wound with the ginberry syrup and change the poultice twice a day. He set some snares so Gulk could catch rabbits for her pot, and in scouting around for good cover for the snares, he chanced upon a place up river from the ford where the Ulbb passed through a deep canyon. But within the canyon the river was still too shallow to have cut into the rock so deeply, so Morgin guessed the nature of the river was far different at the height of the spring thaw.

For some reason it reminded him of the smith's forge back at the castle, and the way the sand molds confined the flow of the steel, channeling it to a specific shape. An idea began to form in his thoughts. The canyon was steep enough that he might be able to use it to his advantage, perhaps leave a little surprise behind as he rode north.

He tore a long, thin, green branch from a nearby willow, sat down on the bank of the river and carefully fashioned the branch into two, twelve pointed stars. Then he cut a lock of his own hair, and between the two stars he tied eight strands of hair, with eight knots in each strand. He then climbed carefully up the north side of the canyon, and at the top of the canyon he sat down to call forth his magic.

This was not a spell composed by another, so it came hard. This was his own spell, of his own composition; he had to sense the natural spirit of it to bring it into the mortal world, and that came slowly. But eventually the strands of hair connecting the two stars began to lengthen and thicken. He worked the spell carefully, lest it evaporate before complete, and when the strands were long enough, he sealed the spell and finished it.

The strands had grown to the thickness of heavy twine. He tied a rock in them close to one star, and wedged the other star into a crevice in the top of the canyon wall high over the river. Then, holding onto the strands, he began spinning the rock-weighted star over his head. He spun it faster and faster, until it was almost beyond his strength to hold onto it, then he released it toward the other canyon wall. It arced out over the canyon and just barely made it to the other side.

He followed the river back down to Gilguard's Ford, crossed the river, then climbed back up stream to the top of the south canyon wall. There, he untied the rock from the strands and wedged the other star into a crevice. And again he called upon his magic.

It seemed to take forever, but slowly the eight strands that now crossed the canyon began to glow and thin out, as if compressed and spread like dough beneath a baker's rolling pin. They flattened until they filled the canyon from wall to wall and top to bottom, and grew so thin they became fully transparent. He extended them down until they touched the water and began to dam the river. But he did not extend them fully down to the river bed itself; some water spilled beneath the veil he had created, though slowly the water was backing up behind it. This was a spell that needed time to develop, to come to fruition.

He returned to Gilguard's Ford, found Mortiss waiting for him. Under the watchful eyes of the three peasants he repacked his saddle bags. As he walked Mortiss across Gilguard's Ford, he heard Ikth call, "Ride with the gods, Lard Morgin."

North of the Ulbb Morgin encountered more refugees fleeing the battle of Yestmark, mostly peasants and farmers. Many were on foot, but often an entire family had trundled its belongings into a two-wheeled cart pulled by a donkey or an ox, or sometimes a man or boy. Shortly before sunset he began to encounter soldiers, many of them wounded, jamming the road in places and making it difficult to move against the flow of refugees.

The first soldiers he came upon were a pair, one with his arm in a sling and the other hobbling on a makeshift crutch. "How went the battle?" Morgin asked.

He with his arm in a sling looked up, and Morgin was struck by the desolation in his eyes. "It was a slaughter. We had twelve hundred men. I doubts there be two hundred left alive."

"What of Eglahan?"

The old soldier shrugged. "Probably dead like all the rest."

Morgin rode on. Before the sun set he questioned more soldiers. All told the same story. One who was older, a sergeant-of-men and probably reliable, gave the bad news that he had seen Eglahan go down.

Once the sun set the refugees on the road thinned out. Morgin was able to travel much faster and reached the fork in the road near midnight, and as Gulk had instructed he took the left road. Throughout the night he noticed small fires in the forest on both sides of the road: refugees unwilling or unable to travel in the dark. But by sunrise he'd reached a point where the road and the surrounding forest were deserted.

He moved with extreme caution, riding in the shadows at the edge of the road and making constant use of his shadowmagic. Shortly after midday he heard a soft rumble that grew quickly into the thunder of hooves on the road. He froze, held Mortiss still and reinforced his shadowmagic. Moments later a mixed patrol of Kulls and Decouix regulars rode past at full gallop.

He waited until they were out of sight, then dismounted. He walked in front of Mortiss and stayed close to the edge of the forest. The sky was clear, the sun bright, and the shadows dark and deep. He walked for another two hours that way, creeping slowly and carefully, freezing into stillness and concentrating on his shadowmagic whenever a Decouix patrol passed by.

He heard it long before his conscious mind recognized it, a faint, soft rumble, like the roar of a distant water fall. As he walked farther it grew into a din that could no longer be ignored. He led Mortiss a good distance into the forest and tethered her there.

He stayed in the wood as he traveled parallel to the road. The going was slower there, but safer. He kept low, followed the smaller game trails rather than the larger, and never relaxed his shadowmagic.

The wood ended abruptly, and the nearby road opened out onto a wide, flat plain. And there, well separated from the edge of the forest, lay the source of the noise that pounded now at Morgin's ears: the camp of the Decouix army, a sprawl stretching for as far as the eye could see, twelve thousand strong with perhaps three thousand horses. Morgin estimated there were a thousand wagons, plus smiths, cooks, wives, children, and the general gamut of camp followers. He stayed within the edge of the forest, moving about and scouting the lay of the camp. He paid close attention to the perimeter, the spacing of the guards, and how they moved. He took note of the location of an elaborate cluster of pavilions near the center of the camp, and especially that which bore the banner of Illalla, Lord of the Greater Clans, King of the third tribe of the Shahot, ruler of the White Clan, foremost of the Greater Council.

When Morgin was satisfied he knew the lay of the camp, he slipped back into the forest to await darkness and the time of shadow.

20

Shadow's Walk

"IT WASSS A grand victory, my lord," the winged snake hissed from its pedestal in the corner of the tent.

"It was not," High Lord Illalla said. His campaign was far behind schedule and his temper was short this night. "It was a rout, nothing more, nothing less. We exterminated some vermin. It was not grand and it was hardly a victory. The real victory will come when I crush that bitch Olivia and her cursed offspring. And cease your condescending flattery, Bayellgae. I'm not in the mood."

"Sssss!" the snake demon hissed. It flapped its tiny wings and extended its body.

Illalla turned upon the demon and pointed a finger at his familiar. "You seem to forget yourself. Must we teach you again who here is master?"

"No, massster. Pleassse." Chastened, the snake averted its eyes.

"Then when you're in the company of your betters, act like it."

"Yesss, massster. Bayellgae begsss forgivenessss."

"If Bayellgae wishes forgiveness, it should beg for it at my feet."

The snake slithered down its pedestal and across the floor, then curled up and laid its head submissively at the tip of the High Lord's slipper. "Forgive me, massster."

"Back to your perch," the wizard said.

The snake sprang into the air, its tiny wings buzzing like a bumblebee.

"Now," Illalla said. "Tell me of the camp."

As the snake spoke, its head and body wove from side to side. "The men have finisssshed celebrating. Sssince you reduced their ration of ale thisss day, they are sssso-ber."

"Will they be ready to travel?"

"Yesss, Your Grace. If you command it."

"I do. I'll issue orders to my captains to be ready to march at dawn."

"Yesss, my lord."

"What of Eglahan? Have you found his body?"

"No, my lord. There are ssso many bodiesss to sssearch. It wasss ssso dissstract-ing."

"And you dallied, no doubt."

"Forgive me, my lord. I cannot help mysssself when there isss ssso much delight-ful death about."

"It doesn't matter." Illalla dismissed it all with a wave of his hand. "Eglahan is of no import. Dead or alive he can no longer hurt me. But what about that bunch of Elhiyne rabble? What have you found out about them, my prescient little beast?"

"They are going to attack usss tomorrow, massster, though they don't know it yet. They believe we don't know they're here, ssso they think they will sssurprissse usss, then disssappear quickly into the foresssst."

Illalla threw his head back and laughed. "So they think they'll surprise us. Well we'll have to prepare a little trap for them, eh? And we'll see who surprises who. Has there been any word of that fool son of mine?"

"Only that the Elhiynesss have retaken their casssstle and Valsssso wasss neither captured nor killed."

"Then he still lives?"

"Perhapsss, my lord. He isss resssourceful and may yet—" The snake stopped its weaving undulations. Agitated by something, it spit and hissed and fluttered angrily.

"What is it?" Illalla demanded.

"We are being obssserved, my lord."

••••

Morgin tensed. He stood hidden within the shadows outside Illalla's tent.

"A spy?"

"Yesss, my lord, a ssspy."

"Then find it, and kill it."

Morgin ran, another shadow among many in the moonlight, but behind him he heard the buzzing of tiny wings and the hiss of the deadly little snake. In desperation he stepped into a shadow and froze, holding his breath, quenching his own magic ruthlessly so that the little monster could not sense it.

The center of the camp exploded in an uproar. Someone shouted for guards and there were Kulls all about. A Decouix lieutenant ran by hollering orders to triple the guard at the perimeter. Bayellgae and Illalla stopped not ten paces from Morgin's hiding place, the snake hovering in the air about its master.

"What was it?" Illalla demanded.

"Sssomething not ordinary, my lord. Sssomething magical."

"A demon?"

"No, my lord. Thisss magic had not the tasssste of the netherlife."

"Then it was a wizard?"

"Perhapsss, my lord. Then perhapsss not."

"What do you mean?"

"There wasss an odd difference to thisss magic, a difference I have not tasssted in a very long time."

"Where is it now?"

"I know not, my lord. It went thisss way, but I can no longer tassste it."

"Then come with me," Illalla said. He moved off into the night and the snake-demon followed.

Wearing his Kull cloak Morgin stepped out of his shadow walking hastily, trying to look like one of many Kulls hurrying toward the perimeter. When he got there he took up a position in the perimeter line with the rest and waited. He was still several hundred paces from the edge of the forest, and to run now, under the eyes of the perimeter guards, would be foolish.

A Kull lieutenant came walking down the perimeter line, inspecting the guard one by one. Soon he would step up to Morgin. He would look him in the face and recognize that he was no Kull. Morgin would die then and there, or worse, be captured alive.

He could wait no longer, so he left his position and walked calmly to the next man in line. Without warning he drew his sword and cut the man down in a single motion.

"Spy!" he shouted as loud as he could. "It's the spy. I've killed him. I claim the reward."

The perimeter broke up as a crowd of men and halfmen gathered quickly. "What reward?" one of them asked.

"Haven't you heard?" Morgin said. "Illalla is offering a thousand gold pieces to the man that kills him. And it's mine."

That sparked their interest. They gathered closely around the dead man as the Kull lieutenant arrived. "Make way," he bellowed in a growling Kull voice. "Let me through."

Morgin obeyed. He stepped aside and moved to the edge of the small crowd, and when the time was right, he slipped into a convenient shadow. The deceit was quickly discovered and the cry rose again, but by that time Morgin had gained the safety of the forest and was making his way back to Mortiss.

••••

Morgin learned that, like his sword arm, the more he exercised his magic, the easier it became to wield. He'd also learned that by relaxing, he gained an awareness of any being nearby, human or not. It was a struggle, though, to relax and yet still concentrate on his horsemanship, for so much of him was devoted to guiding Mortiss stealthily through the night that little remained for relaxation. But then a moment came when Mortiss's soul washed over him, as if to tell him that she needed not the guidance of some stupid mortal, that she was there by her own will, that she had chosen him, and not the other way around. He wondered if he should stop thinking of her as merely a horse. So he let her choose her own path then relaxed, and his consciousness extended outward into the forest around him. That was when he detected the single rider up ahead.

Morgin decided to follow the man, using his magic to allow him to remain at a good distance. The man moved through the forest growth with practiced ease. Like Morgin he was almost a shadow in the night, and Morgin came to realize that were it not for his magic, he would have quickly lost the man's trail.

Morgin followed him to a small camp of armed warriors. The perimeter guards, neither Kull nor Decouix, admitted the man readily, and with his curiosity aroused Morgin tethered Mortiss and went scouting. He pulled a shadow about him and slipped past the perimeter easily, hoping he'd discovered a remnant of Eglahan's army. There appeared to be about fifty men in the camp, most clustered around four fires that were small enough to be safe.

The man he had followed walked quickly toward the center of the camp, and as Morgin moved through the shadows he spotted Abileen, the sergeant-of-men from Kallun's Gorge. He quickly realized that he knew about half of the men present.

When the man stepped into the light of the fire at the camp's center, to Morgin's surprise a woman jumped up and greeted him. "Packwill. Were there any difficulties?"

Morgin had never seen a woman like her. She wore pants like a man, with a sword strapped to her hip; not a lady's dagger, but a full sized battle sword. She stood slightly larger than most women, though still smaller than a man, and even though her appearance was harsh and blunt, she was attractive, and her speech was that of a high born lady.

"No, milady," Packwill said to her as he stepped closer to the fire to warm his hands. "I stayed far enough away to keep out of trouble, though some sort of ruckus started just as I was leaving."

JohnEngine stepped into the light of the small fire. "Come, man. We're all anxious to hear what you learned."

Seated behind the woman was a man whom Morgin didn't recognize. Opposite him, and also seated, were two men with their backs to Morgin. One of them stood to warm his hands over the fire, and when he spoke Morgin recognized Tulellcoe. "How strong is he?"

"Twelve thousand men, Your Lordship," Packwill said flatly. "Three thousand horse, perhaps a thousand wagons."

The man still seated with his back to Morgin spoke, and Morgin recognized France. "How many Kulls?"

"Appears to be one in six."

Morgin listened while the scout Packwill described Illalla's camp in fine detail. He learned that the woman was a twoname named Cortien Balenda, and called Cort by the others. The stranger seated behind her was Valken Surriot, another twoname.

Both had been with Eglahan for many years and had fought at Yestmark, and with a handful of survivors had met up with Tulellcoe, France and JohnEngine. The three led a small band of men with the intention of slowing Illalla's march to Sa'umbra.

"Two thousand Kulls, eh," the Surriot said. "I wish I knew what Illalla planned next."

Tulellcoe turned his back to the fire, edged in closer to the warmth. "Unless he's a fool he'll move out early tomorrow. And he's no fool."

"What's our next move?" the woman demanded.

Morgin could see them all looking to Tulellcoe for leadership. The wizard took a deep breath, thought for a moment. "There's not a lot we can do with sixty men, but I've got an idea. We need axes. We'll use swords if necessary, but axes will be faster."

"Some of the men are from these parts," the Surriot said. "They might know where we can find axes. Better yet, the peasants on the road will have axes. Around here a man has to clear the land, so that's the first thing he gets when he starts a family."

"Good idea," Tulellcoe said. "Take some men and see if you can recruit some peasants to do a little chopping for us. Volunteers only. We need them for half a day, then they can continue south with their families. We also need torches, and oil. Torches we can make, and we can conjure oil, but what do we put it in?"

"How about our water skins?" JohnEngine asked. "There's plenty of streams in this forest so we don't need to carry water with us."

They all looked at Tulellcoe expectantly, and he nodded slowly as if trying to assemble the details of a plan. Morgin wanted to reveal himself, to join them openly, to delay the oncoming army. But of those there, JohnEngine and France were probably the only ones who wouldn't condemn him as a coward. The rest of them would never trust him, so he slipped back into the forest, remembering Illalla's mention of a "... bunch of Elhiyne rabble," and Bayellgae's prediction that they will, "... attack usss tomorrow, massster, though they don't know it yet." He also remembered how Illalla had laughed and said, "So they think they will surprise us. Well we'll have to prepare a little trap for them, eh?"

••••

After leaving the Elhiyne camp, Morgin returned to the Decouix camp in the hope of learning more. Even with the perimeter guards aroused by his earlier visit he found it easy to slip past them, though he dared not go near Illalla's tent; the little snake could apparently sense him. He eavesdropped on some of Illalla's high-ranking officers, and learned nothing new, so he decided to return to the forest and try to get some sleep.

While slipping from shadow-to-shadow toward the perimeter of the camp, it occurred to him he might be able to strike at the invading army in a way no one could have anticipated. He was one, single man, and he'd been racking his brains for days now trying to think of something he could do to make a difference. He could not get close enough to Illalla to assassinate him, not with Bayellgae hovering about. But standing in the midst of the Decouix camp in the stillness of the wee hours, he realized that he could strike at Illalla's men. And while he alone could not kill enough of them to make a difference, common soldiers were a superstitious lot. He could strike such terror in their hearts over the next few days that when the final battle came they would be tired and fearful, their battle skills that much blunted. So before he left the camp he silently slit the throats of two twelves of men in their sleep, and left them to be found by their comrades in the morning.

••••

Illalla et Decouix rode at the head of his army. He had learned long ago that a leader must lead his men, otherwise they might think he had fears like them. Once they began to believe that, they would fear him less, or perhaps cease to fear him at all. The High Lord of the White Clan knew that fear was his real source of power, and he was proud of his ability to wield it like a sword. If only he could induce a little more fear in that fool son of his.

He stood high in his stirrups and turned to look at his army on the road behind him. For as far as the eye could see there were riders, three thousand of them arranged in ranks of four. Behind them clattered eight hundred wagons in single file, and behind that, nine thousand foot-soldiers walking four abreast. It was not the largest army he had ever assembled, but it was an army to be proud of. With it he would crush these upstart Elhiynes, and after them each of the Lesser Clans would have its turn.

"Look, sire," one of the men riding beside him called. "Up ahead."

The High Lord did not at first look, for that would seem as if he was obeying one of his lackeys. He lingered, taking pride in his army, then slowly turned to look forward. Far up the road he saw one of his scouts riding hastily toward them.

When the man arrived he rode past the High Lord a few paces, turned his horse, then matched the pace of his king, saying only, "Sire, the road is blocked by trees. Chopped down and toppled into the road, hundreds of them."

"Call out my escort," Illalla said.

The blast of a horn echoed through the surrounding forest. A short time later the king of the White Clan rode out from the main column escorted by twelve twelves of Kulls. They rode hard for several minutes, but when they rounded a sharp bend in the road Illalla brought his horse to an abrupt halt.

The scout had exaggerated somewhat. There were not hundreds of trees in the road, but there were a great number, perhaps as many as a single hundred. There appeared to be more at first sight, though, because they were not stacked into a neat pile but spread down the road for a goodly distance. Illalla cursed and turned to a lackey. "How long will it take to clear these?"

"Not long, sire. We can take a couple of draft teams from the wagons and have it clear by midday."

Illalla laughed. "Fools," he said. "They probably spent the entire night chopping down trees, and we'll have it clear in a few short hours. Get to it man."

The man bowed in his saddle. "Yes, Your Majesty." He rode off to comply.

Illalla turned to his Kull commander. "The trees are only a feint. Their real target is the wagons. Let them burn a few, and when they retreat east, I want you waiting for them with twelve twelves of your men. I don't want any of that rabble left alive. After you've disposed of them, take your men out to patrol the road for one day's march in advance of the main column. Kill anyone you find on or near the road. Is that clear?"

Illalla watched the halfman smile at the thought of the fun he and his men would have. The Kulls always enjoyed the killing. The halfman nodded, said, "Aye, Lord," then rode off to do his king's bidding.

Illalla continued to speak, but to no one in particular. "Fool Elhiynes. Imbeciles. That old woman Olivia wants time to gather her forces. Well she's going to learn that I cannot be slowed. In seven days I will be at Sa'umbra, and that will be the end of Elhiyne."

••••

Morgin looked down at the road far below and watched the wagons and carts passing slowly by. The train of supplies for the advancing army stretched both up and down the road for as far as he could see. It coiled in and around the mountainous forest like a snake, and for the first time he appreciated the enormity of the host that would soon descend upon Elhiyne.

From his vantage atop a high ridge Morgin had an easy view of the developing scene. Tulellcoe had chosen to attack the wagons at a place where the forest was thin, and the sides of the road sloped upward steeply to sharp ridges on both sides. He had split the small Elhiyne force into five platoons led by himself, JohnEngine, France, Cortien Balenda, and Valken Surriot. He'd spaced the platoons carefully up and down the road so as not to interfere with each other, and he and France, with their respective platoons, hid just above the ridge on this side of the road, while JohnEngine and the Balenda and the Surriot hid above the ridge on the other.

Morgin spotted the winged serpent hovering overhead. He checked his shadowmagic and found that deep shadow already lay about him like a cloak. He'd been living in shadow constantly now for some days. AnnaRail had once warned him to beware of spending too much time in such a nether state, that wizards before him who had made such a mistake had slowly lost contact with reality, and become more nether than mortal. That frightened him, but he had no choice, so he shrugged off the thought and extended the shadow to include Mortiss.

He watched his friends watching the army pass, first the columns of mounted soldiers, then rank upon rank of foot soldiers, and now the wagons. Still hovering overhead, Bayellgae had certainly spotted the Elhiyne forces and reported the fact to its master, though not until much of the army had passed did Morgin spot the company of Kulls sneaking carefully into position behind Tulellcoe and his men.

Clearly, Tulellcoe's intention was to strike quickly, then retreat up a small ravine that led to a large game trail, the only path through the forest growth wide enough for a company of sixty riders. It was there that the Kulls had chosen to wait for them, hiding in the shadows just off the trail. They would attack the Elhiyne force once they recombined into a single unit after the raid. In that way, Illalla could ensure that few, if any, escaped.

From Morgin's vantage he could see quite a ways up the road, and when the leading elements of the army stopped he knew it was time to move. He'd concocted a rather simple plan: sneak up on the Kulls waiting in ambush, use his shadowmagic to slip among them, kill a few and make a lot of noise doing it, then slip away into the shadows of the forest. That should alert Tulellcoe to the danger that awaited him and his band.

He turned away from the ridge, found Mortiss waiting quietly behind him, mounted up and started working his way down toward the Kulls. He knew it would take some time for such a long procession of men and supplies to grind to a complete halt, but he moved hastily nevertheless, conscious that if he were late, or Tulellcoe moved too quickly, the Elhiyne warriors would all die.

He stopped a short distance behind the Kulls and checked his shadows. Then he nudged Mortiss forward slowly, quietly, until he was only a few strides behind the waiting Kulls who sat on their horses in an eerie silence, broken occasionally by a spluttering horse, or the creak of saddle leather. From Morgin's new position he could see only their backs, and a chill ran up his spine.

Down on the road shouts and cries broke the stillness of the forest air. Morgin shifted his position a little until he could see a small stretch of the road. There, JohnEngine's small platoon had charged down the opposite slope and chased away several of the wagon handlers. They quickly commandeered a half-dozen wagons and bunched them together in a jam that blocked the road, then released the teams of oxen and set them loose. They commandeered another half dozen wagons, added them to the already formidable jam, then JohnEngine tossed a water skin on top of one of the wagon tarps, and with a stroke of his sword he split it easily. A shower of glistening oil ran down the tarp and soaked into the material. Each of the other riders split a skin of oil over the jam of wagons, then one rider with a torch touched flame to the oil, and in moments an inferno blocked the road.

Tulellcoe's other platoons did the same, and five infernos now blocked the road. Each would blaze well through the day, the night, and into the next morning, and even then they would still be too hot to clear. Illalla could conjure rain to put them out, but bending an elemental to one's will in that way used incredible amounts of power, and the wizard would be exhausted for days to come. Tulellcoe had done well, for Illalla's army would be stalled for at least two, maybe three days. Now it was up to Morgin to see that the Kull trap failed.

JohnEngine and his men disappeared from Morgin's view as they moved down the road to regroup with the rest of the Elhiyne force. Morgin, with exaggerated slowness, drew his sword, then touched Mortiss's flanks with his spurs and nudged her forward. She moved naturally among the deep shadows of the forest, and without making a sound took a position in the midst of the mounted Kulls, just another shadow among them. And there he waited, wrapped in his Kull cloak and his shadow.

Morgin's ears caught the distant sound of straining men and horses riding hard. The entire company of Kulls tensed, and many reached for their swords. In that moment Morgin picked the Kull nearest him and raised his own sword high over his head. He intended to cut the halfman down without warning, but the sword in his hands flared with red fire and roared into life, emitting a harsh, grating tone that hurt his ears and resonated deep into his bones. Before he could react it sliced down, his hand just a passenger on its hilt. It literally cut the halfman and his horse in two.

Screaming out its hatred of all living things the sword cut through a flat arc and beheaded another Kull, then flashed down and took off the head of another's horse. Then pandemonium erupted in the shadows as the Kull's mounts panicked, while it was all Morgin could do to hold onto the sword and stay in the saddle at the same time.

Mortiss reared and brought her fore hooves down in the face of a halfman, bucked and kicked another out of the saddle with her rear hooves. She worked with the sword as if they functioned together in some way, while Morgin was nothing more than the thread that held them together, fearing he might lose his grip on the hilt and his seat in the saddle. With his free hand he let go of her reins, gripped the saddle horn and held on for dear life, while she and the sword ripped through the company of Kulls without mercy.

••••

As JohnEngine charged headlong up the trail with the rest of the company, he sensed a flow of power, a vast unleashing of energies beyond anything humanly possible. Tulellcoe must have sensed it too, for both of them reined in their horses simultaneously, and the men behind them bunched up as they tried not to override them.

A mounted Kull sprang into the middle of the trail. JohnEngine had his sword out in an instant, but it was not needed, for the Kull's horse was bucking and kicking wildly; out of control it carried the halfman off into the forest. Kulls on panic-stricken mounts were everywhere, and it was all JohnEngine could do to keep his own mount under control. He heard the shriek of some monstrous beast, alternating between a low growl and a wild cry. Then a creature of shadow and death lunged into the trail before him. He sensed evil power flowing from it, and thought that his life was about to end.

It was a monstrous sight, a constantly shifting, undefined shape, streaked with power and darkness. It towered over JohnEngine as it advanced, but another Kull on a panicked mount shot in front of it, and a flaming red talon the length of a sword reached out and cut both halfman and beast in two. Then it disappeared into the depths of the forest, vanishing without a sound, leaving behind a trail littered with dismembered Kulls and their mounts. In the distance JohnEngine heard the scattered, surviving Kulls trying desperately to control their panicked horses.

France said, "What in netherhell was that?"

Tulellcoe looked worried. "It didn't feel like netherlife, and there was something oddly familiar about it. But it was certainly something that doesn't like Kulls."

Valken Surriot looked at the carnage that lined the trail. "Well, let us thank the Unnamed King that it doesn't feel the same way about us. In fact, we owe it our lives."

"Well I certainly appreciate that," Cortien Balenda said, "but I'd rather not stick around to express my thanks. Let's get out of here before it comes back and decides it doesn't like us either."

••••

Morgin spurred Mortiss through the forest, running from something he couldn't define. The sword had come close to JohnEngine, had wanted to taste the blood of his own brother. Had the mounted halfman not come between them, and provided a meal for the sword's hunger, Morgin wasn't sure he could have kept it from devouring JohnEngine's life. He ran from that thought, rode blindly with all the speed Mortiss could deliver, rode himself to exhaustion.

21

The ShadowLord

"THAT WAS A good raid," JohnEngine said. "We didn't lose any men, and we cut further into Illalla's supplies."

They'd bivouacked on a high slope overlooking the road. The men were resting while he and the Balenda, the Surriot, France, Tulellcoe and Abileen held a short council of war. They all needed a good night's sleep and a hot meal.

Tulellcoe shook his head, looked at the empty road far below. "But that's not enough. We didn't slow him down much and he can spare the supplies."

The usually silent Surriot spoke up. "He is being slowed, but not by us."

JohnEngine asked. "What do you mean?"

Tulellcoe twisted slightly, and over his shoulder called out, "Packwill. Please come here."

The scout rose to his feet and joined the small council of war, though Tulellcoe continued to look at the advancing army down on the road as he spoke to JohnEngine. "Haven't you noticed the graves they leave behind each morning when they break camp? They're scattered all the way up and down the length of their encampment. And there's always two twelves of them, never more, never less."

JohnEngine frowned. "That is odd. I'd noticed the graves but I hadn't counted them. I assumed Illalla's men were fighting among themselves."

Tulellcoe shook his head thoughtfully. "Not yet, though that'll begin soon. Packwill. Tell Lord JohnEngine what you did this morning and what you found."

The scout nodded. "Like you told me, my lord, I took two men and dug up a couple of them graves. Their throats was cut. Probably in their sleep. No other marks on 'em."

Tulellcoe pointed at the army below. "Those men are afraid to go to sleep at night. Someone or something sneaks into their camp and cuts throats at random, and Illalla is powerless to stop him. He's quadrupled the perimeter guard, and still it continues. Last night the desertions began; two or three twelves of his men snuck off into the forest. Tonight that number will probably double, and soon they'll begin fighting among themselves."

"Look," the Balenda said, pointing. "This side of that sharp bend in the road. Do you see it?"

Down on the road JohnEngine saw nothing at the point the woman indicated. Illalla's army was approaching from the north, but she was pointing to a spot some distance from a sharp bend in the road that would yet be out of sight of the High Lord and his men.

"What did you see?" Tulellcoe asked.

"I don't know. It looked like a horseman, a mounted rider wearing a long black cloak, but it wasn't. He came out of the shadows at the edge of the road, rode some distance up the road, then disappeared into the shadows again." She shook her head and frowned thoughtfully. "There was the oddest thing about him, as if he and his horse were themselves shadows."

JohnEngine asked, "What did you say?" She started to say it again but he waved her off. "No, I heard what you said. You said shadows."

Behind her France shook his head. "You know, John me lad, sometimes you're not very quick."

"You don't mean Morgin?" JohnEngine said. "He's not even here."

Abileen spoke up. "He crossed alone, Your Lordship. At Kallun's Gorge. Shortly before the rest of you came."

"Why didn't you tell me this?"

The soldier shrugged. "I figured you knew. And he told me not to speak of it. And when I heard he was under sentence of death, I figured best to keep my mouth shut."

In that moment JohnEngine realized he hadn't sensed Morgin's presence because he was so used to having him nearby, like not noticing the air itself.

"He's always around us," Packwill said. "Sometimes I hear a twig break and there's no one there, like he's one of the shadows himself. Maybe he is the Shadow-Lord."

"Of course not," JohnEngine said. "You're a grown man, Packwill. You know better than that. That's a tale to frighten small children. The ShadowLord doesn't exist anymore than faeries and angels do."

Abileen shrugged, tilted his head slightly to one side. "Well maybe he does now."

"There he is," the Balenda said, again pointing down to the road.

This time they all saw him; he'd trotted his horse out into the middle of the road and brought it to a stop. The apparition of a horse and rider, obscured by shadows in broad daylight where no shadows should be, sent a shiver up JohnEngine's spine. But then the shadows disappeared, revealing a lone black rider in a hooded black cloak atop a coal black mount. Illalla and his army were still beyond the bend in the road and had yet to see the rider waiting for them, his horse abnormally still, his sword drawn, gripped in one hand hanging casually at his side. It was the rider's arrogance that was most frightening, for he waited alone in the middle of the road for the on-coming army.

"He's playing a game of terror with Illalla," Tulellcoe said. "And I think we're about to see it ratcheted up to a new level."

••••

Morgin waited in the road trying to control his pounding heart. He could sense Illalla in the distance and the Kulls and the clansmen who accompanied him. Soon, Illalla and his men would round the bend in the road and find a long, straight, narrow stretch, empty of everything but a single black rider seated on a horse standing in the middle of the road. He had chosen this spot carefully for that effect.

It had taken Morgin quite a while to fashion the hood from a strip torn from the bottom of a Kull cloak. His trail kit included a needle and thread, but he was not trained in their use for anything beyond quick repairs, and from up close the results were poor. It only needed to look good from a distance, and if the game he'd chosen to play was to have the desired effect, the hood was mandatory, for in the children's tales the ShadowLord always wore a hooded cloak. It would also serve to shadow his face in the bright sun, adding further to the illusion. Illalla and the noblemen with him would not believe that the ShadowLord had come to life, but common soldiers were, by nature, a superstitious lot, and this day Morgin intended to leave them with a story to tell.

The main column of the Decouix army rounded the bend in the road. They continued to advance for some seconds, but then one of the noblemen near Illalla stood up in his stirrups and pointed. Morgin saw the nobleman's lips move, but the distance was too great to hear his words. Illalla hesitated, allowing more of his army to round the bend, but then he raised his hand and brought the advance to a stop.

Illalla stared at Morgin for several heartbeats, then turned to the nobleman and said something. Moments later the nobleman and two Kulls left the main column and rode toward Morgin at a trot. They stopped a good distance away and the nobleman shouted, "Who are you? What do you want?"

Morgin held his silence, and Mortiss cooperated by remaining perfectly still.

"Speak up," the nobleman shouted.

Again Morgin held his silence.

His patience exhausted, the nobleman turned to the two Kulls and said something. The Kulls drew their swords and spurred their horses forward into a side-by-side charge.

Morgin had picked this spot carefully. Not far from him, between him and the charging Kulls, the branches of a large oak tree extended well out over the road, casting the road and the shallow ditches on both sides in a mottled patchwork of sunlight and shadows that shifted constantly with the soft breezes in the tree tops. He and

Mortiss stood statue still while the Kulls charged, for his timing must be perfect, and not until the two halfmen were at full charge did he finally touch his spurs to Mortiss. But he merely nudged her into an easy trot, and he didn't bring up his sword.

He reached the mottled shadows in the road two heartbeats before the Kulls, and in that instant he cast a deep shadow over him and Mortiss and pulled her off the road into the shadowed ditch. He knew it would appear as if he'd simply vanished.

In mid charge the Kulls sat up in their saddles, lowered their swords and let their horses run slowly down to a trot, passing swiftly through the shadows beneath the tree and out the other side. They came to a complete stop, turned their mounts and looked about. The nobleman stood up in his stirrups and said, "Where is he? Where'd he go?"

One of the Kulls raised his arms in an exaggerated shrug. The nobleman spurred his horse forward into a trot, passed through the shadows in the road and joined the two Kulls. They looked around for a few moments, then turned and began trotting back toward Illalla. But as they passed back through the shadows Morgin pulled Mortiss silently into step behind them. The nobleman and the two Kulls passed into the sunlight, and as Morgin followed them he extinguished his shadowmagic so that it would seem to everyone that he had reappeared just as suddenly as he had vanished. He gave Illalla and the main column just one instant to see him, then he raised his sword, spurred Mortiss hard, and charged between the two Kulls, beheading them with two quick strokes of his sword. He continued the charge, driving Mortiss into the unwary nobleman's mount with enough force to knock horse and rider to the ground.

The nobleman fell in a sprawl. His horse got up faster than he and trotted away in a panic. Morgin brought Mortiss to a stop over the nobleman, leaned over and put the tip of his sword at the man's throat.

The nobleman looked back at the two headless Kulls, then he looked up, and Morgin knew he'd see only shadows where a face should be. "Who are you?"

The shadows within the hood were quite natural, so Morgin cast a shadowspell over his face and head, then slid the hood back. When the nobleman saw that even in the light of day all that remained were shadows, his eyes widened and he asked in a trembling whisper, "What are you?"

Morgin spoke in a low-pitched growl. "Tell Illalla I am the beast that walks the night. Tell him I am the shadow that brings death to his men's dreams. Tell him I am the ShadowLord, and that soon I will come to his dreams." And with that Morgin lifted his sword, trotted Mortiss back into the shadows, and vanished.

••••

That night Morgin made his usual visit to Illalla's camp, but this time he killed all of the guards surrounding Illalla's tent. He wanted to leave the impression that he could have killed Illalla, though he knew that he could not, not with Bayellgae close at hand.

And even had Bayellgae been absent, Illalla was a far more powerful sorcerer than Morgin. Still, the impression would remain, at least as far as Illalla's men were concerned. The ShadowLord was invincible to the point where he could toy with the High Lord of the Greater Clans. And perhaps even Illalla would begin to doubt some of his own power.

The next day Morgin again met Illalla on the road, and played out his role as the mythical ShadowLord. This time Illalla did not hesitate, but sent a dozen Kulls charging up the road after him. Morgin slipped into the shadows at the edge of the road, waited for the Kulls to stop and start milling about in confusion, appeared in their midst, cut two of them down and disappeared again. He did that several times, and in a confusion of shadows and darkness, he cut the halfmen down one by one. That night more than two hundred men deserted Illalla's army even before Morgin harvested his usual quota of slit-throats.

Morgin checked on Tulellcoe and his men regularly, usually slipping into their camp in the early evening. They were badly divided now. France and Tulellcoe wanted to stay out of the way and let Morgin terrorize Illalla's army. The Balenda and JohnEngine thought they should continue to harass the Decouix.

The next morning, with the sun still low on the horizon, and the shadows slanting sharply across the road, Morgin chose a stretch of road and slipped into the shadows to wait for Illalla. The High Lord now had three Kull patrols scouring the road ahead of his army. Morgin watched them pass by several times, and their frequency forced him to wait until Illalla was much closer than usual before spurring Mortiss onto the road.

He decided to give Illalla and his men a bit of a show, and this time held his shadowmagic strongly in place as Mortiss carried him out into the daylight. Mortiss and his shadows saved his life.

Illalla reacted instantly. Morgin heard him shout, "There he is. Now." Too late Morgin realized he was much too close.

Two bowmen, riding beside the High Lord, raised their bows and loosed their arrows almost as one. Both shafts sliced through the air toward Morgin and there was no time for him to react, but at the last instant Mortiss reared beneath him, placing herself between him and the death slicing toward him. The first shaft caught her squarely in the breast; the second slipped past her and buried itself in the meat of Morgin's left armpit.

Morgin almost lost consciousness; it was all he could do to ignore the pain and hold on as Mortiss screamed and collapsed beneath him, sending him sprawling into the shadows at the side of the road. The arrow in his armpit snapped off painfully as he slammed into the ground, leaving a short length of shaft buried beneath his skin. He managed to hold onto his shadowmagic.

He staggered to his feet in the shadows at the side of the road as a dozen Kulls charged toward him, glanced over his shoulder once but could see nothing of Mortiss.

Fighting to hold onto consciousness and his shadowmagic, he slipped into the trees. Behind him he heard the Kulls thrashing about searching for him. He found a small game trail, and as he staggered up it he called for power, digging into the netherworld for it, tugging desperately at any he found. He managed to stop some of the bleeding, and lessened the pain somewhat, but he knew he would not get far on foot.

Up ahead he spotted a large shadow in the game trail blocking it completely. He heard the Kulls getting nearer, but he hesitated, not sure what he faced. Then the shadows dissipated, and Mortiss stood before him.

She seemed unhurt, and he wanted to believe that the arrow had missed her, but he knew in his heart it had struck true. With his left arm useless he struggled to climb into her saddle, then he spurred her lightly, and as she broke into a trot he leaned forward against her neck and passed out.

••••

"There's something wrong here," Tulellcoe said as they crossed the shallows at Gilguard's Ford.

JohnEngine sensed it too, an uneasiness in his soul as if there were some terrible danger nearby. It had come upon them only when their horses had stepped into the waters of the ford, then disappeared as soon as they stepped out of it.

Tulellcoe barked out orders. "John, Cort, Val. Stay here with me." He looked at France. "Take the men down the road a piece, but keep us in sight. There's something magical here, and I want to know what."

France nodded. "Don't take long though. Illalla's not far behind us." He led the men a safe distance down the road.

Tulellcoe dismounted. John and the Surriot and the Balenda followed suit. "Cort, Val, take the other side of the river. John and I'll take this side. Start working your way up river and keep your eyes open."

"What are we looking for?" the Surriot asked.

Tulellcoe started walking, called back over his shoulder. "I don't know."

JohnEngine and Tulellcoe moved slowly up the southern bank of the Ulbb, and the tension in his soul grew with each step. About five hundred paces up the river they found a flat, shimmering wall of water, stretching between the walls of a high rock canyon.

"By the gods," Tulellcoe swore. "This thing must have been building for days. And it's Morgin's work. He must still be alive, otherwise the spell would have collapsed at his death. And what a spell it is!"

"I've been telling you that," JohnEngine said. "I'd know if he was dead."

They heard shouts down at the ford. They both turned and raced downstream, arrived just in time to see a shadow rider on a shadow horse trotting down the road.

France and Abileen, followed by Packwill and the rest of the men, intercepted the horse, caught Morgin as he collapsed out of the saddle. JohnEngine ran across the road, helped them lay Morgin down by the edge of the river. But when he looked into his brother's face the ever shifting shadows that danced there forced him to look away.

He has become the ShadowLord, JohnEngine thought.

The shadows dissipated and JohnEngine saw the pain and fatigue in his brother's face, and the red stain that covered his left side.

"Go away," Morgin gasped. "It's not safe here. The spell!"

"He's right," France said. "Illalla's Kulls will be along any moment."

The Balenda shook her head. "The Decouix isn't scouring the road so thoroughly, now that he thinks the ShadowLord is dead. And this young man has something to do with that spell, so he needs help here and now."

While the Balenda examined Morgin, Tulellcoe sent Packwill back up the road to keep an eye on Illalla. The Balenda stood up straight, and in a bloody hand she held an equally bloody piece of an arrow shaft.

"How did you do that so quickly?" JohnEngine demanded.

She shrugged. "My magic has always seemed particularly effective at healing."

"Get out of here," Morgin said weakly, clearly still in great pain.

"He's right," Tulellcoe said. "Pick him up and bring him with us."

Morgin shook his head. "No. I'm staying." JohnEngine watched him attempt to stand, but he failed miserably, so JohnEngine helped him to his feet. "Get out of here," he said again. "Go away. I have to do this alone."

Tulellcoe shook his head, but the Balenda stepped up to Morgin and gently placed a hand on his wounded shoulder. She held it there for a moment, and JohnEngine sensed something arcane between them. When she withdrew her hand Morgin stood just a little straighter, though he still looked terribly weak. But now the Balenda swayed uneasily, and a red stain had spread near her left armpit. She looked at Morgin and said, "That's the best I can do."

Morgin said. "Thank you."

Tulellcoe pointed a finger at Morgin. "We're leaving, and you're coming with us."

Packwill shouted, "They're coming."

Everyone looked across the ford, saw the scout on his horse pounding toward them.

"Right," France said. "Let's get the netherhell out of here."

They all turned back to Morgin, but he and his horse had disappeared into the shadows of the forest.

••••

When Illalla came into sight on the other side of Gilguard's Ford, Morgin trotted Mortiss out into the middle of the road, trying not to show the slightest hint that he was hurt, for the ShadowLord must appear invulnerable. The effect was immediate and undeniable: Illalla started and reined in his horse.

This time Morgin had been more careful. Illalla was far up the road on the north side of Gilguard's Ford, well out of bow shot, while Morgin sat on Mortiss a short distance south of the ford. Illalla held a hurried conference with his Kull commander. Orders were shouted, and in response twelve twelves of Kulls formed up in front of the main column.

The Kulls charged immediately. Morgin held Mortiss as still as he could keep her, wanted to appear as if he would meet their charge by just standing there. He reached deep into the back of his soul where the river spell had been festering for days. As the water stacked up behind his translucent dam the spell had demanded more of him. It had been like drawing a bow string back and holding it, an easy task at first, but after enough time even the strongest bowman's arm begins to tremble. The pain in his wounded shoulder almost made him release the spell prematurely as the Kulls charged down the road toward him. But he held it, waited until his trembling magic told him he could wait no longer, and in that moment he relaxed.

The bow string in his soul twanged so loudly that any wizard or witch within a league must have heard it. The Kulls were in the midst of their charge, just approaching the ford and oblivious to anything but their target. An instant before they hit the shallows in the ford the ground trembled and the air filled with the sound of snapping trees. The entire company of Kulls was well into the ford when a wall of water, carrying a mass of splintered logs like battering rams, burst into the open flat of the ford. It slammed into the charging line of halfmen and horses, and with screams and cries the Kulls and their mounts joined the logs in the turmoil of water that swept down through the ford.

The last vestiges of the wall of water washed away and an abnormal silence descended over the ford. With the exception of a few dead horses washed up on the river banks, there was no sign that twelve twelves of Kulls had ever existed.

Morgin pitched his voice low and filled the silence with a single, evil laugh. He growled it out, not the laughter of joy or happiness, but a challenge to the High Lord of the Greater Council. He turned Mortiss about, and with his back to the High Lord he arrogantly trotted up the road, melting slowly into a shadow that vanished on the wind.

••••

Standing in Olivia's audience chamber with Roland and AnnaRail, Brandon listened to the old woman relate the information Tulellcoe had sent her: the wall of water at Gilguard's Ford, the desertions from Illalla's army. Olivia beamed with satisfaction. "This ShadowLord ruse that Morgin is playing is brilliant. Ah, that grandson of mine. I always knew he had it in him."

Roland leaned toward her, and when he spoke his voice was tight with anger. "But your condemnation of him drove him to it."

"Yes," Olivia said, "It did, didn't it?" She gave them all an unpleasant, knowing smile.

Brandon could see that Roland and AnnaRail were even more stunned than he by her admission.

Roland said, "You goaded him on purpose?"

Olivia's smile disappeared and her eyes narrowed. "Of course. Someone needed to push him to finally make use of that considerable power of his. And it worked rather nicely."

Brandon was tempted to comment on that, but thought better of it. "Gilguard's Ford, eh? Then we have at least another five days before Illalla can reach Sa'umbra."

"Even more," she said happily, "if Morgin continues to harry him."

"Oh he will," Brandon said unhappily. "You've seen to that. But Illalla is no fool. He'll not sit idly and continue to take this. I only hope that Morgin is prepared when he strikes back. For he will, and soon."

22

The Shadow of Death

ON THE DAY following the flood at Gilguard's Ford, Morgin awoke under the care of the Balenda. He was surprised at how strong he felt, and how weak she seemed, and then he learned that the price she paid for such miraculous healing was to bring the suffering on herself.

Morgin tried to get a few hours' sleep before nightfall. But he now feared sleep, and the dreams it brought. He dreamt again and again of a long dead skeleton king, of strange lands and even stranger beings. There was a great hound that stood as high as any man, with enormous powerful jaws that could swallow Morgin's head whole. It was called a hellhound, and upon its head it wore a crown. There was also an odd beast half eagle, half lion called a griffin, and upon its head it wore a crown.

He always dreamed the same dream, and it brought him to that same grassy plain, seated atop a magnificent war-horse, with that great broadsword strapped to his side. He now knew that it was not he atop the horse, but another who had lived in a far distant past. In the dream Morgin was a captive in the man's soul. He looked through his eyes, listened through his ears, felt through his hands. And it always ended the same: seated atop the great war-horse, facing a vast army, with one equally as vast behind him, Morgin would wake screaming in the night. And never could he remember the dream's end.

He gave up on sleep, opened his eyes and sat up. He stood, walked out of the camp to a small stream. He knelt down near a calm pool, cupped his hands, bent to retrieve some water, and as he did so he looked at his reflection, but all he saw was shadow.

His hands trembled. He sensed his power flowing about him, growing ever stronger with each passing hour, as if building to some arcane crescendo. Perhaps that came from using it almost continuously. Not even Tulellcoe would attempt some of the spells he now cast as a matter of course. And yet, with all the practice, his control was slipping relentlessly away, much like the water that drained slowly through his fingers no matter how tightly he cupped his hands.

He wondered for a moment if it was the killing. Perhaps being the instrument of so much death was affecting his contact with the netherworld.

He splashed water on his face and looked again at his image in the pool. He concentrated, and slowly the shadows dissipated.

"Morgin, lad," France called. "The scouts are returning."

"I'm coming," Morgin said, but he took one last look at his reflection in the water. France had broken his concentration, and the shadows that swirled about his face had returned. Again he banished them, though each time he found it harder to do so.

When he walked into the camp the scouts had already arrived. Their horses were badly lathered and they themselves were breathing heavily. Packwill faced Tulellcoe and spoke rapidly. "Salula has returned from Sa'umbra, my lord, and brought Prince Valso with him. Then Salula left the main column with twice twelve twelves of Kulls at his back. They're riding light; probably journeycake, water, and a blanket, and they're riding hard, my lord, straight for us."

"How much time do we have?"

"Not much, my lord. They're not far behind us."

The Balenda laid a hand gently on Tulellcoe's shoulder. "Do we fight or run?"

Tulellcoe spoke to Packwill. "Find us a good place for an ambush, bows and arrows only. And make sure we've got a good out for a quick retreat."

To the Balenda he said, "First we fight, then we run."

••••

Morgin waited with the rest of them hidden well within the trees. He tried to suppress his magic, fearful that Salula would sense him. He watched the Kulls work their way slowly down the steep slope, Salula foremost among them. They didn't chatter and talk while they rode as ordinary men might, but held to a foreboding silence. They were like gray black shadows in the sun: stark, deadly, malevolent. Morgin had never feared shadow before, but these . . . they were not true shadow.

They had hoped that Salula and his Kulls would come in haste, that they would charge down the slope, over the uneven ground at its bottom, and into the trees where the Elhiynes waited. But Salula was no fool, and his scouts were good. They had detected something at the top of the slope that made them wary, so they came down cautiously.

Salula halted at the bottom of the hill. He stood high in his stirrups and scanned the terrain before him. Morgin could see nothing of his face, but imagined the smile that formed there, the smile he'd seen the night Salula had put the lash to his back.

"ShadowLord," Salula called. His voice, even when raised to a shout, was a low growl. "I am told you are called ShadowLord, enemy of my king. Well your shadows will not hide you from me. I have come for you, and these other men about you cannot save you. They can die beside you, but you I will have, ShadowLord. You I will devour."

Tulellcoe said. "This ambush has no hope of success. Pass the word to slip away quietly. We'll try again, but at another time and place."

••••

Morgin crept up to the edge of the cliff and peered cautiously over its lip. Far below the stillness of the valley floor remained unbroken by movement.

"Well?" JohnEngine asked. "What do you see?"

"Nothing," Morgin said.

"Do you think we've lost them?"

Morgin stared into the distance. "I hope so," he said. "We certainly hit them hard enough this morning."

Cort dropped down beside him. "Aye, Salula walked right into that one. We hurt him badly." There was a smile on her lips. She enjoyed killing Kulls.

Standing behind them, Tulellcoe said, "We lost nine men this morning. How many do you think Salula lost?"

"Thirty," France said flatly. "Maybe forty."

"And yet he's winning," Tulellcoe said. "Because he can afford to lose thirty or forty men, and we can't afford to lose one."

Val shrugged. "No doubt that's his strategy. He'll hound us until he catches us. You've cost Illalla dearly, Morgin. Mostly you've cost him his pride. A few hundred Kulls is a small price to pay for your head."

"I think we've lost them," the Balenda said.

"Perhaps for the moment," Tulellcoe said. "But Val's right. Salula won't give up until we're all dead."

Morgin rolled onto his back, closed his eyes, rubbed them with his fingertips, and noticed the shadows fluttering about his hands. It took a real effort to banish them. Sleep! Other than the occasional catnap, Morgin couldn't recall when they'd last truly slept. Perhaps they should stand now and fight, while they still had the strength to die with honor. But then, maybe Cort was right and they'd lost the Kulls.

As if in answer to his thoughts, Val said, "Look, there they are."

Morgin opened his eyes and rolled back onto his stomach. He had to search for several seconds, but he finally located them: tiny black riders moving slowly across the valley floor.

The rider in the lead stopped, and those following halted behind him. At that distance it was impossible to be certain, but Morgin felt sure it was Salula, and the half-man seemed to look directly at them, as if he knew they were crouched high above, watching him. Again Morgin imagined a smile forming on that rock hard face, then the lead rider threw his head back, and a strange sound echoed off the walls of the valley. Only slowly did they recognize it as growling, inhuman laughter.

Morgin said. "Those Kulls will have to follow the same trail as us. It's the only way up out of that valley, and it's steep. It would be nice if we could arrange some sort of surprise. A landslide perhaps. With a few arrows thrown in for good measure."

••••

Up ahead Tulellcoe reined his horse to a stop. Morgin pulled Mortiss up beside him and wiped a dirty sleeve across his brow. He didn't have to concentrate, for Salula's hatred pulled at him constantly now. "They're almost on top of us," he said. "If we stop now, we must fight."

Tulellcoe nodded. "The men and horses are exhausted. Better to fight now than when our strength is completely gone."

Morgin looked at the troop. They were all gaunt and haggard; little sleep and almost no rest with Salula and his halfmen dogging them relentlessly, and always closer.

The landslide had worked well, killing many Kulls, but when the dust had cleared Salula was still there. He and his halfmen regrouped and they continued their pursuit, leaving their dead behind unburied.

Morgin took a quick head count. There were thirty of them remaining, and Salula had eighty or so. *It is time to die*, he thought.

They were in a small, rocky ravine with steep slopes rising on both sides. "This looks like a good place for it," Tulellcoe said. "We'll ride ahead then split up into two groups. I'll lead one, and you, Morgin, the other. We'll circle back on both sides and hit them here."

Tulellcoe spun his horse about in the ravine and led them up the trail a good distance before reining in. "Split up here," he shouted, then spurred his horse off the trail. Morgin spurred Mortiss off the other side.

In the trees the going was slow. They made it with only seconds to spare before two Kull trackers appeared in the ravine below. Morgin held his breath and prayed that no one would give them away.

The trackers stopped in the middle of the ravine and they paid close attention to the tracks there. Moments later Salula arrived. He stopped to confer with them, and behind him came the rest of the halfmen, stretched out in a long line that led down the trail.

This was the closest Morgin had ever come to Salula in broad daylight. His face could have been chiseled from stone for all the expression it held, a face that had long ago forgotten how to look human. But Morgin would always remember Salula best by firelight, his face splitting into a pleased grimace as he brought the lash down one more time.

Tulellcoe shouted and charged. Morgin spurred Mortiss viciously, shouted at the top of his lungs and charged down the side of the ravine headed straight for Salula. The halfman looked up, surprised, drew his sword in an instant and met Morgin's charge squarely. Their swords crashed together once, and as Morgin charged past the Kull captain he glimpsed again Salula's leering grin. The ravine filled quickly with men and halfmen hacking at one another.

Morgin turned Mortiss in the midst of the melee and cut at anything in gray-black. Salula came at him; their swords met again; both horses slammed against one another and Mortiss went down.

Morgin hit the ground hard, took the fall rolling and jumped to his feet. He ducked beneath a Kull saber, grabbed Mortiss's saddle horn and climbed back into the saddle. He thrust out instinctively, buried his sword in a halfman's chest. Salula came out of nowhere. His sword whistled past Morgin's ear and again they separated.

Val went down nearby. Morgin saw Cort, on her feet without a horse, running to his aid. He spurred Mortiss forward to intercept a Kull trying to ride her down. He swung and his sword bit into the Kull's side, then he locked swords with another Kull, hilt to hilt. They twisted against one another until he raised a boot and kicked the Kull in the side. The halfman slashed downward and Morgin screamed as the sword cut deeply into his thigh.

The air filled with the hiss of arrows in flight. The Kull Morgin faced slumped forward in his saddle, a startled look on his face, a shaft protruding from his back. More arrows filled the ravine. More Kulls went down. Someone shouted, "Morgin, behind you."

He turned in his saddle just in time to see the glint of steel as it cut toward his face. He ducked and threw his own sword out awkwardly. The two blades rang loudly in his ear, and Salula laughed as he charged past.

Salula spun about and charged at him again. The Kull cut a straight line toward him, intending to ram Morgin's horse with his own. Mortiss was smaller than Salula's mount. They both knew that she would go down again, and with a fiery wound in his thigh, Morgin would find it impossible to remount. With no other choice, he spurred Mortiss about and fled into the forest, looked back over his shoulder and saw that his comrades were scattering in all directions. Salula laughed loudly and followed.

Morgin dodged around several trees, spun Mortiss in her tracks, then charged back toward Salula. The Kull continued his own charge and as they passed at full gallop their swords crashed together once.

Morgin pulled back on Mortiss's reins. He spun her about, dodged around a tree and charged again at Salula. Again their swords rang together. Over and over they charged at one another in a test of speed and strength and agility, twisting and turning among the trees in the forest. Morgin tried always to keep at least one tree between them. It forced them both to dodge at the last moment before their swords met, and that gave Mortiss some advantage, for she was lighter and more agile than the Kull mount. With each charge the sounds of battle in the ravine grew fainter, and each time their swords met Morgin's arm weakened, and Salula's grin broadened.

Morgin could finally take no more. As their swords met one last time, he spurred Mortiss on and did not turn back. He no longer heard anything from the battle in the ravine, so he chose a direction at random and spurred Mortiss to the point of cruelty. He swung his sword arm about in a desperate attempt to limber it up, and always behind him he heard Salula's mocking laughter.

Salula caught up with him after a short sprint, so he cut hard to the right, then to the left. Right, left, right, left; he played a game much like that Rat had played in the streets of Anistigh, a game of desperation and adrenaline and fear. Salula gained on him in the straight, but lost distance each time he cut to one side. Again he used the trees and Mortiss's agility, trying always to make a sudden turn within inches of one, then charging straight for some distance before the next turn. Behind him he heard Salula's mount struggling for air, Salula beating it with the flat of his sword and laughing, sounds that came closer with each beat of Morgin's heart. He picked out a tree, and at the right moment ripped Mortiss's reins to the left. He cut too close; his shoulder brushed the tree's bark painfully, and that saved his life, for Salula had anticipated his move.

Salula's sword sliced past his nose and chopped into the tree's bark. Chips of wood stung Morgin's face. He almost fell from his saddle, but he held on and threw his sword out desperately as he shot past Salula and it cut into the halfman's shoulder.

"Ahhh!" Salula cried. He sounded happy. "'Tis good sport you give, Shadow-Lord."

Morgin's stomach lurched as Mortiss charged down an embankment and splashed into a small streambed with a rocky bottom and good footing. Morgin turned Mortiss up it and spurred her madly, swatting her rump with the flat of his sword. He heard Salula close behind him doing the same.

The streambed was a mistake, for it narrowed and grew deeper the higher they went. Mortiss nostrils flared, she gasped and coughed as she fought her way through it, water spraying outward in all directions. Salula's larger horse found the going easier and gained on them.

Morgin pulled Mortiss out of the streambed and up an embankment. Salula halted below them. "'Tis a merry chase you lead, ShadowLord," he called, and laughed. "But our moment is at hand."

Morgin ignored him, charged through the trees, heard the Kull and his horse crashing through the forest behind him, laughing insanely. Morgin, crouched low in the saddle, let Mortiss pick her own way while he looked back to gauge Salula's distance. But the Kull was nowhere to be seen. Fearing some trick, Morgin tried to look in all directions at once, and then there were no more trees. The forest had ended, and Morgin now charged out onto a gray and featureless plain cast in the dim shadows of the dying sun of late afternoon.

Morgin let Mortiss's reins go slack, and the animal, exhausted and no longer spurred frantically by her master, slowed to a trot, then a walk, then stopped altogether. Before him stretched a flat and barren plain without shape or contour, an arid land of sagebrush and brown grasses, a land without end. There were no mountains in the distance, merely a flat sea of land that ended in a thin, straight line of a horizon. Salula and his halfmen had pushed them so far east that Morgin had finally come to the Plains of Quam.

Salula's mocking laughter shattered the stillness. Morgin thought first of running, of giving Mortiss her head and riding like the wind. But out on the open plain Salula would just ride him down. "You must learn to face your fears," AnnaRail had always told him, so he turned Mortiss about.

Salula waited calmly astride his horse near the edge of the trees, his cheeks stretched into that grin of his. "Well, ShadowLord," Salula said. "Our time has come. The chase is done, but it was a good chase, and you fought well, so it will be an honor to personally lay your soul at my master's feet, to tell him that it was I who took your life. For that is what he wants, Elhiyne: the life and the soul of the Lord of Shadow. And I always give my master what he wants."

Morgin thought of all the times he had faced death in the past days, and of how luck had come to his aid time and again. But there was no luck here, only his skill with horse and sword pitted against that of Salula. Salula understood that too, and by the grin on his face he clearly knew whose skill was the greater. If only Morgin had some magic to aid him. But exhausted and almost fully spent, he had no strength to summon the arcane. So with nothing to lose, Morgin wished for a quick and painless death, slapped Mortiss's flank with the flat of his sword and charged at the halfman.

They raced toward one another, bent low in their saddles, sword points held out and forward. Mortiss's hooves thundered on the hard, dry ground with a beat that matched the pace of Morgin's heart. He sensed in her courage far beyond his own, and that shamed him.

With uncanny clarity, he could see the tip of Salula's sword aimed straight at him. He wondered if he could deflect it before thrusting with his own sword, but he'd only have the barest instant, and his timing would have to be incredible. So he held his own sword steady, determined that if Salula was going to spit him like a rabbit, he would at least take the halfman with him.

He and Salula met. Their swords crashed together. The force of the blow ripped the sword from Morgin's hand. It wrenched his arm painfully out and back, and almost pulled him from his saddle. Agony shot up his sword arm and into his shoulder. With his left hand he dropped the reins and grabbed for the saddle horn just to stay mounted. He struggled to sit upright, while streaks of pain shot through his arm from the wrist to the shoulder. Blood welled from a slash on his forearm where Salula's sword had touched him.

He retrieved Mortiss's reins, brought her to a stop, then spun her about to face Salula for the last time, unarmed and without hope.

Salula still rode away from him, took his time to confidently and easily bring his mount to a stop. He sat upright in his saddle, so sure of himself that he didn't even bother to turn and look back at Morgin. He brought his horse slowly from a gallop to a trot, then stopped altogether, and sat there astride it with his back to Morgin, a clearly intended insult.

Salula's horse took a few meandering steps, as if wandering aimlessly without the guidance of its master. It bent its head to nibble on some prairie grass, then turned casually to one side.

In profile, Morgin saw his own sword buried to the guard just below Salula's chin. The hilt protruded upward from Salula's shoulder and forced him to hold his head cocked slightly back and to one side. Like Morgin the Kull had been bent low in the saddle; Morgin's sword had penetrated down the length of his torso, impaling him from neck to waist.

Morgin looked down at his bloody right hand. On it, mixed with his own blood, he saw a thick, grayish-red stain.

He looked back at Salula. The Kull's sword hand opened almost casually and his sword fell to the ground. Then the Kull reached up with both hands and grasped the hilt of Morgin's sword. He held them there for a moment, as if praying to the gods for mercy, then he dropped them to his sides, and Salula, supreme Kull, captain and commander of all Kulls, toppled from his saddle to lay dead upon the Plains of Quam.

Morgin sat atop Mortiss in the dying light of dusk unable to believe what he'd just done. His eyes welled with tears, but he choked them back. He wiped the grayish-red stain from his hand, smeared it on his breeches.

Shakily he dismounted. He tore some cloth from his blouse to bandage his arm and thigh. His eyes welled with tears again. They blinded him and this time would not be stopped. Finally, he crossed his legs and sat down on the plain. He buried his face in his hands, and with Mortiss standing silently over him, sobbed openly, wishing he was a child again so that he might do so without dishonor.

23

Twice the Fool

MORGIN SPENT THE night seated on the plain wrapped in his blanket with Mortiss's reins tied to his wrist. Not that she would wander off, but having her near comforted him as he slipped in and out of dream. His dream was not the kind born of sleep. Instead he sat conscious and awake for a while, shivering with more than the cold of the night air, then skipped into the dream. That happened repeatedly, and he always entered it at some random point in the sequence of events all part of the same whole. At least the dream was taking on a certain terrifying consistency; the bits and pieces of it were slowly falling into place, and understanding now seemed only just beyond his grasp.

Between snatches of dream an undesired flood of power washed over him, a pool of magic that had entered the Mortal Plane unbidden, and that clung to him now with rabid tenacity. It poured through him in waves. It turned his stomach when it crested, left him trembling with fatigue when it ebbed. At one point it reached such intensity that it attracted a cluster of small spirits from the netherworld. They hooted and shrieked about him for a while until he tired of their antics and swatted them out of the Mortal Plane with a flash of power that even Olivia would have envied. Such power frightened him, but before he had time to really consider its implications, he drifted again into his dream.

The first hint of dawn came as a faint glow at the edge of the black night sky. Each time he returned from his dream the sky seemed lighter, until finally it took on a deep blue hue and separated itself from the black earth by a thin, dark line. In his life Morgin had never seen such a featureless and straight horizon. The sight of it was an anchor that held him in the world he hoped was reality. He clung to that horizon desperately while the sun rose and the sky brightened. Then, like a candle extinguished in the night, his power left him and he was again free. He looked carefully at the land around him. He had always wanted to see the Plains of Quam, and now he wanted to rip the memory from his mind.

Salula's horse had wandered off in the night, though Salula still lay not far away, a gray-black crumpled heap among the brown brush and grass. Morgin stood, stretched painfully and yawned. He checked the makeshift bandages on his arm and thigh. He did a quick and sloppy job of rolling up his blanket, fastened it to Mortiss's saddle, then turned to Salula. Time to retrieve his sword.

He approached Salula slowly, fearful lest the halfman be not truly dead. But Salula lay on his back with his eyes open and unseeing, and in death he wore the same expression he had in life. Morgin looked at him and winced at the lump that formed in the pit of his stomach.

The hilt of Morgin's sword protruded just above Salula's collarbone. Morgin bent over, took careful hold of it and pulled. Nothing happened. He pulled harder, then harder still, until he began dragging Salula across the ground. He let go of the sword, sat down near Salula's head, an agonizing exercise since his wounded leg had stiffened during the night. He planted a boot on each of Salula's shoulders, gripped the hilt of his sword with both hands, and put his back into the job of pulling on it.

The sword slid free with a sickening scrape. At the same instant a growl erupted from Salula's throat; blood gurgled from his mouth and he sat up with his back to Morgin. He twitched and thrashed about and screamed his anger and hatred at the heavens.

Morgin brought his sword about in a long, flat arc. It bit into Salula's neck and lodged there momentarily. He pulled it free and hacked at the halfman again, had to chop at the Kull's neck three times before the halfman's head jumped from his shoulders, then hit the ground still screaming, bounced once, came to rest with its eyes on Morgin and its lips twitching a nether cry of hatred. The air filled with the taint of Salula's evil.

Morgin scrambled to his feet, limped to the screaming head, hacked it in two with his sword. It still screamed at him, and laughed Salula's laugh. He chopped at it again and again, and each time his sword touched the head Salula's voice dwindled, but it refused to die. He smashed the pieces with his boots, ground them into the dirt, and yet Salula's laugh still drifted about on a nether wind, an ethereal cry of hatred, an oath of revenge. It did not stop until Salula's head was nothing more than ichor dripping from Morgin's boots, though Salula's evil still clung to the air.

Morgin wiped the gray-red stain from his sword and boots on some prairie grass, then slid his sword into its sheath. Only when the hilt slammed home did the last essence of Salula dissipate, as if somehow the sword itself drew his spirit into this world.

Mortiss stood nearby, nibbling on some small flowers, as if what had just happened were no concern of hers. Morgin limped over to her, climbed painfully into the saddle, but before he rode on, he extinguished the shadows that enveloped him, for he feared what would become of him if he lived forever in shadow.

He turned back toward the forest and nudged Mortiss forward.

••••

"I want him dead," Illalla shouted.

"But what of Sssalula, my lord?" Bayellgae hissed.

"Salula is dead."

Valso jumped to his feet. "No," he said. "That can't be. No Elhiyne pup has the power to kill Salula."

Illalla took pleasure in his son's discomfort. "This one does."

Valso shook his head. "That's just not possible."

Illalla turned on Valso. "But it is, for I felt Salula die myself. And that means the Elhiyne still lives."

"Then he must die."

Illalla nodded. "Yes. And soon. That is why I need someone who is reliable."

"Sssalula wasss reliable, my lord."

Illalla paced the length of the tent. "Salula was reliable only in his cruelty. I need an assassin who can think." Illalla abruptly stopped his pacing and looked directly at Bayellgae. "That is why I have chosen to give the deed to you, my snake."

"But I am no assssassssin, my lord."

"You are whatever I command you to be, snake." Illalla's anger flared visibly and the serpent cringed. "This Elhiyne is a powerful wizard. Think of the pleasure you will have when you feast upon his soul. Think of how his power will taste as you devour it. And think of the agony that will be your punishment if you refuse."

"Yesss, massster," the serpent hissed. Its tiny wings fluttered for balance as it wove from side to side on its pedestal. "There will be much pleasssure in thisss tasssk. And if he isss asss powerful asss you sssay, it will be a joyful death. And I have nothing to fear, for who can sssurvive the venom of Bayellgae?"

"Only I," Illalla said.

"Yesss, my lord. Only you."

"Go then, snake. Now. Seek out this Elhiyne lordling wherever he may be and kill him. After he is dead I give you his body and his power and his soul. You may do with them as you please."

"Yesss, my lord. Thank you, my lord."

••••

Morgin rode west through the forest, though he was quite lost and had no specific destination in mind. He tried not to think of his dead comrades, but his mind kept tormenting him with images of their corpses rotting in the hot sun. He didn't want to think of JohnEngine that way, or France, or Tulellcoe. He wanted just to ride, and not think at all.

The wounds on his arm and thigh proved to be the source of considerable pain, so his mind was far from thoughts of the trail when Mortiss chose to stop. The abrupt cessation of motion, and the impending danger that he sensed, brought him quickly out of his stupor. He was groggy, and in pain, and unable to react quickly. Before he could do more than blink his eyes, a giant of a man, far taller than Ott the peasant, stepped calmly into the trail. He had bone white skin and coal-black hair. He nocked an arrow into the largest bow Morgin had ever seen, drew the string taught, and aimed the arrow's barbed war point straight at Morgin's heart. At such a short distance there was no question of accuracy, and for an instant Morgin thought he was about to die. But the bowman didn't release the arrow, and a soft female voice spoke from behind Morgin. "Off the horse, boy."

Morgin hesitated, fearing for an instant that he had fallen among bandits, and that his best chance might be to run for it.

The giant bowman shook his head. "Don't try it, lad. Just do as she says."

Morgin looked again at the man. He was a freak, enormously tall but thin and spindly, with coal black hair and bone white skin. Not the pinkish skin common in some of the lighter skinned tribes, but the white of bones long bleached in the sun. He was reminded of an expression he'd often heard: *the white face of the black tribe.* Morgin realized then that the man facing him was Benesh'ere, a tribesman of the seventh Ward. He should at least be neutral, and definitely not a bandit.

Morgin dismounted slowly, careful not to make any quick movements. He faced the bowman and held the empty palms of both hands outward. "I bear no weapon against you."

"Name yourself," the bowman demanded.

"I am Morgin, once named AethonLaw et Elhiyne, but no longer."

The bowman's face broadened into a smile. He relaxed the bow string and lowered the arrow. "Well Morgin ye AethonLaw et Elhiyne. We've been looking for you. Your—" His eyes widened. "Blesset no."

The soft voice behind Morgin hissed, "Lying, filthy Decouix!" Something heavy struck him between the shoulder blades. The air whooshed from his lungs and he went down on his hands and knees.

"He's Elhiyne, girl," the bowman said.

"Looks like a Decouix to me."

"Blesset be still," a third voice called out with authority.

The bowman helped Morgin to his feet, where he leaned against Mortiss while he looked at the owner of the third voice. The man was even taller than the bowman and had the same white skin and black hair. He too carried an enormous bow and seemed to be the leader of this group.

"I'm Jerst," the man said. He did not offer to shake Morgin's hand. He indicated a tall, spindly girl with the same white skin and black hair as the two men. "The one with the heavy hand here is my daughter Blesset."

She was shorter than the men, but still taller than the tallest Elhiyne. She too carried a long bow, and like the men seemed thin and gaunt. She looked at Morgin as if he was a piece of maggoty meat. "Forgive the blow, Elhiyne. I thought you were a Decouix. They too are rather short."

"Blesset!" the bowman snapped. "Keep a civil tongue in your head. I'm Jack, lad," he said to Morgin, "Jack the Lesser. Are you all right? Can you ride?"

"I'm fine," Morgin said.

"Then mount up," Jerst said. "You're coming with us."

"Where are we going?" Morgin asked.

Jerst spoke like Olivia when she thought questions were impertinent. "To our camp."

Morgin was in no way misled by the fact that they let him keep his sword. He'd heard of the fighting prowess of the Benesh'ere, and now was not the time to ask if he was their guest, or their prisoner. But he recognized the long arrows they carried, and realized it was these Benesh'ere who had come to their aid in the last skirmish with Salula's Kulls.

A short time later they rode into a large and well-organized camp that had obviously been there for days. He saw heavily trampled trails, and fire pits that showed the signs of repeated use, and about fifty tents that looked to be light weight and easily transportable. They were wide enough to sleep two, and tall enough for an Elhiyne to stand in if he didn't mind crouching a bit.

The camp was a beehive of noisy activity, with tall spindly Benesh'ere tribesmen moving in all directions. There were as many women as men, and like men they carried arms. Everyone seemed to have something urgent to do, and in the doing raised a small cloud of dust from the hot, dry ground.

"Morgin!"

He recognized JohnEngine's voice and brought Mortiss to a halt, stood up in his stirrups and scanned the camp. He spotted JohnEngine running toward him and waving his arms. He seemed unhurt. Tulellcoe trotted beside him, also unhurt, while France hobbled behind them with a bandage on his right calf, and the Balenda walked behind him with one wrapped about her head. With them were six more Elhiyne, most showing some sign of hurt but all able to walk on their own. And they seemed so short among the tall Benesh'ere.

"I knew you weren't dead," JohnEngine said.

Morgin climbed out of Mortiss's saddle. "What about the others?" he asked. "Are they all dead?"

Tulellcoe shook his head. "Val has a broken shoulder and a bad slash across his ribs. And with him are four others who won't do any fighting for a while. We'll have to send them all to Inetka."

Morgin counted the numbers and felt sick. "But we had more than thirty men before the skirmish in the ravine. Where are the rest?"

"Dead," France said without emotion. "We've buried them."

Morgin's stomach tightened. For the first time that day his power came back to him. It seemed to be drawn to death.

Tulellcoe put a hand on his shoulder. "We were all ready to die. That some of us live, we can only be thankful."

They led Morgin to a small fire apart from the Benesh'ere camp, where he sat down wearily on a large rock. Packwill the Yestmarkian scout was there, and so too was the soldier Abileen. There were four men whose names eluded Morgin, but whose faces were familiar. Tulellcoe removed the bandages from his arm and thigh, and Cort examined each wound carefully. "You've taken proper care of the leg wound, I see. All it needs is cleaning and a fresh bandage. But this arm wound. I sense magic there."

Morgin said. "Salula."

Her eyes narrowed. "And yet, the wound appears to be healing nicely regardless of the taint I sense there."

Abileen cleared his throat. "What of Salula?"

Morgin shrugged. "Dead."

"You killed him?" Cort asked.

"Aye," Morgin said. "Twice I killed him. Let us hope I don't have to do it again."

They all gave him odd, sidewise looks.

Tulellcoe set to cleaning and wrapping his wounds. Morgin wanted to know about their hosts. "What of these Benesh'ere? I see both men and women. Is this a permanent camp?"

Val shook his head. "Far from it."

Morgin looked at the twoname closely, wrapped in bandages from waist to neck, moving about with obvious discomfort. Morgin asked, "Do you know about these Benesh'ere and their ways?"

Val shrugged, then winced, having forgotten the pain such a gesture would cost him. "A while back I lived with them on and off for some years. I know their ways, but I know little of the Benesh'ere themselves. This about you is an advanced scouting party, and they're also prepared to act as a war party if need be."

Morgin scanned the Benesh'ere camp. There appeared to be about a hundred of them, all with the same ghostly white skin. Most had the coal black hair that Morgin had seen on Jerst and Blesset and Jack, but it softened to a light gray in some who seemed older.

"If this is a scouting party," Morgin asked, "where is the rest of the tribe?"

"Out on the plains," Val said. "They're just coming in off the Munjarro where they spend the winter months. They'll spend the hotter summer months at the Lake of Sorrows."

Morgin grimaced as Tulellcoe applied healing salve to his thigh wound. While Tulellcoe continued to work on him he learned that the Benesh'ere numbered about five or six thousand. Their leader, Angerah, remained with the main body of the tribe, while Jerst, their warmaster, was in charge of this scouting party.

Morgin said, "In their words I sense hate for the Decouixs. Did I sense rightly? And is this hate a tribal thing, or merely a few individuals who bear some grudge?"

"The hate is common to all Benesh'ere," Val said. "But it's Kulls they hate. They hate Decouixs only because they spawn Kulls and allow them to hunt the Benesh'ere for sport."

Late that evening Jerst invited Tulellcoe to attend a council. They had all been warned by Val to expect something of that nature, for it was customary among the Benesh'ere for two leaders to meet and exchange words over a fire. The custom called for each leader to bring two lieutenants; Tulellcoe chose Val for his knowledge of the Benesh'ere, and Morgin for his notoriety as the ShadowLord and a killer of many Kulls. Tulellcoe hoped to enlist the aid of four thousand Benesh'ere warriors, for then there might be a chance against Illalla, though he'd have to broach the subject carefully, and at just the right moment.

They were directed to a small fire around which Jerst, Jack and Blesset sat calmly waiting. Tulellcoe sat down opposite Jerst, with Val and Morgin on either side of him, and, as Val had instructed earlier, he waited for Jerst to begin. Jerst sat quite still for a long while and looked into Tulellcoe's eyes with a hard expressionless stare, and his white face flickered in the light of the fire.

"Welcome, Tulellcoe of Elhiyne, to a Benesh'ere fire. You and your people may claim guestright if you so choose."

Val had coached them carefully in the ritual of Benesh'ere guestright. The words were simple and to the point, and would be the same between close friends and allies, or enemies meeting under truce. The difference lay in the tone of voice, the cast of eyes, a hundred subtle nuances of hand and body. Tulellcoe, as an untrained outsider, would be given only the slightest benefit of doubt. He and Val had practiced through the afternoon, for his role as distant ally was cast in the hardest of stone, and Morgin could see that he spoke now with great care. "We do so claim, and are honored."

The Benesh'ere remained expressionless. "Then as long as this camp is here, and as long as you are within its bounds, and as long as you remain with peaceful intent, you may rest in the protection of the Benesh'ere."

With the stylized welcome complete Jack and Blesset appeared to relax, though Jerst remained stiffly formal. Tulellcoe spoke further. "We are honored by your hospitality," he said, "and we thank you for your aid yesterday against the Kulls."

For just an instant Jerst glanced angrily at Blesset: some disagreement between father and daughter. But the moment passed quickly and Jerst's face relaxed. He said, "Killing Kulls is always an honorable venture. We are told that you and your men have killed many, and in particular this one here," he indicated Morgin with a nod of his head, "has tasted their blood often. You bring us honor."

Tulellcoe shrugged. "When vermin are about, we kill them."

"Aye?" Jerst said. "And you kill them well, Elhiyne. It's a shame you cannot kill more."

Again Tulellcoe shrugged. "As long as there are Kulls to kill, we will kill Kulls. Believe me when I tell you we will kill many more."

"But this time there are too many for you, Tulellcoe of Elhiyne."

Tulellcoe looked straight into Jerst's eyes. "One live Kull is too many, Jerst of the Benesh'ere."

Jerst nodded. "I stand corrected. But there are still too many Kulls for you. You cannot kill them all. Not before they kill you."

"Then so be it," Tulellcoe said. "But that means there will be Kulls left for others to kill. Perhaps you would be interested in killing some yourself. Illalla rides now with two thousand at his side. There is much honor to be had there."

Jack and Blesset both looked at Jerst hopefully, but he ignored them. "Killing Kulls may be always honorable, but it is not always wise." His eyes shifted for just an instant toward Blesset. "Some of us have much to learn about the right time and place for killing Kulls."

Tulellcoe frowned. "But you killed many Kulls yesterday, and in our defense, not your own."

The anger appeared on Jerst's face again. "Aye. We had divided our numbers into two groups. I was in command of one, and one of my lieutenants the other. Had it been I, I would have regrettably let you die." Morgin got the impression Jerst was taking great care not to look Blesset's way. "But my lieutenant chose to fight, which was her prerogative as leader, but it showed poor judgment. She broke the discipline of the Benesh'ere, and it will be some time before she is allowed to lead again."

"But she saved our lives," Tulellcoe said, "so what harm did it do?"

"One Kull escaped," Jerst said. "When Illalla hears of this, there will be retribution."

"How could one have escaped," Tulellcoe asked, "with so many Benesh'ere arrows hissing about. I am told that a Benesh'ere arrow always finds its mark."

Blesset leaned forward, her jaw clenched in anger. "Salula escaped, chasing this one." She indicated Morgin with a nod of her head, looked at him and asked, "Did he ever catch you? Or do you run from battle so well, Elhiyne?"

"Blesset be still," Jerst snapped. "If none had escaped it would still not excuse your poor judgment."

"None did," Morgin said. "Salula will carry no tales to Illalla. He did catch me, and I left his body to rot on the Plains of Quam."

"Where is his cloak?" Blesset demanded.

Morgin shrugged. "To my knowledge he's still wearing it."

"Then you speak lies."

"Silence," Jerst barked. "I will not have you insulting my guests, child. And remember, it is not their custom to take blooded cloaks."

Tulellcoe added, "I personally have seen this one . . ." He nodded toward Morgin, ". . . kill at least three or four twelves of Kulls. Can you claim such bounty, girl?"

Blesset averted her eyes.

Jerst looked at Morgin. "You bring us honor, Elhiyne."

"Then you will help us?" Morgin asked.

"No. We cannot. We will return to Angerah and tell him that there is war here, a war that does not concern us. We will wait on the plains until there is an end to this matter. We will not war with the Decouix. Perhaps Eglahan may aid you."

"Eglahan is dead," Tulellcoe said.

Jerst shook his head patiently. "There you are wrong, Elhiyne. Eglahan is camped at the Lake of Sorrows with what remains of his army."

"How many men does he have that can still fight?"

"That you will have to ask him yourself. We saw only wounded and dying."

Tulellcoe shook his head. "We need many more warriors than Eglahan can provide. Is there nothing I can say or do that will change your mind?"

Jerst's answer was flat and unyielding. "No."

"Very well," Tulellcoe said. He stood, and Val and Morgin stood with him. "We nevertheless thank you for saving our lives, and we thank you for your hospitality."

Jerst stood and faced him across the fire. "No thanks are needed, Elhiyne. We Benesh'ere will leave on the morrow. You and your men may use this camp as long as you wish."

No one spoke as they returned to the small Elhiyne camp. Cort and the men waited anxiously to hear if the Benesh'ere would aid them, but when they saw the look on Tulellcoe's face, they didn't bother to ask.

Morgin sat down on a flat rock near the fire, too tired to hold back his shadow-magic any longer. It had been a constant struggle throughout the day to hold it at bay, for doing so was like holding a weight at arm's length indefinitely. He gave up, relaxed and let the shadows envelop him.

He stared into the fire in silence, and slowly the men drifted away to their bed-rolls. He wondered if they were tired, or just uncomfortable in the presence of the ShadowLord. JohnEngine stepped into the light of the fire, sat down on the ground and leaned against his saddle. For a long time neither of them spoke, then JohnEngine finally broke the silence. "Illalla's going to destroy us, isn't he? He's going to destroy everything we know and love."

Morgin had no answer for him. He stared into the fire and wished for sleep, to lie down and rest without the haunt of a dream from some unknown past. And while he stared at the fire his magic left him, disappeared from his soul as abruptly as it had come. Then a moment later it flooded back into him. As it grew in strength each day, it also grew more erratic, a symptom of spending too much time in his shadows.

The camp grew silent, and most of the fires dwindled to glowing embers. JohnEngine drifted into sleep, leaning against his saddle and gear. Morgin couldn't get to JohnEngine's blanket without waking him, so he went quietly to his own saddle, unwrapped his blanket and laid it carefully over his brother. Then he slipped into the shadows of the forest, hoping to find peace somewhere in the calm of the night.

24

The Assassin's Bite

THE FOREST AT night was far from empty. The voices of an infinity of small crea-
tures filled the air with a roar, and in the distance the dying fires of the Benesh'ere
camp marked the landscape with faint pinpoints of light. The thick blanket of trees
overhead blocked any moonlight that might have shown, and turned the forest floor
into one infinitely warm and comfortable shadow.

Morgin clung desperately to his shadowmagic, savoring it as other men savored
life. His magic had become totally unpredictable, sometimes flickering like a candle in
a harsh breeze, at other times flooding through him mercilessly, turning his stomach
with its ever-changing intensity. Even now he sensed it building to something.

He tried not to think of that, thought instead of the Decouix army, and of Tulellcoe's plan to seek aid from Eglahan. Victory was out of the question; Illalla would
slaughter the small Elhiyne army at Sa'umbra Gap and Elhiyne would fall. But with
what remained of Eglahan's men they might force Illalla to be satisfied with Elhiyne
alone. If they could do that, Penda, Tosk, and Inetka would remain intact and somewhat independent. And then the Lesser Clans could begin again.

But would Eglahan agree to such a plan? Morgin almost wished that he wouldn't,
for he sensed that something awaited him at Sa'umbra. He sensed his own mortality,
and his own fear, and his own cowardice, and he felt shame.

The world about him shifted sickeningly and he froze in mid stride. His magic
came fully upon him. It tore painfully at his soul and brought tears to his eyes. His
dinner threatened to come spewing up, and only by force of will did he keep it down.

In that instant, the sounds of the forest died and left behind a noiseless vacuum
that made the previous silence seem a thundering roar in comparison. Drowning in
his own magic, Morgin sensed the cause of it all: a presence of nameless evil lurking
somewhere within the Elhiyne camp.

A man's scream shattered the silence, an agonizing wail that rose slowly until it
reached a crescendo of pain, JohnEngine's scream.

Morgin tore through the forest growth, heedless of branches that whipped and
lashed at his face. He reached the Elhiyne fire while the others were still scrambling

for their swords, and by the dim glow of the dying embers he caught one momentary glimpse of Bayellgae coiled like a length of rope on JohnEngine's chest. But in that same instant the serpent saw him, and as he ripped his sword from its sheath it shot in the air straight for his face, spitting venom at his eyes.

Morgin threw up his left arm to protect his face, felt the impact as the winged demon slammed into his arm and buried its fangs in his wrist. A fiery bolt of pain shot up his arm, and for a moment it pulled him deep into the netherlife. He screamed, felt a strange, hideous coldness creeping up his arm to his heart. The snake dropped off his arm, disappeared into the forest, and Morgin fell to his knees near the fire.

He struggled to hold onto consciousness, to ignore the pain creeping toward his heart. JohnEngine lay on the ground in front of him still and lifeless, his eyes open and unseeing, his face a colorless mask twisted in an agony of pain. Morgin let go of his sword, reached out and touched his brother's cheek; he was already cold.

Abileen knelt over JohnEngine, touched his throat seeking a pulse, shook his head sadly. Tulellcoe knelt beside Morgin. "Were you bitten?"

Morgin could only nod. The coldness had reached his shoulder.

Tulellcoe shook his head helplessly. "I'm sorry, Morgin. There's nothing I can do against Bayellgae's venom."

In utter desperation Morgin decided to fight death with death. "Bring me redthorn."

"Do you practice magic here?" a Benesh'ere voice demanded.

Morgin looked up through a sea of pain to find Jerst standing over him. Blesset and Jack stood at his sides, and behind them stood several more Benesh'ere.

"Of course I practice magic," Morgin said. "I am a sorcerer."

"Then we Benesh'ere will leave," Jerst said. "We do not abide magic."

"Go then," Morgin said, grimacing as Bayellgae's venom washed through him. "By all means leave us. Run. And quickly. Lest you find courage nipping at your heels."

Blesset's eyes turned hot and angry. She reached for her sword, but Jerst stayed her hand by gripping her wrist. "Here he is under the protection of Benesh'ere guestright. You will draw no weapon against him."

Jerst looked at Morgin with cold hatred. "But when next we meet, Elhiyne, you will not be so favored." With that he turned his back on Morgin and walked out of the small Elhiyne encampment. And in the faces of those who followed him Morgin saw that if ever they had the chance, they would seek his life without hesitation.

Morgin's stomach cramped and he doubled over. He had to force the words out through his lips, "Where is that redthorn?"

Tulellcoe spoke softly. "There is redthorn here, in my pack. I don't believe that you can do anything, but if you intend to try, then I intend to help you."

Morgin looked at the men surrounding them. When he spoke his voice was weak and without timbre. "Gather all of the firewood in camp. And be quick about it. Then light a ring of fire about us and stand within it to form a ring of men facing outward, swords drawn. Remain alert, and no matter what you hear behind you, if you value your souls do not look back until dawn. And remember the snake Bayellgae is still out there. So if anything comes out of the night and crosses the ring of fire, kill it without warning."

The men dispersed instantly. Morgin turned back to Tulellcoe. "Set your wards within the ring of men. They must be protected from us as well as we from them."

Tulellcoe nodded and bent to his preparations. Morgin collapsed beside JohnEngine. He knew what he must do, and yet he feared the doing, for he knew that in some strange way he had now begun travelling down the road to his fate at Sa'umbra, and even death would be better than that. The turning point had come, he had passed it in ignorance, and he understood now that he was no more than a puppet moving to the strings of some unknown master.

Tulellcoe stood and summoned the first Ward without fanfare. It was not in him to be theatrical like Olivia. His summons was simple, direct, commanding. *Primus* flamed into existence and the Ward's power washed over Morgin. He needed it, wanted it, feared it.

Tulellcoe moved quickly now, summoning each of the twelve Wards in its turn, calling them forth one by one to the world of mortal men. To Morgin each Ward formed a bridge to even greater power, for as each came alight it struck him with a wave of magic that fed on his own power, building upon it, strengthening it beyond any reasonable expectations of mortal capability. He began to fear that his magic would soon be stronger than him, and that it would consume him.

France, standing outside the circle of Tulellcoe's Wards, shouted, "We're ready."

Tulellcoe nodded at him. France and the men lit the ring of firewood and it soon flared high and strong.

Tulellcoe dug into his pack. He retrieved a small pouch, opened it carefully, handed Morgin several wicked looking, bright red spikes. They were a brilliant crimson, not just pink, indicating prime quality. They had been taken from the parent plant at just the right time of year and stored with the proper care and spells.

Morgin started to raise them to his mouth, but Tulellcoe stayed his hand. "Are you sure you know what you're doing?"

Morgin shook his head. "I am sure of nothing, but I have nothing to lose."

Without preparation Morgin placed the thorns, tips and all, in his mouth and began chewing; the redthorn turned slowly into pulp. The taste was bitter. It filled his mouth with saliva, though he was careful not to swallow. The saliva expanded the pulp until his mouth was so full he could no longer chew. The coldness of Bayellgae's venom had reached his chest when he took one last look at the men—their backs turned toward him, their faces turned away—then swallowed the unprepared redthorn.

The reaction was immediate. His stomach tried to reject the poison but he held it down. His mouth filled with an unpleasant metallic taste; his nose burned and his eyes watered. An ache formed in the back of his head and his vision blurred. The ache grew until it overwhelmed the pain in his arm and chest. He closed his eyes, lay on his side and buried his face in his hands, which shook and trembled as excruciating pain tore at his soul. Tears streamed down his cheeks, dripped from his chin. And then he felt nothing beyond the pain.

Looking back he could never remember if the time was long or short. Time seemed unimportant amidst the pain. But at some point awareness returned, and he realized the pain had peaked, was slowly receding, that he could once again function.

His hands were damp with half-dried tears. He waited until the pain was almost wholly gone before he looked up. He opened his eyes carefully, fearful that the pain might return, not believing it was truly gone.

He still lay on the ground as he had lain the night before. But daylight had come, and JohnEngine and Tulellcoe and the men were gone. There was no sign of the ring of fire, no sign that it had ever been. There was no indication of a camp past or present, no indication that man had ever come this way. And yet he knew this small piece of forest in a way he could not explain, and he knew he had not moved since swallowing the redthorn.

He looked again at the sky, an eerie gray-blue day with no clouds to obscure the sun. And yet there was no sun visible, no brilliant, yellow orb hanging in the heavens to light the day. The forest lay in the deathly stillness of an unnatural calm.

"Why are you crying?" a young voice asked.

Morgin started, pulled his eyes away from the dingy gray sky, struggled up onto his knees. A small boy stood directly in front of him next to a tall, beautiful woman. The boy was no more than seven or eight years of age, and dressed as a nobleman's son. The woman wore an elegant gown of rich, blue brocade, and while she didn't wear a crown, she stood with the regal bearing of a queen. And she had striking green eyes that reminded Morgin of someone, but he couldn't quite remember who.

"I'm sorry," the boy said politely. "I didn't mean to startle you. But you were crying. Why were you crying?"

Morgin closed his eyes carefully, then reopened them. The men were still gone; the woman and boy still there. "I was crying for my brother."

The woman nodded her head once. "Your brother. He is walking the Plains of Death at this moment, I believe."

"Where are the Plains of Death?" Morgin asked.

She shrugged. "The Plains of Death are between here and there."

Morgin shook his head. "I don't understand. Who are you?"

The woman smiled as if at some private joke. The boy's eyes widened in surprise. Then he seemed to come to some decision, and said, "First, you tell me your name."

Morgin shrugged. "Sure. I'm . . ." His mouth hung open as if he were slow witted; his voice as still as the forest air. He struggled to speak his name, but the words would not come. The words did not exist. He tried then to just think of his name, but not even in thought would it come to him.

"Ah ha!" the boy said triumphantly. "I knew it. How can you know us if you don't even know yourself?"

"But I do know myself," Morgin said. "I am . . ." Again the words did not exist to be spoken.

"This can't be," Morgin pleaded. "I'm dreaming."

"No," the woman said. "This isn't your dream. If this were your dream you know very well you would be dreaming your one and only dream."

They knew of his dream, but Morgin was certain he had never told anyone of it. "Who are you that you know of my dream?"

"I am Erithnae," the woman said. She looked down at the boy. "And this is Aethon, and this is our dream, not yours."

Aethon added excitedly. "And I am a king, you know. And I rule a vast kingdom. My subjects all call me sire, or Your Majesty."

"Now Aethon," Erithnae said. "You shouldn't boast."

He lowered his eyes sadly. "I'm sorry. But I have no one to play with. A king never gets to play."

Erithnae sighed. "Unfortunately, that is part of being a great king."

She looked at Morgin. "Perhaps Lord Mortal here will play with you. Why don't you ask him?"

Aethon's eyes brightened. "Will you? Please play with me."

"I'm sorry," Morgin said. "But I have to find my brother."

"We can help you find your brother. Then will you play with me?"

"All right," Morgin said. "It's a bargain. But how do we find him?"

"Oh that'll be easy," Aethon said. He reached out and excitedly took Morgin's hand, pulled him to his feet. "You'll have to follow us, and do exactly as we say. There is a lot of power between here and there to tempt one, and it's so easy to succumb to power. But I know the way. You can call me Aethon. I wish we knew your name so I could call you something besides *hey you*. We'll have to ask the Unnamed King, if he is about. He knows all names, you know, except, of course, his own. Poor fellow!"

••••

JohnEngine could think of nothing but water. He would give his soul for just one drink, but water was not a part of this gray nothingness of an existence, only confusion and pain. And even if he found water he would not have time to drink.

He slogged on through a gray landscape with no distinguishing features, and wondered if he would ever find his way. Each step was more difficult than the last, as if he walked in a bog that sucked at his feet in a never-ending effort to slow him. It felt as if he'd been walking forever.

Up ahead he saw a vague outline on the horizon. He trudged on with renewed effort, whimpering almost hysterically. But the feature remained indistinct and his hopes ebbed. Not until he was upon it, almost standing within it, did he realize it was nothing more than a shadow, a singular, dark blotch with no reason or meaning for existence.

A strange creature emerged from the shadow so suddenly that JohnEngine gasped and jumped back. Clearly human, it stood no more than waist high, and it stank beyond belief. It wore tattered brown rags for clothing, and on its face several sores oozed puss. Its hair was a clumped and tangled mass of grease and dirt.

The creature's voice sounded like the croak of a large frog. "I am Rat. Follow me, brother." Then it disappeared back into the shadow.

It had called him brother. And Rat? He had once known of a Rat, from some other life, some other existence, though the memory of that eluded him now.

The shadow that the disgusting little creature had disappeared into began to dwindle. Soon it would be gone, and JohnEngine realized that he must make his choice now.

He shook his head, trying to clear it. "Brother!" he said into the nothingness. "He called me brother." JohnEngine closed his eyes and stepped into the shadow.

••••

Morgin was lost in a gray nothingness that pulled at his soul. It was a struggle just to put one foot in front of another. It felt as he'd been searching forever for an end to this barren landscape, and yet he saw no end in sight.

JohnEngine's spirit fluttered nearby, frightened and confused. Morgin wanted to reassure him, but there was no real communication between them, and in any case his reassurances would be a lie. He was as lost as his brother, and the power of his spirit was weakening with each second he spent wandering aimlessly through nothing. The grayness about him was thick, like honey, and he was so tired, so very tired . . .

". . . Morgin. Wake up, Morgin."

Morgin opened the eyes of his soul. Somewhere Rhianne called to him, and as he made the effort to look he saw an image of her standing over him. There were bruises all about her face and shoulders, and yet she had the strength to ignore the obvious discomfort they caused her. She pulled at him, tugged on his sleeve. "Wake up, Morgin. You mustn't stay here."

It took an effort to speak. "Where can I go? I don't know the way back."

"I'll show you the way."

She pulled him to his feet, and he leaned heavily on her while they walked through the nothingness, clouded by the gray that filled his soul.

••••

Rhianne gasped awake, sat up in bed with her heart pounding. It was several seconds before she realized it had been a nightmare. She sighed with relief and lay back against the mattress. The bruises hurt, and it was some time before she returned to sleep.

••••

Morgin awoke and found Tulellcoe leaning over him, a worried look on his face. He spent a long moment realizing that dawn had come, and that he was still alive. "JohnEngine?" he asked weakly.

Frowning, Tulellcoe said, "I don't know what you did, or how you did it, but he will live. And it appears that so shall you."

Morgin reached up with a trembling hand. "Help me up."

"You should rest."

"I have to see JohnEngine. Help me up."

"Very well. But then you rest."

Tulellcoe pulled him into a sitting position. He got only that far before his head reeled, his stomach churned and he shook violently. He waved his hands, fending Tulellcoe off, unable to speak but signaling that, for the moment, he could go no further.

He sat there for several heartbeats, noted that his tunic was covered with an ugly stain in which he could see the pulpy remains of the redthorn. He remembered swallowing it, and he remembered the pain, and he remembered Aethon and Erithnae. He remembered the nothingness and Rhianne, but he could remember nothing beyond that. There was no memory of how he'd saved JohnEngine, and he wondered now if it was even he who had done the saving.

"Where is Aethon?" he asked. "And where are Erithnae and Rhianne?"

Tulellcoe looked at him narrowly, but said nothing, so Morgin demanded, "Where did you go? You left me alone."

Tulellcoe's look of unease grew. He spoke slowly and carefully. "I went nowhere. I remained by your side through the night. And as you instructed, the men did not relax their vigil until dawn."

Morgin closed his eyes and tried to picture again the still forest with the gray-blue sky, the young boy king and the god-queen. She had looked very much like Rhianne. "Tell me what happened after I swallowed the redthorn."

"Within seconds you cried out and slumped to the ground. You lay through the night near death, vomiting even when your stomach had nothing left to yield. And though I tried many times, I could not help you because you were surrounded by a strong and dangerous field of magic. Dawn came an hour ago. The field of magic disappeared, your illness passed, and JohnEngine began to breathe again. I've been waiting for you to wake."

Morgin decided to say nothing of the discrepancy between his memory and Tulellcoe's words.

"Morgin," Tulellcoe said carefully. There was a sense of urgency in his words, and also a sense of disapproval. "You are not wholly in this world. I can sense it. Part of your soul is still dwelling on the Nether Plane. You're feeding on it, and it's feeding on you, and the longer you remain in contact with it, the harder it will be to break that contact."

For the first time that morning Morgin became conscious of his power. He had not been aware of it before, but now he thought of Aethon's words, "There is a lot of power between here and there to tempt one, and it's so easy to succumb to power . . ." This power had an ethereal sensation to it, as if it were not his own power at all, and deep within his soul Morgin knew that he would be free of it only when it chose to be free of him.

Morgin demanded, "Help me to my feet. I must see JohnEngine."

Once on his feet Morgin could not stop the trembling in his knees so he leaned heavily on Tulellcoe. His stomach continued to churn and his head still ached, and the power pushed at his will as if it were a conscious thing with a will of its own.

The ring of fire had dwindled to smoldering black ash. The men had dispersed, though with his magic fully upon him he could sense each of them nearby.

JohnEngine had been taken aside and wrapped in several blankets. His face remained pale and ashen, but the pall of death was gone and his chest rose and fell with a weak but steady rhythm. Asleep, he seemed like a child that needed protecting. Morgin wanted dearly to protect him, but he knew that was now out of his hands.

"All danger is not over yet," Tulellcoe said. He touched JohnEngine's forehead. "But the worst has passed."

Packwill, the scout leader, and France and Cort came striding across the camp. The scout dropped to one knee before Tulellcoe, bowed his head reverently. "We're ready to leave at your word, my lord."

Morgin looked at Tulellcoe. "Where are we going?"

"I'm sending you and John and Val and the rest of the injured to Inetka now. Val's going to talk to Wylow, though I doubt Wylow's fool enough to help us. Those of us who can ride are going to the Lake of Sorrows to see if we can get Eglahan's help. I have no idea what shape he and his men are in, but we're going to try anyway."

Morgin nodded slowly. "I'll ride with you."

Tulellcoe shook his head and spoke in a flat voice. "No you won't. It's going to be a hard, fast ride, and you're in no shape for that."

Morgin started to speak, but Tulellcoe cut him off, "Don't argue with me. As long as you ride with us, you'll do what I say."

"We'd better get going," France said.

Tulellcoe nodded, looked in France's direction to say something, and Morgin took that opportunity to slip into a shadow. He changed shadows quickly and stopped to catch his breath behind a tree.

Cort gasped. "If I hadn't seen it with my own eyes I wouldn't have believed it. Even up close he literally vanished."

"Damn you, Morgin," Tulellcoe said. "You're getting too good at that. I'm warning you. For your own good. You're spending too much time in those damn shadows."

Packwill asked, "I take it, my lord, that the ShadowLord will be accompanying us?"

Tulellcoe turned on him angrily. "I think we can all take it that the damn ShadowLord will do as he damn well pleases. And stop calling him that."

••••

Morgin found Mortiss waiting for him a few paces into the forest. He climbed weakly into her saddle, but for the first time was unsure of the direction, and the more he thought about it the more confused he became. The netherworld pulled at him, beckoning him to become part of the netherlife, and the power that flooded through him kept his senses constantly overloaded.

He realized he was starting to hallucinate badly when a nearby shadow took on a life of its own. The sun shone brightly in the sky, and a light breeze constantly fluttered the leaves of the trees overhead, sending thousands of shadows dancing about everywhere. But one particular shadow coalesced into a dark wraith shaped much like a man. It had no face to speak of, only the poorly defined shape of head, and shoulders, and arms and torso and legs. It turned toward him, bowed deeply from the waist, spoke with a voice barely above that of a whisper. "My lord," it hissed. "This is the way you seek." It turned and led the way up a game trail.

Without any prompting from Morgin, Mortiss followed.

••••

Bayellgae flew into the tent of its master, fluttered about the room once on its tiny wings, then settled on its perch, coiling its tail tightly about the base.

"Well?" Illalla demanded impatiently. "Is he dead?"

"Yesss, my lord. The deed isss done."

Valso asked, "Are you certain?"

"I do not err in death," the snake scoffed. "Bayellgae'sss venom flowsss thisss night in his veinsss. And none can sssurvive Bayellgae'sss venom."

"Well done, my pet," Illalla said. "This campaign will now proceed rightly."

"But I wasss dissscovered, my lord. I had to kill another."

"Who?"

"The Elhiyne'sss brother, I believe."

"Even better. That is one less Elhiyne that I must deal with."

"But there wasss an outcry in the Elhiyne camp. There wasss no time to sssavor the kill. That wasss to be my reward, my lord."

"Fear not, snake. You have done well this night. And there'll soon be a lot of Elhiyne death for you to feed on."

25

A Bargain in a Dream

PACKWILL DISMOUNTED AND bent to examine the dust of the trail. Many horses had recently passed this way, and their hooves had left a message for the trained eye to read. Packwill was heartened to note that none bore the mark of a De-couix smithy, but still he moved cautiously. If he and the Elhiynes failed to exercise care when approaching Eglahan's camp, they could easily be shot, and their bodies identified after the fact.

He rose from his examination of the ground and turned to look back at Tulellcoe. He could see much of the old witch Olivia in the lines of the sorcerer's face, especially her madness. Two days of hard riding with little rest had hardened his appearance. Packwill raised a hand, signaled for the rest of the party to come forward, and knowing that their lives depended on caution, they came slowly.

"My lord," Packwill said softly to Tulellcoe. "I'm sure the challenge point is just ahead. You must be ready to answer for yourself."

The sorcerer nodded without speaking.

"Wait here, my lord, if you please. I'll check ahead."

Packwill turned and walked up the trail, his sword sheathed, his hands held high, palms out. He knew the moment would come soon, and he prayed that his friends were not too quick with their bows. He'd gone but a short distance when a voice spoke from the edge of the forest. "Stop there if you value your life."

Packwill halted.

"Now speak your name," the voice demanded.

"I am Packwill. A scout. Sworn to Eglahan of Yestmark."

"You lie," the voice said.

"No," a second voice interrupted. "He speaks truth. I recognize him. But you, scout, why are you not now with your liege lord? And who is that behind you?"

Packwill addressed the second voice. "I recognize you, Annen, bastard son of Eglahan, as you recognize me. And I am not with my Lord Eglahan because, like most of his men, I thought him dead. Instead, I joined with Tulellcoe of Elhiyne to seek revenge by harrying the Decouix army. It is he whom you see behind me in the trail, accompanied by what remains of his men. Now why is it I sense distrust in your voice, Annen, whom I have known since you were a boy-child bouncing on my knee?"

Annen stepped out into the trail. Like his father he was a man of average appearance, nevertheless his voice carried the confidence of one who was not easily intimidated. "I trust you, friend Packwill, but not these others who ride with you."

Behind Packwill Tulellcoe dismounted and walked forward slowly, past Packwill to stand facing Annen. Packwill didn't like the look on Tulellcoe's face, and when the sorcerer spoke, his voice cut through the air like a freshly sharpened sword. "I am Tulellcoe et Elhiyne. Your father knows me, and so do many of his men. And if you value your soul, puppy, you will learn to recognize me the next time we meet."

The two men stood eye-to-eye until Annen averted his gaze. "My lord," he said.

"That's better," Tulellcoe said. "Now take me to your father."

••••

The hallucination of the shadowwraiths continued as Morgin followed Tulellcoe's small party, though now he had the impression there were hundreds of them guiding him through the dense forest toward the Lake of Sorrows. He even hallucinated that he could hear them speaking to one another, though their voices were so faint they sounded more like a breeze rustling through the forest leaves.

From the side of the trail he watched the confrontation between Tulellcoe and Annen, watched Tulellcoe's party admitted to the fortified encampment of what remained of Eglahan's army. He dismounted, let Mortiss run free in the forest, stepped into a shadow and slipped easily past the perimeter guards. Oddly enough, or perhaps rightly enough, the shadowwraiths did not follow him into the camp.

He reconnoitered the camp carefully before doing anything else, estimated there were six or seven hundred men present, though many were wounded, and he could sense that the souls of quite a few would soon depart the Mortal Plane. He'd never seen the Lake of Sorrows before, but in the moonlight it was a black mirror reflecting the moon glow.

There was a large tent at the center of the camp. Morgin approached it carefully, stepped into the shadows of a fluttering torch and slipped inside. There he found Eglahan and his lieutenants already meeting with Tulellcoe, France and Cort, and it was obvious they had been at council for quite some time now.

It was no formal council of war. They were not seated opposite one another at a table. The hard ride had taken a heavy toll on everyone in the Elhiyne party, and no one begrudged them a comfortable seat, and a mug of ale.

Eglahan was an older version of Annen, though he sat uncomfortably with one leg heavily bandaged and propped up on pillows. "You know I would join you," Eglahan said unhappily, "if there were any chance at all of stopping Illalla. I don't even require a chance of victory, merely of stalemate, but at best I must have something, not just more death."

"What of this ShadowLord of yours?" Annen demanded. "We've heard wondrous tales of his deeds. What about all this great magic he wields, and all this power? Tell me, where is he? Why doesn't he stop Illalla?"

At Annen's question the Elhiynes all glanced into the shadows that danced about the room. Tulellcoe said, "There was a time when I could sense him if he were lurking in the shadows nearby, but he's now drifted so deeply into the netherworld he could be but an arm's length from me and I would not have the faintest inkling of his presence. I can only guess that he must be here somewhere near."

"Bah!" Annen scoffed. "When I was a child I was frightened by such talk, but no longer. Any man who lurks in shadows is a thief, a murderer, or a coward."

In the flickering shadows of the lamp Morgin chose one going Annen's way, stopped immediately behind him, leaned forward and whispered in his ear, "But Illalla now fears his own shadow."

Annen jumped, started, spun about, but by that time Morgin had moved to another shadow. "What was that?" he demanded.

Cort looked at Tulellcoe. "Is it him, do you think?"

Tulellcoe nodded. "Morgin. Step forward. Make yourself known."

There was a moment of silence while everyone waited for something to happen. Morgin hesitated, not sure whom he could trust. It now took a strong effort to extinguish the shadows about him. After careful thought he decided to remain within his shadows.

Annen shook his head. "The ShadowLord is as much legend as he has always been."

Tulellcoe said, "Illalla might disagree with you on that. And then there's Salula, who's no longer with us. And there are Decouix graves aplenty that line the God's Road from here to Yestmark."

"And the serpent," Packwill said. "I tell you, my lord, he was bitten by the snake demon. I saw the wound myself, and he survived."

Annen opened his mouth to argue, but Eglahan silenced him. "And the desertions. Let us not forget the desertions. The reports I'm getting from my scouts tell me that this ShadowLord alone has cost Illalla more than I and my entire army." Eglahan closed his eyes, sucked in a long, tired breath and exhaled slowly. "But he hasn't cost Illalla enough. Roland is lucky to have levied three thousand men, half of them farmers with pitchforks for weapons. And I have about four hundred men who can still fight. But while Illalla's men are deserting him in droves, he'll still have at least six to nine thousand when he gets to Sa'umbra, and they're all seasoned veterans. I'll not order my men against those odds again."

Eglahan rubbed his eyes, ran his hands through unkempt hair. "My leg is hurting me. And it's late. We'll talk about this more in the morning. Please leave me now. I need rest."

They all filed out of the tent. At Eglahan's orders Annen carefully extinguished all of the candles in the tent but one, and then he too left. Only Morgin stayed, waiting in a shadow, finding it hard now not to succumb to the constant pull of the netherworld.

Eglahan peered into the darkness as if he sensed Morgin's presence. He tilted his head like a blind man cocking his ear toward a sound. The silence grew thick, and then he said, "Tell me, ShadowLord. Why do you linger?"

Morgin struggled to pull himself out of the netherworld. And then, with great care, like a barefooted man walking near glass shards, he stepped into the dim glow of the candle. He knew that for some seconds he appeared as a specter of shifting, flowing shadows, but then with an effort he extinguished his shadowmagic and stood before the old warrior as one man to another. "You must help us," Morgin whispered. "Without you and your men it will be a slaughter."

Eglahan shook his head sadly. "With me and my men it'll still be a slaughter. We're not enough. There has to be something more. You have to provide something more. You, ShadowLord."

Morgin looked into the soft flame of the candle. The air in the tent remained so still it didn't flicker, and like the candle's flame Morgin felt lifeless and empty. He'd played the game of the ShadowLord to its conclusion, and it turned out to be an empty game, with no substance or meaning.

"I'll make a deal with you," Eglahan said into the silence. "I'll bring my four hundred men to Sa'umbra if you can convince that bastard Wylow to bring four hundred of his own, and if you match his warriors and my warriors each with a warrior of your own. Do that, oh ShadowLord, and I'll come."

Morgin was desperate, even to the point of lying. "It's a deal," he said flatly, wondering what price he would have to pay when Eglahan finally learned he'd been deceived.

Eglahan flinched. He had not expected Morgin to agree to such a ridiculous proposition, but he recovered quickly. "Where will you get eight hundred men?"

Morgin extended his hand. "Leave that to me. You have the word of AethonLaw et Elhiyne, the ShadowLord."

Eglahan reached out warily, clenched Morgin's hand with almost crushing force, and in that instant Morgin extended his shadowmagic, let it encompass both him and the Yestmarkian Lord. Eglahan gasped as the shadows surrounded him. "But remember, Eglahan ye Elhiyne. If you break your word; if you're not there at Sa'umbra, then you will see me next in the shadows of your dreams."

Morgin left Eglahan in his tent, taking with him his shadows.

••••

Mortiss ran like the wind, gusting at times into bursts of blinding speed, then cutting back to a steady, inexhaustible gale that blew on and on and on. Morgin clung desperately to her back as she charged through the shadows of the night, never quite sure if she rode the ways of the netherlife, or galloped beneath the glow of a mortal moon. Time and distance seemed unimportant on the roads that Mortiss traveled, for the sun never rose to clear the perpetual shadows that enveloped them, and the leagues were devoured beneath her hooves as Inetka grew closer with each passing shadow.

There came a time when the shadows cleared, though a thick blanket of cloud obscured the moon overhead. Mortiss trotted down the God's Road at an easy pace, and Morgin was relieved to find that the night air he sucked into his lungs was mortal, though a large part of him remained well within the netherlife no matter how hard he tried to withdraw from it. From the terrain he guessed they must be somewhere near the fork in the road that led to Sa'umbra.

Morgin sensed another rider on the road up ahead. He pulled Mortiss to a stop, closed his eyes, listened to his soul as the man approached, recognized immediately that he'd come upon the messenger they'd sent to Inetka with JohnEngine and the rest of the wounded.

Morgin waited in the middle of the road with Mortiss. He didn't want to startle the man, but since no light from the moon penetrated the cloud cover, he cast a faint glow about him and Mortiss. The rider ahead turned a bend in the road, saw the glowing apparition waiting there for him and pulled his horse to a halt. He hesitated, then asked, "Who are you?"

Morgin spoke softly. "I am Morgin et Elhiyne."

The man relaxed and nudged his horse forward, stopped before Morgin and bowed his head. "ShadowLord."

"Are you bearing a message?" Morgin demanded.

"Yes, my lord," the man said uncomfortably. "From Lord Wylow to Lord Tulellcoe."

"Speak this message to me."

"Yes, my lord," the man said. "But please remember that the words I speak are those of Lord Wylow, who commanded me to speak them exactly as he did."

Morgin nodded. "You will not be held accountable for repeating Wylow's words."

"Thank you, my lord. Lord Wylow told me to tell Lord Tulellcoe that he was a bloody idiot if he thought Inetka would allow itself to be slaughtered with Elhiyne. He said we could all go to the Ninth—"

"Enough," Morgin said. "I get the gist of the message."

Morgin wasn't sure how he could convince Wylow when Val had failed. "Continue north," he told the messenger. "You'll find Tulellcoe and Eglahan riding south with the remnants of Eglahan's army. Deliver Wylow's message to Tulellcoe exactly as it was spoken to you. Then give Eglahan a message from me. Tell him I want him to remember our bargain. Tell him I still intend to keep my part of it."

The man bowed his head. "Yes, my lord."

While the messenger's head was bowed, and his eyes were averted, Morgin slipped a shadow over him and Mortiss and disappeared. He turned Mortiss toward Inetka, and a short time later it began to rain, a cold, wet, driving rain that soaked through the Kull cloak he wore, and he hoped that if Mortiss chose to travel the ways of the netherworld, it would at least be out of the rain. But if she did carry him there for a time, it was in no way obvious, for it rained there too. The night and the rain lasted all the way to Inetka.

•••

With Morgin astride her, Mortiss walked the Nether Plane into Castle Inetka, a path that left no traces in the world of mortal men. In the netherworld the stone of the castle seemed insubstantial and ill-defined, though Morgin had no trouble treading its halls. He found Wylow abed with his wife, lying on his face with an arm thrown haphazardly over her. The Inetka lord snored loudly, grumbled something in his sleep.

Still deeply in the netherworld, Morgin climbed up on the footboard of Wylow's bed, sat there irreverently with his muddy boots crossed in front of him making a mess of the blankets near Wylow's feet. Morgin watched his hand move of its own accord, as if he was a puppet dangling from a web of strings with his actions dictated by some puppet master looking down from afar. His hand settled on the hilt of his sword, pulled it silently from its sheath, extended the tip toward Wylow's face. He pulled the Inetka leader into the netherworld with him, then nudged the man on the cheek with the dull side of the blade.

Wylow growled something incoherently, swatted at his face as if brushing away a bothersome fly, settled back into sleep. Morgin nudged him again. This time his eyes opened with a start, and though the room was dark, they settled instantly on the sword tip only inches from his nose. Morgin withdrew the sword to a safe distance.

Wylow rolled over on his back, sat up, squinted into the darkness and could obviously see nothing more than a faint silhouette at the end of his bed. "What the hell are you doing in my dreams?"

Morgin laughed. "What are you doing in *my* dreams?"

Wylow threw his head back and laughed heartily. "So the ShadowLord has a sense of humor. What do you want?"

"I want you to come to Sa'umbra."

"Not on your life, lad. There's no reason Inetka should fall with Elhiyne."

"And why does Elhiyne have to fall?"

"Look at the facts, lad. The odds are against you."

"What if I get Eglahan to come to Sa'umbra. He still has four hundred mounted men that can fight."

Wylow squinted at Morgin distrustfully. "So that old fool's still alive, eh? Four hundred men, eh?" Wylow seemed to consider the situation, but Morgin sensed the scheming going on behind his eyes. The Inetka leader appeared to come to a decision that he liked. "All right, lad. I'll make a deal with you. I'll bring four hundred men to Sa'umbra if you can convince that bastard Eglahan to bring his four hundred, and if you match his warriors and mine each with a warrior of your own. Do that, oh Shad-owLord, and I'll come."

Morgin couldn't believe his ears. The bargain Wylow offered was identical to that Eglahan had offered, and spoken in almost the same words. He wondered for a moment if the two old warriors had conspired against him, but they couldn't have known in advance that he would play such a role in the coming events, nor had they had the opportunity to communicate since the battle at Yestmark. In any case, while Morgin had no hope of coming up with eight hundred warriors of his own, if he agreed to the bargain it would at least get Wylow and Eglahan to Sa'umbra with their warriors. He had no idea how he'd convince them to actually join the battle once he failed to fulfill his end of the bargain.

"It's a deal," he said flatly. "But remember this, Wylow et Inetka. For the Shad-owLord, a bargain made in a dream is still a bargain."

Wylow's confidence faltered, and he looked at Morgin with growing fear. "If you break your word," Morgin said, and for some reason Wylow's face twisted with terror, "If you're not there at Sa'umbra, then I will ever haunt the shadows of your dreams."

Wylow seemed near hysteria, but before he could shout or cry out, his eyes drooped heavily, he lay back and returned to sleep.

26

War Magic

MORGIN DANCED CAUTIOUSLY from one moon-shadow to the next. He moved slowly, with infinite care, sword in hand, ready to be discovered and killed at any moment. As he stepped to the next shadow he stumbled over something, caught the branch of a nearby tree to keep from falling, then froze into stillness like that of the night air.

He waited for an outcry, his heart pounding with fear, knowing that a Decouix sentry must surely have heard his fumbling. But luck was with him, for the silence about him remained unbroken.

He looked down at the crumpled heap he'd stumbled into, another dead warrior, though whether Decouix or Elhiyne he could not tell. The man had been partially stripped by camp followers, and what little clothing remained was insufficient to identify his clan. Many corpses littered the moonlit ground of Sa'umbra.

Without warning the power of the sword surged within him. He looked at his hands with some idea of what to expect: they glowed softly in the dark. He concentrated on his shadowmagic, trying to obscure the eerie light that emanated from his skin, and as a shadow swirled about his hand the glow there diminished. It was joined by others, and soon he was enveloped in a never-ending dance of ghostly half-images that flittered from head to foot.

The sound of many horses broke the silence of the night. They came as a thunder in the distance, approaching quickly, building to a crescendo as a Decouix patrol neared, then dying slowly as they rode on. The sound took forever to disappear on the night air, but when it was gone Morgin moved on, dancing among the shadows that had become so much a part of him, dancing in a landscape of darkness, moonlight and death.

The battle at Sa'umbra had been raging for four days now. Eglahan, with his four hundred men and horses, had arrived just that evening. His scouts had found a place to camp hidden within the forest far down from the gap, and he was waiting now for Morgin and Wylow. Wylow had not yet shown. During the intervening days and nights Morgin had spent his time scouting out the battle, and had chosen to avoid contact with everyone.

It was well past midnight, and Morgin longed for a place to stop and rest, but it was slow work travelling on foot, lurking from shadow to shadow. He was forever in danger of discovery, and now that he knew the lay of the pass and had the information he sought, the danger was even greater. He had a tendency to move hastily, rushing from the horror that lay about him. One poorly chosen step might cost him his life.

Whenever possible he had stayed within the confines of Eglahan's camp, hidden within a shadow and unable to show himself, hungry for human companionship nevertheless. This night, wrapped within his shadows, he slipped past Eglahan's sentries easily, and noticed a commotion at the center of camp. Wylow and his men had arrived and a council of war was in progress.

Eglahan sat near a small fire with Annen and his lieutenants at his side. Opposite them sat Wylow, SandoFall, Edtoall, and Wylow's sons and lieutenants. To one side sat Tulellcoe and France and the Balenda. France sat on a rock a short distance back from the rest, so Morgin sat down in a shadow beside him.

France neither looked nor turned Morgin's way; he whispered softly, "Beware, lad. There's bad blood and swollen pride here."

Morgin nodded, then realized the swordsman could not have seen the gesture. And he wondered how France had known he was there at all.

The council of war had clearly been going on for some time now. Annen and Edtoall were into a hot argument. Wylow looked ready to pick a fight with someone, and stared unhappily at Eglahan. Tulellcoe remained silent, apparently unwilling to join in the clash of wills. The dispute between Annen and Edtoall grew more angry with each word, and as the two men stood facing one another over the fire, they held the focus of the council. From what Morgin had seen of interclan councils, this was typical.

Eglahan had kept his silence, but as the heat of the argument grew there came a moment when he could obviously contain himself no longer. He raised his right hand to demand their attention; it was stiff and flat like the steel blade of a knife. "Enough," he shouted. "We should be working together, not fighting among ourselves."

Annen and Edtoall stared at each other for a moment, then sat down, though the look that Wylow gave Eglahan bode ill for any cooperation between the two leaders.

"Where's the damn Elhiyne?" Wylow demanded. "ShadowLord or no, we have a bargain."

Eglahan shrugged. "I believe he'll show up."

"And will he keep his end of the bargain?"

Again Eglahan shrugged. "I hope so. I believe so."

Wylow spoke loudly so that all could hear him. "If he doesn't, we're gone from here. But if he does, I still say we wait until the final battle, then hit Illalla from behind and destroy his wagons and supplies. He'll not be expecting that."

Annen yelled hotly, "And I say we attack now. We can force him to split his troops and form a battle line at his rear."

"What will that buy us?" Edtoall demanded. "Illalla has enough men to defend his rear and still take the gap."

"Exactly," Wylow said flatly. "And that is why my men and I will wait until the main battle. We will attack only then, and destroy Illalla's supplies."

Eglahan shook his head sadly. "And by that time the Elhiynes will be exhausted. Most will be dead and the main battle will be a rout."

"It seems to me," Annen said to no one in particular, "that the Inetkas seek to save themselves by destroying the Decouix supplies. With that done Illalla cannot carry his campaign to Inetka, though of course it will be too late for Elhiyne."

Wylow squinted at Annen. "What are you implying, Elhiyne?"

Annen feigned simple ignorance. "Oh nothing at all, Inetka. Only that you could then hide safely behind your women and your castle walls with no—"

Edtoall leapt up, drew his sword and shouted, "Elhiyne lies!"

Annen jumped to face him. "Inetka coward!"

A young Inetka cursed and lunged at Annen, but Annen sidestepped quickly and clubbed him in the face with the hilt of his sword. As the young Inetka went down, Edtoall leapt past him, landed squarely before Annen, struck down hard with his sword. Annen deflected it, but the sound of the two blades crashing together seemed to be a signal to the entire camp, and hundreds of blades were pulled from their sheaths with an ominous scrape of metal against metal.

Morgin wanted to run, to get out of the way and let the fools kill each other. He wanted to disappear into the forest, to return to his original idea of assassinating Illalla in the night, but his arms and legs were no longer his to command. He remained seated on the ground and reached for his own sword, but he slid it only a few inches from the sheath, far enough for him to touch the steel of the blade with the flesh of his hand. It stung his flesh like a hot brand with a power that was foreign and evil, but he endured the pain and called upon the power of the blade, let that power flood through his soul and used it to form a shadow larger and darker and deeper than any he had ever attempted before. He brought the shadow down over the entire camp, the light of the moon died and the glow of the campfires dwindled to nothing, throwing everything into blackness. A cold, deadly wind whistled through the camp; it cut to the marrow and chilled men's spines. There were cries of terror and loathing, and all fighting ended in that instant.

Morgin held the shadow in place while he walked through the camp and stopped in front of Annen. Then he released his grip on the blade and the wind died, leaving behind a silent and deadly calm. The enormous shadow cleared from the camp to reveal almost everyone standing with sword in hand, though most were looking over their shoulders and no one seemed inclined to do any fighting.

Finding Morgin standing directly in front of him as if he'd materialized out of thin air, Annen gasped, started, stepped back into the fire, stumbled over the coals and raised a shower of sparks. He recovered quickly, stood up straight and faced Morgin squarely. Morgin heard murmurs throughout the camp.

Morgin looked at Eglahan, then Wylow, and hoping to avoid the issue of his end of the bargain, he said simply, "I've scouted the gap quite extensively. Is there anything you'd like to know?"

"Yes," Wylow said. "What in netherhell am I doing here?"

Someone demanded, "What did you see out there?"

Morgin thought of the moonlit landscape he'd just crossed, and the human debris that littered it. "Death," Morgin said. "Death everywhere."

"How far did you go?" someone else asked.

"How has the battle gone?"

"Where is the battle line now?"

"Silence," Eglahan shouted. "One question at a time." He looked at Morgin anxiously. "Tell us what you can."

Morgin nodded and spoke slowly. "This side of the gap is narrow, treacherous in spots, and the Elhiynes have used that to advantage. They've kept the Decouixs bunched so that Illalla can't make use of his numerical superiority. It appears to have been a long, drawn out battle of attrition. Illalla is winning, but not with the speed I'm sure he anticipated."

Eglahan asked, "How much longer can your father's men hold?"

Morgin shook his head. "They're not holding at all. They lose ground with each skirmish and are slowly forced westward. Eventually they'll have to withdraw onto a wide glen near the summit of Sa'umbra. It's the only place where the gap isn't so narrow. The final battle will probably take place there."

"Did you see this glen?" Wylow asked.

"Yes. From a distance. It was broad daylight and there was fighting at the time. I couldn't find a way to cross the battle line, but I climbed to a good vantage and was able to see it from this side."

"Was there an enormous stone, about the size of a large castle or holding, sitting all by itself on the far side of this glen?"

"Yes. A massive black rock. Very impressive."

Several of the Inetkas nodded their heads knowingly. "Csairne Glen," Wylow said. "I know it well."

That name clearly held some significance for just about everyone there, but for Morgin it held no more than a slight ring of familiarity.

"When will your father be pushed out onto the glen?" Eglahan asked.

Morgin shrugged. "Two days hence, perhaps three."

"What kind of rear guard has Illalla established?"

"Nothing extensive. He must believe that the only enemies he has to his rear are what's left of my uncle's men. He's placed a few sentries here and there, and a guard of about fifty men on the road."

"And where are your warriors?" Wylow demanded. "We have a bargain, you and I."

Morgin looked at the Inetka leader and lied without hesitation. "They'll be here when the time for battle is at hand."

····

Mortiss waited for Morgin just beyond the light of the fire. He was checking her saddle harness when France, Tulellcoe and the Balenda approached him, and the Balenda voiced the obvious, "You won't be able to keep Wylow waiting for two days."

"If he's still alive in two days," France said. "If he keeps shooting off that big mouth of his, Eglahan's likely to kill him."

Morgin turned to face them. Tulellcoe looked at him squarely and demanded, "What bargain do you have with them?"

Morgin carefully explained the bargain he'd struck with both Eglahan and Wylow, and oddly, not one of them questioned his ability to fulfill the terms, nor did they even ask how he would do so.

"Wylow won't wait two days," Tulellcoe said. "We've got to get Roland to start giving ground now, to retreat as if his forces are already spent. If he withdraws onto Csairne Glen tomorrow, while his men still have strength to fight, and while Wylow is still here to fight with us, then maybe we have a chance. But how do we contact Roland? I can't reach him, not with Illalla and Valso watching the netherworld so closely."

Morgin felt sick to his stomach at what he was about to say. "Maybe I can. Shadows are just as effective there as here."

"Are you sure you want to try that?" Tulellcoe asked.

Morgin shook his head. "I don't think I have a choice. Will you help me?"

Tulellcoe shrugged. "Do I have any more choice than you?"

"No," Morgin said. "You don't."

····

"There is an intruder," *that other* said to Valso. Valso started with surprise. *That other* had actually spoken to him. It had formed true words within his thoughts. Always before their communication had consisted of mind images that, while not vague, sprang from an undefined otherwhere. But now it spoke to him with words. True words! Such a phenomenal change in their relationship could have only one meaning: *that other's* power had begun to grow. It was preparing to come forth, make itself known again on the Mortal Plane, and soon it would reveal its mastery.

"There is an intruder," *that other* said again.

For the first time Valso paid attention to the meaning within the words, and his excitement ended quickly. "An intruder? Where?"

"In the netherlife."

Valso knew fear. "That can't be."

"Nevertheless it is," *that other* said. "It walks upon the soul of the netherworld, and such an affront must not be tolerated."

"Then crush it," Valso said. "Destroy it. You have the power."

"No," *that other* said. "It is much too early to make myself known."

"But if you destroy it, it will know nothing."

"But if I intervene directly, there are others who will sense that. And that is why you must destroy it."

"Me? But I don't have the power."

That other smiled deep within Valso's soul. "I will give you the power, and you will become the most powerful mortal alive."

••••

Roland sat in his tent staring unhappily at the four canvas walls. Dawn approached much too quickly, and with it would come another day like the last: more fighting and more dead. Illalla would use his men without mercy, and so the Decouixs would die in greater numbers, but they would still gain ground. The Elhiyne army would retreat: reluctantly, slowly, but inevitably. Roland had considered the situation carefully time and again. There were some things he could try: tricks that might delay, traps that might hinder. But he had come to the bitter realization that delay and hinder were the only tactics left to him. Nothing would change the final outcome.

Hope! They needed hope. Some kind of hope. They needed a plan, something with some possibility of success, not this doom and delay, knowing it was useless, hoping for a miracle they knew would not come.

Morgin! Why did his mind keep returning to Morgin? For all they knew he was dead by now. Poor Morgin! And damn Olivia!

Roland sensed AnnaRail's arrival. He stood to greet her. She, knowing that he would be aware of her coming, entered without preface. They spoke no words, but wrapped their arms about one another and held each other close for a long moment. He loved her softness, and her strength.

When they separated she spoke softly. "You sent for me, my lord?"

"Yes," he said. "I need your help. I had a dream last night, and I can't remember it."

"This dream was important?" she asked, almost more of a statement than a question.

"I don't know. But it's been nagging at me since I awoke. I can't put it out of my mind."

Another woman would have reminded him that now was not the time for inter-
preting dreams, that dawn would come momentarily, that there were more weighty
matters to consider. "Can you tell me something about this dream?" she asked.

"No," he said, shaking his head with frustration. "I remember nothing."

"Very well," she said. "Let us sit down then. Here, on your cot."

He did so, and she sat down beside him. She took his hands in hers and spoke
softly. "Now darling, I want you to close your eyes and relax. Let your mind wander
and tell me of the first thing that enters your thoughts."

"I've already done that," he said more harshly than he intended. "Morgin comes
to mind. Morgin and nothing else. Just Morgin. Over and again Morgin."

She looked thoughtful. "Hmmm! That is curious." She reached into a fold of her
dress to some hidden pocket there. She withdrew a small linen pouch that opened at
the touch of her fingers, and from it she took several small pieces of tattered cloth.
She chose one particular scrap, saying only, "This one was his, I believe," then she
replaced the rest. From another pocket she produced a small piece of charcoal
wrapped in dried leaves. With it she wrote Morgin's name upon the scrap of cloth,
then returned the charcoal to the leaves, and to her pocket. She crumpled the cloth
between her hands, rolling it into a tight ball, then turned to Roland and said, "Think
now of Morgin. Think of him and no one else."

Roland thought of the last time he'd seen Morgin, riding away on the black mare.
He concentrated on that image as AnnaRail extended her left arm with the crumpled
piece of cloth resting in her upraised palm, and with her right hand she began making
passes above it. As she did so, she muttered some incantation that Roland could not
understand.

After several minutes of conjuring she drew her right hand back, snapped her fingers, and the piece of cloth in her hand burst into flames. The flames sparkled for a
moment then died, leaving a small cloud of gray smoke that swirled upward, rising
slowly toward the roof of the tent.

The cloud moved with a life of its own, bunching here, thinning there. Then it
coalesced slowly into an image of Morgin. Roland realized then that he was looking at
his dream.

The image swayed and shifted sickeningly. It was poorly defined, though definitely
Morgin, but a changed Morgin. The face was the same—young, boyish, open—but the
eyes had lost the innocence of youth and now seemed haunted and distant, a bit insane.

"Father," the smoky image pleaded desperately. "Please listen to me. I haven't
much time. I can't hold this existence for long, and there are those about me that
would end it prematurely. When the battle begins anew, retreat to Csairne Glen. Do
so slowly, as if your strength is finally depleted and you must reluctantly withdraw.
Illalla must be made to think that you have weakened early, that he is about to win—"

Morgin's image flickered out of existence, then returned slowly. Now it was
smaller, hazier, blurred. The weakened image spoke on as if unaware of the

interruption, though Roland knew that some of the message had been lost. ". . . some of your forces until the right moment. Trust me, father, please. We—"

Morgin's image staggered, not a thing of AnnaRail's magic, but part of the dream. His face twisted with pain, he put a hand to his head and groaned, then disappeared altogether. Roland waited for more, but none came. The dream was gone.

"What did you see, husband?" AnnaRail asked.

"Didn't you see it too?"

"No, my love. It was your dream, not mine. Would you like to tell me about it?"

"I think I saw hope," he said. "Maybe hope for us all. Come. We must find the others, and quickly. We have some changes to make before the fighting begins anew."

27

Death Magic

MORGIN SHOT AWAKE, sat up with his heart pounding in his throat. With the memory of many such awakenings he realized instantly that he'd been dreaming his dream. His mouth was filled with an odd metallic taste, his ears rang, and the forest about him glowed with an eerie light. His only memory of the netherworld was a choice he'd made somewhere deep within a dream, a choice between retreat before reaching Roland, or the temptation of vast power.

France sat nearby watching over him, staring at him oddly. The swordsman seemed different, far away, detached. "Are you Morgin?" he asked, an odd tone in his voice.

"Of course I'm Morgin," he said, though even he recognized that something had changed. "I think."

"You're Morgin all right," France said. "The others want you to join them when you're ready."

Morgin looked at France, and sensing the distance between them he asked, "Stay close, France, will you? I need you."

France nodded, the distance remained, though the swordsman tried to hide it. "Sure, lad. You an' me eh? But we'd best be joining the others."

Morgin found it impossible to hold his shadows at bay; his time in the netherworld had strengthened their hold on him, and as he followed France toward the center of the camp he didn't like what he saw in the eyes of the waiting troops that parted to make way for him. He could see that they'd actually begun to believe the legends, that to them he was now some sort of supernatural freak, a strange netherlord out of myth that might at any moment explode in their faces.

Wylow and Eglahan and their respective lieutenants waited for him, their anger and impatience easily visible. Wylow turned on him, though he hesitated for a moment at the prospect of addressing a specter of shadow. He recovered quickly and asked, "Where are the warriors you promised? We have a bargain, and I'm waiting for you to live up to your end of it."

Morgin ignored him, turned to Eglahan instead. "What's the situation up in the gap?"

Eglahan said, "The battle has been progressing all morning. My scouts report that the Elhiyne forces have weakened earlier than anticipated and are just now retreating onto Csairne Glen. They've formed the final battle line across the width of the glen. The Decouixs act as though they're at festival, laughing and joking. They should begin the final battle shortly, and it will be a slaughter."

The message had gotten through. Roland had done exactly that requested of him. He had put his faith in Morgin and placed his army at the mercy of Illalla and his hordes, and now it was up to Morgin. At all costs he could not betray that faith.

"What of Illalla's heavy cavalry?" he asked. "The armored knights. How will he use them?"

Eglahan frowned and answered hesitantly. "His heavy knights are preparing for a charge. It appears Illalla wants to weaken your father's men quickly; I'd guess he intends to use his heavy troops right away, in the first skirmish. He'll then withdraw them to rest while his lighter forces nibble away at the Elhiyne battle line. That'll leave time before nightfall for one last charge with the heavier knights. The second charge will break the back of your father's army, and for all intents and purposes the battle will be over."

"Might he try some trick?"

Eglahan shrugged. "He has no need of tricks, not with the overwhelming forces at his command."

"But enough of this," Wylow demanded. "The bargain. Without your warriors, I and my men will not join the battle."

"Nor I and mine," Eglahan added calmly.

Morgin nodded his head slowly. He had to stall for time. "Our bargain will be fulfilled when the time is right, and not before."

Wylow was getting angrier with each second. "And when will that be?"

"Before we go into battle."

"Blast you! When will that be?"

"Shortly," Morgin said. "But for the moment I want to see the main battle for myself, from some vantage."

Wylow opened his mouth for more shouting, but Eglahan quickly interjected, "That's good enough for me, as long as I don't have to commit my troops before that time."

Wylow hesitated, thought about that for a moment, then snarled in Morgin's face, "All right. Same goes for me. I don't commit until I see these wondrous warriors of yours, ShadowLord." He turned his back on Morgin and stormed away.

"Packwill," Eglahan said. "The ShadowLord wants to see Csairne Glen from a vantage." He turned to Morgin. "My head scout will show you the way."

••••

Morgin lay still and held his breath; he was transfixed by the battle below, though it was not the sight so much as the sound, for even at this distance his ears were pounded by a din that raised hackles on the back of his neck. He tried to identify the individual components of that noise. He could hear the screams of both men and animals; the clash of sword against sword and sword against shield; the clop of horse's hooves and the pad of running feet; the grunt of extreme exertion. He couldn't hear the twang of crossbows or the hiss of arrows in flight. Nor could he smell the sweat and fear of battle—at least not that beyond his own.

"ShadowLord," Packwill said, lying beside him. "Look yonder. Illalla is withdrawing his heavy cavalry."

From their vantage atop a small hill the heavy knights were easy to distinguish in their plate armor and ankle length mail. There were about two hundred of them, and they trotted gaily off the field of battle in small groups, their backs turned confidently to the bloodletting, laughing at the ease of the day's kill, displaying proudly to one another trophies of combat such as the hand of a vanquished foe.

Morgin and Packwill could see all of Csairne Glen, and more. The Elhiyne camp lay on the far side, situated where the road from the west opened out onto the glen. From there a grassy plain sloped gently downward to where the battle raged, then back up to the Decouix camp. Behind Illalla's wagons and tents the road to the east disappeared over a small rise. If Illalla cared to look, he'd find Wylow and Eglahan and their eight hundred warriors waiting not far from there, hidden just off the road in small groups.

"Packwill," Morgin said. "Run quickly and tell Lords Wylow and Eglahan to get ready."

"Aye, my lord," Packwill said. He jumped on his horse and raced out of sight down the back of the hill.

Morgin waited, wondering if he might hope, carefully watching the Decouix heavy cavalry as they sauntered casually toward their camp. They arrived in ones and twos, were assisted from their large and ungainly war-horses by servants and retainers. They removed their helmets, then sat down in chairs and lounges to rest while servants brought them chilled wine and adjusted umbrellas over their heads to shield them from the hot sun. Most wore heavy mail, though the richest wore plate, but few chose to remove it, preferring instead to rest for some moments before going to the trouble. They sat in moderate comfort, sipping their wine and watching the extravaganza of death taking place before them, occasionally wagering on individual combats that became separated from the whole.

A shadow lay down beside Morgin. It looked at the battle carefully for some moments, then turned to Morgin and whispered a question, "Has the time come, my king?"

Morgin tried to ignore the shadow, but again it asked, "Has the time come, my king?"

Finally, resigned to the inevitable, Morgin nodded. "Yes. I believe it has."

The shadow disappeared as Morgin inched back from the lip of the hill. He climbed into Mortiss's saddle, spurred her hard in Packwill's wake, and on the way down the hill he began gathering his power.

Wylow and Eglahan were waiting for him, neither of them happy. Wylow said, "You don't have any damn warriors, do you?"

Eglahan spoke carefully. "You'll have to produce them now."

"Right," Wylow said, "Or we withdraw."

Morgin looked up at the sun. It was well past noon, and half way down toward the horizon, but still bright and hot, and the lengthening shadows it cast were sharp and well defined. Morgin relaxed some of his resistance to the pull of the netherworld, let part of his soul sink into its depths, felt an answering surge of power flow into him.

He spoke to Wylow and Eglahan. "Order your men to mount and line up in single file down the length of the road."

Wylow started to protest, but Eglahan gripped his arm viciously and growled in his ear, "By the gods, man, do as he says."

Wylow frowned for a moment, then shut his mouth, turned to his lieutenants and gave the necessary orders.

The men had been waiting anxiously so it didn't take long to get them in their saddles and lined up in the road. Beside each one the sun cast a shadowed replica of both rider and mount.

Morgin concentrated his power further, pulled it out of the netherworld, pulled it out of the trees and the bushes of the forest about him, pulled it out of the life of the soil itself, and then he started feeding it into the shadows that mimicked the movements of the eight hundred warriors. He tried to speak, but his voice came out in a whisper, sounding to him like the voice of the shadowwraith, "Tell them to draw their swords."

Eglahan did so, and the warriors obeyed, and the shadows that mimicked them followed suit. As the swords cleared their sheaths Morgin drew more power and poured it into the shadows. The horse of the rider at the front of the line neighed and reared high, and its shadow followed suit. Morgin continued pouring power into the shadow and the horse sidestepped skittishly, but this time its shadow did not move with it, and it broke free of its master. While the real horse and rider remained still, the shadow horse whinnied and bucked for a moment, then calmed itself and became still. Now the shadow warrior and horse moved independently away from the rider and horse. All up and down the line of warriors the shadow riders broke free and calmed their shadow horses.

The shadow warrior closest to Morgin nudged his shadow mount with his shadow spurs and trotted the apparition forward. He stopped in front of Morgin, saluted with a shadow sword, bowed, and when he spoke his voice came out in a whisper. "We heard your summons, my king, and we have come."

Morgin looked at Wylow and Eglahan, and in their eyes saw no more argument, only naked fear. He said, "The bargain is complete. Do either of you dispute that?"

Both shook their heads nervously.

Morgin pulled Mortiss about, looked up the road. Ahead it took a turn to the right before coming upon Illalla's rear guard. Beyond that there was a slight rise, then the road opened out onto the glen, and there lay the Decouix camp.

Morgin stood up in his stirrups and twisted about to look back. Behind him waited France, Tulellcoe, Cort and Abileen. Then there was Eglahan and Wylow, and behind them their eight hundred warriors who looked nervously upon their shadowwraith counterparts. Some of their faces showed fear, most showed distaste and uncertainty.

Morgin touched his spurs to Mortiss's flanks and she broke into a trot. He fought to restrain her, but as he approached the turn in the road he eased up on the reins a bit and she broke into a canter. Slowly he let her have her speed and the tempo of her hooves pounding on the road increased until she charged at full gallop. He bent low in the saddle, the point of his sword held out before him, behind him the thunder of sixteen hundred charging horses filling his ears.

He made the turn in the road and up ahead the Decouix rear guard came into sight. They turned in surprise, drew their swords, then thought better of the odds, spun about and scattered into the forest, and with the wind in his face Morgin passed them by without a thought. His stomach lurched as he topped the rise where the road opened out onto the glen, and he charged down into the midst of the enemy camp where the Decouix servants looked at him once, then fled in all directions. He picked out one seated figure and watched as the man tried futilely to stand, weighted down by the heavy chain mail he wore.

Morgin swung his sword out to the side, leveled it like a scythe set for a harvest of blood, and as he passed the enemy knight he swept the blade forward, his arm jerked outward and back with a sickening thunk. He caught a fleeting glimpse of the man's head tumbling through the air. He pulled on Mortiss's reins, brought her to a halt and spun her about. The knight still lounged in his chair, dressed in his fine garments and chain mail, headless. Up and down the line of the Decouix camp there were many more like him, still seated in their finery, unable to move quickly enough. Some few had managed to get to their feet, but heavily armored knights on foot were helpless against mounted troops. Morgin was not needed here.

A strange prickly sensation touched his soul. It called to him from the main battle, so he turned from the pandemonium of the Decouix camp to face a field of unending death.

He was closer now, and the din cut at his nerves like a knife, but in the sight of the thing his mind refused to distinguish individuals, preferring instead to lump it all together into one shifting, swaying mass of arms, legs, men, horses, swords, pikes, spears and shields. He was strangely drawn to it and unable to look away, as if this were his destiny, the culmination of his training, the ultimate purpose of his magic and power. His magic was almost palpable now, swirling about him, fed by his intimate contact with the netherworld, building to some unknown end. It frightened him, filled him with the desire to throw his sword away, to spur Mortiss and flee from this festival of death.

As he watched, unable to look away, an individual warrior separated himself from the melee. He walked slowly and unevenly up the shallow slope that led to Morgin, and from a distance Morgin could distinguish almost no detail about the man. He wore Elhiyne livery, carried no weapons, walked with a bad limp. In his clothing there was a garish amount of Elhiyne red. But as the distance between them narrowed Morgin realized that the red the man wore was not cloth, but a cloak of blood that covered him from head to foot.

Morgin shivered as the stranger hobbled slowly toward him, but could not look away. One of the man's legs was crooked, broken in many places, with sharp splinters of bone protruding from the skin. His leather jerkin was slashed everywhere with sword cuts, many of which must have penetrated to the skin, and beyond. But of all the wounds he bore, the most terrible was the enormous hole in his chest where a steel tipped war lance had shattered his torso. The wound was mortal, yet this stranger still walked as if he were among the living.

Morgin looked reluctantly at the man's face. It too was covered with blood, some of it dried and caked, some of it fresh and glistening in the afternoon sun. There were wounds on the man's face, small slashes and cuts, but Morgin's eyes were drawn to three small scars long ago treated and healed, ghostly reminders of a faraway past where filth and degradation grew childhood diseases.

Morgin's heart climbed up into his throat, and even though he sat astride his horse, his legs felt weak and yielding. In the face of the apparition that stood before him, mutilated and crooked, he saw the scars of his youth; he saw his own face, twisted into an expressionless stare of death. And he knew now that he was living his dream, that the nightmare he had dreamed so many times in the past was no longer a dream, but life itself. And soon he would know its terrifying end.

Morgin's sword lifted itself slowly, carried his hand with it. The blade shimmered and glowed with power; he could feel it swirling through the air about him. He saw little motes of it dancing down the length of the blade, trickling between his fingers, scurrying up his arm. It tickled the hairs in his nose and made his eyelashes feel alive.

The apparition that wore his face stopped just beyond reach. It bowed formally to Mortiss, then looked at Morgin.

With what little control Morgin had over his power, he pointed the tip of his sword at the ghostly specter. He could not hide the tremble in his voice as he followed the path of his dream and whispered, "Name yourself, demon."

The apparition stared at Morgin through cold, dead eyes buried in a stone, dead face. It shrugged, opened its mouth and said, "I am MorginDeath, my lord, and I have come for you."

Morgin now knew the end of his dream. He finally understood that it was not he in the dream, but a great king who had allowed Morgin to see the dream through his own eyes. And when the king had faced AethonDeath, he had shrugged uncaringly and said, "So be it." But Morgin could not be so cavalier. "Be gone," he said, his voice cracking with strain. "Leave me. You cannot have me."

The ghostly specter shrugged again. "As you wish, my lord. But I am your destiny." It glanced over its shoulder at the carnage in Csairne Glen, then looked back at Morgin. "I will await you on the battlefield below," it said, then disappeared without trace.

Morgin imitated that long dead king from his dreams, and whispered, "So be it."

"What?" Tulellcoe demanded. "What's wrong?"

"Did you see it?" Morgin asked.

"See what? I saw nothing. What did you see?"

"A dream," Morgin said. "Just a dream. Tell me, uncle. What is Csairne Glen known for? Why have I heard the name before?"

Tulellcoe looked at him suspiciously, as he did so often now. "Legend has it that Csairne Glen was the scene of the last battle of the Great Clan Wars. It is said that Aethon died here, and was then entombed in Attunhigh."

"Of course," Morgin said. "It had to be."

"Are you all right? Is something wrong?"

"My lord," Wylow called before Morgin could answer. "We're ready."

Morgin turned in his saddle and looked at the warriors behind him. The shadow warriors waited astride their shadow horses motionless, while the mortal warriors held themselves apart and glanced at them nervously. It would not be wise to have them ride together.

"Lord Eglahan," Morgin said above the din of battle. "You and your men take the right flank. Lord Wylow. You take the left."

Both men nodded and said nothing. Each turned, raised his sword as a signal, spurred his horse, and, followed by his warriors, rode out to his assigned side of the glen. Morgin was left with his shadows, and he felt so alone.

Morgin looked again at the battle in the center of the glen, which raged on, seemingly oblivious to any threat Morgin and his companions might offer. He picked out Illalla's banner, a target he would aim for. If he and his shadows could split the Decouix line, then Eglahan and Wylow, each with their warriors, would charge from both sides and try to split the halves again. Only the gods knew if it would do any good.

Morgin cast a spell for courage, and one to banish fear. Then he began to purposefully draw on the power of the sword. He put a cloak of shadow about Mortiss to protect her, though since he was starting to glow with an eerie, blood-red light, he didn't bother for himself. France! At the last moment he thought of France.

As if reading his thoughts, the swordsman said, "I'm right here, lad. Right behind ya. You an' me eh?"

Morgin turned about in his saddle and found Tulellcoe, France, Cort, and Abileen waiting with his shadow warriors. And as if in answer to the question on his face, Cort said, "We ride with you, my lord."

Morgin nodded, turned back to the battle, cast shadows about all four of them and their horses, added a slight variation to the spell so they wouldn't be aware of it. He held his eyes targeted on Illalla's banner and nudged Mortiss forward into a walk. Behind him the creak and groan of the saddle leather of eight hundred shadow warriors answered his lead. He held his sword casually, letting it dangle at the end of his arm.

He touched his spurs to Mortiss's flanks; she changed her pace to a trot. There came a second's delay, then the tempo of the hooves behind him changed likewise. Behind him the shadows closed their ranks to form a wedge, the head of a spear with Morgin at its point.

Another touch of his spurs and Mortiss moved up to a canter. She tried to break into a run but he held her back. She was jumpy, skittish. She sensed her master's mood, and she smelled blood and death on the air. She wanted to surge forward, to release her energy in a blinding flash of speed, but it was imperative that Morgin keep his warriors bunched tightly, not strung out by an overlong charge.

The sword also pulled at him, was not unlike Mortiss in that. It wanted to be given full rein to wreak carnage among friend and foe alike, and he struggled to control it as well. Timing was of the essence.

Mortiss still struggled against him, so he gave her a little rein and let her break into a gallop. The battle line in front of him seemed no closer, as if it were more reluctant than he to meet this fate. But when the time was right, when the distance was right, he swung his sword out in front of him and dug his spurs into Mortiss's sides. She exploded, almost tore Morgin from his saddle, and behind him the war cry of the shadow warriors was a whisper of death as they fought to keep up with him. The power of the sword pushed at his will like Mortiss pulled at her reins, but still he held it back.

Morgin's sight narrowed to the seething mass of pain and death that was the rear of the Decouix battle line, and his hearing lost all sounds but the thunder of Mortiss's hooves. He braced himself. Then, in that eternity of an instant of impact, he released the power of the sword fully and they struck with a deafening roar, eight hundred riders colliding at full charge with the rear of the Decouix line.

In the first seconds after impact Morgin's sword was useless. He could do nothing but charge forward, using his power to shield himself and Mortiss from injury. Then a Decouix sword sliced past his face. He deflected it, struck out blindly, cut off the man's arm. The air about him was filled with screams of pain and cries of fear.

He deflected a pike, slammed his sword against a shield and hacked down at someone's shoulder. To his amazement his sword lengthened magically, taking on the attributes of a full-length broadsword. He gripped the hilt in both hands, stood in his stirrups and hacked downward at anything that came within range. He spurred Mortiss on, knowing that if he stopped, he would die, though the density of the battle was slowly pulling her to a grinding halt.

Something stung at his arm. He slashed outward, downward, tried to fight in all directions at once. A Kull officer on horseback reared in front of him. For a short time his battle narrowed to that one Kull. Then he saw an opening, smashed the edge of his blade into the Kull's rib cage, and the Kull died then and there. He kicked at the Kull's riderless horse. It snorted fearfully and bucked away from him.

Behind the horse a foot soldier leveled his pike at Morgin. Morgin raised his own sword to strike the man down, but they both froze in wonder, for the man was Elhiyne. "ShadowLord!" he cried excitedly and raised his pike over his head.

"To me," Morgin shouted. "To me." Then he spun Mortiss about and charged back into the seething mass of men and horses, and for the first time he felt hope.

He met a Decouix wizard face to face. The man threw the fires of magic at him, but his own magic was fully upon him, and the Decouix's power was as nothing against that of the sword. He cut the wizard down almost casually and turned to look for another.

He was surrounded by them, isolated from his comrades. He fought, for there was nothing left but battle and death. He used his power and his sword as if they were one. He was bleeding from small cuts and wounds in a dozen places, and he was weakening. The past weeks of fighting, days without food and rest, were all taking its toll.

His right leg lit up with fire and Mortiss screamed and stumbled. The shaft of a long arrow protruded from his thigh, though little of it was visible for it had gone through his leg and well into Mortiss's side. She stumbled again, tried to rear up but only staggered, stayed valiantly on her feet. A Decouix pikeman stepped out of the melee and rammed his pike deep into her chest. She shuddered, then toppled to the left.

Morgin, with his right leg pinned to her side by the arrow, could not jump clear. She landed on his left leg and he felt and heard it snap. He screamed. She kicked and jerked, and her death throws ground his leg between her weight and the rocky ground.

Morgin felt his leg snap and splinter again and again, and as the bones grated against one another he almost lost consciousness. His world narrowed to a universe of pain and oblivion. The battle became a world of pandemonium in which he could no longer distinguish friend from foe. But then the confusion of bodies about him parted to make way for a Decouix warrior mounted upon a charging steed. In his arms he clutched a steel tipped war lance aimed at Morgin's heart. In that instant the apparition MorginDeath coalesced into being. He stood nearby, watching without expression.

The steel tipped lance approached, and Morgin was powerless to stop it, though the sword in his hand jerked spasmodically, as if to make one last try at defending its master. But it too was spent, able to yield only one, final, halfhearted effort.

The lance struck, splintered into his chest, washed his soul in a sea of pain, and in that instant the mists and confusion of battle cleared, as if in his last moments of life Morgin finally understood the trial of his power. But then it all slipped away from him, receding to a distance far beyond measure, and he heard MorginDeath speak, and his words rang sharp and clear: "Now we are one, my lord . . . my king. Now we are one."

28

God Magic

THE SUN'S RAYS crept over the mountain peaks that surrounded Csairne Glen, and morning came possessed of an eerie calm. Where only the day before the battlefield had been filled with the screams of hate and death, it was now immersed in a murky stillness that hung over the carnage like morning mist.

Brandon no longer needed the light of his torch so he smothered it in the cloak of a dead warrior. In the light of day he could now see the full extent of the battlefield and its harvest of death. He marveled at their numbers. In places they were piled waist high; they looked like toy dolls dropped by some careless giant of a child, their arms and legs twisted at odd angles. But their faces shattered that illusion; in death, they revealed the true horror of the previous day's violence. And he had looked closely, throughout the night, searching, forever hoping that the next face would not be the one he sought.

He came upon a young boy seated on the rump of a dead horse, one of many such people: women and children and old ones seeking sons and fathers and husbands among the dead, fearing, yet desiring to know for certain the fate of a loved one. Most of the wounded had by now been removed, or, if they were Decouix, dispatched to their final rest, though AnnaRail had put a stop to that when she heard it was being done.

The young boy asked Brandon, "Who are you looking for?"

Brandon frowned, and looked at him closely. He wore the clothing of a nobleman's son, and yet Brandon did not recognize him.

"You look tired," the young boy said. He patted the horse's rump next to him. "Sit here with me and rest."

Not long ago Brandon would have been appalled at the thought of using the carcass of a dead animal for a seat. But the long night of searching among the dead had numbed him. He dropped down beside the boy and was grateful for a place to rest.

"I asked who you're looking for."

"Oh!" Brandon said, still shaken and confused. "I'm sorry. It's all so ... overwhelming."

"It's just the dead," the boy said with wisdom beyond his apparent age. "What do you expect when you put ten thousand men to chopping at each other? So who are you looking for?"

"My cousin. Morgin was his name."

"Did you lose lots of kin?"

"Not in this battle," Brandon said. "No. Only him. But before that, back in the castle, they killed my brother and wounded my father, though he died later." Tears began to well in Brandon's eyes so he quickly changed the subject. "Who're you looking for?"

The boy spoke sadly. "A king. He's out here somewhere. I know it."

He's crazy, Brandon thought, but he kept his thoughts to himself. The young boy, like all of them, was probably a bit unhinged by the magnitude of the carnage.

Brandon stood. "I'd better be moving on. I still have to find my cousin. He's the only member of the family we haven't accounted for yet."

"Who was it you said you were looking for?"

"My cousin. His name was AethonLaw, but he liked to be called Morgin."

"Ah!" the young boy said. "The ShadowLord, was he not?"

"Yes," Brandon said. "They call him that. Do you know of him?"

"Aye. Everyone knows of the ShadowLord. I thought he was my king, but then he died. Dead kings don't rule much, do they?" The young boy laughed bitterly at some private joke. "Dead kings can't even rule their own souls, eh?"

"He is dead then?" Brandon asked. "You've seen his body?"

The young boy rolled his eyes as if dealing with an ignorant child. "He's not dead, at least not anymore."

This young boy had a strange way of speaking. "I . . . I don't follow you. Not dead . . . anymore?"

"Aye. Now you're catching on."

Brandon grabbed the collar of the boy's tunic, though he did so more violently than he intended. "Where is he?"

"Right here," the boy said, patting the rump of the dead horse.

Brandon looked carefully at the carcass; only its rump and hind legs were visible, the rest buried beneath a pile of dead warriors.

Brandon let go of the boy's robe and climbed frantically onto the pile of bodies. Both Decouix and Elhiyne had died here. He pulled at a set of shoulders, but the dead had stiffened during the night so it was difficult work. He'd just managed to pull the first dead warrior loose when he realized that the young boy couldn't have seen Morgin, not buried under this pile of dead. He spun toward the horse's rump to accuse the boy of lying, but now he stood alone in a field of dead.

Brandon scanned the horizon in all directions. The glen was quite flat so he could see far, much farther than the boy could have moved in the few seconds his back had been turned, and yet there was no sign of him. Only then did Brandon stop to listen to his soul. There was a taint on the air, as if something old beyond imagining had recently passed nearby, and he realized that the missing boy had been steeped in the arcane of ancient lore. He nodded, turned unerringly back to his task of digging among the dead.

••••

"A messenger comes," one of the guards at the Inetka battlements cried.

JohnEngine jumped to his feet, a mistake since his leg still pained him badly. As he limped down the stairs to the main floor, everyone rushed past him. He joined AnnaRail in the castle yard just as Abileen rode through the castle gates and reined his horse to a halt. He dismounted, tossed his reins to a groom, and approached AnnaRail.

Abileen's voice trembled. "Milady . . ." A tear touched his eye. "I bear ill news. Your son . . ." He faltered momentarily, hesitated long enough to compose himself, then straightened. "Lord Morgin is sorely wounded and very close to death. Lord Brandon says he will not survive the journey here. You must come to Csairne Glen."

AnnaRail staggered as if that simple, flat statement was an arrow striking her heart. "I don't believe it. If he was dying I would know, and he is not dying."

She spun about, barking commands as she hurried back into the castle proper. "Prepare a horse for me while I gather my things."

With his leg still badly swollen JohnEngine could not mount a horse, so he was forced to wait at Inetka. He watched AnnaRail and Abileen depart with a small escort. He had to sit nervously through the day, waiting, questioning anyone who came down from the mountain for word of his brother.

It was just before nightfall, as dusk settled upon a gray, still day, that they brought Morgin's twisted and mutilated body down from Sa'umbra. A hush fell over the throng that waited. They'd bundled Morgin onto a litter between two horses, accompanied by a long and winding procession that stretched down the road.

AnnaRail walked beside his litter, hovering over him, snapping instructions at everyone. As they carried Morgin into the castle JohnEngine stopped her and asked, "Will he live?"

Her complexion had turned gray with fatigue and worry. "I know not. Death is very close at hand."

There was nothing JohnEngine could do but get in the way, so as night settled over Inetka he limped down to the castle yard and out through the main gates. He stopped there and looked out into the blackness of the night beyond the walls of the castle, tried not to hear the cries of the wounded that littered the landscape there. There were so many wounded that not even the castle itself could hold them all, and more arrived with each passing moment. The moon had yet to rise, so those caring for them carried candles or lanterns, and in the inky darkness they appeared as lonely sparks of life bobbing about on a field of pain and death.

Morgin loved the night, JohnEngine knew. For him it was an ally, but not this night, not a night filled with the cries of dying men. Morgin loved nights of peace and solitude. The cloak of darkness was his friend, the moonlight his companion. Through Morgin's eyes JohnEngine had learned to view darkness in a new way.

JohnEngine sat on the dirt with his back to the outer castle wall and cried like a child. He sat in a dark shadow far to one side of the main gate. He wanted to be alone, and understood why Morgin was always drawn to the solitude of shadow.

France's voice interrupted his thoughts. "JohnEngine, lad. Are you out here?"

France stood within the light that splashed outward from the open main gates of Inetka. He peered blindly into the darkness and called softly, "JohnEngine?"

"I'm here, France. In the shadows at the foot of the wall."

France stepped out of the light and felt his way along the wall slowly. When he found JohnEngine he sat down beside him, and for a long time neither of them spoke. Then France said, "Your grandmother is commissioning a bard to write a song about the great battle of Csairne Glen, and about the mighty warrior AethonLaw."

"He didn't want to be a hero," JohnEngine said. "Especially not the kind the old witch is going to make him into."

France made no answer, and again they sat without speaking. The night was lonely and cold.

"John," France said. "Your mother needs you. She's exhausted her magic on him and now sits there, refuses to rest herself, refuses to admit he's dying. She's not thinking clearly, not right in the head, John. She needs you."

"All right. I'll come in shortly, after . . ." JohnEngine hesitated, for he sensed magic in the air.

"Look," France said, pointing up the road.

There appeared in the distance a soft, white glow set against the blackness of the moonless night, a rider, mounted on a black horse walking slowly toward the castle. Both rider and horse appeared to be encased in an aura of some kind, and about them hovered a hot, brilliant spark that darted in every direction at once.

As they approached JohnEngine saw that the rider was a woman. She wore some filmy, gauzy thing more like a nightgown than a dress, and yet the coldness of the night air seemed not to touch her. Her feet bore neither sandals nor slippers. Her long, golden hair hung past her shoulders, and she was by far the most beautiful woman he had ever seen, though it was a cold, inhuman beauty. About her hung an aura visible to the eye, a soft, warm illumination that called happily to one's soul. But more powerful than the aura, a sense of goodness and kindness beckoned to JohnEngine's heart. She had enchanted him, bewitched him. He stood and limped toward her.

France gripped his arm painfully, spun him about, slapped him hard across the face. "Keep your wits, lad. Look at her horse."

The spell was broken. JohnEngine shook his head to clear it, then turned to look back at the woman's mount. There could be no mistaking the coal-black mare, the horse Morgin had ridden into the battle at Csairne Glen, a horse that was now dead, by all reports. Suspicious now, JohnEngine tried to look at the hot spark darting everywhere about the woman, but it moved too quickly for him to discern any detail.

The horse stopped in the middle of the road just in front of the castle's main gate. JohnEngine and France approached cautiously.

For what seemed an eternity the woman failed to notice them. Then slowly she turned her face upon them, a face of unnatural beauty, marred only by her vacant expression and the inhuman look she cast upon them.

JohnEngine bowed deeply. "My lady. May I ask to whom I have the honor of speaking?"

At his words her face softened and showed a bit of emotion. Her eyes came to focus and she said, "I am . . ." She hesitated, confusion and distress visible on her face. She put her fingertips to her forehead as if to think carefully, then her eyes brightened and she nodded. "Yes," she said. "Yes. But it has been so long since I existed on this plane. It is so hard to remember."

"Milady?" JohnEngine asked politely. "I don't understand?"

Her attention turned back to him. "Ah mortal! Yes. Your question. I am the Archangel Ellowyn." She nodded again, as if she needed to confirm that statement by agreeing with herself. "Yes. I am Ellowyn."

"Lies," France said. He stepped back warily. "Nothing but lies."

JohnEngine tried to intervene. "No, France. I think she's telling the truth."

France ignored him. "Well you'll not have him," he said. "Not as long as I live to protect him." He stepped back another pace to stand blocking the castle gateway, and drew his sword in a single fluid motion.

The hot spark of light shot toward his face, darted about him and dove at him again and again. He raised an arm to protect his eyes and slashed his sword blindly about.

"Laelith stop," Ellowyn cried. Her voice cracked through the night like a whip, and the spark obediently retreated from France to hover over the archangel. "Swordsman," she said. "Put away your sword. You cannot harm us."

France hesitated, then obeyed, and when his sword was sheathed Ellowyn slipped off the horse's back. She turned to the animal, curtsied and said, "Thank you, my lady."

One moment the coal-black horse was there, the next it was not.

Ellowyn turned to France and approached him. He stood ready for battle, but JohnEngine could see that there was only peace in her heart. She held up a finger and called to the spark, "Come, little one. Alight."

The spark descended, landed on the outstretched finger, and for the first time it was still, a tiny little girl no larger than the finger on which she stood, with shimmering, translucent wings. She seemed unable to remain still for longer than a second or two, fluttering her wings nervously and moving about.

"There, there, little one," Ellowyn said. She stroked the back of its neck. "The swordsman means no harm. He feels great sorrow, and he only wishes to protect his friend."

The archangel looked at France. "Forgive her, swordsman. Her intelligence is not great, and she understands even less than you." Ellowyn looked again at the spark on her finger, then back at France. "France, the swordsman, meet the faerie Laelith."

JohnEngine asked, "Why are you here?"

"And you, wizard," Ellowyn said, turning to JohnEngine. "Why do you ask so many questions?"

"I belong here. You do not. Again, why have you come?"

The confused distress returned. "I am Ellowyn," she said, as if that alone was answer enough. "I was summoned to this moment. But I'm not sure by whom."

Her back straightened; her chin lifted. "Where is the one called Morgin? I have an unpleasant task to perform."

"You're too late," France spat. "He's dying. And no one can heal those wounds."

Ellowyn shook her head sadly. "No he's not, unfortunately. He has his own task to perform, and until he does so, he cannot be granted such peace."

JohnEngine touched France's arm gently. "France. Who would summon an archangel?"

France turned his anger on JohnEngine. "What in netherhell are you talking about?"

"I'm talking about an archangel, France. Who would have the power to command an archangel? Who would dare?"

France's eyes softened as comprehension hit him. JohnEngine continued, "I think, my friend, that death means very little to whoever summoned this angel."

France pleaded, "Can't we just leave him in peace?"

JohnEngine shook his head. "I don't think it's up to . . ."

••••

JohnEngine awoke to the bright morning sun slicing through the open window of his room. For a time his mind refused to believe that the angel had been only a dream. She had seemed so real, and he so wanted something to come and make everything right: to save Morgin and bring MichaelOff and Malka back to life. But dreams and wishful thinking were not going to change the reality he faced each morning, even if it was the same dream night after night.

JohnEngine sat up, swung his legs off the edge of the bed, rubbed circulation back into the leg where the remnants of Bayellgae's bite were a constant and painful reminder of the little viper. He pulled on his breeches, a blouse and a pair of rabbit fur slippers Wylow had lent him, made his way to the kitchen for a bite to eat. There he found France and Abileen seated grimly at a small table with a setting of cold meat, hard bread and cheese. Both men chewed silently, and neither spoke as JohnEngine pulled up a chair and sat down with them. A serving maid brought him a mug of flat ale. He cut off some cheese and meat, tore off a hunk of bread.

JohnEngine asked, "Any change in Morgin's condition?"

Abileen answered with a silent shake of his head.

France asked, "You going to talk to your mother today?"

JohnEngine looked at France, was reminded of the swordsman's words of the day before: ". . . refuses to rest herself, refuses to admit he's dying."

JohnEngine rubbed his eyes tiredly. "Yah. I'll talk to her. Maybe if I agree to take her place by his side she'll get some rest."

"You look tired, lad."

JohnEngine nodded. "I slept poorly last night."

"I didn't sleep much either."

"Oh I slept," JohnEngine said. "I just didn't sleep well. I keep having the same dream over and over again."

"I know what you mean, lad. Damn dreams been keeping me awake too. Strangest kind of dreams: angels, faeries, things that don't really exist—"

JohnEngine started and looked up, spilled his mug of ale across the table. He locked eyes with France and said only, "Ellowyn? Laelith?"

The swordsman rocked back in his chair as if he'd been struck. "Outside the castle wall? At night? And Morgin's horse?"

JohnEngine climbed out of his chair, was half way across the kitchen headed for Morgin's room, cursing his injured leg for slowing him down. The swordsman sprinted past him.

••••

"I don't want to go back," Morgin told the skeleton king. They both sat on an old, rotted log in a forest in some lost memory of a dream. "Please don't make me go back."

The skeleton king sighed and adjusted the crown on his head. He looked at Morgin with eyeless sockets. "The choice is not mine, Lord Mortal. It is yours. But if you don't go back now you'll spend the rest of eternity like me, going neither forward nor back, forever waiting."

"That doesn't seem so bad."

The skeleton king shrugged. "No. It isn't. Not at first. But I just sit here and wait, and the days turn into years, and the years into centuries, and the centuries into millennia. And ever and ever I wait."

"What are you waiting for?"

"I've been waiting for you to release me."

"To release you? Me?"

"Yes. You. Only you can release me, and then I can go on." The skeleton king looked upward wistfully. "I'm frightened of what I'll find there, but anything will be better than this."

"But how can I release you?"

"By going back."

"But I don't want to go back."

"But you must. If not for yourself then for me."

Morgin thought long and hard for a moment. He was tired of the pain and the sorrow that awaited him. But deep within he knew he must go back. He turned toward the skeleton king to tell him his decision, but the king was gone, and so were the log and the forest, and all sight and sound and existence. Only darkness remained.

29

The Pride of Fools

"MY LORD," ELLOWYN said. "It's time to light a—"

"No," Morgin snapped angrily. He took in his surroundings quickly. He lay in a bed in a very normal bedroom in some castle, but the presence of the angel, and the lack of pain, warned him that he was dreaming. But sometime soon he would have to leave the dreams behind, and face Rhianne and her treachery.

Ellowyn winced. "Why may I not light a candle, my lord?"

Outside it was early dusk, a world of long, lean shadows cast by the last remnants of the setting sun. Morgin stared at the darkness of the open window. "Because I said so."

Ellowyn looked away from him. Laelith sat fearfully on the end of his bed, eyes downcast, her wings for once still.

"This is unhealthy, my lord."

Morgin didn't answer.

"You must love her very much."

"No," Morgin said. "I don't love her at all. I hate her."

"That too," Ellowyn said. "I'm afraid I will never understand you mortals. How you can hate someone whom you so dearly love—"

"I told you I don't love her."

"You mortals are also good at believing your own lies."

"Please be silent. I'm trying to think."

Ellowyn stood. "Come, little one," she said to Laelith. "We're not wanted here." She turned and left the room; the faerie followed.

"Go," Morgin whispered after them. "You're nothing but the stuff of dreams anyway."

••••

For many days Morgin lay in a stupor, unknowing and uncaring. And then one morning he awoke lying in the arms of his Rhianne. "My lord," she said softly, tracing her fingers across the enormous, ugly scar in the center of his chest. "It gladdens me to see that you have chosen to rejoin the living."

Rhianne! By that he knew he was no longer dreaming. By that he knew he would now face a painful reality.

When next he awoke Rhianne sat in a chair near his bed. She was asleep, her head bowed, her hair loose and draped about her face, her mouth open in a very unladylike way. And yet, she was still so beautiful. Not Ellowyn's kind of beauty, which was a cold thing to admire from afar; Rhianne's was the simple beauty of a pretty girl with a smile on her face and a twinkle in her eye. He longed to see her open her eyes, to see that mischievous glint that seemed to imply the two of them shared some hidden secret. But he hadn't seen that look in a long time.

She started, opened her eyes, blinked several times in that moment of confusion that comes with waking in a strange place. She yawned, extended her arms and stretched, arching her back, and Morgin wondered why everything had gone so wrong between them. Yes, she'd slighted him, humiliated him. But he had more than paid her back with two years of pure grief. Only a few moons ago it had been time to mend the rift between them; he'd been looking forward to that with joy, and then he'd watched her go willingly to Valso's bed, and all of his longing desire crashed around him.

She stood and took a moment to straighten her dress, still not aware that he'd awakened and was watching her. When she did finally look his way she froze.

"Morgin!" She crossed the room in an instant, hovered over him. "Are you in pain? What should I do?"

He wanted to forget that she'd betrayed him, wanted it to be a dream with no truth to it so he could rest in her arms and drown in her eyes. It hurt to speak, but he would let nothing stop him from saying the one thing he needed to say. "You betrayed me. You betrayed us all. I heard you bargain with the Tulalane, then go to Valso's bed. Get out of my sight."

She blinked her eyes several times, clearly confused. Obviously, until that moment, she had believed he was unaware of her treachery. A tear rolled down her cheek, and she stood there silently for several heartbeats, her mouth open, tears now flowing freely. It didn't give him any joy to see such pain in her eyes. But then her face hardened with anger.

She leaned toward him and said, "How dare you? You know nothing." She trembled with rage. "You have no idea what I went through for this family, this revered House. You— You—"

She sobbed once, turned, and marched out of the room.

Morgin struggled to understand what he'd just seen. Her reaction had not been that of someone guilty of such betrayal, and yet he'd witnessed it himself that night in Elhiyne. The evidence was clear. He'd seen the truth with his own eyes.

••••

Morgin lay in bed, staring at the doorway through which Rhianne had left in tears, replaying the scene over in his mind. When JohnEngine and AnnaRail walked in it took an effort of will to focus on them.

"You're awake!" AnnaRail said.

She leaned forward ever so slightly, as if she might hold him and nurture him, but she hesitated, looked at him as if he were a stranger; and in that hesitation he saw distrust.

"Mother," he said softly, which was as loud as he could say anything.

"Morgin?" she said, speaking his name as if it were a question. She reached out, touched his face gently, but the comfort he'd expected was not there. "You are Morgin, aren't you? You are my son?"

He tried to nod. "I am as much your son as I have ever been."

That was the wrong thing to say. Her brow wrinkled as she clearly wondered if there was some hidden meaning there. But then she smiled and touched his face. "Yes. You are my son," she said. Still, he heard doubt in her voice.

She sat down in the straight-backed, wooden chair that Ellowyn—or was it Rhianne—kept near his bed.

JohnEngine said, "What happened to Rhianne? We passed her a moment ago, and she was crying."

"She betrayed us," Morgin said. "I heard her bargain with the Tulalane, and then go to Valso's bed to gain his favor, all so she could save her own precious life."

JohnEngine's eyes hardened and he demanded, "And did you say anything of this to her?"

"Of course," Morgin said. "I told her I witnessed her treachery—"

JohnEngine shouted, "You great bloody fool."

AnnaRail turned to JohnEngine and put a hand on his shoulder. "Calm down, JohnEngine. There's been a mistake here."

JohnEngine ignored her, stepped past her to lean over Morgin. "You heard her agree to go to Valso's bed, but it was a ruse to get close to him. She took poison to his chambers and tried to kill him. But she failed, and no one can fault her for that, you bloody idiot."

Morgin couldn't believe what he was hearing. "But, I heard—"

JohnEngine leaned even closer. "You heard, but you didn't see. She saw you standing in the shadows nearby, and she didn't betray you. It was her witness, along with Nicki's, that proved you were not the coward grandmother believed. And she paid a brutal price for her loyalty to us, her loyalty to you. You bloody, bloody idiot. You're not the only one who was hurt in this. She bears scars as well, though not as visible as yours."

JohnEngine turned and stormed out of the room. "You stupid fool."

Morgin's thoughts raced frantically through his memories of lurking in the shadows of Elhiyne. The night she'd agreed to go to Valso's bed she had glanced his way.

He'd watched her do so, feared at the time that she might have seen him, knew now that she had, knew now that JohnEngine was right, he was a bloody, bloody idiot.

AnnaRail stood and said, "You've done a terrible thing, Morgin."

"Go to her," he said. "Please. Tell her I didn't know. Tell her I'm sorry. Ask her to forgive me."

She looked at him for a long moment, then turned and left the room.

She didn't return until late that afternoon, saying only, "Rhianne needs time. And I think . . . so do you."

••••

The next day AnnaRail and Tulellcoe seemed abnormally cautious, and everyone avoided speaking of Rhianne. Seated in a comfortable chair near his bed, with Tulellcoe standing beside her, AnnaRail said, "We thought you were dead."

Morgin shrugged. "There are moments when I thought I was dead."

She frowned. "You were found buried under dead Kulls, pinned to the ground by a broken lance. There seemed little life in you, though life is a curious thing. The healthiest of men will suddenly die for no apparent reason; or the sickest of the old will live on and on. With the will to live, who can say how close to death one might venture and still return to the living?"

She sounded as if she were trying to reconcile Morgin's miraculous recovery, hoping to convince herself he had simply been wounded and survived.

He said, "Lately I've thought of that a lot. And sometimes . . . I wonder if maybe I didn't actually die out there . . . and then somehow return to the living."

Tulellcoe shook his head, and without conviction said, "You were wounded—horribly—and you survived. It's as simple as that."

Morgin heard suspicion in Tulellcoe's voice, and while he saw none in his eyes, it seemed Tulellcoe shared AnnaRail's unease. Again, one who had been close to him seemed now far and distant.

Tulellcoe said, "There is talk of the ShadowLord carrying this war to Durin. Some even speak of uniting the Lesser Clans to do so."

Morgin shrugged indifferently. "I thought this war was done. And besides, it will be a long time before I am healed sufficiently to return to war. And then I doubt that I will want to."

AnnaRail said, "I'm glad to hear that."

"Let's hope he has a choice in the matter," Tulellcoe said.

••••

As Morgin recuperated, a continuous stream of clansmen, family and friends, came to wish him well, but never did he see Rhianne. And politely worded notes asking her to come to him were rebuffed without an answer. One afternoon, he had a pleasant chat with Tulellcoe and Cort. Morgin hoped the distance in his uncle's demeanor was slowly dissipating, though as they left, Tulellcoe did seem oddly relieved to be gone.

Cort stopped at the threshold, looked back and said, "I pray that you heal quickly, my lord."

"My lord?" Morgin asked. "Why so formal? Why am I no longer just Morgin?"

She shrugged. "It has been a long time since you were just Morgin. After all, you are the ShadowLord."

"That's just a name," Morgin said. "Nothing more."

"Oh, but you are wrong. It is far more than just a name; it is a symbol. It represents honor and power. It was the ShadowLord who opposed the Decouix menace, and it was he who defeated them."

"You act as if I did it alone."

"In a way, you did, for without you it surely could not have been done."

"I don't want to be a symbol," Morgin said.

"Then you should have allowed Illalla his victory."

"I couldn't do that."

"No," she agreed. "You couldn't. Your destiny was written in the blood of Csairne Glen long before you fought there."

"Damn you!" Morgin said. "You're starting to sound like all the rest."

She was not an expressive woman, and a shrug seemed to be one of her most prolific gestures. "I speak only the truth, ShadowLord. But if you wish, then I will call you Morgin, but only among friends."

••••

Morgin awoke just after dawn, in that in-between time when the servants were quietly preparing the morning meal, but the general hustle and bustle of the castle had yet to commence. He'd slept poorly, thinking of Rhianne and trying to find some way he might mend the rift between them. But she refused to have anything to do with him, and he hadn't seen her since she ran from his room in tears.

On a small table next to his bed he spotted a half-finished cup of tea from the night before. He sat up carefully, retrieved the cup, and of course the tea was cold. No need to bother a servant at this very busy hour of the morning, for any clansman could remedy the situation.

It should have been a simple spell, an every-day kind of spell. A short incantation, a few words and a bit of power, and steam would once again rise from a warm cup of tea. But when Morgin tried, no power came at his bidding.

He tried again, and again, and again. His power and arcane abilities were gone as if burned out of his soul, and he realized that he must hide that fact from everyone. There was an emptiness in his soul, a vacuum of nothingness that left him alone and cold. Somewhere between the horror of Csairne Glen and the pain of his awakening he had lost his power, and its absence left an ache in his soul, a sorrow that consumed him. He was a wizard without magic, a sorcerer without power.

30

Magic's End

THEY'D GIVEN MORGIN a room high in Castle Inetka, and it was a painful struggle to negotiate the stairs down to the ground floor with just a cane. At AnnaRail's insistence, he'd recently begun taking short walks about the castle. But today he was on a mission, with a clear and well defined purpose. France was avoiding him; everyone but the swordsman had come to see him. He'd learned that France had taken up residence in the common soldiers' barracks, and he hoped to find the swordsman there.

Inside the barracks he found a long room furnished with a great number of cots and a large table at the far end. Seated at the table were several common soldiers and a few clansmen of the lowest caste, but with the exception of France, the room was otherwise empty. They tossed dice back and forth on the table, cursed loudly, and told the kind of jokes that one heard only in a soldiers' barracks. None of them noticed Morgin as he stepped into the room.

France sat on one of the cots, his back to Morgin, methodically sharpening his sword. Morgin walked slowly down the aisle between the cots and stopped a few paces short of the swordsman.

"Aye, swordsman," one of the soldiers playing dice bellowed. "Are you sure you won't try your luck?" He looked up for an answer, but instead saw Morgin. His eyes shot open and he stood. "My lord," he said, bowing deeply from the waist. Taken by surprise, his comrades jumped to their feet and followed suit. France stood also and turned slowly to face Morgin, though he did not bow.

One of the soldiers stepped forward, obviously their leader. "Forgive us, Lord. We didn't know you was there. No offense intended."

"And none taken," Morgin said. He reached into his pocket and retrieved a silver coin, more than a month's wages for one of these men. "I'd like to speak to the swordsman alone," he said, and flipped the coin onto the table where it chinked among a few copper coins. "If you'd do me the favor of continuing the game elsewhere, that should sweeten the pot for your trouble."

The soldiers thanked him and left quickly.

"Hello, France," Morgin said. He wanted to stand and face the swordsman squarely, but he tired quickly. His knees began to tremble. Moving with great care he sat on a nearby cot.

France stood stiff and formal before him. "My lord," he said, and bowed deeply from the waist. "How may I serve you?" He spoke without any trace of his usual accent, addressing Morgin in the same stilted way he conversed with Olivia.

"So you're going to do it to me too?" Morgin asked.

"Pardon, my lord? Do what?"

"You know damn well what."

"Forgive me, my lord, if I have offended you. I—"

"Damn you!" Morgin said. "Stop calling me that. I'm not *my lord*. I'm me. Morgin."

France looked at him for a long moment, then carefully asked, "Are you?"

"What do you mean by that?"

"Nothing, my lord." France's face remained expressionless.

Morgin buried his face in his hands. "Damn you," he whispered, thinking of AnnaRail and JohnEngine; her distant unease and his uncomfortable formality. Both of them had tried repeatedly to break through the invisible barrier that made them all strangers, and neither had succeeded. "You've changed just like all the rest," Morgin said.

France's answer came in icy and distant tones. "It is not we who have changed, my lord."

Those words hung on the air like smoke in the dead stillness of the morning. "Have I changed that much?" Morgin asked. "I'm still Morgin . . . I think."

"The Morgin I knew," France said, "came down from Csairne Glen bearing wounds no mortal man could survive. Who, or what, you are, I do not know. But I will not be friend to some demon who haunts the body of my dead friend."

"Damn it I'm not dead. I never was. I don't know what happened to me up there. I . . . Damn you!" He almost started crying, thinking of the gap in his memory, of that time when he was dead, or near to it. "I don't even have my magic anymore."

"What?" France said. "What did you say?"

"I said I no longer have any magic. It's gone, torn from me. I'm as powerless as any peasant."

"Gone, you say?" France asked. "Completely gone?"

Morgin nodded. France sat down beside him and threw an arm about his shoulders. "Don't ya see, lad? That's a blessin', not a curse. It was your witch powers that was always your curse. It brought nothing but trouble, and now you're free of it."

France stood, began pacing back and forth in front of him. "Who knows about this?"

"Just you, and maybe Ellowyn and Laelith, if Laelith even understands—"

France hissed angrily. "Don't mention them two. They don't exist, never have. They was just a dream."

Morgin shrugged, decided not to argue the point. France continued. "But it's good no one knows about your magic. And you be careful not to tell no one. Not even your mother or that brother of yers. The fewer who know, the better. If this gets out, Valso won't be the only one trying to kill ya."

"Valso?" Morgin asked. "Trying to kill me?"

"Sure. He's been sending assassins quite regular. In fact the whole damn Greater Council wants your head on a pike. Take a look around. Wylow's still got this place under heavy guard. And there's more than a few Elhiynes among them. Your grand-mother's been sending him troops to help out."

"But why are they after me?"

France shook his head. "You ain't changed, have ya? Still can't see it even when it's right in front of your nose. You're a big hero. And your grandmother's getting everything out of that she can. She's pushing you real hard, gonna make sure you're a public figure before she gets done with you. Maybe even try to unite the Lesser Clans under you, especially if she thinks she can control you."

"Me?"

"Of course, you. You're the ShadowLord. You beat Illalla's army when we was outnumbered four to one. You got a reputation and she's making sure it gets bigger every day. If I was you, the first thing I'd do when I got back home was cut Valso's throat."

"Valso?" Morgin asked. "At Elhiyne?"

"Yah. He and that chop-faced father of his got caught trying to sneak away from Csairne Glen. Your grandmother's holding 'em for ransom or something. That wom-an sure likes to play her games."

Morgin's head spun crazily. It was all too much too fast.

France said, "You don't look so well, lad."

"I'm tired," Morgin said.

"Better get you back to bed, eh?"

France almost carried him back to his room. It was frustrating to be so helpless, to find his knees weak, his eyelids heavy. But he'd learned the hard way that in his present condition, exhaustion came all too quickly. And the mention of Valso's name had reopened the wound in his heart. He'd wronged Rhianne so terribly, he wondered if she would ever forgive him.

••••

Morgin stood in front of the full-length mirror in his room and looked carefully at his image. He looked ridiculous. He felt like a clown, dressed all in red: red breeches, red blouse, red cape. He understood that red was the ceremonial color of House Elhiyne, and that Olivia had arranged for high ceremony that day, but red from head to foot? And the lace! White lace at cuffs and collar! He looked like a dandy, and felt like a fool. At least the knee-high boots and the hip length doublet were black leather. He put his hands on his hips and scowled. "Must I wear this in public?"

Avis, kneeling beside him, making last minute adjustments to his sleeve, spoke around a mouth full of needles. "It is customary, my lord. And it was the outfit chosen for you."

Avis was being diplomatic. Olivia had chosen the outfit, and sent it with the servant to Inetka. But Avis knew better than to mention the old woman's name around Morgin.

"Very well," Morgin said. "Let's get this over with."

"Another moment or two, my lord." Avis worked feverishly at a small leather button on Morgin's cuff. It looked all right to Morgin, but something about it offended the man's sense of propriety. Finally, satisfied, he stood, stepped back a few paces, and carefully inspected Morgin. "That should do it, my lord. Shall I tell them you're ready?"

"Yah," Morgin said. "Go ahead."

"Very well, my lord." Avis bowed deeply and turned to leave.

"Oh," Morgin said. "There's one more thing."

Avis stopped just short of the door. "Yes, my lord?"

"I haven't forgotten that you were one of the few who had faith in me when everyone else thought I was a coward."

Avis smiled, a rare breach of his own private etiquette. "Thank you, my lord."

"No, Avis. I thank you."

Avis's formality returned and the smile disappeared. "Will there be anything else, my lord?"

"No. I guess I'm ready."

Avis bowed and left.

Morgin, alone now, turned slowly through a full circle and surveyed his room carefully, making sure that everything of importance had been packed. He felt no regret at leaving, for there were no fond memories to look back upon. But after a season of continuous residency he had grown accustomed to the place. He turned back to the mirror.

It was customary for a clansman to wear something of his clan's colors on ceremonial occasions. And the higher the clansman's station, the more of that color he wore. If it weren't for that, and the fact that he'd seen his brothers and cousins wearing something similar on other occasions, he would have refused to wear such outlandish clothing.

His eye caught a hint of movement in the mirror. He spun about, found a tall stranger leaning casually against the far wall. The man wore black leathers, with long dark hair framing an aristocratic face that could only be described as beautiful, though darkness clouded his features as if he bore some great sadness. Morgin realized instantly that he stood in the presence of another angel, a dark angel.

The angel shook his head and glanced about, as if dazed or confused. Then he looked at Morgin and frowned. "Ah!" he said. "Lord Mortal. I am Metadan, and I—"

Before he could speak further Ellowyn materialized in front of him, broadsword in hand, her anger a livid and bright halo about her shoulders. "You," she hissed, and Morgin would never have thought one could put so much hatred in a single word. She swung her sword in a flat arc, but Metadan side-stepped and eluded it easily.

"Ellowyn," he said. "I am unarmed."

"You and your evil are never unarmed," she said. She lunged forward and swung again, but this time he was backed against the wall, with no room to step out of range. Her sword sliced through him cleanly, but in the instant of contact it touched only a column of gray smoke formed in the shape of a man. The blade whooshed through it with no discernible resistance, and slowly the smoke began to dissipate into the air of the room.

"What is that smell?" Morgin asked.

Ellowyn stared at the spot where the dark angel had stood, and after a long pause she spoke absently. "Brimstone, my lord."

"I suppose . . ." Morgin said, ". . . that you're going to tell me that that was just another dream."

"No, my lord," she said. "This now is a dream."

"Are you going to tell me who he was?"

"No, my lord."

"Do you refuse to tell me? Is that it?"

"No, my lord. It is not by my choice."

"Is that the difference between us, Ellowyn, the difference between mortal and angel? We have a free will, and you do not?"

"No, my lord. The difference is only that you believe you have free will." Then, without preamble, she disappeared, and Morgin stood alone in the room.

He collected his sword, buckled it to his waist, stepped into the hall and found it crowded with a large number of servants and retainers all dressed in the ceremonial yellow of Inetka. The soft murmur of idle conversation ceased quickly, and in silence they all bowed. Again he wondered why he must go through with this.

Roland, AnnaRail, JohnEngine and Annaline awaited him at the bottom of the stairs. He and Roland had had their private reunion several days earlier. Roland had been warm and close, without that distant reserve that Morgin sensed in the others. And Annaline was just Annaline, more of an Inetka now than an Elhiyne.

Wylow and his sons were there, and Edtoall and Matill and Rhianne's sisters and their husbands. And too there was Val and Cort and Tulellcoe and Eglahan. And behind them all, far to the back, stood Rhianne, alone, with an almost vacant look of unconcern on her face. She too wore Elhiyne red, with her hair piled high on top of her head, and as always there was an unruly lock that had come loose to tease the edge of her cheek. Morgin remembered the night they first met in Anistigh. She had been beautiful then, with a twinkle in her eyes that hinted at a spark of mischief and strong will. She was beautiful now, but the twinkle had disappeared.

For just an instant she looked his way and their eyes met. In hers he saw a tear, a question, maybe even forgiveness, but then her look turned hard and angry. For this grand ceremony of Olivia's she had her role to play as well. She couldn't avoid him, and, if need be, he would use that to advantage. So slowly, carefully, he walked toward her and the crowd parted before him. When he stopped in front of her he offered her his arm. She looked at him with cold indifference and took hold of his arm with a proud and strong grip.

For Morgin's return to Elhiyne, Olivia had sent with Roland an escort of twelve twelves of crack, mounted troops. They were the best in the tribe, having competed for the honor of accompanying the ShadowLord on his triumphant return. When Morgin stepped into the Inetka castle yard they startled him by snapping to attention, with each man standing beside his horse. They were an impressive sight, dressed all in red, with brass and silver hardware polished and gleaming in the sun, men and horses lined up in the yard in twelve rows of twelve.

Their sergeant-of-men stepped forward and dropped to one knee in front of Morgin. He bowed his head as he said, "ShadowLord. My men and I are at your service."

"Abileen?" Morgin asked. "Is that you? Stand up and look me in the face."

The soldier rose, stood proud and strong. "I am honored that you remember me, my lord."

"Of course I remember you," Morgin said. "You rode beside me at Csairne Glen."

Abileen bowed deeply. Morgin noticed then that he wore a black armband. He asked about it.

"The arm band signifies that I was in your original troop, my lord. There are few of us left, but we are all here today to ride in your escort. My lord, the men would be honored if you would review them."

This ceremony was taking a turn Morgin had not prepared for. "Of course," he said. Then he whispered quietly so only Abileen could hear. "I'm not used to doing this kind of thing so you'd better lead the way."

Abileen turned about smartly. They passed down each row of soldiers, and Morgin paused and looked each man in the eyes, though only for an instant.

As Abileen had said there were few wearing the black armband, all too few. With each, Morgin went to the extra trouble of stopping and extending his hand. The first tried to bow and kiss it. "No," Morgin said sharply. "We're comrades, you and I, so just shake it."

The soldier beamed with pride at the rare honor. He shook Morgin's hand happily, and kept shaking it until Abileen nudged him forcefully.

When he finished the review Morgin turned to Abileen in front of the men and shook his hand. Then he reached out and embraced him tightly. The soldiers let out a single great cheer, then subsided into silence as Wylow ushered Morgin to a reviewing stand erected for the occasion.

Wylow made a rather long-winded speech, praising the glory of the ShadowLord's victory over the Decouix army. He spoke of more war, and painted a vivid picture of the price the Greater Council would pay for their aggression.

Roland's speech was quite different. He spoke of truce, an end to war, and he painted a picture of the good harvests that would come without soldiers tramping through the fields. He received polite applause, nothing like the raucous cheers that had accompanied Wylow.

Then it was Morgin's turn. Olivia had prepared and written a speech for him, and sent it with Roland with instructions that Morgin should not deviate from it by so much as a single word. Morgin knew her arrogance was not Roland's fault, and while he considered refusing to accept the old witch's instructions, that would have been unfair to his father. So he accepted the written speech without comment, then later, with no one to observe him, he tore it up without reading it.

He stepped up to the podium, looked down upon a sea of faces. Everyone had come to see the ShadowLord: the lords and ladies of Inetka, peasants from the countryside, soldiers and merchants, rich and poor, all come to bid farewell to him as he took leave of their lands. And in those faces he saw that they expected far more of him than he could ever give.

Silence descended. They waited for him to say something wise and profound, and he forgot the few carefully chosen words he had prepared.

A voice far back in the crowd cried, "Long live the ShadowLord!"

Abileen's soldiers took up the cry and chanted, "ShadowLord . . . ShadowLord . . . ShadowLord . . ."

The assembled throng joined in and their shouts quickly became a deafening roar. Morgin raised his hands to silence them, and they shouted even louder, calling his name as if it was a badge of honor, or a cry to war.

A hand touched his shoulder softly. He turned and found Roland there. "Perhaps now is the time to go, son."

Morgin said, "I didn't want this."

"I know, son."

Wylow used his household troops to open a path through the crowd to Abileen, who waited at the far end of the yard with his men and horses, and pack animals, and Morgin's retinue, and some spare mounts for Morgin and Roland and JohnEngine, and a carriage for AnnaRail and Rhianne and the ladies that would accompany them. Abileen held the reins of a large black mare, a tall, sleek, beautiful animal. But as Morgin approached more closely the sight of the animal sent a shiver down his spine, and when he finally stood beside her the magic of her touched his soul.

Morgin shook his head and looked at Mortiss; it felt good to have his old friend back, and yet her presence frightened him. She snorted and looked back at him as if to tell him he was a complete fool for not realizing she would be here, even if that meant returning from the dead.

He took the reins from Abileen, grasped Mortiss's saddle horn. He still limped a bit, and had to bat a few retainers away when they tried to help him mount. He carefully and painfully climbed into the saddle. Roland, JohnEngine, Val, Cort, Tulellcoe, and Eglahan mounted up and clustered about him, for they would ride beside him. Abileen's soldiers mounted up in a single motion, and with a shout and a cry they rode from the castle along a road lined with cheering people.

France was nowhere to be seen, and Morgin wondered where he'd gone. He asked those about him, but none there had seen the swordsman that day. But as they trotted down the road, well past the last of the cheering crowds, they came upon him waiting patiently by the side of the road. As they approached, he mounted his horse and brought it up to a pace that matched theirs, merging with them without a single missed step. He rode beside Morgin without comment.

31

The Song of the Betrayer

MORGIN AWOKE TO the sound of pipes, an eerie, faint sound, far in the distance, originating deep within the forest that surrounded the Elhiyne camp. The pipist was good; the notes he blew told of years of practice. The tune he chose was a sad one, almost a dirge, and it spoke of sorrow, unhappiness and regret.

Morgin looked up at the inside of his pavilion. He rolled groggily out of bed, pulled on a pair of plain, brown, loose fitting breeches, a white blouse and a leather doublet, then fought his way into his boots. The morning air in the mountains was always cold so he threw a cloak about his shoulders. He peered out through the flap that separated his sleeping chamber from the rest of the tent. No one else was about, which was typical for one of his dreams.

The guards outside his tent leaned drowsily on their lances. Morgin tiptoed past them and was gone. The sentries at the edge of the camp seemed oddly inattentive— again he reminded himself that this was just a dream.

A thin sliver of sun had just appeared over the mountain tops that surrounded Csairne Glen. The grass beneath his feet was green and wet with dew, the air about him cold and crisp, with a gray mist that hung close to the ground and made the sun-beams visible, but so faint that only the most distant objects were blurred by the haze. One would never know that this peaceful, grassy glen had recently been the scene of so much death. But the pipist knew; it was in his song.

Morgin followed the sounds of the pipes until he came upon a small clearing and stopped near its edge. The dark angel Metadan sat on a large boulder in the center of the clearing, playing his sad tune. Morgin hung back, hiding just within the wall of trees at the edge of the clearing. He wondered why the angel felt such sadness. A tear touch Morgin's cheek.

The angel's tune ended slowly, as if it drifted away with the morning mist. He lowered the pipes from his lips and looked at them wistfully. "Ahhh!" he said. "If only I could spend eternity piping such notes." Then he blinked his eyes and the pipes van-ished. He stood, and for the first time Morgin saw that he wore a sheathed broad-sword strapped to his waist. He jumped down from the boulder, and turned to look directly at Morgin's hiding place. "Lord Mortal," he said, bowing at the waist like the most elegant of couriers. "Tell me, did you enjoy my tune?"

Morgin thought of running, but the angel could catch him easily so he stood openly and stepped into the clearing. Since he had no weapon, he kept his distance.

"I am not here to harm you," Metadan said, as if sensing Morgin's unease. "And you have not answered my question, ShadowLord. Did you enjoy my playing?"

Somehow Morgin sensed that the angel placed great store in the answer to that question. "It was beautiful, and very sad. But tell me, why are you haunting my dreams?"

Metadan smiled and said, "Your dreams, my reality."

"You're playing games with me," Morgin said.

"No, my lord. I seek to play no games, merely to deliver a message."

"A message from whom?"

"My master."

"And who is your master?"

The angel merely shook his head.

"You will not tell me who your master is?"

Before either of them could speak further there came a thrashing in the trees as if a large animal charged headlong through the undergrowth. Ellowyn burst into the clearing, with a broadsword gripped in both hands. She halted abruptly and pointed her sword at the dark angel. "My lord," she said to Morgin. "Do not trust this deceitful traitor."

Metadan held out his empty hands. "Ellowyn, I've come in peace."

She stepped protectively between Morgin and the dark angel. She slashed out and the tip of her sword hissed past Metadan's nose.

He back-stepped and halted, and stood straight and proud. "I have come only to deliver a message. Let me speak it and I'll go."

"Speak nothing here," Ellowyn said, her voice cracking with strain. "Your tongue curls about false words like a snake about its prey. And it is long past time it was silenced once and for all."

Her words stung him visibly, as if her hatred inflicted a far more painful wound than that of any sword. "I do not want to fight you, Ellowyn," he said. "But if you will not let me speak, then I must."

He drew his sword in one smooth motion. Morgin gasped, for drops of fresh blood dripped continuously from the entire length of the blade.

Ellowyn and Metadan began their battle by circling one another slowly, both holding their swords high in a two handed grip. Ellowyn attacked with a swiftness Morgin could not follow. Their swords rang together again and again, then they separated and circled once more.

Ellowyn fought hot and angry, the dark angel cold and confident. She attacked again, and again Metadan repelled her, but this time Morgin saw how easily he did so, and he realized that Metadan was in command of this battle, not poor Ellowyn. The dark angel gave her a pained and unhappy smile. "I was always able to best you with a sword, my Ellowyn."

Now Metadan attacked, though not with Ellowyn's swiftness, but with a deliberate determination that bode ill for her chances of victory. He brought the bloody sword around and down, raining blow after blow upon Ellowyn's faltering defenses. She retreated slowly across the clearing, now on the defensive. She stumbled on something, faltered, and as she tried to regain her footing Metadan stepped within her guard and brushed her sword aside. But instead of cutting her down, he slammed a mailed fist into the side of her head, and she slumped to the ground in a stupor.

He stood over her for a moment, breathing heavily and watching her closely, his expression hard and angry. But when she did not move he frowned. He reached down and touched her cheek, then he sighed and his shoulders relaxed; his expression changed to relief. He dropped to one knee beside her, lines of sorrow etched on his face. He caressed her cheek softly, with a tenderness Morgin would not have believed had he not seen it himself. "Oh my Ellowyn!" the dark angel said to her as she lay unconscious at his feet, and a tear ran down his cheek. "My dear Ellowyn. I have loved you since before time began, and I will love you long after it ends. I was such a proud and stupid fool. Can you ever forgive me? Must I endure your hatred through eternity?" Then he closed his eyes and wept openly.

Morgin was touched by pity, but fear warned him to move cautiously. He edged his way carefully toward the sobbing angel. He stopped well out of reach of the dark angel's bloody sword, and asked softly, "Is she dead?"

Metadan started and looked up at Morgin. The anger returned to his face. "You!" he cried. He stood upright and swept the bloody sword in a broad slash. Morgin backstepped, stumbled on something and landed on his butt. Metadan lowered his sword and held the tip the width of a small finger from Morgin's nose. Blood dripped from the blade onto Morgin's chest, and the angel shook with anger.

Unarmed and at the angel's mercy, Morgin knew his only hope might be boldness. "You can't kill me. This is just a dream."

The angel shook his head. "And every dream yields its own reality."

"But this is my dream."

The dark angel nodded. "Aye. But your dream is my reality."

Without warning, Metadan pressed the tip of the broadsword into Morgin's cheek, and cut the flesh there deeply and painfully. Morgin cried out.

"Forgive me, my lord," the angel said sadly. "But you must know and understand the reality of your dreams, and so I give you that token."

"Who are you?" Morgin asked.

The angel looked at him narrowly. "I am the Fallen Angel. I serve the Dark God who sits upon the throne of power in the ninth hell of the netherworld, and I have a message for you, mortal."

Morgin asked. "Why would the Dark God have a message for me?"

"Do not presume to know the source of the message, fool." Metadan touched the tip of the bloody sword to Morgin's chest. "It is the Unnamed King whom you should seek, and his consort the god-queen Erithnae. But in your stupidity you will seek the god-sword, and you will fail. And finally, in the city of glass, beneath the fires of the eternal sun, you will ask three questions, and you will gain three answers, and in them you will know yourself far more than any mortal should."

Morgin frowned. "What does all that mean?"

Metadan looked at him as if he were a foolish child. "That is a question you should ask of the Unnamed King." And then, without another word, he stepped back, touched the bloody sword to his lips, and bowed deeply. In the instant that he stood upright, he became a column of smoke in the shape of a man. The smoke held its shape for a moment, then dissipated slowly into the forest air, and once more Morgin smelled the scent that Ellowyn had called brimstone.

He climbed to his feet, looked down at his chest and examined it carefully. There was no sign of the blood that had dripped there from Metadan's sword, and for an instant he questioned his own sanity. But pain from the cut on his cheek made this dream seem very real, and Ellowyn's temple still bore the bruise from Metadan's mailed fist.

He sat down by Ellowyn; she lay still and unconscious. Her breathing and pulse were normal, so he lifted her head and shoulders and laid them in his lap. And as he waited in silence for her to regain consciousness, he heard far off in the forest, so faint it was almost not there, the sound of beautifully sad pipes.

Ellowyn's eyelids fluttered and blinked open. She looked at Morgin, confused and disoriented for a moment, but then her eyes filled with recognition and she smiled.

"Who is Metadan?" Morgin asked.

Her smile vanished. "Please do not speak that name to me, my lord."

"He loves you very much," Morgin said. "It hurt him to hurt you."

Ellowyn began to weep, soft, silent tears. Morgin put his arms about her and tried to comfort her. "Tell me about him," he said. "I must know."

Ellowyn forced back her tears and drew a ragged breath. "Long ago," she said, "in a time so distant its measure has no meaning, he was the greatest and mightiest of the twelve archangels. He commanded the first legion, and by his might and glory they were the greatest of the twelve legions of angels. All of us looked to him for wisdom and guidance, and we honored him, and the gods favored him by making him lord and commander of us all, and we followed him gladly, joyfully. He was so proud, and grand, and his glory inspired us all.

"But he wanted more. He wanted power, the power of the gods, and to gain it he allowed himself to be seduced by the Lord of the Seven Sins. He betrayed us to the nether god, and we were devastated by his armies. The first legion, his legion, was massacred, and fell even to the last angel—it is their blood that forever drips from his sword. And now the eleven legions that remain are but remnants of what they once were."

"And yet you still love him," Morgin said.

"No," she said. "I hate him."

Morgin nodded. "That too. But it was not too long ago that you wondered how I could hate someone I so dearly love. Well, my Ellowyn, now you know."

She began to weep again. "I am an angel," she said. "I am not meant for such mortal emotions. It's not right that I should know hate."

For once Morgin felt very wise, and also very sad. "But if you would know love, Ellowyn, then you must know hate. For one without the other is meaningless."

The sound of the pipes ceased. It had been hardly noticeable, but was now conspicuous by its absence, and in the silence that followed Morgin heard cries far off in the distance. He listened carefully, recognized JohnEngine's voice calling his name.

"They're looking for me," he said. "We'd better go and help them find me."

They stood, he and Ellowyn, and walked together out of the clearing, Ellowyn leading, Morgin following. At its edge, on impulse, he looked back, and was not surprised to find only uninterrupted forest. The small clearing had vanished, leaving no mark upon the land, and no trace of its passing. And, of course, when he turned back to continue up the trail, Ellowyn too had vanished.

••••

It was a simple spell that DaNoel cast, the kind of spell a child could master, and of course the kind of spell the whoreson always found so difficult. It was not a spell meant to twist the forces of nature, nor to manipulate great powers, but only to make one simple-minded clansman of a guard drowse at his post. It had to be a simple spell, for if it weren't, and Olivia ever examined the guard carefully, she'd know he had been tampered with, and eventually she would trace that tampering to DaNoel.

Olivia had fortified the guard's own magic against Decouix tampering to protect him from Valso. It had never occurred to her to fortify him against Elhiyne tampering, so DaNoel's spell worked well. The guard's eyes drifted slowly shut, and eventually, in an effort to get comfortable, the man wedged himself awkwardly between his lance and the stone wall of the castle corridor. If he were discovered that way he would be in some trouble, but it would not be the first time a guard had been caught sleeping at his post, so the trouble would be no more than one of Olivia's tongue-lashings.

DaNoel tiptoed carefully past the guard, then through the lone door at the end of the corridor. Beyond the door he encountered a circular stone stairway, but he paused before climbing it. Now he had to be exceedingly careful, for this spell would be neither simple nor easy.

He closed his eyes, expanding his sense of magic slowly, lest it collide with Olivia's veil of containment and alert her immediately. He sensed the veil in its netherlife as a shimmering curtain of power on the stairway before him, of such intensity that not even Valso dare touch it. But DaNoel knew he could pass, for he was of Olivia's blood.

To avoid the need for extensive preparations on the spot, he had prepared his spell well in advance. But it could easily fail if he were to move incautiously, so he took a deep breath, then touched his spell to the veil in the most delicate way.

For an instant he feared he had failed, or worse, that he had been indelicate and Olivia would know of his tampering and come storming up the stairway to demand an explanation. But then he saw a wrinkle form in the veil, and as he looked on his spell took hold and the wrinkle grew into a well-defined and distinct flaw. A little more power and the flaw opened quickly into a rift large enough for a man to pass. He stepped through the flaw without hesitating, then released his power and quenched the spell mercilessly, for once begun such spells had a tendency to run away from their makers. As the veil closed behind him he breathed easier.

He climbed slowly to the open door at the top of the stairs, but hesitated before stepping into the room beyond.

"Come in, Elhiyne," Valso called out casually. "Don't hide in the shadows like your infamous brother."

DaNoel stepped angrily into the room, found Valso seated casually by a warm fire. "The whoreson is not my brother."

Valso shrugged. "I meant no insult. To me he is the whoreson, nothing more, and in deference to you I will not again call him your brother." Valso shivered, stood, moved closer to the fire, stopped with his back to DaNoel and rubbed his hands together. "Ahhh! Your Elhiyne nights are cold even in summer."

"Fall is almost upon us," DaNoel said. "It'll get colder yet."

Valso shivered again. "I'll be glad to get back to Durin."

"And what makes you think you'll ever see Durin again? My bro—the whoreson returns tomorrow. He'll probably kill you."

"No. Your grandmother won't let that happen. My father and I are too valuable alive."

DaNoel shook his head. "My grandmother has always had difficulty controlling Morgin."

"But she will control him in this. Believe me."

"You're awfully confident for one who might die tomorrow."

"No one will kill me tomorrow, least of all him."

"You'll be horribly humiliated."

Valso laughed, and turned to face DaNoel. "Humiliated? Here? With only Elhiynes looking on. No. There is no humiliation in that."

"But grandmother intends to have the whoreson take you back to Durin where you'll be dragged through the streets and ransomed publicly to your family."

Valso nodded. "Aye. That will be humiliating. And of course Morgin will gain even more stature among the clans."

DaNoel couldn't hide his anger. "Damn him! ShadowLord bah! He has everyone but me fooled. I know him well. He's a guttersnipe who pretends at nobility. And he thinks he's better than me."

Valso nodded and agreed. "Yes. He does. He thinks he's better than us all."

DaNoel slammed his fist down hard on the table. "Damn him!"

"If only I could escape," Valso said as if speaking to no one in particular. "He would gain little stature if he entered Durin with only my father as captive."

DaNoel frowned. "What do you mean? Your father is king of the Greater Council?"

"But he was defeated by that guttersnipe, and lives now in unredeemable disgrace. No. My father's days as a ruler are ended."

"But what of his power?"

"After Csairne Glen there will be no support for him in my family, especially if I can get there before him. And alone his power is not enough to hold the throne."

"This is all academic," DaNoel said, "You can't escape. At least not with your life."

"But what if someone were to help me?"

"Only someone of Elhiyne blood could get you past that veil."

Valso nodded. "I know. And it must be someone of great power."

"I could do it," DaNoel said, then stopped. He certainly hadn't come up here to help the Decouix escape. But the whoreson's victory had eclipsed anything DaNoel might ever hope to accomplish. He would need help from someone powerful if he ever hoped to shine on his own, maybe even shine brighter than the almighty ShadowLord. And who better than Morgin's greatest enemy?

"Will you help me?" Valso said.

DaNoel hesitated. He would wait to see what happened when the whoreson returned. "Like all Elhiynes, I'll stand in the Hall of Wills tomorrow and laugh as the whoreson kills you."

"And if he doesn't kill me," Valso asked, "will you then help me escape?"

DaNoel spun about and left the room, but he glanced back and saw Valso smiling.

32

Dream Magic

MORGIN STOOD ON the lip of a high plateau overlooking the valley of his home-land. The *token* that Metadan had given him, the cut on his cheek, was very real. He'd explained it away with a lie about falling and gashing his cheek on the sharp edge of a shield. It was a good reminder that he should be more careful in his dreams.

Far in the distance Castle Elhiyne dominated the valley, nestled with the nearby village and the small wood that separated them. Together they formed a distinct and separate blotch on the gently rolling landscape of the surrounding fields, a land ripe and overflowing with wheat and corn and rye.

More than once, as a boy, he had stood on this same spot looking down upon the valley below. But now he was, almost regrettably, a man. Then he had worn the clothes of an adolescent, and now he wore the red of a great Elhiyne lord. The old woman's ambition propelled him, and he knew that it was his responsibility to temper her machinations. He felt that his inability to do so reflected a lack within himself.

It was still well before noon, but down below he could see the crowds forming along the road that led across the valley floor to the main gates at Elhiyne. Olivia knew well that his homecoming would be today; riders had been sent forward daily to keep her informed of his progress, and she would not miss this opportunity for a show. Today the ShadowLord would come home in victory and triumph.

Morgin heard the soft fall of Ellowyn's footsteps as she approached behind him. That was odd, for ordinarily she seemed to walk as if her feet did not touch the floor. Recently she'd taken to imitating mortals, though her efforts were stilted and unnatural. Without turning from his view of the valley floor, he said, "Each day you are among us you walk more like a mortal, my Ellowyn."

"Yes, my lord. I know. And so I must go."

He had been expecting that. "Go? Why?"

"Because it is right, my lord. You are healed. You no longer need me."

"Oh but I do," he said, refusing to turn and face her. He knew he could not win this, their last argument. "I need you more now than ever. I need you more with each passing day, for who will explain what's happening in my dreams?"

He heard her sigh. "That too is why I must go. It is not good for you to become so dependent upon me."

"And what of you, Ellowyn? Do you ever need me as I need you?"

"Oh yes, my lord. And that too is not good."

"Where will you go?"

"Wherever my master bids."

Ellowyn's master! Morgin itched to know the identity of this mysterious master, but he knew better than to ask. "Will I ever see you again?"

"That I do not know, my lord."

"Go then," Morgin said softly. "Leave me, if you will. But remember I do need you."

She made no reply. He turned to face her, and was not surprised to find her gone, vanished as if she had never been, leaving only a shimmering in the air to mark her passing.

He stood silently for a long time, until Abileen approached, glancing about, clearly wondering why his master would stand alone facing nothing. The soldier did not voice his thoughts, but dropped to one knee and bowed his head. "My lord."

"What is it, Abileen?"

"We are ready to ride, my lord."

Morgin nodded. "Then lead the way."

Abileen's men stood by their horses, dressed in their own finery and milling about. In Morgin's absence the camp had disappeared, packed up and loaded on the backs of sixty pack horses. Such a waste, Morgin thought. To carry a pavilion merely for his comfort, and pillows to sleep on, and soft sheets and blankets. A small tent would have been sufficient to keep out the rain, and they could have made the trip in a quarter of the time. With sixty pack animals he could keep twelve twelves of fighting men provisioned for a month. But then, without such a retinue the old woman's show would be far less impressive.

Abileen led him to a small rise where Roland, AnnaRail, JohnEngine, Val, Cort, Tulellcoe, and Rhianne waited with their horses and his. He stood by while the women were assisted into their saddles, then climbed into Mortiss's saddle. He stood high in his stirrups and scanned the waiting soldiers for France's blond head. But of course, on a day such as this, the swordsman would choose to make his own way to Elhiyne.

Morgin spurred Mortiss forward into a comfortable trot. She snorted and blustered, and seemed to be enjoying the spectacle. He crossed the lip of the plateau and began his descent into the valley; the wind felt good on his face. His family rode behind him, and behind them Val and the other lesser clansmen, then Abileen and his men, with the pack train and servants in the rear. It was an order that Olivia had specified; she had orchestrated today's event in the finest detail, including, no doubt, instructions that the peasants should line the road and cheer raucously. "Tell them to have a good time," the old witch had probably commanded, "or I'll have them whipped."

Morgin tried to picture himself as the peasants might see him now: a distant blotch of red riding down into the valley. He wondered if beneath their forced exuberance they were laughing at him. Then again, the old woman had probably declared a festival and day of feast for all. With that kind of bribe the peasants would cheer anyone.

As the road leveled out onto the valley floor he came upon a cluster of peasants waving red banners and shouting. He wanted to speed past them, to avoid seeing the derision in their eyes, but just then a young girl ran into the road in front of him.

He yanked back viciously on Mortiss's reins. She screamed angrily, reared, and he just missed trampling the girl as Mortiss brought her fore hooves down in the middle of the road.

"ShadowLord," the peasant girl cried joyously as she stuffed a bouquet of ripe wheat into his saddle harness. It had been dipped in red dye, which was a custom among the peasants since colorful flowers were rare thereabouts.

The girl was buxom and fair, with large, jiggling breasts that threatened to burst from her dress. She had full red lips and big round eyes filled with honest and sincere joy. She tugged on his sleeve, almost pulled him from his saddle. To keep his balance he bent low toward her until their faces touched. She whispered in his ear in a voice hot and sensuous. "ShadowLord," she said. "I am yours." Then she kissed him passionately, scandalously, with no regard for the propriety of the situation.

Morgin broke free of her, realized he had been surrounded by a small clutch of peasants, all stuffing colorfully dyed bouquets of wheat into his pockets and harness. They touched him reverently and cheered, until he broke away from them and spurred Mortiss forward. "Long live the ShadowLord," they cried after him.

His next encounter with a cluster of peasants was little different, and so too was the next, though he took care to be certain the earlier incident was not repeated. He slowed as he approached each group, but did not stop, and in response to the joy he saw in their faces he found himself waving at them triumphantly, exactly as the old witch would want him to.

Well short of the village the spectators were no longer grouped in clusters, but lined the road on both sides all the way to the castle. The shouts of individuals blended into a continuous indecipherable roar, and among the peasants Morgin saw clansmen and women, merchants of high and low caste, laborers, farmers. They all shouted and cheered.

The village headman waited for him in the center of the village, standing in the middle of the road leaning heavily on an old staff. Morgin stopped, but did not dismount.

The headman raised his staff and slowly the crowd quieted. "Ye have come home, ShadowLord," the old man said in a voice far stronger than Morgin had expected.

"We owe ye much, ShadowLord, for Illalla would have cost us grievesome hurt. We owe ye our lives, and our fields, and our crops, ShadowLord. But more than that, we owe ye our lands."

A long silence followed the old man's words. On impulse Morgin dismounted, crossed the short distance between them and stood before the old man as an equal, thinking of Rat who could not have even claimed the stature of a peasant. He reached out and took the old man's hand, then bowed deeply and kissed it.

A hushed gasp floated through the crowd, for clansmen did not humble themselves to a peasant. "I am deeply honored," Morgin said, and the old man smiled.

Someone cheered, a single voice that drowned the silence of the crowd. Then a second voice joined the first, and they all screamed and shouted. They mobbed him, reminding him painfully of his wounds as they pulled him toward the castle gates.

He'd been careful not to let go of Mortiss's reins. He fought his way to her side, managed to get hold of the saddle horn, to find a stirrup. He struggled for a moment, unable to mount in the moving, shifting throng. But then someone in the mob gave him a rather rude helping hand and catapulted him into the saddle. He spurred Mortiss lightly, and caught only a momentary glimpse of France's grinning, mustachioed face as she trotted forward, clearing a path through the mob.

Ahead of him the crowd waited obediently along the sides of the road, and as he passed they spilled into it behind him, forming a jubilant unruly mob that Olivia would never approve of. He could leave them behind, he knew, by applying his spurs a bit harder, but perversely he chose not to.

The castle gates were open, and beyond them he saw the old woman waiting amidst several clansmen of high caste, among which were representatives of the other Lesser Clans. Morgin pulled Mortiss to an abrupt halt just outside of the castle wall, and the crowd behind him crested like a wave on a rocky shore. But where they had mobbed him before, they now held back, reluctant to stand between him and the old witch. An uncomfortable silence descended upon them all.

Olivia's patience had not improved with time, and she barked some whispered command at Brandon, who obediently trotted across the yard and through the castle gates. "Cousin," Brandon asked. "What are you waiting for?"

Morgin dismounted, stood squarely before his cousin, and both he and Brandon had the same impulse. They abandoned propriety and wrapped their arms about one another in a heartfelt hug while the crowd cheered them.

"It is good to see you," Brandon whispered in his ear. "But don't spoil the old woman's show. You know how she is when she doesn't get her way."

"Come now, grandson," Olivia interrupted them impatiently. "We are waiting."

Morgin pulled free of Brandon's embrace. Olivia too had crossed the courtyard and stood just within the threshold of Elhiyne. He did not move to enter.

Olivia's brows slowly narrowed. "Well?" she demanded.

Morgin shrugged. "When last we met," he said, speaking softly and with care, though his voice rang loudly through the silence around them, "you accused me of cowardice. You condemned me to a death that would not be fit for the worst criminal, and swore by the gods that should I ever return, you would order my death."

Olivia's eyes went stark with anger.

"Now I know you to be a woman of your word," he continued, "so I stand here now, at the threshold of my home, and I wonder: Have you changed your mind, or will I fall to treachery?"

This was in many ways the moment he had lived for: to see the old witch eat her words, to see her for once humbled as she chose to humble others. But just as her anger seemed ready to explode and shower down upon them all, she smiled warmly; she stepped forward and embraced him, though it was a gesture for public viewing, cold and lacking the love that had been in Brandon's embrace.

"All is forgiven," she announced loudly, somehow turning the tables so that it was she who forgave him for her own sins. "Let it not be said that Elhiyne does not welcome the return of its wayward son. We rejoice that you have come home to us, oh ShadowLord."

She released him, turned to the crowd, lifted her hands high to demand the attention that she already commanded. "The grandson of Elhiyne is home; AethonLaw et Elhiyne; ShadowLord; hero of Csairne Glen; and now, by my command, Warmaster of the Council of Elhiyne. From this day hence the ShadowLord will attend all council of Tribe and Clan and House Elhiyne. The ShadowLord has come home."

The crowd cheered and shouted, but Olivia silenced them with a wave of her hands. "Come," she said to them. "Let us adjourn to the Hall of Wills. It is time for the ShadowLord to meet his enemies, for by his own hand they are now his prisoners in defeat."

She spun about and strode across the castle yard, leaving Morgin and the crowd behind. The crowd was now hers, and would have trampled Morgin had he not followed. They allowed him only the barest instant to move out ahead of them, forcing him to match Olivia's pace. They drove him through the gates, across the castle yard, up the steps and into the main entrance of the castle proper. And only when he entered the Hall of Wills did they slow, for even peasants could sense the power that waited there.

Clansmen of middle and high caste filled the hall, and Olivia was nowhere to be seen. For an instant Morgin saw nothing but another milling throng blocking his way. Then, as if the entire thing had been rehearsed, the crowd before him parted slowly like calm, still water cut by the bow of a ship. They withdrew to the edges of the Hall and left Morgin at one end, facing Olivia at the other where she sat upon her throne; and between them, in the center of the Hall, two lone figures, on their knees, facing him, their hands bound behind their backs. Illalla and Valso looked at him, Illalla with uncertainty, and Valso with no expression at all.

Morgin felt ill and numb. Everyone there waited to see what he would do, what he would say, but he could find no grand speeches within him, nor could he think of an appropriate action, or gesture, or command. He wanted merely to disappear into a shadow, perhaps go hunting in the mountains, or fishing by the river. He decided that he would do exactly that. *To netherhell with all of them!* he thought. Olivia could play her games without him, and damn the crowd's need for a show.

Oddly enough, Valso stopped him. Valso must have sensed his hesitation, for at that moment Valso's lips curled slowly into a triumphant grin, a smile that reminded Morgin of Salula's evil pleasure with the lash.

Morgin had crossed half the distance to Valso before he realized what he was doing. He could not remember drawing his sword, but it was in his hand now, alive with such power that the clansmen about him stepped back. It was a mistake to bring that weapon to life with no power of his own to control it, but with the memory of Valso's grin etched on his mind he no longer cared.

Olivia cried, "No. I forbid you," and the sword flared even more powerfully in his hands until even she cringed back from him. And in that instant, as he stood over Valso and Illalla about to take their lives, he saw fear in Valso's eyes, stark, naked terror, and it pleased him.

The air between them shimmered, and Erithnae appeared, in every way a goddess that did not belong among mortals. Morgin understood that she was there only for his eyes. She held up her hands. "No, Lord Mortal. Please. You must not."

His voice cracked and trembled as he spoke. "Out of my way, Erithnae. Go back to your king and your world of dreams."

"Please, Lord Mortal," she begged.

Morgin advanced another step. "What care you for this offal that calls himself a man?"

She shook her head. "I care not for them, but for you, Lord Mortal. You must not harm yourself so by killing them."

"Be gone," he shouted, and at his anger she reluctantly disappeared.

Something tugged at his sleeve. He looked down and found young Aethon standing next to him. "Please, Lord Mortal," the boy begged with tears in his eyes. "Please don't harm them. For you will harm yourself far more."

Aethon held Morgin's sleeve in one hand, buried his face in the other, and his shoulders shook with sobs as he cried openly. And while he cried he slowly faded from sight.

No more phantoms appeared to replace Aethon. The power had left the sword in Morgin's hand and it lay dormant and peaceful. He looked at it, then sheathed the blade.

The crowd cheered him. Olivia stood from her throne and crossed the room to where Morgin stood over the two Decouix lords. She raised her hands to silence the crowd. "The ShadowLord has chosen to consult the gods, and from them he has learned the wisdom of mercy for his enemies."

"ShadowLord," the throng chanted. "ShadowLord . . . ShadowLord . . . Shadow-Lord . . ."

In the midst of all the noise Olivia looked at Morgin and her eyes narrowed. As always, when she was near, he felt the ghostly fingers of her power probing at him. She leaned toward him until their faces almost touched. "You are hiding something, oh ShadowLord," she mocked him, though he heard no joy in her voice. "You wear the fear of discovery about you like a cloak."

Her eyes flashed as if she looked into the depths of his soul, and for an instant he thought he saw a hint of sorrow touch her face.

She said, "Keep your secrets for now, but as in all things in this house, the truth eventually trickles my way. And you will do my bidding, ShadowLord. That you will."

33

Dream's End

A SWORD POINT sliced past Morgin's nose and he back-stepped desperately, then foolishly lost sight of the blade for just an instant. He found it again only by the glint of the sun on the steel point as it cut straight for his heart. He dodged to one side barely fast enough to elude it, and brought his own sword down against it with a loud ringing clang.

"You're concentrating too much on me point, man," France said between strokes, "and not enough on your form. Know where it is, but don't let it rule your fight."

Morgin threw his sword up, caught the back of France's blade, then hit the ground in a low charging roll. He came up beneath the swordsman's guard and slammed into his stomach like an enraged bull.

France spit out a sharp "humph" as he lost his wind and collapsed on top of Morgin. Morgin tried to press his advantage by lifting France off his feet, but France's sword hilt came out of nowhere and crashed into the side of his head. Morgin's world lost its stability and they both collapsed into the dirt.

He staggered to his feet knowing France would recover almost instantly. He coiled to spring at the swordsman again, but he faced only empty ground. He spun about to look behind for the wily swordsman, but France was not there either. He spun full circle, ready for the attack to come from any direction, but France was nowhere to be found. He had quite plain and simply vanished, and for that matter so had everyone else.

Morgin stopped, scratched his head, came to the slow realization that he now stood alone in an empty practice yard. The yard, the castle, the smithy, the stables, all were deserted. The place felt empty and dead.

The first faint notes of a pipist's tune settled upon the air and sent a shiver crawling down Morgin's spine. He turned toward the sound to face the pipist, and of course he found Metadan, dark, handsome, intent upon his playing, leaning casually against a wooden pillar in the shade of the long, shadowed porch.

Morgin demanded, "What are you doing here?"

Metadan started and stopped playing. He looked about for a moment with a worried frown, then nodded, looked at Morgin and bowed.

"I asked what you're doing here."

Metadan smiled. "It is I who should ask you what you are doing here."

"Don't speak riddles to me."

"There is no riddle in this, oh King of Dreams," Metadan said, then frowned, clearly no longer so self-assured. "You have come, have you not, to take your throne?"

"I don't know what you're talking about. Are you going to try to kill me again?"

Metadan shook his head. "I guess not," he said, then began to melt into the stone of the porch.

To Morgin the castle itself seemed unreal, as if part of some strange, indistinct, and poorly defined dream.

"Wake up, lad. Wake up."

Someone slapped his face hard enough to sting a little. Then they slapped him again, and again, and again . . .

"Leave me alone," he said.

Someone started shaking him. "I didn't mean to hit you so hard, lad. How's your head?"

Morgin opened his eyes. France and several of his kinsmen leaned over him, all looking mildly concerned. "You've been out for some time, lad."

Morgin sat up, but went no further as his head began to swim. "Take it easy there, lad."

"Help me up," he demanded.

France and one of the others helped him to his feet. He staggered to the porch and sat down in the shade there. The crowd of onlookers dispersed and France sat down beside him.

"Where's Metadan?" Morgin asked.

"Who?"

"Metadan."

"Don't know no Metadan."

"The archangel."

France shook his head. "Ain't no archangels here, lad."

"But he was here. I saw him."

"Like you seen them gods in the Hall of Wills that day, eh? No one saw them neither."

France threw an arm over the back of Morgin's shoulders. "Listen, me boy. I hit ya perty hard. I didn't mean to, but you know how it is when the blood's up. You went down and out, like a candle in the wind. I ain't surprised you saw all sorts of things."

"Is that all it was?" Morgin asked. "Another dream. Seems like my whole life is one giant hallucination. I sometimes wonder if any of it was real."

"Aye, lad. It was real. Too real sometimes."

"But nothing's changed."

"Well, you're a great Warmaster now." France made no effort to hide the fact that such titles did not impress him.

Morgin sneered. "Warmaster bah! That's only when grandmother wants to impress someone. I so tire of her games."

"Tell her that."

"I've tried. But when I do she ignores me."

"How are things going with the little lady?"

Morgin thought of Rhianne, and none of Olivia's scheming mattered. He shook his head sadly. "I made a mistake, friend. A horrible mistake, and I can only hope that, with time, she'll forgive me."

France said nothing. Morgin turned to look at him and found that he had again vanished. Morgin looked about the castle yard, and again it was deserted. "Damn!" he swore. "These dreams are getting ridiculous."

He waited for Metadan to appear again, but that didn't happen and he remained alone. Eventually he grew bored. "Well," he said. "At least I have power in my dreams." He held out his hand, and the red fire of Elhiyne magic danced among his fingertips, something he could do only in his dreams.

Yes. That confirmed it. He was dreaming. He was in no mood for dream walking now, but since there was nothing he could do about it, he resolved to sit patiently and wait for this dream to end.

••••

And so ends *Child of the Sword*, the first book of *The Gods Within*, in which Morgin has learned the limits of his power. In the second book, *The Steel Master of Indwallin*, Morgin learns the limits he must face in the past.

The Levels and Planes of Existence

Level	Celestial Plane	Mortal Plane	Nether Plane
12	7th Heaven		
11	6th Heaven		
10	5th Heaven		
9	4th Heaven	4th Mortal	1st Hell
8	3rd Heaven	3rd Mortal	2nd Hell
7	2nd Heaven	2nd Mortal	3rd Hell
6	1st Heaven	1st Mortal	4th Hell
5			5th Hell
4			6th Hell
3			7th Hell
2			8th Hell
1			9th Hell

Acknowledgements

I'D LIKE TO thank Durelle Kurlinski for fixing all my dotted t's and crossed i's, Kelley Eskridge for helping me turn an ok manuscript into something I can be really proud of, Karen for both supporting my dream and being my most valuable critic, and Steve Himes, and the whole team at Telemachus, for getting a quality product out the door.

Books by J. L. Doty

Series: The Treasons Cycle
Of Treasons Born
A Choice of Treasons

Stand Alone Novel
The Thirteenth Man

Series: The Gods Within
Child of the Sword
The SteelMaster of Indwallin
The Heart of the Sands
The Name of the Sword

Series: The Dead Among Us
When Dead Ain't Dead Enough
Still Not Dead Enough
Never Dead Enough

Series: The Blacksword Regiment
A Hymn for the Dying
A Dirge for the Damned
A Prayer for the Fallen
A Requiem for the Forsaken

Series: Commonwealth Re-contact Novellas
Tranquility Lost

Series: The Deck of Chaos
The Thief of Chaos
Chaos Unraveled (working title)

About the Author

JIM IS A full-time SF&F writer, scientist and laser geek (Ph.D. Electrical Engineering, specialty laser physics), and former running-dog-lackey for the bourgeois capitalist establishment. He's been writing for over 30 years, with 15 published books. His first success came through self-publishing when his books went word-of-mouth viral, and sold enough that he was able to quit his day-job, start working for himself and write full time—his new boss is a real jerk. That led to contracts with traditional publishers like Open Road Media and Harper Collins Voyager, and his books are now a mix of traditional and self-published.

The four novels in his new hard science fiction series, *The Blacksword Regiment*, were released in July 2020, and *The Thief of Chaos*, the first book in *The Deck of Chaos*, is scheduled for release in early 2021. Right now he's fleshing out ideas for the next book in *The Dead Among Us*, he's writing another episode in *The Treasons Cycle*, and he's working on the second book in *The Deck of Chaos*, a Regency fantasy of seduction and dark magic.

Jim was born in Seattle, but he's lived most of his life in California, though he did live on the east coast and in Europe for a while. He now resides in Arizona with his wife Karen and three little beings who claim to be cats: Tilda, Julia and Natasha. But Jim is certain they're really extra-terrestrial aliens in disguise.

Visit the author's website at http://www.jldoty.com
Contact the author at jld@jldoty.com

Printed in the USA
CPSIA information can be obtained
at www.ICGtesting.com
LVHW040314080823
754564LV00004B/404